D0179419

Robert C. Gruen

About the Author

SARA GRUEN lives in northern Illinois with her husband, three children, two dogs, three cats, two goats, and horse.

FLYING CHANGES

FLYING CHANGES

SARA GRUEN

WITHDRAWN

HARPER

NEW YORK · LONDON · TORONTO · SYDNEY

HARPER

This book is a work of fiction. The characters, incidents, and dialogues are drawn from the author's imagination and are not to be construed as real. Any resemblance to actual events or persons, living or dead, is entirely co-incidental.

First published in 2005 by HarperTorch, an imprint of HarperCollins Publishers.

FIRST HARPER PAPERBACK PUBLISHED 2007.

Library of Congress Cataloging-in-Publication Data
Gruen, Sara.
        Flying changes / Sara Gruen.
             p. cm.
        Sequel to: Riding lessons.
        ISBN: 978-0-06-124109-3
        ISBN-10: 0-06-124109-1
        1. Mothers and daughters—Fiction. I. Title.
PS3607.R696 F58 2007
813/.3 22   2006052982

08 09 10 11 ❖/RRD 10 9 8

To Bob,
as always

Acknowledgments

I am indebted to a great many people for seeing me through the birth of another novel:

To my critique partner, Kristy Kiernan; and my first readers—Elizabeth Graham, Maggie Dana, and Karen Abbott.

To Carrie Feron and Selina McLemore at HarperCollins, for wonderful support and the type of editorial guidance for which all writers hope.

To Seana Pope, for taking me under her wing and showing me New Hampshire, and for her many other tireless efforts on my behalf.

To Teresa Paradis, for answering my questions about the transport of PMU horses, and to all the volunteers at Live and Let Live Farm, for their hospitality and for sharing their stories with me. Special thanks to Heather Evans and Teresa Gladstone, who will recognize hints of their own horses herein.

To Margaret Odgers, for providing information about Nokotas.

To my writing group, who propped me up and

generally kept me going with consistent love and support.

To Emma Sweeney, agent extraordinaire.

And to Bob, whose contributions are too vast to enumerate.

"And God took a handful of Southerly wind, blew his breath over it, and created the horse."

Bedouin legend

FLYING CHANGES

Chapter 1

I awake with a start—one moment I'm riding Harry, my zephyr half, my phantom boy, and the next my eyelids flicker and I'm staring at the ceiling. When I realize I'm not on his back at all—I'm huddled under an eiderdown in the freezing bedroom of the apartment above my mother's stable—I close my eyes and lie perfectly still, trying to coax him to stay. But it's no use—his body dissolves, the reins melt in my hands, and he gallops off, ephemeral as breath on the wind. I move not a muscle, listening as his hoofbeats fade into the ether.

I hear them. I swear to God I do.

Harry wafts into my sleep with a regularity that's astounding considering how effectively he used to elude me. For years after his death I longed for him so badly that I'd squeeze my eyes shut at night and cycle endlessly through visions of him—Harry, with his head high and nostrils flared, cantering through a meadow; Harry, sniffing the wind, his ears perked and chest as solid as bedrock; Harry, flinging those magnificent brindled limbs forward like a Saddlebred—hoping they'd seed a dream.

But they never did. No matter how fiercely I clung to him, at the critical juncture when I lost control he'd slip away to wherever he was, whatever was left, in that place I wasn't allowed. The few times he did come to me were unbidden and horrifying, and always at the precise moment he crashed to his death beneath me all those years ago.

No more. Now he comes to me in plain view, healthy and whole. And I'm thirty-nine, not eighteen. Sometimes I'm on his back and we're cantering through fields of swaying grass. Sometimes I'm standing at his shoulder and he's blowing into my hand, rumbling a greeting from deep within his chest. Sometimes we're even taking fences, one after another in perfect rhythm.

More than two decades gone, and he looms as large in my dreamscape as he did in my life.

A psychologist would probably say that he's always been there and it's only now that I'm letting him come. That I am finally at the point where I can think about him without falling to pieces. This is what I think a psychologist would say. But I can't be sure, because I won't see one.

Both Mutti and Dan have suggested it, separately, although for the life of me I can't figure out why. Both times my reaction was a combination of sputtering indignation and hurt tinged with anger. That, and an instant replaying of all my recent actions and comments to try to discover why, exactly, everybody around me always thinks I'm nuts. But I must confess that later—in the privacy of my room, when there was no longer any need to feel defensive—I found the idea intriguing. Not intriguing enough to actually consider it, of course, but intriguing enough that I began trying to guess what a psychologist would make of me. It's probably not the healthiest pastime for someone who already analyzes things to shreds, but there it is and there's no stopping it. You can't pluck an idea out like you can a sliver.

But while Pseudo-Psychologist Me has decided that my dreams are filled to overflowing with Harry because finding his brother has allowed me to heal, there's another part of me that believes in some way I cannot define and would never admit to that Harry has found a way to come back to me, is giving me his blessing, is glad I have Hurrah safely in a box stall beneath me.

I hug my pillow and sigh, my heart swollen and tender as if I've dreamed of a lover. It's a feeling that will take the length of the day to wear off, and I'm grateful.

It is his gift to me.

• • •

I dress quickly, hunched against the cold. I left the window open a crack last night, and my breath comes in puffs as I pull on my jeans, sweater, and quilted vest. I pause at the door and then go back to my dresser to drag a brush through my scraggly hair. I'll make myself properly presentable later, but at nearly forty you don't just roll out of bed and go even if you're not expecting to run into anyone. Particularly if you have a sixteen-year-old daughter who is mortified when, as Eva puts it, she catches me "looking like a sea hag."

I cleaned my brush only the day before yesterday, but it is once again full of hair. The tangled mess rips free with a noise like Velcro opening. I examine it, analyzing the white-to-blonde ratio. Still mostly blonde, thank God—although I have to hold a couple of the hairs up to the light to make sure. Then I lean forward and peer into the mirror, studying both hair and face for general impressions.

A minute later I hurry down the stairs, booted feet thumping the wood. The main floor of the stable is even colder than the apartment. It's heated, but not to house standards because the horses go out without blankets and we don't want to compromise their winter coats. I rub my hands together, hoping to warm them by friction. I slip into the lounge, which is heated separately, twist the thermostat to a sizzling seventy-four degrees, and start a pot of coffee.

And now, for my early morning tonic.

Three or four times a week, fresh from dreams of his brother, I slip downstairs and ride Hurrah. I ride other horses during the day, usually in the context of giving a lesson and finding it easier to show rather than tell, but never Hurrah. Hurrah I ride in private.

I'm not the one "making an issue of it," as Mutti puts it. It's everyone else who's making an issue of it, and that makes it impossible for me to behave normally. It's a vicious cycle, I know. But how can I ride Hurrah in front of them when I know they're scrutinizing me for signs of obsession? When I know they're interpreting my every look and movement? Given what happened last year, I guess I can forgive them for that. But the end result is I can't ride Hurrah in front of them.

The only exception to this is the stable hands. If I'm still on Hurrah when they arrive, I don't immediately slip off and lead him back to his stall, and that's because they know how to give a girl her privacy. They don't pretend they don't see me. They simply nod a greeting and leave me alone with my horse; and in gratitude, I always make sure there's a warm lounge and a pot of coffee waiting for them when they arrive in the morning.

My horse. The words are so sweet my eyes still prick with tears when I think them. And contrary to popular opinion, I'm well aware of which horse this is. Hurrah may be a virtual doppelgänger of his uniquely marked brother, but he is very much his own boy. I'm amazed at how different Hurrah is under saddle—or under leg, since I always ride him bareback. And I don't mean on a bareback pad, either. I mean on a bare back.

If someone asked me why, I'd say it's because I'm too lazy to tack up, but that's not the reason. And it's also got nothing to do with improving my seat, although as an instructor I prescribe riding bareback on a regular basis. The reason is simple: I want nothing between me and my horse.

With my knees and calves pressed against his warm, solid muscle and my hands connected to his mouth through a rein that buzzes like a Ouija board, I sense his thoughts as they occur to him. I'd feel clever for that, except he anticipates mine before they've even arrived. At the very moment the concept of canter occurs to me, he arches his neck, brings his hindquarters in, and rocks forward in a gait meant for the dressage ring—a slow gait, collected and floating, a gait that betrays his Olympic past.

Hurrah transports me, and I give myself over to him. When I ride him I'm a different person—confident, competent, operating at a level somewhere below latent thought and in absolute concert with the magnificent animal beneath me. When I slide from his back, I am recharged and whole. How could I possibly let anyone witness that? It would be like letting someone watch me make love.

I head for his stall now, heart thumping in anticipation.

As I round the corner, my eyes light on the open door. I stop, confused, blinking because it doesn't make sense. I checked the horses myself last night. When I realize that I'm not seeing things—that the door to his stall really is open—I break into a run and crash to a halt in front of the sliding-door track.

The rising sun spills through the bars of his window. Dust swirls in the shafts of cool light like sperm in a Petri dish, but the stall is otherwise empty.

My head whips back and forth as I assess the possibilities. The doors to the outside are closed, so if the latch wasn't shut and he somehow nosed his door open, he's still in the stable—hopefully not working his way through a bin of feed. Images of laminitis and colic flash through my head.

I bolt to the cubby that contains the feed bins. They're shut tight.

Okay. Okay. He's loose, but he's not exploding with grain. The blood vessels to his feet are not constricting. His bowels are not compacting.

I sprint to the top of each aisle—all empty—and then run to the arena. He's not there, either. Finally, over jets of breath whose size and frequency betray my growing panic, I rush to the corridor where we keep the tack. I can't imagine that Eva would take him out without asking, but I'm running out of possibilities.

Her helmet is on a hook. Her saddle is on its rack. I bring my hand to my mouth, but not before crying out.

He's been stolen.

With the outside doors closed, there's no other possibility. Unless—

I run toward the outside doors, listening to the little meeping noises that seem to be coming from my mouth. I'm not aware of making them, but there's no denying I'm the source.

Outside, my last shred of hope vaporizes with the empty parking lot. It was an implausible situation anyway—that the hands had somehow arrived without me noticing, turned out Hurrah and only Hurrah, and then closed the doors and remained inexplicably outside.

I'm frozen to the spot, paralyzed with fear.

I've got to snap out of it, got to call the police, but from where? I opt for the house, where at least I'll have Mutti at my side.

I'm halfway there, chugging and puffing uphill just as fast as my thirty-nine-year-old legs can manage, when thundering hoofbeats burst out of nowhere, from utter and dead silence, somewhere off to my left. I stop and turn, facing two fields where no horse has any business being because we reserve both for mowing in the fall in an attempt to minimize reliance on bought hay— a parsimony of Mutti's at which I scoffed until I tried, briefly, to manage the stable.

Now, in late March, the tan stubble resembles straw more than hay, lightly frosted and mashed into a flat weave by the weight of the snow. The snow itself is gone, but the ground remains frozen. The hoofbeats are hollow, pounding in the relentless four-beat rhythm of a gallop and amplified by the field's slightly concave surface. They come from nowhere and everywhere, and I can't see a damned thing—distinct patches of fog dot the field, dozens of clouds dipped down to rest.

I hold my breath and keep watching, trying not to blink, and just as I'm thinking that surely at some point the noise will have to materialize into horse, *Boom!* out of a fallen cloud flies a centaur—or, more precisely, my daughter with her long legs wrapped around my horse, bareback, helmetless, her naturally-blonde-but-currently-black hair streaming behind her, shoulders rounded and urging him forward with her hands, galloping as though a horde of Mongols are behind them. Galloping so hard, in fact, that I don't think she's noticed that they're headed straight toward one of the whitewashed wood fences that enclose our pastures.

My heart lodges somewhere in my esophagus and stops. I can neither breathe nor cry out.

Eva, please see the fence.

Please God, make her see the fence.

Eva, for Christ's sake, *see the fence*!

And then it dawns on me that of course she sees the fence. She's looking right at it, and so is Hurrah. She's going to take it at a full gallop, bareback, on my seventeen-year-old one-eyed horse.

In that absurd slow motion that precedes accidents, I prepare for all the possibilities—Hurrah will throw his front legs in front of him, locking his knees and sliding chest-first through the wood, which will splinter and snap, bursting like firecrackers. The impact will send my daughter flying over his head and over the fence and into the ground. She will crumple like an aluminum can, and—if she survives at all—will suffer cata-strophic injuries to her head and spine. The split planks won't withstand Hurrah's massive body weight, and he will hurtle through with spears of wood studding his chest like banderillas in a hapless bull. And then his twelve hundred pounds will crash to a stop on top of Eva's one hundred and twenty, crushing her rib cage, her lungs, her everything.

Or Hurrah will attempt the four-foot fence and my daughter—who, granted, has a wonderful seat, but what the hell does that matter when you're approaching a four-foot fence at a full gallop without so much as a bareback pad beneath you?—will come unseated. Where she'll be thrown is crucial: if she comes off during the takeoff, she'll fall sideways and probably clear of Hurrah. This is the best case scenario, because while there's no question she'll break something, chances are relatively good it will be a limb, hip, or collarbone instead of her neck.

The final thought that runs through my head as they barrel toward the fence without any sign of stopping is that they'll clear the fence but miss the landing. Hurrah's front feet will come down and instead of finding purchase will skid forward on the frozen earth until his radius bones snap. Eva will have no hope—she'll simply slide around his shoulder, as I did on Harry, and hit the ground headfirst at almost thirty miles an hour.

I watch helplessly, cold hands pressed to my cheeks.

Hurrah raises his head and brings his chin toward his chest. His nostrils flare, his ears prick.

I try to beam him a message: Don't do it Hurrah. I know what she's telling you, but don't do it.

But there's no stopping them. Eva pumps her arms like a jockey in the homestretch, her strong young legs clinging to his rib cage. When they're within twenty feet of the fence I utter a whimper, and just as I wonder whether I have the strength to watch or am going to have to turn away from the carnage, Eva suddenly turns her head and sees me. She leans back, yanks Hurrah hard to the left, throws an arm in the air, and screams a whoop of victory. With both hands back on the reins, she slows to a canter, and then further to a trot. She posts effortlessly, bareback. I can't help noticing this even as my heart is still decidedly upwards of its normal position.

"Oh hey, Ma," she says, coming to a stop in front of me. "What's up?" Hurrah's nostrils flare in and out, flashing red. His striped rib cage heaves like a bellows, his flanks speckled with foaming sweat.

I stare with my mouth open. My legs are tingly and liquid, and it's only through sheer force of will that I manage to remain upright.

"You okay?" says Eva, leaning over and peering into my face. "You don't look so good. Did you even brush your hair this morning?"

It takes me a few seconds to find my voice. "Eva, what are you doing?"

"Duh. I'm riding. What does it look like I'm doing?"

Again, I'm too stunned to speak right away. "Get off," I finally say.

"What?"

"Get off!"

In the space of a split second, her face morphs from alarmed surprise to impervious belligerence. With eyebrows raised and lips pursed, she swings her right leg over Hurrah's back and slides down. She makes a point of not looking at me during this whole operation.

I close my eyes and compose myself, willing my heart to slow. When I look again, she's pulled the reins over Hurrah's head and is straightening his forelock.

"I don't see what you're so mad about," she says casually.

I explode. "You were riding bareback! Without a helmet! Galloping toward a fence on frozen ground! On a one-eyed horse!"

"So?" she says, completely unfazed. She clicks her tongue and walks toward the gate. Hurrah plods along beside her, blowing hard.

"So?" I say in disbelief. *"So?"*

I fall into step with them but on the opposite side of the fence. I glance nervously between the planks, watching Hurrah's legs closely. No sign of a limp. I straighten up. Even though they're both okay, I still have a distinct sense of vertigo. My breath is shaky, my body buzzes with adrenaline.

"I have no idea why you're so upset," she says, coming to a stop in front of the gate. "I ride bareback all the time. Okay, maybe I should have been wearing a helmet, but it's not like I jumped anything."

"But you were going to, weren't you?"

She opens the gate with nimble fingers and thrusts it toward me.

It creaks forward and I catch it, holding it open until she leads Hurrah through. Then I shut it. As I fumble with the chain that secures it, she marches toward the stable.

"Eva, please wait!"

Of course she does nothing of the kind. She continues on without so much as a backward glance.

I hate it when she does this. The person following is never in control, which she knows full well and which is exactly why she does it. I drop the chain, which my cold fingers can't make work, and jog a little to catch up with her. The gate creaks open behind me.

"Eva!" I say, falling into stride behind her. I feel like Smike, shuffling and mewling behind Mr. Squeers. "Don't walk away from me! Eva, please!"

She gives every indication of being deaf.

"Eva! I asked you to stop!"

Finally, I've had enough. I fall back long enough to run behind Hurrah and jerk the reins from her hands.

Hurrah's head shoots in the air, turning his left eye to see who's got hold of him. I stroke his face and murmur until he calms down.

Eva betrays a flash of surprise but recovers almost instantly, placing her hands on her waist and throwing her weight on one hip. She exhales loudly, rolling her eyes at the sky.

"Tell me the truth. Were you going to take that fence?"

Her brown eyes glom on to mine. She waits a few beats before responding. "Maybe," she shrugs. "Okay, fine. Yes. I was."

"Oh God, Eva. You'd have been killed."

"No way," she scoffs. "I've never come off a horse in my entire life."

"That means nothing!" I shout. "Nothing! He hasn't taken a jump since he lost his eye. What if he misjudged? What if he slid through the fence? What if he refused? You had no protection whatever. No stirrups, no helmet. Nothing."

"You need to calm down, Ma."

"I beg your pardon?" My hand drops to my side. I stare into her eyes, seeking understanding. I'm baffled and I'm traumatized and I'm facing an adolescent who has absolutely no idea what nearly transpired.

Hurrah dances nervously, taking several steps backward. The white of his left eye, which he's taking pains to keep trained on us, is showing.

I step forward, shushing, stroking his cheeks and the crest of his neck. "Go back to the house and wait for me," I say to Eva.

Her face compresses into a scowl. "Why?"

"Because we're not finished talking about this."

She turns and stomps up the drive. "Shit," she mutters, just loud enough for me to hear and just low enough for her to argue that I misheard, particularly as she kicks a spray of gravel into the air at that exact moment.

"Stop right there!"

She stops, and drops her head back. "What now?" she says.

"What did you just say?"

"I didn't say anything," she says, still without turning around.

"Yes you did, and you know it."

No response.

"You're grounded," I say.

"Well, there's a big surprise," she grumbles. And off she goes, periodically kicking up gravel with the toes of her boots.

I watch her entire progress. She climbs the ramp that leads to the porch and enters by the back door, slamming it behind her.

Poor Mutti. If she's in the kitchen, she's already getting an earful.

I turn to Hurrah and slide a hand between his front

legs. His chest is slick with sweat and I feel another pang of anger toward my daughter, although in my heart I know she would have cooled him off properly. Eva knows and loves horses as I do. It's me she has a problem with.

I take Hurrah into the indoor arena and walk him slowly around its perimeter, periodically stopping to feel his chest and assess his breathing. After he's completely cool, I take him back to his stall to await his morning pellets. The other horses are shifting and nickering in anticipation of theirs, too. I could start feeding them myself, but the stable hands have their routine down to a science and I don't want to mess with it.

As I leave the stable, they arrive in two ancient cars that rattle and bang down the lane. I lift a hand in uninspired greeting and trudge toward the house and whatever awaits me.

About halfway there, it dawns on me that the hoofbeats I heard as I awoke this morning were not Harry's at all. They were Hurrah's.

• • •

I lay my hand on the doorknob and pause for a moment, staring down at the bristly doormat and steeling myself in case Eva is still in the kitchen. Then I take a deep breath and enter.

To my relief, Mutti is alone, scooping coffee beans into the electric grinder, her blonde hair pinned into its usual tight coil. Her quilted turquoise dressing gown is zipped right up to the soft loose flesh under her chin, and I find myself wondering whether she's ever caught it in the zipper, whether it was terribly painful, and whether it was hard to work free.

Mutti glances at me, frowning as though she's read my mind, and turns back to the grinder. Its growl fills the kitchen, relieving us both of the pressure to speak. I peel off my paddock boots, hang my vest on one of the hooks by the back door, and take a seat at the table.

Mutti puts the grinds into the coffeemaker and flicks the switch. It begins to gurgle immediately, which means she used hot water to fill it.

Of course she did. She's Mutti.

She glances back at me, eyes narrowed as if she's once again read my thoughts. I blush and look down, cowed, and resolve to never again think about Mutti while in her presence.

She turns and wipes her hands on an ironed dish towel hanging from the oven door and retrieves two mugs from the cupboard. She sets them on the counter and joins me at the table.

"So," she says, plopping her hands on the table in front of her. With her accent, it comes out *Zo*.

"So," I say glumly.

"You want to tell me what happened?" Her eyebrows are raised. She examines her hands, twisting her plain gold wedding band round and round. Her knuckles are prominent, her hands pale but mottled with age spots.

"What did Eva say?"

Mutti stops twisting her ring, folds her hands neatly, and looks at me. "She says she decided to take an early morning ride on Hurrah, and that you came out and"—she frowns and looks away as she tries to come up with the word—"I believe her exact phrase was that you 'wigged out completely.' "

"I don't suppose she mentioned that she was galloping bareback on frozen ground with no helmet straight toward a solid fence on my one-eyed horse?"

A slight pause. "No."

"Well, she was."

"So what happened?"

"She saw me at the last second and veered away."

Mutti rises and sails to the counter, standing in front of the coffee machine as it sputters into silence. Although the mugs look perfectly aligned to me, she adjusts them again before moving to the fridge to get the pitcher of cream. On her way back, she picks up the sugar bowl. She is the picture of dignity. Always calm. Always cool.

She doctors my coffee in the same unhurried manner, leaves hers black, and brings both mugs to the table.

"Thanks," I say as she sets mine in front of me.

I wrap my icy fingers around the hot ceramic and stare at the steam rising from the liquid's surface. Its center is still moving, a whirling indentation. I lean down and take a small sip and end up slurping because it's so hot. I look up quickly, expecting Mutti to disapprove.

She seems not to have noticed. She's staring straight through me with her cool blue eyes, waiting for me to continue.

"I did not 'wig out.' In fact, under the circumstances I think I was relatively calm. I thought I was going to watch her die."

Mutti watches me silently, and then reaches over to pat my hand. "So where do things currently stand?" she asks.

"Who knows? She walked away from me. As usual."

Mutti lifts her coffee, takes a sip, and then sets it

back down. She runs her forefinger round and round the mug's rim, as though trying to make a wineglass sing.

"I think you should let her go," she says finally.

"I know you do."

"You won't even consider it?"

"No! Whose side are you on, anyway?"

"I'm on both your sides, of course."

Where Eva wants to go—in fact is entirely desperate about—is the Strafford International Young Rider Horse Trials. It's my fault. I let her compete at the Canterbury Horse Trials in Florida last month. The problem is that while I viewed Canterbury as a one-off—a reward for staying out of trouble and getting her grades up—Eva viewed it as the start of a competitive career. The campaign to enter Strafford began almost immediately after, and quickly became both an assumption and an imperative.

"There's no point, though, is there?" I argue weakly. "The best horse we have is Malachite, and he's nowhere near good enough. Besides, he's nasty. He'd swipe her off under a branch given half a chance."

"Malachite is not our best horse. Hurrah is."

"He's *blind*, Mutti!"

"He's only half blind—"

"He's seventeen years old," I say. "Even if I let her ride him, he'd have to retire soon."

Mutti shrugs. "So buy her more horse."

"We can't afford more horse," I say. "More horse, as you put it, translates into at least forty thousand dollars. *At least.* I don't have that kind of money and neither do you."

"You could ask Roger."

"No, I can't," I snort.

"Why ever not?" she says. "He's her father."

"Because he's got plenty else to spend it on, what with his brand-new house, brand-new wife, and their brand-new baby."

There's a moment of uncomfortable silence as I realize just how bitter I sound. I flush and look down at my twisted fingers.

"You don't know until you ask him," Mutti says softly.

She watches me carefully. Then she leans forward across the table, reaching for both my hands. "*Schatzlein,* I don't want to argue any more than you do, but think about this for a moment. You took the child away from everything she knew—her home, her friends, her father—and plunked her down on a horse farm in the middle of nowhere. Against all odds, she excelled anyway. Her grades are up. She's riding every day. And now—when it's starting to pay off for her—you're putting on the brakes? It makes no sense. Never mind what the repercussions will be, because you know she'll find a way to punish you."

I stare at her for a long time, my eyes and cheeks burning. "I know," I whisper.

"So let her."

"I can't, Mutti. I wish I could. But it scares me too much."

"Then it's time you talked to someone about it."

"Counseling wouldn't help."

"And how do you know, since you refuse to try it?"

I stare silently at the table, my cheeks burning.

Mutti grows impatient, waves a hand dismissively. "Fine. Whatever. You're a grown woman."

I stand up so abruptly my chair legs screech against

the linoleum. "I'm going to take a shower. Can I use your shampoo?"

"You can't be out yet. I bought you some last week."

"It's back at the stable."

Mutti leans back and folds her arms across her chest. "This is ridiculous, this trekking back and forth between the house and stable. Why don't you just move back into the house?"

"Because," I say, writhing with embarrassment.

"Honestly, Annemarie. You're forty years old."

"Thirty-nine!"

"Sure, for four more weeks."

"I'm thirty-nine until the stroke of midnight on April twenty-eighth. Besides, it's not like I've actually *moved* out there. I just sleep out there."

Mutti arranges her features in sour judgment. "Exactly. It makes no sense whatever."

I march to the sink and dump my coffee. It was a gesture, of course, and I regret it immediately, not just because the coffee was excellent but also because it leaves a milky film in the sink—which I can't leave, because Mutti is an Austrian Cleaning Machine and I'm the World's Biggest Slob. And so I am forced to follow my grand gesture by slooshing water around the sink until it is clean. Then, since my gesture has lost all its oomph anyway, I decide to just go ahead and pour myself another cup.

Such a symphony of amplified noise: never has cream glugged so loudly, nor spoon tinkled so shrilly. I swear I can hear each grain of sugar as it melts into the liquid. When I'm finally finished, I set the spoon on the bottom of the sink—with a deafening clink—and retreat upstairs.

I haven't looked at Mutti, but there's no doubt in my mind she's sitting with arms crossed and mouth pressed into a thin line. And shaking her head.

• • •

I climb the stairs, muttering to myself but being careful to keep it under my breath since I know Eva is holed up in her room on high alert. Since I'm at a clear disadvantage—I have no idea what I'm going to say to her and she's had ample time to frame her arguments— I decide to take my shower while I consider my approach. Besides, letting her stew a bit longer might be helpful, might soften her up. Of course, it might also have the opposite effect. One never knows with Eva. I thought fifteen was difficult, but sixteen is shaping up to be at least as volatile. It's been a hard year for us both.

I stomp past her door and march to the bathroom, grumpy at both daughter and mother. Daughter, for reasons that were more obvious before I talked to my mother; and mother for being painfully astute about some things and hopelessly obtuse about others.

I can't move back into the house. There are only two bedrooms, and with Eva occupying my childhood room, that leaves only my parents' upstairs bedroom and the dining room, which my parents converted to a bedroom when my father became ill and could no longer manage the stairs. My father's life ended in that room, and because of that—even though Mutti was practically mule-like in her determination to continue sleeping there—I finally reached the point where I couldn't stand it anymore. The thought of her spending her nights alone down there where he died was keeping *me* awake. I considered the possibility of sleeping there myself for all of twelve seconds, but that was also out of the question. Too much of Pappa remains in that room, and although changing its configuration back from bedroom to dining room obscured that cosmetically, we all feel it keenly. It hasn't escaped my notice that Mutti now serves dinner in the kitchen even on formal occasions.

But if I'm really honest with myself—and I'm trying hard to do that these days—that's not the only reason I started sleeping out at the stable. Because if it were, I could have just taken up residence on the lumpy foldout couch in the study, in spite of the metal bar that runs across the middle of my back.

I know that I'm thirty-nine and divorced and entitled to sleep with whomever I like, but somehow the idea of making love with Dan in a room above, below, or even down the hall from either my mother or daughter has the same effect on my libido as a raging case of cholera. We tried on several occasions, and despite heroic effort on Dan's part, it just didn't work. And so for the two months before I finally upped stakes and started sleeping in the stable, we snuck around much like we did as teenagers. This worked fairly well—and even added a certain *je ne sais quoi* to the mix—until the night my dachshund decided I was an armed intruder.

I knew Dan was coming, so I was waiting by the window in my parents' old bedroom. When he flashed his headlights, I rushed silently down the stairs.

I had the routine down pat—tread lightly down the left side for the first three steps, skip the fourth entirely, cross over to the right for the next five, skip the tenth, and then tromp down the rest of the stairs however I want because none of them squeaks.

I was wearing a thin cotton nightgown with small blue flowers—an ankle-length, blousy thing with no waist in the style of Laura Ashley, which I thought was romantic in a Victorian type of way. It was entirely unsuitable for the weather, which was already below freezing, but I knew that if I hurried down the drive, Dan would be waiting for me in the stable lounge with the heater going and a down comforter.

I swung by the fridge, grabbed the bottle of champagne I had hidden under a plume of collard greens, pulled my rubber boots over my bare legs and feet, and opened the back door as quietly as I could.

At this precise moment, Harriet—my thirteen-year-old selectively deaf dog, who slept like a top through my departure from our shared bedroom—came tumbling down the stairs snarling and yapping like Cerberus using all three heads. Since Mutti was still sleeping in the dining room at this point, it took her only a few seconds to appear and flick on the kitchen light. And there I was, busted, in my blue-flowered nightie and rubber boots, holding a bottle of contraband bubbly. Harriet shut her snout so quickly she left teeth outside her lips and assumed an expression of great confusion. After a moment she wagged her tail uncertainly.

Mutti scrunched up her face to adjust to the light, ran her eyes over me, and said, "What in heaven's name are you doing?"

"I'm, uh," I said, flushing from my head to my toes. Then I glanced behind me.

Mutti cocked her head to see around my blousy self, caught sight of Dan's truck through the screen door, laughed uproariously, and disappeared back into the dining room.

I moved out to the stable the next night.

• • •

On second thought, I decide to deal with Eva before my shower. What's the point in leaving everybody miserable? I put my coffee on the antique dresser in the bathroom—setting it on the white lace runner only after first checking that the bottom is dry—and then go back to Eva's room. I stand outside her door with my hand raised, hesitant.

"Eva?" I say without knocking. "Honey?"

There's a muffled response from the other side of the door. Since it didn't sound like "Go to hell," I push the door open.

I pause in the doorway. Eva sits at her vanity, her muck-caked boots up on its surface, crossed at the ankle. Beside them is a silver-framed picture of Jeremy, her shiny new half brother. He's nestled in a molded car seat under cheerily patterned baby blankets, beaming at the camera with fat round cheeks and toothless gums.

Eva leans back so her chair is balanced on two legs. This is entirely for my benefit, and is incredibly effective: in my mind's eye I'm already watching her fall backward and crack her skull open.

I press my lips shut and perch behind her on the bed—close enough to intervene if she topples over.

As the mattress sags beneath my weight, our eyes lock in the mirror. Hers are fierce and bright and peer out at me from under a fringe of straight blue-black hair. It's been a couple of months since she dyed it, so the hair next to her scalp is blonde again. Left to its own devices, which it never is, her natural hair color is one countless women spend hours and fortunes to achieve. But I don't argue hairstyles. Unlike the Hated Tattoo, hairstyles grow out.

As Eva glares at me, I drag one foot up over my opposite thigh and then try to do same with the other. I was aiming for the lotus position, but my hamstrings immediately suggest that cross-leggedness would be a more practical choice.

How depressing. I used to be able to put both my feet behind my head at the same time. Of course, I also used to be able to do the splits and back walkovers.

After trying in vain to arrange my folded self into a comfortable position, I give up and set my feet back on the floor.

"So what do you want?" says Eva, glowering at me from the mirror.

"We need to talk."

"So talk."

I draw a deep breath and let my cheeks inflate. "Okay, fine," I say. "I need you to promise me that you'll never do that again. You know the rules—no riding without a helmet, ever."

"Like that's what you're mad about."

I stare at her for a moment, rubbing my chin. "It's a large part of it. Hurrah has one eye. What if he refused? Or slipped on takeoff? Or missed the landing? My God, even if he took the jump perfectly, you were completely unprotected! You didn't even have stirrups!"

Eva blows a raspberry. "He'd have cleared it. Easy."

I lean forward, speaking urgently. "Eva! Honey.

Please listen to me. I know you think you're invincible, but what you did this morning was incredibly stupid."

"Thanks, Ma."

"I'm not trying to insult you. I'm just trying to make you see things from my viewpoint."

She raises her eyes to mine. "Okay fine. So you wanna try to see things from my viewpoint for half a second?"

I blink at her image in the mirror for a few seconds. "Uh . . . okay. Yes. Sure."

"I worked my butt off all winter. I got my grades up. I did really well at Canterbury, and now, for no good reason at all, you're pulling the plug."

"Honey, I . . ." I stare at her for a moment, and then drop my head into my hands, wanting to cry. I'm utterly exhausted, and I've already run out of arguments, which strikes me as a singularly bad sign. "Look, I know it seems like I dangled a carrot, and I'm so sorry. It's just . . . I really appreciate all the work you've done—you have no idea how much—and I knew how badly you wanted to go to Canterbury. I thought I could deal with it. But my heart was in my throat the whole time."

"This is all because of your stupid accident, isn't it?"

"Eva!"

"Oh please, Mother. It happened in the Stone Age. Besides, it was freakish. It's time to let it go."

Her words cut deeper than she can imagine. Yes, it was freakish—it was completely inexplicable. But what the people around me don't seem to understand is that this is precisely what makes it so scary. Neither Harry nor I did anything wrong. When we came over that jump, his left foreleg blew apart for no reason whatever, sending both of us crashing into the ground. I nearly didn't make it. And Harry? Well, they shot Harry.

I pause, reflecting. "Would you consider doing just dressage?"

"No."

"Because if you did, I'd let you go. I'd even let you ride Hurrah."

"No!" she says in exasperation. "I want to jump! Why is that so hard for you to understand?"

Why indeed. I am silent, drumming my fingers against my lips.

"I want to do this," she says, her eyes burning into mine.

"I know you do."

"I want it more than anything I've ever wanted before," she persists. She drops her feet from her desk and swings around to face me.

"I know."

"So let me ride at Strafford and just keep shutting your eyes."

"I beg your pardon?" I say feebly.

"In Canterbury. You closed your eyes every time I took a jump. Just keep doing it."

I am speechless with shame. How did she find out?

Other parents. Other parents sitting in the stands must have told their kids, who in turn told Eva. I'm a freak and my kid knows it.

"Eva, I'm so sorry," I whisper.

"Yeah, whatever. So are we done here?"

I blink.

"I said, are we done here? Or am I supposed to try to

make you feel better and pretend we've shared a 'moment' because you've admitted that it 'seems' like you dangled a carrot? Because you know, maybe it makes you feel better, but it sure doesn't help me."

"I . . . uh," I say, straightening up and trying not to blink because if I do I'll set free the tears that quiver along my lower lids. "Yes. I guess we're done."

She turns to the window, folds her arms across her chest, and then crosses her legs. One foot bobs violently. "Figures," she says.

As I reach the door, she calls after me. "And by the way, Ma, it doesn't 'seem' like you dangled a carrot. You did. A big fat one."

I head back to the bathroom, fighting tears, and having accomplished absolutely nothing.

• • •

I slug the rest of my now-tepid coffee down like bourbon—indeed, wishing it were—and undress.

As I stand naked in front of the tub fussing with the taps, I ponder in a dispirited fashion about how low my breasts hang when I'm bent at the waist. I'm not exactly falling apart, but I'm well aware of what side of the mountain I'm on. I'm melting like a candle. I weigh exactly the same as I did four years ago, but everything's sliding downward.

Our house was built in 1843, and the pipes moan and screech like the innards of a tanker. One second the water is too cold; the next, it's hot enough to blanch a peach. I finally lose patience and just stick the plug in the drain. Why shouldn't I take the time for a bath? Joan, our other trainer, is doing today's lessons, and Dan won't be back until at least tomorrow, so I can wait another day to wash my hair. Besides, a bath might help me decompress.

After the tub fills, I turn the taps off and lean over, swirling the fingertips of one hand through the water. It feels good, so I climb in.

As soon as my feet and lower legs are submerged I realize I've seriously underestimated the temperature. I stand perfectly still, debating whether I'll be able to get used to it or have to do something.

After a couple of seconds, the answer is clear. I shuffle forward so my feet are directly under the faucet and turn the cold on full blast. The relief is instant. I allow the cold water to pool around my stinging legs, and then crouch down to mix it into the rest of the water.

I should know better than to test a bath like that—one of the permanent souvenirs from my accident is a slight decrease in sensation at the very ends of my fingers. But my legs seem happy now, so I lower my body into the tub and lean back until my head rests against its rim.

I love this tub. I don't think it's original to the house, but who knows? New England houses have their own secret histories. Whether original or not, it's an antique claw-footed beast of a thing that's long enough for me to stretch out completely and is sloped at such a forgiving angle I can lie comfortably back.

I grab the facecloth from the towel rack above me and drop it into the tub. As it saturates and sinks, its corners spread like a manta ray, I sit forward and splash my face repeatedly. Then I lie back and drape the washcloth across my forehead and eyes. Water streams over my mouth and chin, drips from the end of my nose.

Poor Eva—she has every right to be upset with me. Since even I don't entirely understand my reactions, how can I possibly expect her to? And why shouldn't she think that being allowed to compete at Canterbury was the start of something larger?

My ambivalence stems from what happened to me, of course, and I realized this long before my recent addiction to self-analysis. What mother wouldn't want to protect her daughter from the type of devastation I suffered? If someone had asked me when Eva was first born whether I'd ever let her on the back of a horse, I'd have laughed. Indeed, if I recall correctly, Mutti did just that and was entirely unamused by my response.

Of course, this was back when I still foolishly believed I could control what Eva would or wouldn't want to do. It took just under two years for my daughter to disabuse me of *that* notion. From the moment she uttered her first words, it was clear that although I had married Roger and moved to Minnesota largely to escape anything and everything to do with horses, our daughter was gravitating toward them as inevitably as a salmon to spawning grounds.

It shouldn't have been a surprise. As far as I can tell, the only thing Eva got from Roger is her brown eyes. Everything else—from her blonde hair to her impetuous nature to her factory-installed love of horses—came from me. I could have moved her to Alaska and homeschooled her or taken her by canoe to deepest Borneo and set us up in a cave. It wouldn't have made a damned bit of difference. She would have wiggled her way into a stable from the South Pole.

She was a barnacle. Clinging to ponies' legs at petting zoos, kissing the television screen every time a horse appeared and then giggling at the static that zapped her lips, cutting out every picture of every

equine she ever saw—including, to Roger's dismay—
the ones from our encyclopedias, typing rope "reins"
around the end of a thick branch and then skip-
cantering around our backyard neighing to herself.

And so it went. The year Eva was six, the photograph
on our Christmas card showed her grooming her favorite Shetland pony while wearing a tutu, fairy wings,
and purple muck boots. I believe I was the one behind
the camera.

It wasn't until she was ten and began jumping that
Roger had to take over lesson duty. I was happy enough
doing it as long as she was riding on the flat, but I simply couldn't bring myself to watch her jump. At first I
tried to prevent it, but even at ten Eva was formidable.
But it wasn't the cosmic explosion of outrage that per-
suaded me, or even the long and reasoned arguments
presented by my ever-patient ex-husband. When Eva
realized I planned to prevent her from jumping anything, ever, I saw myself reflected back through her
eyes and I hated what I saw. I never figured out what
that was, exactly, but I hated it nonetheless.

And so Roger began accompanying her to lessons.

Of course, when I left Roger and returned to my family's horse farm in New Hampshire—

Wait a minute. I've got to stop doing that. Why do I
keep doing that? I didn't leave Roger. He left me.

Okay. Deep breath—

When Eva and I moved *without* Roger to my family's horse farm in New Hampshire, she found herself
in hog heaven. Horses everywhere, a whole barn full,
hers for the taking twenty-four hours a day.

Throw near-daily lessons into the mix and I guess it's
no real surprise she excelled. And it did pull her back

from the brink—she's not exactly a straight-A student, but she's a nearly straight-B student, and that's good enough for me. One of the main reasons I fled Minnesota was that her school career was so clearly in the toilet. I got a note from the principal informing me that she was flunking spectacularly only three and a half weeks before she was expelled for truancy.

Considering that she subsequently suffered a move and parental split, it's a miracle she's doing as well as she is, and there's no question it's because she turned to riding.

There's also no question she's good. Scarily good. And that, of course, is the problem.

If Pappa were still alive, he'd have already taken control of the situation and put her into training. I'd have been left watching, swinging my head back and forth with horrified whiplash, as though at some nightmarish tennis match, as he orchestrated one final campaign toward his—or, as he'd phrase it, "the family's"—Olympic dream.

But even if I can move beyond my fears, deciding to do this in any kind of serious way would require major changes to all our lives.

Just the logistics are a nightmare: Eva and me schlepping around the country in a pickup truck hauling whichever horse behind us in a beat-up slat-sided Kingston trailer is not going to cut it on the eventing circuit. To do this, we would need people, equipment, a paradigm shift. Even if I could bring myself to act as Eva's trainer—which is a really big if, considering that my inability to watch her take a fence is the entire reason we hired Joan—we'd need to either take Joan on full-time or hire someone else to replace me while we were on the road. And unless I want to homeschool Eva, we'd also need a tutor. Never mind that we'd spend so much time on the road I'd see even less of Dan than I already do. And poor Mutti would be left on her own for all but the off-season.

And unless we want to keep the model we used on our way to Canterbury—the one in which I sleep in the parking lot of the motel with the horse while Eva snoozes comfortably in a bedroom inside—we would also have to buy a trailer with a living area. Something like a Sundowner, with a couple of beds, a kitchen, and a bathroom. And if we bought a Sundowner, we'd also have to buy a truck with a dual axle and conversion engine to pull it. And each of those pieces of machinery costs at least as much as the horse we would have to buy to replace Malachite, and all of this would naturally translate into a closer association with Roger and Sonja, because by necessity they'd be bankrolling this whole endeavor.

I strip the washcloth from my face and, even though I'm sitting alone in a bathtub, look guiltily from side to side. And then I slide back into the water, sick with guilt and desperation.

There is another option, but neither Mutti nor Eva knows about it. And since I never followed up on that phone call, I reckon it will stay that way.

I do so want to do the right thing. I really do. I'm just never sure what that is. And the problem with the phone call is that it feels a lot like Pandora's box—I'm afraid that once I tell someone about it, I'll set something in motion that I won't be able to stop.

Chapter 2

I'm simultaneously investigating whether I can stop the faucet from dripping by plugging it with my big toe and examining my prune-wrinkled fingers when I'm interrupted by a violent thumping on the door.

"Ma!" Eva yells through the slatted wood. "Hey, Ma! Phone!"

I sit forward, sloshing water dangerously close to the tub's rim. "Who is it?"

But she's gone, stomping down the hall. A moment later her door slams with such force the toothbrushes rattle in the holder above the sink.

I had been considering adding more hot water and extending my bath, but since Eva isn't giving me the option of calling whoever it is back, I pull the plug and climb out, holding the tub's edge carefully until I have one foot planted squarely on the thick pile of the bathmat. I grab a towel and tuck it around myself.

On my way to the door, I catch sight of myself in the full-length mirror.

It's too bad you can't just walk around in towels, because this one is the perfect length for me. It comes just far enough down my thighs to cover my difficult areas while leaving the lean parts exposed. If you didn't know what was immediately above it, you might think I had slim thighs. I might try to find some skirts in this length, although I have almost zero opportunity to wear anything other than jeans or breeches these days. It's not something I repine; it's just something I hadn't really noticed before.

Come to think of it, maybe I do repine. I can't remember the last time Dan and I went out.

• • •

I stump my way to Mutti's bedroom, leaving wet footprints all the way down the hall. Eva has left the door open, has tossed the receiver on top of Mutti's bed. I pick it up and settle carefully on the edge of the eiderdown. Mutti believes in hospital corners and smooth covers, and I want to limit the repairs I'll have to make later.

"Hello?"

"Hey, babe." It's Dan, his voice crackly above the static of a cell phone.

"Dan! Where are you?"

"Still in Canada."

The smile falls from my face. "Why? What's going on?" I try not to let disappointment color my voice, but I had figured he'd be as far as Ohio by now.

"Got hold of seven more horses and am waiting for the results of the Coggins tests, that's all. Should be on my way in a day or two."

Dan is a veterinarian by trade, but his passion—his calling—is running Day Break, his horse rescue center.

He's been gone much of the winter, hauling truckloads of horses away from the hundreds of pee farms that are going defunct. Back in the heyday of hormone replacement therapy, it was the foals that needed saving. Now it's all of them—mares, foals, and stallions—and Dan, and every other rescue operation we know, is scrambling to get them out before they end up either as dog food or on a meat counter in Asia.

"Oh," I say in a small voice. I feel guilty for my disappointment, but I've been counting the minutes until his return. I had been hoping to talk to him about the phone call—to ease my conscience, to hear him tell me I'm doing the right thing. Because of course I'm not sure of this at all.

There's an uncomfortable pause.

"Sweetie," he says, "are you okay?"

"Yes, of course," I say, dropping my forehead into one hand. I want to cry, and hope I can hide it in my voice. "I just miss you."

"I miss you, too. Is something else going on? You sound funny."

"It's not important."

"It's important if you're upset."

"Eva's mad at me. And I miss you. That's all."

"Hang in there. I'll be back in a couple of days, tops."

"Good." I swallow over the lump in my throat and smile, beginning the mental adjustment.

"Listen, there's another reason I called. I need a favor."

"Oh?" I say. "What's that?"

"Is there any way you can spend the next couple of nights at my place?"

"Sure. Why?"

"Maisie's set to foal anytime. Chester was staying with her, but all three of his kids came down with strep and his wife was threatening to leave if he didn't come home. Can you take over until I get back?"

"Um . . . sure," I say, trying to keep the panic from my voice.

"What's the matter?"

"Nothing," I say.

"You've been at a foaling before, right?"

"Well, no. Not exactly."

"Oh." There's a pause. "Do you want me to try to find someone else?"

"No, no! I'll be fine."

"Are you sure?"

"Positive," I say, winding the phone cord so tightly around my fingers that the ends of them turn white. "Just tell me what to look for."

"Restlessness. Discomfort. Check her vulva for swelling or discharge."

"Okay," I say, nodding vehemently. "Swelling and discharge. What else?"

"Her udder may leak. Or get waxy."

"Leaking, waxy udder. Got it." Continued bobbing of my head. "What else?"

"That's about it. When she goes into labor she may lie down and get up a lot. And seem uncomfortable. Pawing the ground and so on."

"Well, yes. I should think so." I swallow hard. "And, um, if she starts? What then?"

"Well, it's fairly straightforward. You want to make sure that two hooves are presenting, followed by a nose. If that's not the case, call the backup vet immediately.

His name is Walter. I left his name and number in the foaling kit."

"All right."

"Chances are good it won't happen until I get home, but she's far enough along I need someone to check on her once an hour. Oh—and at night, you can use the foal-cam. I usually just sleep in front of the TV."

"Will I be able to figure it out?"

"It's dead easy. Ask Judy to show you." Dan's voice softens, turns gravelly and low. "Thanks, babe. I'll make it up to you."

"Sure. If you ever come home," I say.

"I'll be home in a day or two. We'll catch up then. I promise."

"Maybe I'll cook you dinner," I croon into the receiver.

"What? Why? What did I do?" he cries in mock desperation. "Whatever it is, I'm sorry!"

I snort. "All right. I won't cook. But I'm warning you, I plan to be Velcro woman when you get back," I cradle the phone in both hands, rocking it gently. "I really miss you, Dan."

"Miss you, too. I'll be home soon, sweetie. I promise."

• • •

Mutti throws me a questioning look when I appear with a duffel bag. She's wiping the table with a pink sponge. The kitchen smells of bleach.

"What's up?" she says.

"I'm spending the night at Dan's."

"Is he back?"

"No. He's got a mare set to foal, and no one else can stay."

Mutti's arm stops for a second—just the slightest hint of a pause, but enough for me to see. Then she continues wiping the table with wide, broad strokes.

"*Schatzlein*," she says, "have you ever seen a mare foal?"

"Er, no," I say, dropping my duffel bag on the floor.

"And what will you do if she starts?"

"I'll call Walter, that's what."

"Who?"

"Dan's backup vet."

"Ah," she says. She walks to the sink, rinses out the sponge, and centers it precisely behind the faucet.

"Dan says she'll probably hold off until he gets back anyway," I say. "But I'm sorry to leave you with Eva in a state. Do you think you'll be okay with her?"

Mutti turns from the sink and approaches me. She lays her bleachy hands on either side of my face and kisses my forehead.

"I will handle Eva. Don't you worry," she says. "Now go help your *Mann*."

Which of course is the German word for husband. As I scoop my duffle bag from the floor, a hollow pang runs right down my middle.

• • •

The road that leads to Dan's property is long and winding and passes through pine trees so crowded and tall the bottom thirds are scraggly and naked from lack of sun. The road is dirt, full of pot holes, and in the winter occasionally blocked by a fallen tree or branch. These have been cleared and set off to the side, where they'll either rot or get collected at some point in the summer.

I'm driving my Camry—which has almost no sus-

pension left and never really did recover from its alter-
cation with the truck last year—and I wince as it
kerthumps into yet another large hole. There's no
avoiding them. The best I can do is try to have only one
wheel in one hole at a time. This isn't the most practical
car for this part of the world, but of course I wasn't living in this part of the world when I bought it.

The property itself consists of two barns—the one in
front, built in 1811, is tall and red and handsome. Not
far from it stands (in a manner of speaking) the original
house, which had not been occupied for probably a
century before Dan bought the place, and which collapsed promptly upon his signing the papers. Fifty
years of assault by carpenter ants and powder-post bee-
tles plus one heavy snowfall did the job. The local old-
timers gathered around the next afternoon muttering
things like, "Aye, yup, knew it would go real soon,"
puffing their corncob pipes, clapping poor miserable
houseless Dan on the back, and chiding him for not
having insurance.

Its fieldstone fireplace and the boards at three of the
corners still stand upright, but the rest of the structure
lies where it fell, a dense heap of spindly wood. It looks
like the collapsed hull of a sunken galleon, the protrud-
ing rib cage of a weathered corpse. Dan has been selling the wood to local carpenters, who treasure the grain
and color, which apparently only reveals itself after a
clear coat of polyurethane. I wish they'd treasure it a
little faster and get rid of the damned thing.

Behind these two structures is a flat concrete building with eighteen stalls that is both Dan's quarantine
barn and his surgery, although the two operating rooms
at the back, with their hydraulically powered tables,

haven't seen much use this year. The end result of Dan's desperate scramble to rescue the PMU horses involved in the production of pregnant mares' urine is that he's been backing further and further away from his veterinary practice, which I can't help finding alarming. His finances aren't officially my business, but I'm hoping they will be soon.

Behind all of that, past a thin line of anemic trees, is Dan's trailer. He bought it before the house collapsed, thinking that he and Jill—his late wife—would live there temporarily while he worked on the house. The trailer was used at the time, and that was eleven years ago. To this day it rests on concrete blocks with assorted garbage, junk, and God only knows how many rodents' nests beneath it. I shudder at the thought.

I find Judy alone in the main barn with the tractor parked in the aisle, tossing steaming piles of manure into the back with a pitchfork. When I enter, she looks up, startled. I think. It's hard to tell with Judy.

She's a string bean of a woman, tall, with long feet and hair even more calamitous than mine. Her glasses are thick and round, which magnifies her eyes and makes her look slightly cross-eyed. She has deep creases beside her mouth and across her forehead, and squints continually.

"Hey, lady—want a hand with that?" I say, grabbing a pitchfork from the wall.

She wipes the back of her hand across her forehead, smearing it with manure. "Oh, yeah. Hallelujah."

"Where's Chester?"

"Gone."

"I thought he was supposed to stay the day?"

"Teresa was pretty desperate. All three kids were up

all night, and now she's coming down with it too. Was threatening to run away if he didn't get home right away."

"Well, can't blame her for that," I say, ducking into a stall and observing the mess with horror. The stall belongs to Ringo, who was a show horse in his previous life and never got turned out. The end result is that he never relieves himself in the pasture. He holds it all in until he comes in for the night, and then lets loose with a deluge. Then he turns circles, making sure he spreads it into every corner.

"Ugh," I say.

"Ha," says Judy through the stall wall. "Finders keepers."

"Ugh," I say again.

"Might want to get yourself a shovel. You won't be able to save much."

Judy and I spend the morning mucking out, scrubbing and refilling buckets, mixing feed, wiping dust and cobwebs from stall windows, dumping the contents of the tractor at the muck heap, topping up the shavings, and finally watering down and sweeping the aisle. At the end the barn looks much too clean to let the horses back in. It's kind of like my experience with kitchens. The second you get one clean, it's time for another meal.

When we're finished with the chores, Judy and I sit in Dan's office gobbling a late lunch of Ruffles, Twizzlers, pepperoni sticks, and Coke. We're covered in filth; from manure and water-bucket slime to shavings that cling to our hair and clothing. I remove a boot and whack it against the beat-up couch, pick the remaining shavings off my sock, and then scratch the bejesus out of my ankle. Then I plop my feet up on a tack box and lean back into the couch.

"So how's Maisie look?" I ask around a mouthful of soda and licorice. I try to sound casual, but I'm watching Judy hard from the corner of my eye.

"Looks fine to me." She lines up three pepperoni sticks and bites off the ends. "Say, you're not nervous, are you?"

"Maybe a little."

"It's easy," she says brightly. She points a forefinger into the air beside her head. "Just remember, the goal is a foal!"

"I'm sorry, Judy, but that's helpful how?"

She stops chewing and stares at me, her magnified eyes enormous. She leans forward, arms on her legs. "You really are nervous, aren't you?"

"No. Yes." I glance up, and then down again, embarrassed. "Yeah, okay. Maybe a little."

"You've had a baby. You know what to expect."

"That's just it. Things don't always go as expected."

For example, uteruses rupture. My hand moves unconsciously to my belly.

Judy's eyes follow it and linger there. After a moment, she raises her eyes back to mine. "I can't spend the night because the kids drive Todd bonkers," she says quietly, "but if she starts and you get nervous, call and I'll come right on over."

I chew my Twizzlers in embarrassment, grateful almost to the point of tears. "Thanks, Judy. I may just do that."

• • •

After lunch, Judy heads out to run some errands. Since it's ages before the horses have to come in again, I hang around the office and boot up Dan's computer. He's so sweet—his password is my birthday.

I may not know anything about foaling, but I sure do know a thing or two about Googling. Before long, I've had a crash course in foaling and its most common problems—breech birth? Got it. Dystocia? Retained placenta? I am *so* on the phone to Walter. But mostly I'm relieved to learn that in the vast majority of cases you're supposed to just leave the mare alone to get on with it. Not only that, you're actually *encouraged* to leave her alone in order to leave the umbilical intact as long as possible—the better to achieve maximum placental blood transfer to the foal.

In late afternoon, when I find myself skimming passages because I recognize the information within them, I shut the computer down and head back to the barn. Then I mix a bucket of bran mash, stick a dandy brush in my pocket, and wander out to the back paddocks to see Bella.

Bella is my personal project, a thirty-four-year-old Morgan mare who came into Dan's care a few months ago. She'd had a good life until about a year ago when her owner got into a spot of trouble with a shotgun and ended up in prison. A neighbor who knew nothing about horses took over his twenty-six mares and geldings, turned them all out together, and tossed hay over the fence in one big pile. Bella, being old and arthritic, was driven away by the other horses, and since the ground was covered in snow, there was no grazing.

With her person suddenly missing, her arthritis untreated, and no food, Bella simply shut down. When the neighbor finally noticed something amiss, he sent the emaciated old mare to auction. Dan intercepted right before the gavel came down, paying three cents a pound more than the killer buyer.

He brought her home on Christmas Eve, the saddest sack of bones I'd ever seen. Her chestnut coat was run through with gray, her mane and tail straggly. Her head hung low—as did her bottom lip, as though she couldn't be bothered to keep it closed.

I've seen Dan coax horses back from the brink when anyone else would have given up, trying everything from equine massage to acupuncture to aromatherapy when traditional veterinary care fails—but in this case everything was failing. Since there was no medical reason for it, Dan finally concluded she wanted to die.

I couldn't accept that. Something about her eyes haunted me. They were hollow and glazed, which is certainly not uncommon in horses when they first arrive here, but I saw something else, too. Since Joan and I were teaching on alternating days, I started spending my off-days here, working with Bella.

Dan was immensely grateful, because he was working fourteen-hour days trying to get his latest load of rescued horses adopted. His gratitude made me all the more determined to save the old mare, because I want him to know I support his work. I want him to know that I'm willing to do this with him. Hell, what I really want him to know is that I'm ready for us to start our life together.

I put Bella in a paddock by herself so she'd have no competition for food. I put Barney, an equally ancient Thoroughbred gelding, in the paddock next to her, for company. I brought her pellets, oats, apples, carrots, mints—I tried all the tricks I used on Hurrah last year, but she was having nothing to do with any of it. She grew thinner and thinner, until it was hard to believe she could remain upright.

Naturally, the breakthrough that led to her recovery came on one of the days I was teaching at Maple Brook. Life's like that sometimes.

Dan was in the quarantine barn, mixing up buckets of bran mash to disguise the taste of medications for his surgical patients. Somehow, Bella got free and her nose led her to Dan. Apparently she was quite insistent on the matter. I wasn't there, of course, but Judy's description of the commotion as Dan danced from medicated bucket to medicated bucket trying to keep Bella's nose out of them was hilarious, particularly since Judy acted out the parts of both horse and man, flinging her long arms and legs about like a marionette.

And so began Bella's recovery. She loved her bran mash so much she'd lick the bucket clean with her eyes shut, ears twitching in ecstasy. And she began eating hay again.

We realized she was going to make it the day we came out and caught her nuzzling Barney over the paddock fence.

Now they share a paddock, inseparable friends. They spend much of the day standing head to rump, snoozing in the sun.

As I approach with her mash, Bella lifts her head and lets loose a low rumble, a throaty *huh-huh-huh, huh-huh-huh.* It's a greeting of honor, the one reserved for a horse's chosen person.

"Hey, sweets," I say, opening the gate and coming through. She plods over and shoves her head in the bucket. I haven't even set it down yet. Barney turns to look and resumes snoozing. He couldn't care less about bran mash. They're a perfect couple. Jack and Mrs. Spratt.

As Bella eats, I pull the dandy brush from my pocket and run it over her coat. Then I pick some tangles out of her tail with my fingers. She ignores me, continuing to lick her bucket long after the bran mash is gone, pushing it up against the fence with her eyes squeezed shut. When she finally gives up on it, she pulls her head out, turns to look at me, sniffs my hand, gives it a quick lick because it smells like bran mash, and wanders back to Barney.

As I turn to leave the paddock, I see Judy approaching. She stumbles on a clump of dirt.

"Whoopsy," she says, staring back in consternation and then tripping over something else. She comes to an abrupt stop just outside the paddock, pushes her glasses up her nose, and places her hands on her hips. She squints even though the sun is behind her, shining through her hair so that it looks like a halo of steel wool. "Mind if I take off now?"

"What's left? Just evening feed?"

"I got it ready. All you gotta do is bring them in."

"Thanks, Judy. You're a doll."

"Don't I know it." She turns to go.

"Oh, hey, Judy," I call. "When did you last check Maisie?"

"Just now. She's sulking, so I think you're safe."

"I beg your pardon?"

"She's attached to Dan, and he's gone."

Apparently I look baffled, because Judy continues.

"Prey animals. They have a smidgeon of choice when

things happen. But check her once an hour anyway, just in case. Say, you know how to work the foal-cam?"

"Uh, no." I say.

"Put the TV on channel three, and then press the Input button on the big clicker."

"Sounds easy enough."

"It's not brain surgery," she says, walking away.

I wince, because she's probably just jinxed me. In my experience, those words have always been the precursor to some disaster.

• • •

A quarter of an hour after Judy leaves, the sky splits with a resounding crash of thunder and *SLOOSH!*—an entire ocean's worth of water drops on my head. Why, I can't imagine, because the last time I looked up there was nothing up there but rolling puffy clouds. In retrospect, I suppose they *were* suspiciously tall and lumpy.

The water comes in sheets, sideways, never in the form of rain. Instead, it vacillates between hard sleet and clumpy snow, which melts the second it hits the ground and turns it into great squelching catfish mud whose many gaping mouths are constantly trying to suck off my boots. I rush back and forth from pasture to barn, desperate to get the horses in before they're soaked through.

They huddle at the gates, shivering, with snow gathering along their spines and manes and wondering what the hell is taking me so long.

When they're all safely inside, rubbed down and dry and munching on alfalfa hay, and after I've made sure I've been forgiven by each—because Lord knows I'm the only human here and therefore responsible—I poke my head outside the main barn and gaze mournfully at the quarantine barn, where Maisie resides.

But since I think I should probably assess the swelling and discharge—not to mention the Leaking Whatevers—in person before relying on the foal-cam, I grab an empty feed bag, hold it over my head, and sprint out into the squall. Halfway there, one foot skids out from under me. I throw both arms out in an attempt to regain my balance, sending the feed bag flying from my head. On its way past, it sluices water down my back. The mud offers no resistance whatever and I crash to the ground. Something snaps in my hip just before I hit. I cry out and clutch it with both hands, my fingers curled into wet, slimy denim. The pain is severe, and for a moment I wonder if I'm going to be able to get up and keep going. When it occurs to me that if I don't, nobody will find me, I steel myself and struggle to my feet. After ascertaining that I can, indeed, bear weight, I whimper and limp onward, with teeth clenched and the heel of one hand pressed against my hip. I leave the stupid traitorous feed bag in the mud, where I will no doubt slip on it in the morning and break my neck.

I finally reach the quarantine barn and stagger inside.

Maisie is the only horse in the barn, although the other stalls are set up and ready for the ones Dan is probably hauling behind him at this very moment.

She's in a foaling stall, which is just two regular stalls with the partition removed. She's a black-and-white draft mare, mostly Percheron, with feathered feet and long whiskers framing her large-boned face. She's already been adopted, but her new family was nervous about having her give birth at their place, so here she is.

I peek into her stall and find myself facing a large black-and-white rump. Beyond it is an enormously swollen belly. Her tail is wrapped, presumably to keep it out of the way of the action, and she's in deep straw instead of shavings so that wood particles won't get inside the foal's delicate nostrils.

Maisie pretends she doesn't notice my arrival, but her ears flicker and then settle decidedly further back than they were. Her official greeting is to shift her weight and rest her right hind foot on its rim, daring me to come in.

Since there's no way I'm opening the door with her foot cocked like that, I crouch down to investigate the foaling kit parked just outside her stall. Actually, I don't crouch down so much as topple over and crash to the floor, adding a bruised tailbone and wrenched wrist to my list of complaints. I thought I could lower myself on my one good leg, but I guess I haven't been working out enough. Or at all.

Anyway, I end up on the floor by the foaling kit, which is a blue plastic laundry basket covered with a folded bed sheet and stuffed with all sorts of objects: short and long gloves, a tube of KY Jelly, iodine, Purell, a plethora of fluffy towels and canvas sacks, surgical scissors that must be sterilized because they're zipped inside a freezer bag, a flashlight, long bulb syringe, clamps, garbage bags, thermometer, stethoscope, loaded hypodermic needles, dental floss, and a cell phone. I extract and identify each artifact, filing it in my head. When I get to the bottom, I put everything back and rise, gasping at the pain that shoots through my lower body.

Maisie still has her rear end to the door. I stare at her

wrapped tail, wishing she'd flick it off to the side since it's blocking my view of the very thing I have to assess. But she doesn't. I look both ways down the aisle, wondering if I'm going to be discovered in the morning with my face missing.

I push my filthy wet hair away from my face with filthy wet hands and slip the latch on the door. Maisie's eyes pop open. She adjusts her weight, still leaving one foot conveniently free for kicking.

I stay put and click my tongue. "Go on, girl. Shove over. Go on! Go on!"

Despite my clicking and pleading, she doesn't move. I open the door a crack, reach inside to the full length of my arm, and give her a little push. She pins her ears flat and I retreat.

I look from side to side down the aisle, resign myself to my fate, slide the door open and hobble past the menacing hoof.

Once I'm inside, she sighs deeply and cocks her ears in an unmistakable gesture of *Oh, all right. Fine. Just get it over with and leave me alone.* And then I begin to remember how I felt when I was hugely pregnant, and before long, I'm awash with pity for the poor girl and her heavy load.

I approach Maisie's head with the intention of introducing myself, because I don't want to be like the rude doctor who came into my labor room and didn't think to tell me his name until he was in up to the elbow—and even then it was only because I reminded him rather sharply that I also had a head.

I cup both hands beneath her muzzle and coo, but Maisie is not in the mood. Her ears swivel back and her eyes glaze over.

All right, so she's grumpy. That's completely under-standable for a lady as pregnant as she is. At this point she probably wishes she could be like the lazy Mayzie-bird and leave her egg for Horton to hatch.

I stand by her shoulder—indeed, I brace myself against it since I don't want to risk keeling over again—and peer beneath her. Her udder is full, but doesn't ap-pear to be leaking. There's also no evidence of wax, so I think we're good there. I approach her rear end some-what more timidly and after a moment of contempla-tion grab her wrapped tail. This sets off a strenuous round of tug-of-war, with me yanking and her clamp-ing, until eventually she gives in and lets me move it off to the side.

I observe for a moment, cocking my head and assess-ing. Certainly things are more engorged than what I'm used to seeing on a mare; but then again, she is hugely pregnant, and a draft horse to boot. I take a last look—mental flash photography, if you will—and drop her tail. Then I go back around to her head and thank her for not kicking me.

Since she still hasn't forgiven me for having the so-cial ineptitude to show up without so much as a carrot, I ask her nicely to please not have her baby until Dan gets home, skulk past her cocked foot, and stumble off through the mud and pelting sleet to Dan's trailer.

The stairs are difficult to manage, particularly since I have to avoid the rotten middle one. When I fling the screen door open, it bangs against the outside wall and stays there. I stagger inside, ready to weep with relief at finally being indoors and able to stay there. And for not having to dig mud out of anybody else's feet, or rub anybody else down, or check anybody else's udder.

I peel off my boots and socks, leave them at the front door, and hobble down the pumpkin orange carpet to Dan's bedroom. I change into a pair of his sweatpants and a T-shirt. The extra material gathers in rolls on my legs, but I'm warm and I'm dry and my mood is infinitely improved.

I decide my clothes are too wet to put inside his laundry hamper and head down the hall to the bathroom to toss them in the bathtub. I almost reconsider after finding algae-like stuff growing around its edges, but since the floor is no cleaner, I drop them in anyway.

Then I dig through the medicine cabinet looking for painkillers and trying to ignore the mildew spot beside it. I find all sorts of medicine, but, alas, none of it seems to be for people. And so I go in search of alcohol.

I thump across the kitchen with my eyes glued firmly on the refrigerator, awash with guilt and for good reason. I set Dan's kitchen on fire last year, and his strategy for repairing the damage was to "air things out a bit," buy a secondhand stove and range hood, and finally— the *coup de grâce*—to throw a coat of paint over the blackened walls and ceiling. He repeats this at regular intervals because the greasy streaks eventually work their way back to the surface of the paint; as indeed, they're doing now.

I wanted to have the kitchen redone, but Dan refused. I begged him to at least let me replace the stove, but he refused even that.

And so now he has a rust brown 1980s era coil-top stove in place of the avocado green 1970s one I set on fire.

I reach the fridge, having successfully avoided looking at either the stove or the recurring black streaks. My eyes sweep its empty shelves quickly and with increasing desperation: there's a large jar of Klaas pickles, which, upon closer examination, turns out to be a single pickle swimming in generous brine, two bottles of Odwalla soy protein drink whose swelling sides suggest they're of questionable vintage, a box of baking soda—whose vintage I know because he threw the previous box on the flames—a squeeze bottle of French's mustard, a baffling jar of Kim Chee, and Oh! Merciful Gods! Three cans of beer! Boddingtons, too, bless his heart.

I remove one of the tall yellow tins and get a glass ready. I learned the hard way that one has to be prepared when opening a Boddingtons—the cans contain a floating thing called something like a sprigget or a widget, but as far as I can tell its purpose in life is to make the beer explode forth and spill over the sides of the can the second you open it. And so I prepare, setting the glass next to the can, sliding my thumbnail under the tab, and leaning so my lips are within slurping distance.

Just as the seal breaks and the beer surges forth, the phone rings. I glance at it, back at the quickly rising foam, and decide to take care of business first. I snap the tab completely open, lean over, and suck the beer as it rises from the can. With the situation thus under control, I wipe my lips with the back of my hand and stump, wincing, to the phone.

"Hello?"

There's a shuffling at the other end.

"Hello?" I repeat, glancing at my beer, which is still rising. My stomach gurgles, and I'm reminded of my dim dinner prospects. Perhaps he has cereal or something stashed away in a cupboard? Macaroni and cheese? Anything?

"Hello?" I say again.

I'm just about to give up when a female voice says, "Oh . . . uh . . . Who's this?"

"Who are you trying to reach?" I say, propping the phone between my head and shoulder and reaching oh-so-far for my beer.

Success. I snag the glass with my fingertips and tip it, pouring the beer slowly down its angled side. It's a lovely rich brown and its foaming head cascades down the interior in rolling waves. I'm drooling like Pavlov's dog, but I think I'm entitled—I've had what Eva would call "a day." Besides, I need some Dutch courage if I'm going to spend the night alone in the trailer with all the mold and fungus, not to mention the rodents underneath.

"Never mind," the woman on the phone says. "I'll try again."

"But—"

There's a click at the other end.

I shrug, hang up, take a long sip of beer, and head for the living room area, progressing carefully because I'm off-kilter and don't want to spill my beer, which may well be the closest thing to dinner I get.

It takes me a while, but I reach the couch with my beer intact and set it on the coffee table beside the television's remote control. At Mutti's house, I'd use a coaster; but I'm not at Mutti's house, I'm in Dan's trailer, where the coffee table is made of something that only looks like wood.

I pull my ailing leg up onto its laminate surface and

settle back into the couch cushions. Then I reach for the remote control, determined to figure out the foal-cam.

The screen zaps to life. A man is holding a long floppy tube-like thing, tearing chunks off with his teeth with obvious and great disgust. Whatever it is, it's tough and stringy and he chews with his lips pulled back and eyes scrunched shut. The people around him scream things like "Puke! Go on! You know you wanna!" and then groan, looking as though they're going to do so themselves.

I realize—with immense and overwhelming horror—that I'm watching *Fear Factor,* Eva's favorite TV show, and that the current competitor is attempting to eat some type of disembodied penis. I scan the remote control frantically for the Input button so I can make it go away.

But there is no such button. Judy's words—"the big clicker"—come back to me.

"You can do it!" encourages the show's host, although even he's grimacing. He recovers with a shudder. "Three more minutes!" he shouts in a raw baritone. "Don't listen to them! Force it down! Just think of the fifty thousand!"

I scan the room quickly for the big clicker, and then dive elbow-deep into the couch, frantic to find it.

"Think of where it's been, dude!" shrieks another contestant, then apparently does so himself because his face contorts and he spins so that his back is to the camera, clutching his chest and stamping his leg up and down like a country fiddler.

I'm now gagging. I sweep my hands beneath the cushions with increasing desperation and encounter nothing but encrusted bits of God-knows-what, a couple of energy bar wrappers, and some coins. Since I'm now in serious danger of actually throwing up, I grab the smaller clicker so I can just turn the damned thing off. Just as I poke the power button, the phone starts ringing again. I leap to my feet, still feeling distinctly ill, and hobble toward it. But apparently I pressed the power button with such force that I double-clicked it, because the television has turned itself back on. And on it must stay, because I'm almost at the telephone now, clutching my hip and gritting my teeth in pain.

"Hello?" I shout into the mouthpiece, plugging my other ear to keep out the groans of disgust coming from the other room, which is really only separated from the kitchen by a counter.

"Oh, crap," says the same distant voice. "I've done it again."

"Who are you trying to reach?" I ask impatiently. I can't help it—my hip is seizing, people are eating penises behind me, and a most horrifying thought about female callers who don't want to identify themselves when I answer Dan's phone has just occurred to me.

"I was trying to reach the horse rescue," she says.

I shut my eyes with relief and make the sign of the cross, even though my Catholicism is definitely of the lapsed variety. "Then you've succeeded. This is the Day Break Horse Sanctuary."

"In that case you should say so."

My eyes spring open in surprise. "The phone line is also for a residence. Is there something I can do for you?"

"I have to get rid of my horse."

"Uh, okay," I say, frowning. That's a mighty strange

way of putting it. So strange, in fact, that it puts me on alert. "Let me get some information from you. Hang on while I find a pen." I yank the handle of Dan's junk drawer, which sticks shut because of the multiple layers of paint. When I finally jerk it open, loose batteries, screwdrivers, computer labels, and a tube of bute—an equine analgesic—crash to the floor.

I scrabble through the remaining Banamine granules, expired coupons, hoof picks, and assorted other junk until I find a pen and Post-it notes.

"Okay, I'm ready," I say, scribbling on the top sheet to get the ink flowing. "What's your name and number? I'll have the owner call you when he gets back." I glance back at the television, which has fallen blessedly quiet, the penis apparently consumed.

"What do you mean? When's he getting back?"

"In a couple of days. He's up in Canada getting a load of horses."

"I can't wait that long."

"Well, I'm sorry, but that's when he's coming back. I can get the ball rolling, though. Do you have a fax number where I can send the surrender papers? Or do you want to pick them up?"

"I'm selling him, not surrendering him."

I put the pen down on the pad. "You realize this is a rescue center, yes?"

"Yes."

"We don't buy horses."

"What about them PMU mares? You buy them, don't you?"

"Well, yes," I say, frowning. "But that's only so they won't go to slaughter."

"That's why I figured you'd buy Squire. The dealer

I talked to said he'd give me three hundred and fifty for him."

"Which dealer?" I say with a sinking feeling.

"Jack Harrison."

"He's a killer buyer!"

"Well, exactly. That's why I thought you'd want first shot," she says matter-of-factly.

"Listen," I say, pressing the heel of my hand to my forehead. "I don't think you understand the way this place works. It runs on a shoestring. We depend on do- nations of hay, wormers, grain—everything. Farriers donate their work for free. Volunteers do the barn work. I highly doubt we even *have* three hundred and fifty in the bank. We'd be happy to take your horse and give him a good home, but we can't pay for him."

"Well, I can't afford to give him up for nothing, so I guess that's that."

I press my lips together and rub my hand back and forth across my forehead. After a long pause I say, "Okay. Call him back and tell him the deal's off." I'll pay for the horse myself and consider it a karmic op- portunity to pay Dan back for the stove.

"So you'll take him?" she says, brightening audibly.

"Yes," I say.

"You'll have to come out tonight."

"Why?"

"Cuz the dealer's coming first thing in the morning."

"Just tell him the deal's off."

"How do I know you won't back out?"

I sigh deeply, grievously. "Okay. Fine. Where are you?"

"You won't be sorry. He's a real nice horse. A fifteen- hand Appy, although he's built more like a Thoroughbred. Real slim, real athletic. He'd make a good sport horse."

"I said, *where are you*?"

There is silence on the other end of the line.

I take another deep breath and force my voice to soften. "Please tell me how to get to you. I'll come out tonight."

"With four hundred?"

My jaw drops. "You just said Harrison offered three fifty!"

"Well, I figured being a rescue and all you'd pay a bit more," she says coyly, "so that . . . you know . . ."

"Okay. Fine," I say wearily. "Just tell me how to get to you."

And then she does, interspersing her directions with assurances about how I won't be sorry to have this horse because he's such a nice horse and worth so much more than I'm getting him for and it's just *killing* her to give him up but right now she really needs the money and all sorts of other stuff that I don't hear because I've tuned her out.

It doesn't matter a damn what kind of horse he is. I'd go get that poor creature tonight if he were a llama.

Chapter 3

Forty-five minutes. That's how long she told me it would take to get to her place. So far I've been on the road for an hour and a half, and I still haven't seen the designated landmark—a large maple with a black lightning mark on its trunk.

I finally catch sight of it—in my side-view mirror as I sail past. I pull off on the practically nonexistent shoulder, throw the car into reverse, and back up to it. This is only possible because I'm not hauling a trailer—the second I stepped outside at Dan's place, I realized I'd driven the Camry and therefore had no way of hauling a horse. I figured I'd better come anyway, pay the woman, write up a bill of sale, give her a stern warning about the legal ramifications of double-selling and how much more than seven hundred and fifty it would cost her if she tried, and then return in the morning to claim the horse.

At least the rain has stopped. The road is narrow and twisting, hemmed in by thick and tangled trees. Fat disks of pale fungus cling to their trunks up near where they split into branches. I've always thought of them as tree mushrooms, although I have no idea what they're really called.

The driveways are hard to make out, unpaved as they are and with night falling. I lean forward in the driver's seat, squinting and trying to count. I turn into what I think is the fourth driveway, discover that it's the beginning of a trail, and reverse back out to the road.

I stop tentatively at the mouth of the next possibility (two wheel tracks that lead into the trees), and turn. It snakes sharply a few times, then opens onto a clearing that is so muddy I hang tightly to the tree line, circumnavigating the lot in an effort to keep at least two of the car's wheels on solid ground.

I climb out of the car, glance down at the deep and slippery mud, and reposition my feet on little islands of rotting leaves.

The house is small and weathered with a dilapidated porch. It was white at some point, but the color is now merely suggested by streaks of paint embedded in the grain. There's a small paddock on one side, and its fence is a mess; some of the boards are missing entirely. Others are broken in half, their splintered ends resting on the ground. There's no way it could contain a horse.

I look around with widened eyes, wondering where the hell he is. There are a few small outbuildings, but nothing that looks like it could house a horse. It dawns on me that if he's not in one of the buildings, he must be wandering free. I'm starting to seriously regret not making a detour to get Mutti's pickup and trailer.

I approach the house, taking in the broken windows and toothless blinds with growing trepidation.

A little girl sits on the front porch. She's no more

than three, with dark curly hair, a yellow dress, and a bleached-out blue snow jacket that is unzipped. She has shoes on, but no socks. She's manipulating a Barbie doll with a crew cut. More disturbingly, Barbie has no clothes. The peach-colored body, with its wasp-waist and oh-so-perky breasts, is covered with ballpoint pen marks that look like varicose veins. Upon closer examination, Barbie is not entirely naked—she's wearing pink rhinestone-encrusted high heels.

The girl looks up at me, startled.

I lean over. "Hi, sweetie," I say, conjuring up my warmest smile. "Is your mommy home?"

She clambers to her feet and runs past me into the house. The screen door, with a two-foot rip in it, slams shut behind her. Its springs hang free from the hinges, which are crisp with rust.

A moment later a woman comes out the front door. She is small, with dark hair pulled back into a messy knot. She looks frail and wan, nothing like I expected.

"Hi," I say, stepping forward and sticking my hand out. "I'm Annemarie Zimmer. From Day Break."

"Hi," she says. All bravado is gone. She offers me a limp-fish hand and stares at the floorboards of her porch. "Eugenie Alcott."

"So," I say, putting my hands on my waist and looking around for something positive to comment on. "Is that your little girl?"

"Yes."

"She's adorable," I say.

"Thank you." There is no proud smile, no cute anecdote, no offering up of a name. "So I suppose you want to see Squire."

"Um . . . sure," I say. I look in alarm toward the

house, wondering if I can stall a bit because now I'm at least as concerned about the child as I am about the horse.

"Hang on," Eugenie says before turning and disappearing inside the house. When she returns, a man's flannel shirt hangs around her shoulders.

"He's this way," she says, walking past me and down the stairs.

She leads me around the side of the house toward a white cement-brick building that looks like a garage. I limp behind, as quickly as my hip will allow.

She comes to a stop outside the garage. It's even more dilapidated than the house—surely the horse isn't in here?

I glance at her with wide eyes and step up to the doorway. That's when the smell hits me.

"Sweet Jesus!" I exclaim, stepping back and gagging. And it's not just that I've been primed by *Fear Factor*—the interior reeks so fiercely of ammonia my eyes and nostrils sting.

"I know it's not the cleanest," she says.

"Not the cleanest?" I stare in disbelief. She gazes at the ground in either indifference or defiance.

I throw her one final look of incredulity, take a deep breath, and step inside.

There's one window at the very back of the cement brick structure. By its dim light I make out an enclosure and step closer.

It's a makeshift stall set up in the corner, the boards nailed haphazardly to a wooden post. I catch sight of white hide and a single shining eye. I'm almost out of oxygen, but I lean forward and peer through the slats.

Inside is a tiny creature, no more than thirteen hands

high, bedraggled, and clearly skeletal despite his hugely distended belly. His feet are completely obscured by slimy muck. It's at least a foot deep.

I've run out of breath without noticing and gasp in a lungful of contaminated air. I turn back to the doorway, toward the woman who lets him live like this. "Get him out of here."

"What?"

"Please. Just get him out," I say, staggering past her to the fresh air. I stand doubled over, hands on my thighs, struggling for breath.

Eugenie disappears around the side of the building and returns with a piece of knotted twine.

"What's that?" I say, pointing at it.

"It's a halter."

"No it's not."

"It's all I've got," she says.

She approaches the stall slowly, timidly even. She fumbles with the latch, which appears to be stuck. The second she gets it open, the pony blasts through the door and out of the building. His parting gesture is to shoot a hind hoof at my face—I fall back against the outside wall to avoid being hit.

Despite his initial steam, he comes to a stop about thirty feet away, at the first clump of sorry grass.

His legs are wet and dark almost up to his knees. His hipbones stick out like wings behind a belly as grossly swollen as Maisie's. He eyes us warily, swirling his ropy tail in circles. Out in the open, he looks so much worse I realize I can't possibly leave him here tonight. The paddock wouldn't hold him, and there's no way I can allow him to go back into that garage.

I spin around to Eugenie. She's scowling into the wind, hugging the flannel shirt against herself.

"What?" she says, as though she has no idea.

The second I get out of here, I'm calling Child Protective Services.

I turn away from her and step toward the pony, carefully, approaching from the side. He keeps working the tuft of grass, but his left pupil is aimed right at me. When I get within eight feet his ears fall back.

"Easy, boy," I say, stopping. "Easy."

I take a few tentative steps forward, holding out my hand.

He lifts his muzzle a few inches from the ground and holds it there, pinning his ears. Then *WHOOSH!* A hind leg snaps out, narrowly missing my ear.

"Whoa!" I take a long step backward and look over my shoulder at Eugenie, who is still scowling. "Got any grain?" I ask.

"No."

"Why am I not surprised?"

"What the hell is that supposed to mean?"

I sigh and walk back to her. "Let's just go inside and draw up a bill of sale. I'm going to need to borrow your phone to call for a trailer. Will you take a check?"

"Cash only," she says quickly.

I throw her a murderous glance.

"I can't do it through a bank account," she says. "My husband would get at it."

"Okay. Fine. I'll get cash. Let's just get this over with, okay?"

She leads the way to the house in silence. I follow, limping like Quasimodo and glancing back at the starving pony to make sure he's staying put, although I'm not sure what, exactly, I would do about it if he didn't.

Once we're inside the house's dismal interior, Eugenie waves me at the phone and climbs the stairs with hunched shoulders.

I glance around the living room. A single bulb is suspended from three wires in what was once an ornate ceiling fixture. The wallpaper hangs off in shreds, revealing crumbling plaster and strips of lath. There's a couch and matching chair, with ornate woodwork and red upholstery. At one time it was glorious. Now it's tattered and lumpy, with springs sticking through the seat. Loose garbage and stacks of newspaper tied with twine line the walls.

The little girl sits at the very bottom of the stairs playing with her Barbie. She gives no indication of being aware of my presence. Her dark hair is greasy, and flattened at the back. I watch her for a moment, fingers pressed to my mouth in thought.

Then I turn back to the phone and dial our number.

Eva answers immediately, so quickly that from this end it didn't even sound like it rang.

"Hello?" she says breathlessly. Obviously she's hoping I'm her boyfriend Luis.

"Eva, it's me," I say. "Get Oma."

"Can you call back later?" Eva hisses. "I'm expecting a call."

"Honey, please—this is important."

She sighs dramatically. "Okay. Fine. But I really do need a cell phone."

"Point noted. Now get Oma."

"So I'm getting a cell phone?"

"Get Oma!"

She slams the receiver down and her footsteps recede. "Oma," she calls in the distance, "it's Mom. Says it's . . . '*important.*' " There's a clear pause before the final word.

Hurried footsteps approach the phone.

"What is it? Is everything all right?" says Mutti in clipped Teutonic. She can't help it. Her accent gets stronger when she's worried. "Is it the mare?"

"No. But I do need help."

"What? What is it? Are you all right?"

"Not really. I need you to come out to Gum Neck with the horse trailer. And four hundred in cash. And a pony halter. And a bucket of grain."

There is silence at the end of the line as she takes this in. "I will come. Where are you?"

I'm just getting to the part about the burnt maple when I hear heavy footsteps on the porch. I turn just as a huge man crashes through the front door. He throws it open with such force that its knob lodges in the wall behind it, and then he stands in the doorway, wild-eyed and panting. He's at least six foot three, and well over two hundred pounds.

The little girl looks up and screams. He trips over her in his rush to mount the stairs, which he takes three at a time. The child scrambles over to me on all fours and grabs me by the legs, shrieking into the back of Dan's sweatpants.

Eugenie appears at the top of the stairs and opens her mouth, but before she can make a sound, the man cups her throat in one hand, claps his other over her mouth, and throws her back against the wall.

"Hey, Buddy!" I bellow. "Yo! Buddy!"

He freezes and does a double take down the stairs.

He passed right by me on his way up the stairs, but apparently failed to notice my presence.

"I've got nine-one-one on the line here!" I say, still pressing the receiver to my ear.

"*Mein Gott,* Annemarie! What is going on?" cries Mutti.

"Hang it up!" he roars. "Hang it up or so help me God—"

"You'll what?" I scream back at him. "The second I dialed it, they traced the call. They're already on their way and they're listening to every damned word you say!"

"Eva! Eva! Get my cell phone! *Schnell! Schnell!*" screams Mutti from the other end of the phone. "Annemarie," she continues, her voice an urgent whisper, "I'm calling nine-one-one on my cell phone. I've got your instructions. They are coming. They are coming! Do not hang up!" Then again, her mouth away from the receiver, "*Schnell,* Eva! *Schnell!*"

The man drops Eugenie, who crumples to the floor like a rag doll. He turns and stares at me, his expression frighteningly blank. He takes a step toward the top of the stairs. Then another.

The little girl whimpers, her face still buried in the back of my legs. I reach around and press her against me.

The man comes to the top of stairs, slowly, his eyes locked on mine, his massive hand gripping the banister.

"They're listening to the whole thing," I say, forcing myself to meet his gaze. My voice is hollow and deep, fueled by God only knows what. "The dispatcher confirmed your address. It's all over," I say.

He stares at me for what seems an eternity. Then his face falls, his shoulders slump, and he comes down the stairs slowly, one at a time. When he reaches the bottom, I take a couple of steps backward, still pressing the child against me.

But we might as well not be in his world anymore. He passes right on through the open door, which is still impaled in the wall, and takes a seat on the top step of the porch.

"Mutti," I whisper into the phone. "I'm hanging up now. I'm calling nine-one-one for real."

"I already have, *Schatzlein*," she hisses. "They are already coming, and so am I."

• • •

Twenty minutes later, the police arrive. I'm sitting on the tattered couch with both arms wrapped around the child. She's curled into a ball on my lap, sucking her thumb. She still hasn't said a word, but her little body is relaxed. Her head is tucked beneath my chin, and I stroke her hair even though the scent of unwashed scalp is overwhelming.

Eugenie is still upstairs, crouching against the wall where she fell. She appears catatonic. The man is still on the top step of the porch and has dropped his head into his hands. Because of the open door, I have a clear view of him and I wouldn't have it any other way. His shoulders are rounded, and he may be crying. I don't know and I don't care.

At first there are two cruisers, but before long other vehicles start to arrive. The man is handcuffed and bundled into the back of a car. Kindly women in plain clothes pry the little girl off me—it takes some doing, since she seems to have associated me with safety— and take her into another room. Others go upstairs and kneel beside Eugenie. I am taken to the kitchen by two uniformed officers to fill out a statement.

When I've added every last detail I can think of, I sign it and push it across the table at the officer sitting opposite me.

"What's going to happen to them?" I ask as he picks it up.

"He'll be cooling his heels for a while, that's for sure." He runs his eyes across my handwritten statement. "What's this say?" he asks, leaning forward and pointing at a word.

"Sockless."

"And this?"

"Unwashed. Sorry. My writing's not great at the best of times, and I'm still a bit shaky."

"That's understandable," he says. He clicks his pen open and prints both words above my loopy handwriting. Then he hands the sheet back to me. "Here. Initial both places."

"What's going to happen to the little girl?" I say, taking the pen.

"Child Protective Services is evaluating the situation now."

"And Eugenie?" I say.

The other officer, who is filling out a form, sets his pen down and looks at me. His stark gaze is accusatory. "Why do you want to know?"

"No reason. Just curious," I say quickly, looking from officer to officer. "I mean, I did kind of get thrown into the middle of the whole thing."

"So you're taking that horse, right?" says the nice one, giving me an opportunity to look back at him—which I do, gratefully.

"Yeah. I guess so," I say. "My, uh, boyfriend runs the Day Break Horse Sanctuary."

Boyfriend. That word becomes troublesome when you're nearly forty.

"Is it registered?" he says.

"Yes. He gets called out to cases like this all the time."

"Good. Then I won't have to—"

"Annemarie!" cries a hoarse female voice.

I twist in my chair and see Mutti cross the kitchen at a near-run. When she reaches me, she puts a hand on the back of my chair and runs her eyes frantically over my body. "*Mein Gott,* what is going on here? What happened?"

"A 'ten-sixteen,' " I say, reading from the top of the evil officer's report. "A domestic disturbance," I continue.

Understanding dawns on her face. "That brute out front? Did he touch you? Because so help me God, I will rip out his spleen!"

The eyebrows of both officers shoot up.

"Mutti! I'm fine. He never touched me."

Mutti halts, presses her lips together, and continues investigating me with her eyes. When she's finally satisfied that I'm fine, the lines disappear from her forehead. She makes the sign of the cross and takes a seat in the only remaining chair.

The men exchange glances.

I sigh. "Officer Pitts, Officer Ewing; my mother, Ursula Zimmer."

Mutti nods at each of them. "It is very nice to meet you."

"Likewise," Pitts says unsurely. His eyes dart sideways.

"Are we finished here?" I ask. "Because that pony's chariot just arrived, and I'd like to catch him before he wanders off."

"I think we've got everything we need. I assume we can call? I'm pretty sure we'll be laying charges about the animal as well."

"I should hope you would. And yes, by all means, call anytime," I say, pushing my chair back and rising. I grimace and grab my hip.

"He hurt you! I knew it!" cries Mutti. "I'll kill him!"

"No he didn't!" I hiss. "I slipped in the mud. In the rain. Back at Dan's place." I add each detail separately, watching her fury deflate in stages. "Really," I say firmly.

She stares at me for a moment longer. When she's finally sure she believes me, she rises and places her hands on her hips. "So, where is this horse?"

"God only knows at this point," I say. "With any luck, not out on the highway."

"He's still out back," says Officer Ewing. "And he's got a bit of a temper from the looks of it."

"Yeah, well, you would too if you'd been living like him," I say grimly. Then I turn and limp from the kitchen.

Mutti follows me, watching my progress carefully—I can feel her eyes all over me. When we get to the living room I lean back and whisper, "Mutti, could you *please* refrain from threatening to kill people in front of police officers?"

"*Hrrmph,*" she snorts, raising her chin and making it pointier.

I've never known how she manages that.

• • •

When we round the corner and the bedraggled little horse comes into view, she stops in her tracks.

"*Mein Gott.* He is full of parasites."

"I know. He's a mess."

"Go get in the car. I will catch him."

"No, I'll help."

"With that leg? Get in the car."

"It's my hip. Besides, he's full of piss and vineg—"

Her arm shoots straight out, index finger pointing through the house. "In the car, Annemarie!"

I make my way carefully around to the front yard. It's full of vehicles, the porch buzzing with activity.

As I climb obediently into my car, Mutti marches back to her truck. She opens the passenger door, removes a bucket, halter, and lead rope, and disappears behind the house. Moments later she reappears with the pony plodding beside her, stretching his nose out toward the grain. He follows her straight into the trailer without so much as a moment's hesitation.

I shouldn't be surprised. Everybody obeys Mutti.

• • •

In a few minutes, we're on our way. When we get back to Day Break, Mutti stops, opens her window, and beckons me forward with her hand. I pull up beside her and run my passenger window down, leaning over so I can see her.

"Where should I put him?" she shouts over the sound of our combined engines. "The quarantine barn?"

"No, Pregzilla's in there."

"Who?"

"Maisie. The pregnant mare. Put him in the paddock on the far northeast side, the one with a shelter. I don't want him anywhere near the other horses till we've had him checked out. Think I should call Walter tonight?"

"No. He'll be fine until morning. You go on back to the house." She runs up her window and wends her way behind the quarantine barn.

By the time Mutti joins me in Dan's trailer, I've found the larger clicker and am watching a bluish gray image of Maisie sleeping.

"Well," says Mutti, coming to a stop and putting her hands on her waist. "At least everything there looks okay. How's your hip?"

"Pretty sore."

"Have you iced it yet?"

"No. I'm not sure Dan even *has* ice."

Mutti goes into the kitchen and opens the freezer. I hear her wrestling with something—particles and shards of ice ping and tinkle as they hit the interior walls of the freezer, and then she appears with a frost-covered bag. She bashes it against the side of the sink a few times, and then brings it to the couch.

"Someone needs to defrost that thing." She hands me a bag of peas. "There is nothing in it but snow."

"Maybe I'll do it tomorrow," I say, leaning to one side and pulling open the waistband of Dan's pants. I insert the bag of peas and press it against my hip. "Ooh! Aah!" I say, sucking air in through clenched teeth.

"Mmmm," says Mutti, looking dubious. "Be careful you don't flood his kitchen."

"Mutti!"

"I'm just saying . . ." she says, casting her eyes

around the room. She points at my beer, which is looking sad and flat. "Is that new?"

"No. Alas."

She whisks it away, washes the glass, and puts it back in the cupboard.

"Is the ice helping?"

"Not really. Now it feels like a toothache."

"Try heat. Take a bath."

"Are you kidding?" I snort.

Mutti shoots me a glance.

"I would have cleaned it, but with my hip and all . . ." I look sheepishly into my lap, letting the sentence trail off.

Mutti disappears down the orange carpeted hallway. She returns immediately, rummages under the kitchen sink, and goes back with a sponge and canister of Comet. The sounds of vicious scrubbing, sloshing, swishing, and slooshing emanate from the bathroom, punctuated by water running full blast.

Sometime later, I'm relaxing in a deep bath with my eyes closed and a wet washcloth over them.

"Here," says Mutti.

I yank the washcloth from my eyes, prepared to be outraged that my mother has entered the bathroom and is standing beside my perfectly naked self. But when I see that my mother is handing my perfectly naked self a freshly poured beer, I sit forward, feeling effusively thankful instead.

"Oh, Mutti," I say. "Whatever would I do without you?"

"Indeed," she sniffs. "I'm leaving now. There's spaghetti on the counter. It was all I could find. Call if you need help with that mare."

. . .

After my bath, I return to the kitchen on a considerably loosened hip and snarf the spaghetti. Then I bring Dan's pillow and comforter from the bedroom to the couch—after first covering said couch with two layers of sheets to protect myself against potential dust mites. It's not Dan's fault—the thing's just old.

The incident with Eugenie has left me feeling a little ill. Even if the authorities are now aware of her little girl, whose name I never found out, what can they really do? How much harm has already been done? And will they send her back to one or both of her parents? The thought makes me weepy for Eva.

My daughter has never gone sockless, has never had hair matted from neglect, but neither has her life been idyllic. I suppose it probably looked that way until last year when Roger and I divorced, but even before then I'd racked up fifteen years of parental faults. Roger racked up a few of his own, to be sure, but in a way he's lucky: he'll get to use the benefit of our combined experience raising his second family, an option that's closed to me.

But as unfortunate as that is, it's largely beside the point because I'm nowhere near finished with Eva. She's not just the concentrated point of all my hope—the one and only repository of my DNA—she's a good kid, a smart kid, who just happens to act out in all the currently fashionable ways when frustrated. And what frustrates her is me.

Hell, I frustrate myself. I'm starting to feel stolid, lumpish, and definitely in the way.

So what's wrong with me? Am I so fearful that she'll

be injured riding that I'm willing to let her skid off the rails in every other aspect of her life? Because that's completely ridiculous. I might as well keep her from riding in cars.

Maybe it is time to see a therapist. Not because I'm crazy, but because maybe it's time to get the opinion of someone who can objectively weigh the statistical chances of a crippling accident against the advantages of structure, goal, and harmony. Certainly I—with my reconstructed face—am not that person.

I consider calling Eva tonight, but some deep inner switch warns me against it. This train of thought is too new. I don't want to make a proclamation I'm going to regret.

I turn on the foal-cam and watch Maisie snooze for a while. Then I switch to the eleven o'clock news and help myself to the other beer. For medicinal purposes, of course. Then I lie back against the pillow, which smells like beautiful, beautiful Dan, and pull the covers up to my chin.

• • •

Birds are singing. A male voice blares in the background. I blink a few times. A predawn glow suffuses the room.

"—we're expecting a beautiful day, Louisa, with almost no chance of precipitation and highs of almost fifty-six degrees—"

Springing upright, I seek the large clicker. I snatch it from the floor and stab the Input button. The screen switches to black and white.

Maisie is on her side on the ground. Her uppermost hind leg is stiff, quivering.

"Oh shit!" I scream, leaping off the couch.

I stuff my feet into my mud-encrusted boots, snatch Dan's lumberjack coat from the coat tree, and bolt across the thickening mud, too full of adrenaline to take anything other than vague notice of my screaming hip.

Please let her be okay, *please* let her be okay, *please* oh *please* Lord, please don't let anything be wrong—

I stagger into the barn, flick on the light, and approach Maisie's stall as quietly as I can, although I'm breathing heavily from my sprint. I peer through the bars of her stall with trepidation.

She grunts as a contraction hits and her hind leg stiffens almost like in rigor mortis. A white bubble appears at her vulva, and disappears when the contraction ends.

It's the amniotic sac—the birth is imminent.

"Okay, okay, okay," I chant, sliding the door open. "Everything's going to be okay." Despite my protestations, my heart is pounding.

Maisie jerks her head up and looks at me. I freeze, worried that she'll try to get up. I'm about to back away when she groans and drops her head into the straw.

"Good girl, good girl," I say, leaning over and dragging the foaling kit in behind me.

I kneel behind Maisie and tuck the sheet from the top of the kit, still folded, beneath her haunch as a landing strip for the foal. Then I fumble through the kit, seeking the flashlight.

Maisie lifts her head and grunts, rolling slightly onto her back.

"Oh, I know, Maisie. Believe me, I know," I croon, although in fact my own labor went terribly wrong before it ever progressed this far. Her grunt turns into a groan, and her body seizes. The bubble reappears.

I crouch behind her with the flashlight, urging her on. "Come on, Maisie! Come on!"

This time, when the contraction ends, the bubble stays. The clear membrane is veined and filled with swirling opalescent liquid. In the center is a small dark thing.

I scooch closer, aiming the flashlight at it from various angles. It's a tiny hoof.

"Oh!" I say, clapping my hand to my mouth in delight when I realize that the patch of white above it is a sock.

Another contraction, and a gush of liquid. The leg comes further out, and another appears, slightly behind the first. This one is sockless. I have to remember to breathe, gazing in wonder as the foal reveals itself by inches.

Another contraction, but this time the legs don't move. When this happens again, it suddenly occurs to me that I haven't seen the head. I shuffle forward to get a better look at the legs.

I gasp, horrified. They're hind legs, and with the foal this far descended, the umbilical cord is almost certainly compressed. In a normal presentation, the head would already be out and the foal could start breathing. But in this case, the foal's head is buried deep in Maisie's abdomen. I have approximately two minutes to get it out.

Whimpering, I scrabble through the kit for the Purell. I squirt generous amounts onto my hands, rubbing them furiously. Then I tear open one of the packets of sterilized gloves.

I make the sign of the cross and glance at the ceiling. Then I take a deep breath and grasp a tiny foot in each hand. They're too slick for me to get a good grip, so I reach behind me for a towel. I rub them hard—so hard one of the feet objects, and I cry out with relief because it means the foal is alive.

"Okay, okay," I say as much to comfort myself as Maisie.

I climb to my feet and stand with my knees bent, grasping the foal's feet and waiting for another contraction.

When it starts, I pull with all my might. The foal descends by almost a foot, but then lodges, remaining in the birth canal.

"Oh no," I say, my face contorting. "Oh no. Come on, Maisie," I urge. "Just one more. Come on, Maisie!"

It feels like an eternity. I'm watching her so closely that I forget to blink. I sniff and wipe my nose on my shoulder, holding the feet, waiting.

When I see her abdomen tighten, I heave with all my might. The body moves, sliding toward me, but once again stops. I keep pulling, clenching my teeth and growling with the effort even as my feet slide out from under me. Since it's now or never time, I stick my left leg out and brace it against the wall—still grasping the tiny hooves, still pulling with everything I've got.

The foal slips out and lies there, a black mass, completely limp. I crawl to its head on my hands and knees, desperately swiping the amnion away from its nose and face.

"Come on, baby," I plead. "Come on!"

I reach for the towel, rubbing the foal's head and body roughly.

"Come on, baby. Don't do this to me! Breathe! Breathe, dammit!"

The foal suddenly comes to life, lifting its head and sucking a great lungful of air.

"Yes!" I shout. "Oops, sorry Maisie," I continue, addressing the concerned mare, who has lifted her head and is looking behind her to see what's going on. "Here," I say, grasping the foal by the rib cage. I hold its wet fuzzy self close to my chest and turn it around, being careful not to pull or step on the umbilical cord.

"Here's your baby, Maisie. Look—"

Maisie snorts and rumbles in recognition, nuzzling and licking her baby. The foal—a black filly with one rear sock and a perfect diamond of a star—squeals a high-pitched greeting.

I watch long enough to realize that not only are they both just fine, but any further involvement on my part would be interference. And then I retreat to a corner of the stall and sit on a feed sack, crying like a baby and watching one of the most beautiful things I've ever seen.

Chapter 4

"Eva!" I burst through the back door of our house already shouting her name. "Eva! Are you up yet?"

She and Mutti appear in the doorway of the kitchen at the same moment, a study in contrast. Mutti is dressed and neat, her hair pulled into its usual bun of solid steel. Not a strand is out of place. Eva is wearing baggy pink pajama bottoms and a cropped T-shirt that displays plenty of belly. Her eyes are puffy and she's barefoot.

"What?" she says, rubbing her eyes. She squints at me, looking me up and down. "Geez, Mom, did you even brush your hair? You look like a sea—"

"Get dressed! There's something I want to show you!" I say, too excited to be offended. Besides, I probably do look like a sea hag.

"What?" says Eva, still suspicious, still scowling.

"Just get dressed!"

"I wanna know why!"

"Maisie had her baby. It's a perfect, beautiful filly!"

Eva squeals and stamps her feet. Then she turns and disappears into the hallway.

"So, everything went fine then," says Mutti, passing

me on her way to the coffee machine, which is full and steaming.

"Actually it was a breech birth," I say.

Mutti's head jerks around. "What happened? Is everybody okay?"

"They're fine. Fortunately both legs presented, so when I realized that the foal was backward—not headless—I got to work and pulled her out. It took me a second to get her going, but she was up and nursing in half an hour."

Mutti keeps looking at me. Then she turns back to her coffee. "Well, good for you," she says, nodding proudly.

A blur of denim and pink fleece streaks through the kitchen, thumping on thick Nike soles. It stops by the door.

"Mom! Come on! What's keeping you?" says my daughter, pulling the back door open. Her expression is of pure excitement.

"Wait, Eva," says Mutti. "Annemarie, do you want a cup of coffee to take with you?" she says, opening the cupboard and reaching for my stainless steel travel mug.

"No, she doesn't!" squeaks Eva. She dances with desperation, like a child who needs to use the washroom. "There's no time for that!"

I burst out laughing, shrug at Mutti, and limp to the door, through which my daughter has already disappeared. By the time I'm stepping out onto the back porch, her car door is slamming shut.

• • •

"Oh my God!" Eva whispers as she stares through the bars of Maisie's stall. "Look at her! She's gorgeous! And so fuzzy!"

The filly is lying in the straw behind Maisie. She gazes back at us, her chocolate eyes shining. Then she unfolds her impossibly long legs and clambers to her feet, peering at us from under the safety of her mother's belly.

"Isn't she just?" I say. Prompted by who-knows-what, I put my arm around Eva's shoulder. She reaches up and squeezes my fingers.

Maisie observes us, her eyes cheerful and inquisitive. With her ordeal behind her, she is bemused, calm, and pleased as punch with what she's done. And the baby is perfection itself, in a fuzzy daddy-long-legs kind of way. Her mane and forelock are cashmere fluff, her tail a fat pipe cleaner that alternates between standing on end and twirling furiously. Her muzzle is tiny, her face angular, her eyes fringed with long lashes.

Eva suddenly looks strange. "Are you *sure* it's a girl? Because, uh, isn't that a . . ." she says, pointing.

"That's the umbilical cord, honey."

"Oh."

From outside the barn, there's the crunching of tires on gravel. A moment later a car door slams shut.

"And I'll bet that's the vet," I say.

A man wearing a cowboy hat appears in the doorway of the barn, carrying a kit. "Good morning, ladies," he says. "I hear there's been a blessed event."

"Indeed there has," I say.

He comes up beside us and sets his kit on the floor. "Annemarie, I presume?"

"Yes."

"I've heard all about you," he says, winking. "Walter Pennington."

"How do you do," I say, blushing and taking his hand.

"Don't worry, it's all good," he says, noting my discomfort. "And congratulations, you handled this situation like a pro."

"Well, you know," I say, feeling suddenly bashful. "I did what I needed to."

"You saved her life is what you did," he says. "Possibly the mare's, too. If you'd called me instead, it would have taken me at least half an hour to get out here."

I call the Hutchisons—Maisie's adoptive family—on my cell phone while Walter checks the new baby. He allows Eva to act as maternity nurse—tying off the filly's long umbilical cord with dental floss, dipping the stump in iodine, and fitting her with a tiny pink halter. He listens to her heart and lungs, and then lets Eva do the same, telling her what to listen for. However, when Walter kicks through the straw and locates the placenta, Eva allows as to how he can have the honor of disposing of it.

Not long after, the patter of feet on concrete announces the arrival of the Hutchisons, whose three daughters race into the barn amid excited squeals.

"Everything looks perfect with these two," Walter says, coming into the aisle as the girls barrel past. He reaches out and grabs an arm. "Whoa there. Slow down. You don't want to make the mother anxious."

The girls collect themselves with obvious effort.

Walter turns to me. "You said there was another horse you wanted me to look at?"

"Yeah, he's a real mess. I got him last night. He's out back, because I wanted to keep him as far as possible from the other horses until you'd run a Coggins and so on," I say.

I turn to tell Eva that we're leaving, but she's otherwise occupied, kneeling in the straw and introducing the Hutchison girls to the filly. She's also regaling the entire family with vivid details of the birth and how brilliantly I handled it. I can tell how this is going to go down in our family's mythology: it's already taking on the proportions of a full-fledged fish tale.

I hurry from the barn, leading Walter to the northeast pasture.

He stops and whistles as Squire comes into sight. "Oh my-my-my-my-my-my-my," he says. He sets his kit on the ground and ducks between the boards of the fence.

"Should I have called last night?"

He shakes his head. "No. A few hours either way won't have made a difference. Fact is, someone should have called me a year ago. It never ceases to amaze me what people are capable of."

Mutti was right, of course. Squire's distended belly is due to parasites, and despite how large it is he's seriously undernourished. He also has one of the worst cases of thrush Walter has ever seen, along with ulcers on all four legs.

He's fast with his feet, and more than willing to use them. Walter is clearly an expert at dodging hooves, but Squire eventually makes contact with an audible crack.

"Shoot!" Walter leaps backward, clutching his arm.

"You okay?" I ask, tightening my grip on Squire's halter.

He flexes his fingers, bends his elbow. "Seem to be," he says, grimacing.

"Do you want me to twitch him?"

"Yeah. I guess you'd better. There's one in the second compartment."

I dig the twitch out and catch a portion of Squire's upper lip in its looped cord. Squire peers resentfully up at me as Walter finishes treating the wounds on his back legs.

"We're just trying to help you, you know," I say, stroking his forelock with my free hand. I smooth it and lift it off to the side, revealing a long scar on his forehead. It's at least six inches long, healed over, but bald and a raw pink.

"Walter, come look at this."

Walter wipes his hands on his pants and comes around. "What is it?"

"His face. Check this out."

When he gets out of range of Squire's back legs, I release the twitch.

"Oh my-my-my-my-my-my-my," says Walter again, and I think two things: first, that if I were his wife that phrase would drive me bonkers; and second, whether he says it because he doesn't want to swear (the kick would have elicited at least a "shit" from me). And then I try to remember if I've sworn in front of him.

When Squire has been wormed, washed, twitched, injected, slathered in ointment, bandaged, had his ears flushed and teeth floated and been generally insulted in a million different ways, we leave him feeling slightly better about life through a simple bribe of bran mash. He has Bella to thank for that.

Walter packs up to leave, and I return to the quarantine barn. I am halfway down the aisle, moving silently

on soft-soled shoes, when I hear Eva segue from how
wonderful-marvelous-beautiful the filly is to how
wonderful-marvelous-beautiful her new baby half
brother is. Of course, she doesn't say "half." She just
calls him her brother.

I do an about-face and go see Bella.

• • •

On the evening of the next day, Eva and I are in the
kitchen making tabbouleh, one of the dishes I have
managed to master since she became a vegetarian.

She's being sweet. Too sweet. She's planning something, that much is sure.

"Mom," she says, looking studiously at the parsley
under her knife. *Chop, chop.* Pause. Quick glance up,
and then back down.

"Yes?" I say, bracing myself.

"I'm sorry about the other day." *Chop. Chop.*

I stare at my own cutting board and the tomatoes
upon it, waiting. Here it comes—

"If you let me ride at Strafford, I'll let you get my tattoo removed."

"What?" I laugh out loud. "You'll *let* me? For your
information, getting a tattoo lasered off costs thousands
of dollars."

We're silent for a moment, chopping our respective
vegetables.

I glance up at her. "Really?"

She smiles, sweetness personified. "Sure."

"Huh," I say, pondering. Another pause. "Eva, what
do you want to do with your life?"

"I want to ride."

"I know. I meant later, as a career."

"So do I."

"You don't want to be a vet anymore?"

"No. I want to compete."

"Are you sure? You know the money's not very good, right? I mean, when you consider how much it costs to campaign even just one horse, a fifty-thousand-dollar purse starts to sound a whole lot less—"

"I know. I figured I'd take students in the off-season. I kind of thought I might do it here," she says, throwing me a shy look.

Another pause, as I teeter on the precipice, both arms spread and wondering whether I have the courage to just let myself fall. I take a deep breath and lean into the void—

"Eva?"

"Yes, Mom?"

"I know it's probably too late for me to do anything about getting you a horse in time for Strafford, but I'll see what I can do, okay?"

"What?" She looks stricken.

"You heard me."

She stares at me for a long time, waiting for the punch line. When it doesn't come, she slams her knife down and bounds across the kitchen, nearly knocking me down with the force of her embrace. "Mom! Are you serious?" she shrieks, taking my shoulders in both hands and searching my face with her eyes.

When I nod, she whoops, and dances an impromptu flamenco with one arm thrust in the air. "You're the best! What made you change your mind? No, never mind—I don't want to know!"

The obvious subtext being that she doesn't want me to reconsider.

She spins me around, plants a sloppy kiss on my cheek, and disappears into the hallway.

"Don't forget, young lady—you owe me a tattoo!" I shout after her.

She crashes up the stairs and slams her door with such force the glasses rattle in the cabinet behind me.

Mutti sails into the kitchen. She stops, glances at the bubbling bulgur and abandoned cutting board and assumes the worst. This is understandable, because amazingly Eva sounds exactly the same in the throes of great happiness as she does when on the rampage—which is to say three times her body weight.

"What now?" sighs Mutti.

"I just told Eva that I'll see what I can do about entering her in Strafford."

Mutti stares at me for a moment, and then takes her place behind Eva's parsley. She picks up the knife and begins chopping, lightning quick.

"And what are you going to do about a horse?" she says finally.

"I don't know yet."

Mutti doesn't answer. I consider telling her about the phone call, but decide I'm not ready to leap off that particular precipice yet.

• • •

When the table is laid with hummus, pita, and tabbouleh, I go to the bottom of the stairs and call Eva.

I hover by the kitchen doorway, listening. After a few seconds, her door squeaks open, and shortly thereafter she thumps into the kitchen.

"Hey, Ma," she says cheerfully.

The phone rings. I look expectantly at Eva. She

breezes right past and comes to a stop by her backpack, which hangs from a hook by the door.

I look at Mutti, who raises an eyebrow. I shrug and answer the phone.

"Hello?"

"Hello, Mrs. Zimmer. It's Luis. Is Eva there?"

"We're just sitting down to dinner, but you can talk for a couple of minutes." I turn toward Eva and hold out the telephone. "Eva, it's Luis."

"I'm not home," says Eva, rummaging around in the backpack's outer compartment.

My eyes spring open. I clap my hand over the mouthpiece of the phone.

"I can't tell him you're not here," I hiss. "He heard you! What's the matter with you?"

"Nothing. I just don't want to talk to him," she says. She extracts a cherry-flavored ChapStick and applies it to her lips in a single round sweep. Afterward, she smacks her lips.

"Eva! He knows you're here."

"Yeah, well, now I'm not," she says, grabbing her jacket and exiting. The screen door slams behind her.

I blink in horror first at Mutti, then at the phone in my hand. Mutti spins to look out the kitchen window as I bring the phone reluctantly back to my ear.

I clear my throat. "Uh . . ." I say.

"It's okay, Mrs. Zimmer. I heard."

"I'm so sorry, Luis. I have no idea what's going on."

"It's okay," he repeats gloomily.

Wait a minute. He's not surprised. Why is he not surprised?

"Luis? What's going on? Did you two have a fight?"

"No."

"Then what's going on?"

"I have no idea."

"Well, something must have happened!"

"Not on my end, it didn't," he says, sounding exasperated. "She stopped calling about a week ago, and now she won't talk to me at all. I don't know what the heck is going on."

"I'll talk to her."

"No!" he says loudly.

I frown, thinking I should probably be offended.

"I'm sorry," he continues quickly, picking up on my feelings. "I didn't mean to be rude, but please don't. I'd really rather deal with this myself."

Huh. All right then. We say our goodbyes.

"Where did she go?" I ask Mutti after I hang up.

"The stable."

I cross the kitchen and grab my jacket from the hook.

"Leave her alone," says Mutti. "Come. Eat."

I pause.

Mutti points a finger at my chair. "Come. Eat," she repeats. "There's nothing you can do."

I hesitate, watching as she spoons food onto the plates. Then I hang my jacket back up and join her at the table.

"You must let them work it out themselves," she says, leaning over and pouring me a glass of wine. "Anything you do will seem like interference. Do you remember what happened when you were a teenager and I tried to help smooth things over with Dan?"

Boy, do I ever. If Mutti hadn't loved Dan and hated Roger, I probably would have married Dan in the first place. I lift my wineglass and take a deep slurp.

"Besides, the semester ends soon," Mutti continues, spreading her napkin across her lap. She rips a pita apart and uses it to scoop up hummus. "Perhaps they'll sort things out when he returns for the summer."

"Perhaps," I say miserably.

Despite my initial misgivings about their relationship, Luis has been a wonderful influence. I should have known it was too good to last.

• • •

At eleven o'clock, Mutti rises from the table, takes Eva's dish to the counter, and puts plastic wrap over it. Harriet follows hopefully, but after Mutti puts the plate in the fridge, she sighs and collapses to the floor. Fortunately, her legs are short and she doesn't have far to fall.

Mutti turns to me and rubs her hands in front of her. "Well, I'm turning in. And so should that girl of yours. It's a school night."

I'm still sitting at the table, working on my second glass of wine. "I'm headed out in a minute. I'll send her in. Good night, Mutti."

"Good night, *Schatzlein.*"

When she disappears into the hallway, Harriet rises immediately and follows.

"Good night, Harriet," I call out as she scrabbles around the corner. I stare after my fickle dog, listening as her toenails click up the staircase. I sigh, put my wineglass in the dishwasher, and head out to the stable.

When I first started sleeping there, Harriet automatically came with me. After a month or so, she started spending the occasional night with Mutti. Now she spends virtually every night in my mother's room. I like to think she's only making a statement about being forced to take a cold, dark walk last thing at night. But still, she's my dog, and dogs are supposed to be faithful.

I crunch my way toward the stable, which looms like a sleeping giant at the bottom of the long graveled drive. I stick my hands deep in my pockets and hurry, puffing like a steam engine.

When I get there, I slip inside and follow the only light in the building.

Eva has Flicka, her two-year-old Arabian filly, in the cross-ties. Flicka's long winter coat is spotless, a glossy jet black, the result of regular and thorough grooming. Eva is finishing up, pulling Flicka's long tail off to the side, catching up a section with the brush, running through it, and then letting it fall. I see a flash of metal handle, and lean forward, squinting.

Eva is using my hairbrush—my forty-dollar, ionically charged hairbrush—to detangle her horse's tail.

Chapter 5

"Lean further back, Jenna. Further. Good. But don't stick your feet out in front of you," I say, walking a small circle in the center of the arena as my student thunders around the perimeter on Tazz, who is quite possibly the most patient school horse ever put on this earth.

Jenna is a middle-aged mom who took up riding again after a twenty-year lull, like I did. Perhaps because of this coincidence, I feel an unusual affinity toward her. She is cantering for the first time since she was nineteen, and is scared out of her wits, holding on to the pommel and leaning so that her center of gravity is in her upper body instead of her seat. This causes her to bounce out of the saddle with each stride and then reunite with it so violently it's painful to watch.

"Okay, good, now bring him back to a posting trot," I say, for the sake of both Tazz's spine and Jenna's rear. "Good. Only sit a beat, because you're on the wrong diagonal . . . One beat, Jenna. Not two. Try again . . . Good. Now you've got it. Cross at *B* and change directions . . . Sit one beat right in the center. Good. And again, at *E*."

Her riding is more than rusty, by which I mean that I don't think the hiatus is responsible for the way she rides. I believe this is probably the level she was riding at before she quit, and that's fine with me. When we hired Joan, I made a conscious decision to take the students who were doing this for pleasure and to leave the competition-minded ones for her.

My cell phone buzzes in my pocket. I pull it out and flick it open, scanning the glowing blue display. It's Mutti, calling from the house.

"Jenna, keep doing figure eights. Sit one beat right in the center when you change directions. I'll be right with you." I bring the phone to my ear. "Hi, Mutti. What's up?"

"Annemarie, come back to the house. I need to speak to you right away."

"I can't. I'm in the middle of a lesson."

"Annemarie, please. This is important."

"Why? What's going on?"

"I will tell you when you get here."

"Mutti, for God's sake—just tell me. Did something happen? Is Eva all right?"

A heavy sigh, followed by a pause. "Yes and no. They caught her smoking marijuana at school. The police are there now. You need to go right away."

I gasp and cover my mouth with my hand.

Jenna does a double take as she passes at a trot.

"I'll be right there," I say, my voice and hands shaking. I snap the phone shut and stand staring at the spiffy new Surefoot rubber granule footing that covers the floor of the arena. Black-and-white checks invade my peripheral vision. Eventually my eyes flutter shut.

"Annemarie? Are you okay?"

Jenna's voice snaps me out of my stupor. I open my eyes and find myself looking at Tazz's dapple gray chest. Jenna stares down at me, the edges of her eyes creased with concern.

My response is to burst into tears.

• • •

After Jenna assures me that she is perfectly capable of removing Tazz's tack and putting him back in his stall, I rush to the house to change. I have no idea whether my appearance is likely to influence the police and their ultimate decisions, but I would rather not show up at the school in muck boots and breeches smeared with green saliva.

I stumble down the stairs in my unfamiliar high heels, dragging a brush through my hair. It's full of Flicka's long black tail hair—damn it, Eva! There are how many grooming kits in the stable and you had to use *my* hairbrush? I make a mental note to check myself in the rearview mirror once I get in the car, to make sure I haven't given myself black extensions.

As I flee through the kitchen, struggling to tuck my pressed white blouse into my tweed skirt, Mutti and I exchange rushed words, the gist of which is that while I'm at the school trying to beg, wheedle, or otherwise persuade the police not to press charges against Eva, Mutti will try to scare up Joan to take over the rest of the day's lessons; or, failing that, she'll stay at the stable herself and come up with any excuse other than the truth to explain my absence as students arrive.

The school is one of those uninspired designs from the sixties; functional and plain, with little else to distinguish itself. But at least it doesn't have a slew of trailers out back, as so many do. It does, however, have three police cruisers parked in front. When I see them lined up against the curb, I feel physically ill.

The hollow *tap-tap-tap* of my heels on the linoleum floor sounds almost otherworldly, and it's not just the misplaced sound of authority—I'm trying to remember the last time I wore heels. I have an uneasy feeling it was at Pappa's funeral, and for some reason I can't quite fathom, this makes me miss Dan so fiercely that tears spring to my eyes.

Classes are in session. Each of the wooden doors has a single eye-level window, and as I pass, I see teachers gesticulating, expounding, pontificating. They are fresh and enthusiastic, and surprisingly young. It reminds me of just how much depends on perspective.

My heart quickens as I approach the office. The secretary's area is exposed to the hallway by windows, and each of the wooden chairs is filled by either a dour, blank-faced teenager or pale, grim-faced parent. Three uniformed officers lean against the walls.

Eva is sitting at the end of a row of chairs. When I enter, she looks up and then immediately away, her face drained of blood.

"Eric! Get up and give the lady a seat!" snaps a man with a crimson face. His eyes are bloodshot. A vein pulses so violently at his temple it looks like he's about to keel over from an aneurysm.

His son, a bone-thin teenager with short dark hair and a ring through his eyebrow, is sitting beside Eva. He shoots me a hateful look and then slides slowly off his chair. As he passes me to take a place against the wall, I have to twist sideways to keep our shoulders from banging. His heavy gray jacket smells earthy and sweet—I take a deep breath, memorizing the smell in case I ever need to recognize it again.

I sit beside Eva, who shrinks away. I turn and stare at her, willing her to meet my gaze. But she doesn't. She stares studiously at the feet of the people sitting opposite. Only her crooked brow betrays her fear.

The principal's solid wooden door opens, and a pimply boy in a camouflage jacket spews forth, propelled by the flat of his father's hand. The man's jaw grinds back and forth, and his eyes burn with anger. The mother follows a moment later, honking into a tissue.

A weary-looking woman appears in the doorway. "Mr. Hamilton, Eric," she says, reading off a piece of paper.

The bone-thin boy and his father disappear into the office. There's an uncomfortable settling in the ensuing silence. Kids steal fearful glances at their parents, who shift uncomfortably in their seats.

Fifteen minutes tick interminably by before the office door opens again. This time the father exits first, striding out and through the door without so much as a backward glance at his son, who follows with an amused, self-satisfied look. He throws Eva a glance as he passes, lifting the corner of his mouth into a smirk.

I turn so quickly something snaps in my neck. Eva is smiling coyly up at him, watching through the windows as he recedes down the hall.

Everything is entirely clear to me now.

"Mrs. Zimmer, Eva," says the woman in the doorway. She pokes at a wisp of loose hair, sighs, and slips back into the room to let us pass.

• • •

We don't exchange a single word in the car on the way home. I mean, really—what is there to say? I'm so disappointed and overwrought I'd probably just end up crying.

In a way, Eva was lucky. She and the others were caught smoking pot in the forested area behind the school, but since no drugs were found in Eva's locker, she's not being charged with anything. She has, however, been expelled. The school has a zero tolerance policy, and—despite my impassioned entreaties—apparently zero tolerance means exactly that. So here she is, expelled from two schools in as many years.

As we pull into our drive, I catch sight of Joan's car in the parking lot by the stable. Thank God for that—at least Eva hasn't also cost us an afternoon's revenue.

I see the kitchen curtain fall, and the door opens before we reach it. Mutti stands aside as I enter. Eva follows me—slinking, disgraced, and yet somehow radiating anger, as if this were someone else's fault.

"What happened? What's going on?" cries Mutti, closing the door and hovering.

I throw my purse on the table. It slides across and onto the floor, scattering its contents everywhere. A coin skids across the linoleum, spinning. I stand utterly still, blinking at it. Then I turn to Eva.

"Give me your backpack," I say quietly.

"What?" she says. Her eyes widen. She takes a step backward.

"Give it to me."

Her fingers tighten around its pink vinyl strap. I lunge forward and rip it from her shoulder.

"Mom! Stop it! Give it back!" she screams.

I whirl around—first this way, then that—switching

direction as necessary to avoid Eva, who leaps around me, snatching at it.

I clutch the backpack to my chest, fumbling with the zippers that meet in the middle, still doing my dervish dance.

"Mom!" Eva is desperate, shrieking. "Give it back! You can't do that!"

One side unzips and I tear the other open, removing most of a fingernail in the process. Then I dump its contents, which hit the floor with a splat—three textbooks that land with their pages mashed; a binder that explodes, sending lined paper and colored class schedules flying; a hairbrush, a compact, a plastic tampon container—and finally, a foil-wrapped condom.

All motion ceases. In the background, a single drop of water hits the bottom of the sink.

I lift my face to Eva's.

She stares at me, her rib cage heaving, her face growing redder and redder. "I hate you!" she screams. She turns and runs from the room.

"Eva! Get back here!" My voice is raw, catching in my throat. "Eva!"

She stomps up the stairs. A door slams.

I turn to Mutti. She is pale, staring at the condom on the floor with the fingers of one hand pressed to her throat and her other arm wrapped around her chest. She is trembling.

• • •

Mutti and I are still on our hands and knees, collecting the things from Eva's backpack and my purse, when we hear gravel crunching under tires. We look up at the same moment, locking eyes.

Above us, a door opens, and Eva's footsteps thump down the stairs. She crosses the floor between us and grabs her jacket.

"Eva! Don't you dare leave! Eva!" I shout, lunging for her ankle. "Where do you think you're—"

The door bangs shut behind her. A car door slams, a motor guns, and then there is silence.

I am left on my knees in the middle of the kitchen floor, one hand reaching for my absent daughter, the other perched on a condom's foil packaging.

After a stunned pause, I open my mouth and wail, a low moan that rises and ripens into a howl.

There's the muffled thumping of knees on floor, and a moment later Mutti wraps her arms around me from above.

• • •

Mutti installs me in one of the deep winged chairs in the living room, hands me a Jägermeister, and kneels down to light a fire. Harriet sits beside her, sniffing suspiciously.

I watch Mutti's slim back as she fusses with the kindling, alternately staunching my leaky nose with the edge of my sleeve and sipping my drink. I'm not all that fond of Jägermeister anymore—I've become more of a chardonnay girl—but when Mutti hands me a glass, it's a friendly gesture. At this point, I'm just grateful for its effect. As its warmth spreads through me, I pull my knees up onto the chair and allow myself to sink into its velvety embrace.

When the fire is crackling and licking its lazy way up the logs, Mutti puts the poker on the hearth, wipes her hands, and rises. Then she takes a seat in the chair opposite me. Harriet follows, slumping down on Mutti's feet. I stare into her deep brown eyes, beaming guilt signals, hoping she'll come to me, but Harriet is oblivious. She heaves a sigh and closes her eyes, shifting to a more comfortable position.

"Well, it could be worse," says Mutti, reaching for her glass.

"How?"

"She wasn't arrested."

"Well, yes," I sigh.

"And at least she's using protection."

"Mutti!"

"Would you prefer she weren't?"

"I'd prefer she weren't doing it at all!"

"Well, of course."

"She's probably doing it at this very moment," I say miserably.

"She can't have been doing it for long."

"Why do you say that?"

"Because this Eric is a new development. I heard her talking quite happily to Luis last week. And we know she wasn't sleeping with Luis because he lives in Henniker."

"Oh, great. So she's been seeing this Eric creep for a week and she's already sleeping with him?"

Mutti stares at me, tapping her lips with her finger.

"What?" I say irritably.

"Are you going to tell Roger?"

"About what? The pot or the condoms?"

"Yes," she says simply.

I drain my glass in a single gulp.

Mutti rises instantly and refills it from a cut glass decanter.

"I can't tell him," I say. "If I tell him, he'll want her to come live with him."

"And is that such a bad idea?" she says, topping up her own glass before heading back to the side table.

"Yes! It's a horrible idea."

"Why?"

"Because I can't stand the thought of her living away from me. It's the whole reason I never called Nathalie Jenkins back."

Mutti freezes, the decanter suspended an inch above the table's surface. "What?"

I stare at her, but what can I do? The words are already out there.

"What did you just say?" Mutti says.

I look guiltily into the fire.

"Did you just say Nathalie Jenkins called you?" Mutti sets the decanter down and turns so she's staring at me full on. She puts both hands on her hips. "Annemarie!"

"What?" I say.

"Why? What was she calling about?"

I sigh and turn back to her. "About Eva potentially coming to train with her. She watched Eva ride in Canterbury and was impressed. She wanted her to come try out."

"And you didn't call her back?" she says, her voice incredulous.

I shake my head, utterly miserable, two inches tall.

"Annemarie Costanze Zimmer! She is a three-time Olympic medalist! Why didn't you call her back?"

Mutti watches me for a moment, and then leans back in her chair. "Annemarie. You must listen to me. This is a godsend. It solves everything—the horse, the boy, school, everything!"

"I suppose so," I say.

"Then why in heaven's name do you sound glum?"

"Because she's the only child I'm ever going to have, and I'm not finished being her mother."

"Oh, *Schatzlein.* You will not stop being her mother. Look at us—you are forty and still living with me."

"I'm not forty! I'm thirty-nine!"

"Pssh!" says Mutti, waving her hand.

"And besides, I lived away from home for twenty years before I came back." I feel a bit petty for having to point that out, but it's an important distinction. Otherwise I'm just a forty-year-old loser who never left home.

Mutti leans forward, seeking my eyes. "Do you think it was easy for me to let you go train with Marjory?"

I frown. Strangely, this had not occurred to me. I had seen Eva's potential experience as a parallel of mine, but I had not looked at it from the other direction.

"It was one of the hardest things I've ever had to do," Mutti continues.

"Really?"

"Of course! You wanted so badly to go. You couldn't get out of here fast enough."

"That wasn't because of you, Mutti. Pappa was making me miserable."

"I was so hurt," she continues. "And think of how your father felt. It was hard for him, too—to admit that she was the better trainer and that you belonged there rather than here? But he did. He knew what was best for you and he worked hard to persuade me, because I did not want you to go. I was absolutely sure that Marjory would take my place in your life. And of course she did not."

I stare at her in amazement.

She's right. I loved Marjory. I loved living with her, loved training with her, loved everything about that period in my life until the accident ended it all; but despite this, I haven't been in contact with Marjory in almost eighteen years. Instead, I'm sitting in my mother's living room.

"*Schatzlein,* Eva is in serious trouble."

"I know that. Believe me."

"The best thing we can do is remove her from the situation. You say you don't want her to go live with Roger. Fine. I understand. It's too far away. But Nathalie—she works out of where? Columbia?"

"Yes," I say staring at my lap.

"That's an hour away at most. Please, please, for God's sake, call her back."

"I will, Mutti."

"Do you promise?"

"Yes." I look up and find her scrutinizing me. "I will, Mutti. Things are different than they were when she first called."

Mutti nods deeply, agreeing with me so vehemently her drink sloshes from side to side in her glass. "It is the right thing. And absolutely, without question the best boy repellent in the world. This will save her. You will see."

"Unless she breaks her neck."

"Annemarie!" snaps Mutti.

"All right, all right, I'm sorry," I say, draining my glass for the second time.

This time, Mutti doesn't refill it.

• • •

Eva returns at just past eleven. She walks in the back door, peels off her jacket, hangs it up, and goes straight upstairs. Mutti and I exchange glances and immediately go over to the row of coat hooks.

I lift a sleeve and press my nose against it. "Just tobacco. Thank God."

Mutti sniffs the air at various points around the jacket.

"Yes. Cigarettes," she nods. She delves into Eva's left outside pocket and comes out with a fistful of stuff. She opens her palm and examines it—two peppermints, various coins, and a crumpled piece of paper, which she carefully unfolds.

"A movie receipt. From tonight. So."

"Well, thank God for that," I reply, up to my wrist in Eva's right outside pocket.

The phone rings.

"I'll get it," I say.

Mutti shrugs and stuffs everything back in Eva's pocket. "Okay. Now that everybody's accounted for, I'm turning in."

"Good night, Mutti."

She pads off into the hallway. Harriet, who is doing her dead-dog routine—lying flat on her back with her belly exposed—lifts her head, considers following, and then decides against it. As she plops her head back down, gravity pulls her lips away from her teeth in what looks like an upside down snarl. Her whole body shudders in a mighty sigh.

"Oh, good girl!" I croon, giving her a quick caress as I pass. "You *do* love me, don't you?"

I grab the phone. "Hello?"

"Hey, sexy lady."

"Dan!" I squeal. "Where are you? Are you home yet?" I press the phone closer to my ear, listening for clues. There's a bit of crackle, so he's on his cell phone, but I don't hear any traffic noises in the background. That's a good sign.

"I'm not, no."

"Oh, Dan," I say. My jaw begins to quiver. I'm in serious danger of melting down right here and now—he's been gone so much, and I've never needed him more than I do at this moment.

"Not anymore, that is," he continues in a slow drawl. "See, even though Mike and I just drove a couple of thousand miles straight through in shifts, and all I've been thinking about for the last eighteen hours is getting home and into bed, when I got there, it turned out that the bed I wanted to be in wasn't there . . ."

"What?" I say, perking up. "Dan, where are you?"

"Where are you?" he parries.

"At home, of course."

"Where?"

"In the kitchen."

"Look out the back window."

I rush forward until the phone cord yanks me to a halt. Then I roll onto my tiptoes, peering over Mutti's lace half-curtains.

The roof of Dan's truck picks up glints of moonlight in the stable parking lot.

"I thought you'd already be in bed," he says. "Was hoping to surprise you. Are you turning into a night owl on me?"

I'm halfway to the stable before I realize I've left

Harriet behind. After a moment of hesitation, I go back for her.

. . .

Dan and I lie in bed, limbs entwined and feet tangled with the mulberry eiderdown. Before long, we'll have to reach down and get it, but for now we bask in the aftermath of passion.

Harriet is behind me, desperate to wiggle her way between us. Our nocturnal activities worry her—she doesn't know exactly what we're up to, but she knows it doesn't involve her and she doesn't like it. When we're finished, it always takes her a while to recover.

She lays her head across my neck so that her nose is between our faces. When she pushes hard enough to impinge on my windpipe, I shove her away. She reappears instantly, burrowing, twitching.

"So what made you change your mind?" says Dan, ignoring the dog and running his fingertips up and down my back.

"About what?"

"Letting Eva compete."

"It's largely so she won't end up pregnant or in the slammer," I say.

"Yeah, but you didn't find out about any of that until after you'd already agreed. Unless I've got it backward."

"No," I say quietly. "You've got it right."

Harriet has crept forward enough that her belly covers my whole face. I lift her up and toss her behind me. She reappears within seconds, nudging insistently.

"I dunno," I continue. "I was tired of fighting, and my position was full of holes. Besides, she's very clear that it's what she wants to do, which I guess in the long run is more important than what I want for her."

"And what do you want for her?"

I take a moment to eject Harriet again, and then pause, considering the question while tracing loop-de-loops on Dan's chest.

"I want her to be happy. I want her to not hate me. I want her to be successful."

"What do you want her to be successful in?"

"I don't know. Medicine. Law."

"Law. Like her father?"

"No," I scoff. "Not patent law. Not criminal law either," I hasten to add. "Okay, forget I mentioned law at all. Medicine. Paleontology. Astronomy."

"Not astrology?"

I whack him. "I want her to be successful in something where she can't break her neck."

"I'm sorry, but I think astrology qualifies—"

"Dan!"

He wraps his arms around me, pausing first to rebuff Harriet, and rocks me against his chest. "I know how hard this was for you. For what it's worth, I think you're doing the right thing."

I lie against him in complete surrender.

"I hope so, Dan. God, I hope so."

Chapter 6

When I call Nathalie, she is gracious and happy to set up an audition, although I also get the impression that most people don't make her wait three weeks while they waffle.

When I break the news to Eva, she is so ecstatic she flings her arms around me. (Twice! In forty-eight hours!)

Eva bounces happily on the car seat beside me. She has reason to be upbeat; she might well have expected to be driven to boot camp, not the famed Nathalie Jenkins's farm for an audition. She's so excited and so pleased that she neglected to bring the portable CD player and headphones that are normally required to drown out my presence.

"What did she say again?" she says, looking at me with glistening eyes.

"I've already told you three times!" I laugh.

"Come on, Mom, I want to hear it again!"

"She said that she saw you at Canterbury and was impressed at how you got Malachite through the final stage."

I pause, smiling, waiting.

"Because . . ." she prompts.

"Because obviously he was in way over his head, and yet you managed to get a clear round out of him anyway."

I sneak a glance at her. She's waiting, staring out the windshield, pretending to be patient. After a few seconds, her eyes dart over to me. Her fingernails dig into the seat's upholstery. She starts banging her knees together.

Her head swivels toward me, her mouth open, but before she can speak I continue. "And that clearly you've got huge potential. 'Natural born talent,' were her exact words, and she wants to see what you're capable of on another horse. A good horse."

Eva sighs dreamily and leans back in her seat.

A moment later she says, "Is that all?"

"Isn't that enough?" I say, laughing again.

She sits forward again. "So obviously she doesn't want me to bring Malachite."

"Clearly not."

"And you're not going to let me bring Hurrah."

"No."

"So will I be riding one of her horses?"

"I would imagine so. That's one of the things she and I will be talking about."

I glance at her—quickly though, since I don't want to run off the road. Her eyes sparkle as she revels in the possibilities.

"And I'll be living there?"

"If she takes you on, yes."

"Oh, she'll take me on all right," says Eva, nodding confidently. Her bravado breaks my heart.

She flops back into her seat. I'm not looking at her, but I can sense her. The air around her throbs with anticipation and energy. I feel a pang of guilt, because if I had only followed up on this when Nathalie originally called, there probably would have been no Eric Hamilton, no pot in the woods behind the school, no condom in the purse and all that little piece of latex implies.

But even now—when there is not a shadow of doubt that this is not only the best choice but the only choice—I can't allow myself to think ahead to the moment when I drop Eva off with her bags.

Instead, I parcel that whole concept off in the back of my brain and rattle and thump toward Columbia in my dear old Camry that has almost no suspension, sharing a welcome moment of closeness with my daughter.

• • •

Wyldewood Farm is enclosed by a brick wall. When we pull up to the tall wrought-iron gates, I roll my window down. The black box embedded in the gatepost crackles at me.

"I beg your pardon?" I say.

"Kccchchhchcchch e weccchhhh e schguu?"

"I, uh—I'm sorry, I can't understand you, but my name is Annemarie Zimmer and I'm here with my daughter, Eva Aldrich. We have an appointment with Nathalie for four thirty."

"Kcchcchchh e wuuu," says the box. Then the gates swing slowly inward. I roll my window back up and drive through.

Wyldewood is better described as an operation than a farm. The buildings—two barns and an indoor arena—are huge and new, with cedar siding instead of vinyl.

The walls are red and the trim a pewter gray—some painter's attempt at capturing Wyldewood's stable colors, which are crimson and silver. Windows dot the long sides of each barn.

The property is sectioned off into individual paddocks and outdoor schooling rings. About half of the paddocks contain horses, each turned out singly, which is the fate of horses in truly competitive barns. There are Thoroughbreds, Dutch and German Warmbloods, Oldenburgs, Hanoverians, and one that looks like a Holsteiner, although I'm judging purely by height, face, and neck since the legs, body, and feet of the horses are completely obscured by red coverings. But what I can see is magnificent: their necks are thickly muscled and gleaming, their faces noble, with the bemused expression of creatures who are entirely sure of their value on this earth.

Behind everything, at the top of a steep hill, is a house—an impressive white colonial with large shade trees whose original outline has been obscured by many additions, including a four-car garage. I can't help but wonder whether it contains the lemon yellow Maserati Nathalie won at last year's Jumper Classic. Lined up beside the garage are three shiny gooseneck horse trailers, each of them crimson and silver and probably capable of hauling six horses.

Even though Nathalie does double duty as a Grand Prix show jumper and four-star eventer (as I did back in the Cretaceous period), and even though she's won some of the biggest purses both disciplines have to offer, it wouldn't be anywhere near enough to support what's going on here. There's definitely income from somewhere else—and plenty of it.

As we wind our way to the parking lot, Eva's face is glued to the window. A patch of fog furls and unfurls on the glass in time to her breathing.

I pull into a spot at the end of a long line of cars and get out. To my surprise, Eva remains in the car.

"Annemarie! Eva!"

Nathalie herself strides toward us in tan breeches, leather paddock boots, and the ubiquitous quilted vest. She is in her mid-forties, wiry, with dark brown hair pulled back at the nape of her neck. "Glen called down and said you'd arrived. How are you?"

"Good," I say. "Cold. Beautiful place you have."

"Thank you." She turns to Eva, who has finally climbed from the car. "And how are you, young lady?"

"Fine, thank you," she says in tiny voice. I do a double take, checking that it's still Eva who is standing next to me.

She's blushing, looking down and scrubbing her toe in the dirt.

Nathalie turns to the barn entrance and cups her mouth with her hands. "Margot!" She waits a minute and then calls again, "Margot!" Another pause, with her head cocked. "Bah! She can't hear me. Come on inside," she says, turning and leading the way.

The interior of the barn is as warm as our house—no wonder the outside horses are all in blankets and leg wraps. There's not a single winter coat among them.

The aisle is wide and airy, and lined with huge box stalls. The concrete floor has not a speck of hay or mud on it, and when I look up, I realize there are skylights in the peaked roof. Birds twitter happily in the rafters.

About halfway up the aisle a tall horse is in crossties, surrounded by young women.

"Margot!" calls Nathalie.

"Yes?" answers a woman crouching beside the horse. She stands up and turns toward us. She's in her late twenties, also a brunette, and also slight.

"Come meet Eva. And her mother. Annemarie, Eva, this is Margot, my head groom."

"Stable manager," says Margot.

"Right. Stable manager. Anyway, I'd like to talk to Annemarie for a while. Can you show Eva around?"

"Sure," says Margot.

"Relax, kid," says Nathalie, giving Eva a friendly whack on the shoulder. "No one's gonna bite you. Except maybe Pinocchio. You'll want to watch yourself around Pinocchio."

Even though Nathalie winks, Eva barely cracks a smile. Seeing Eva so completely starstruck fills me with unspeakable tenderness.

"Come on," Margot says, leaning toward her in a conspiratorial fashion. "We'll show you the apartment first."

Eva, Margot, and the other girls—all of whom are roughly Eva's age—make their way down the aisle, leaving me alone with Nathalie and the horse.

He's an enormous chestnut, seventeen hands if he's an inch. He regards me curiously. I extend the back of my hand for him to sniff and then lay it on his neck. It's rock solid, as is the rest of him.

"Is he a Trakehner?" I ask.

"Yes."

"He's gorgeous."

"Beauregard's my champion eventer, a two-time Olympic medalist. Silver and bronze."

"Really? What year?"

"Ninety-two," she says. "And ninety-six."

I freeze mid-pat.

"I hear you've got his teammate in your barn," says Nathalie.

A prickle of dread shoots up my neck and across my cheeks.

"I read about it in the papers last year," she says in a steady voice. "Besides, word kind of got around the circuit, if you know what I mean."

My shame is hideous. People have been talking about me all winter, and I wasn't even aware—although I suppose that's a blessing. I wonder if Eva caught wind of it at Canterbury? And what on earth will she hear from this point on?

I drop my hand from Beauregard's shoulder.

"No need to be uncomfortable," Nathalie says. "Quite frankly, you came across as something of a hero. McCullough's a bastard and we all know it. So how is the great striped Hanoverian anyway?"

"He's fine, thanks."

"He lost an eye, is that right?"

"Yes."

"Otherwise he's sound?"

"He's perfect," I say.

"Well, good for you. McCullough can fry in hell, for all I'm concerned."

"Me too."

There's a moment of awkward silence. I turn to face her, still feeling the heat of my blush.

"So," says Nathalie, clapping her hands in front of her. Beauregard yanks his head up, startled. "Let's get down to brass tacks. I saw Eva ride at Canterbury. I think she has huge potential. Her lineage doesn't hurt," she adds, looking pointedly at me.

"She's worked very hard this year."

"So why haven't I seen her before Canterbury?"

"I—I . . . uh . . ." I stammer, rummaging through my head for an excuse. But it doesn't matter, because Nathalie has moved on—

"What's her history? How long has she been riding?"

"Her whole life, really. But she only began training seriously this year."

"And you're the one who's been training her?"

"No. We have another trainer."

"Huh. I'm surprised, given your history," she muses.

"Actually it's because of my history," I say softly.

"Ah . . ." she says, as understanding dawns on her. "Okay. Fair enough. Anyway, she's got a rock solid seat, and that's the kind of foundation I look for. It's not something that can be taught. I mean, you can teach a good seat, of course, but then there's the other kind, the kind you're born with. You know what I'm talking about."

I nod, picturing Eva stuck to Hurrah's bare back like glue.

"I have two programs for students. Normally I don't have a preference, but in this case I do. Ultimately it's up to you."

"What are they?"

"Boarders bring their own horses and pay a fee, both for board and lessons. Working students campaign my horses and live here. They earn their keep around the barn. Either way, if the student is still in high school the parent has to pick up part of the cost of the tutor. And everybody goes home on Sundays. Unless they live too far away, of course. You're only about an hour away, right?"

"Uh, yes," I say. "We're probably looking at the working student option."

"So you don't plan to have Eva campaign Hurrah?"

"No," I say quickly.

"Why?"

"Because he's only got one eye."

"That doesn't disqualify him."

"I beg your pardon?" I say weakly, because a terrible thought has just crept into my head. Is Nathalie feigning interest in Eva to get at Hurrah?

"As long as he has full sight in his other eye, he's fine," she says matter-of-factly. "Horses can't see the jumps they're going to take once they get within six feet of them anyway."

"*Please* don't tell Eva that," I say miserably. I glance from side to side, seeking my daughter. We've been duped. I want to go home. Where the hell have they taken her—

"Don't tell Eva what?" says Nathalie, apparently completely unaware of my distress.

"About the regulations. I really, really don't want to bring Hurrah out of retirement. He's seventeen, he's got some issues with his legs, and, well, just no. He's earned his rest, and he's going to get it."

Nathalie's brown eyes bore shamelessly into me. Then she nods. "Good. I was hoping you'd say that. Because I have a specific horse in mind for Eva."

My eyes widen.

"Follow me," she says, ducking under Beauregard's cross-ties and marching down the aisle.

After a second's hesitation, I duck under as well. She's walking so fast I have to jog to catch up.

"But what about him?" I say breathlessly.

"Who?" says Nathalie, marching onward.

"Beauregard!" I say in amazement. "Are we just going to leave him there?"

"The girls will get him."

"But they just went off with Eva."

"Oh, honey, that was just some of the girls. I've got girls coming out my ears," she mutters, waving both hands. "Girls, girls, everywhere girls."

She steps into the indoor arena. Before following, I turn and look back down the aisle.

Beauregard has been swarmed by girls. Two are cooing into his face and three are adjusting leg wraps.

• • •

Nathalie leads me straight through the enormous arena and through a door on the far side into another building full of box stalls. She comes to a stop in front of a plaque that says SMOKY JOE.

"Here he is," she says.

I peer inside. My eyebrows shoot upward.

"Here, I'll take him out." Nathalie grabs a lead rope from a hook, and slides the door open just a crack.

A blue roan face with black forelock and intelligent eyes immediately pushes itself into the space, nudging the door further open. Nathalie hooks up the lead rope. I can't help noticing that she threads the nose chain across his muzzle.

I stand back as she leads the horse from the stall. He's a true blue roan—white and black hairs evenly interspersed all over his body, with scattered black flecks and a black mane and tail. His face is wide, with large, well-defined nostrils, his tail set low off a sloping croup. His body is so compact it looks short, but it's not. He's just extremely solid, his shoulders and flanks huge, his neck as cresty as a stallion's. I glance underneath. Gelded—but I'll wager it happened after he was fully mature.

But more surprising is that I haven't the foggiest clue what he is. I flip through my internal database trying to come up with a breed—or even a combination of breeds—but his shape is utterly unfamiliar to me. Finally I give up. "What is he?"

"Ha! Good for you," says Nathalie, keeping her chin out of the way because the horse is using her as a scratching post. "So many people pretend they know everything. He's a Nokota."

"A *what*?"

"A Nokota," she says, pushing the horse's face away and then straightening his wavy forelock. She puts her other hand under his muzzle. He starts licking her hand.

"I've never heard of them," I say.

"They're wild horses from the Badlands of North Dakota."

"This is a wild horse?"

"Well, not Joe, personally. But yes, they're descendants of the Indian plains ponies. In fact, Joe here is a direct descendant of the horses confiscated from Sitting Bull. A few bands of them got inadvertently closed into Theodore Roosevelt National Park in the forties when the government was rounding up and shooting wild horses. It's the only reason the breed survived."

"No kidding," I say, taking a closer look at this horse. His legs are stocky, his head heavy, his low tail wavy and thick. There are hints of Mustang, of Andalusian, of Friesian about him. He gazes back at me, bemused. "Well, he certainly looks tough."

"Tough as nails. Have to be to survive in the Badlands. Eventually the government agreed to leave a demonstration herd in the park, but they also decided they were too ugly and tried to change the phenotype—"

I gawk at Nathalie.

Phenotype? Did she just slip *phenotype* into the conversation?

"—wanted to replace all the herd stallions with modern breeds. Said that any breed with this many blue roans had to be inbred, or some nonsense like that. I mean, look at this guy," she says with obvious outrage, swooshing a hand through the air. "Does he look inbred to you? Anyway, in the end two brothers basically saved the breed. It's an interesting story—I can give you some articles if you want. They're amazing horses. They give their entire heart and soul to the task at hand, whatever that is, from roping to dressage to whatever."

"And this is the horse you have in mind for Eva?"

"Yup."

"Why?"

"Because I saw her ride that other horse—what was his name?"

"Malachite."

"I saw her take him through a course he had no business being on at all—sorry, no offense," she says, glancing at me quickly.

"None taken," I say. "I have absolutely no ego wrapped up in Malachite."

"And she got a clear round out of him anyway,"

Nathalie continues. "She's a strong rider, and that's what Joe needs."

Tiny little pings of warning register on my maternal radar. "Why's that?" I ask warily.

"He's very well-trained indeed—I got him from Yvonne Richards. He's got enormous potential. Simply enormous. But he's young. Seven. And strong-willed. And stubborn."

"I thought you said Nokotas give their heart and soul," I say slowly.

"They do, but not to just anyone. It's got to be the right person. So far, he hasn't taken to anyone here."

Larger flares now pop in the periphery of my brain. "When you say, 'hasn't taken to anyone,' what exactly do you mean?"

"I mean that he won't let just anyone ride him."

The alarm bells are shrieking now. "You know, on second thought, I'm not sure I think this is such a good—"

"Follow me," Nathalie says, heading for the arena with Joe clip-clopping beside her.

Eva is on the far side of the arena in the center of a group of giggling girls. The top two buttons of her shirt are undone, and she's pulling it aside, showing off her tattoo. The girls lean in, making admiring noises. A couple trace the unicorn's outline with their fingers. Another girl lifts the edge of her sweatshirt, displaying her navel piercing. More oohs and ahhs.

"Margot!" shouts Nathalie, striding toward them.

The girls straighten their carriage and clothing and fall silent, waiting until Nathalie and Joe stop in front of them.

"Show Eva where Joe's stuff is. Eva, I want you to tack up Smoky Joe and bring him back here."

Margot steps forward to take the lead rope.

"No," Nathalie says firmly. "I want Eva to lead him."

Margot shrugs and falls back.

Eva's eyes widen, and there's a second's pause before she steps forward. When she does, Joe's ears swivel forward, perked. They're fluted, large as tulips at the bottom. I'll bet he could hear a bird fluttering from a mile away. He lifts his nose, stretching it forward, sniffing.

Nathalie hands Eva the lead rope and steps out of the way.

Eva's eyes sparkle, swooping across the whole of the blue roan Nokota, and then going over each inch of him again, and again, and again, as though she can't believe what she's seeing. She offers him her hand and he presses his nose into it, nostrils flaring in and out.

And then from deep in his throat he rumbles: *huh-huh-huh, huh-huh-huh, huh-huh-huh*.

Oh dear God.

I'm doomed. Eva's doomed. We're all doomed.

I glance at Nathalie, who watches the meeting with greedy eyes.

• • •

Nathalie takes me to the lounge. Or rather, leads the way to it, because she always manages to stay a dozen steps in front of me.

Nathalie's lounge is much like ours, an enclosed room with a large window that faces the arena. And like ours, it's outfitted with mismatched furniture that ranges from worn-down couches to hastily constructed plywood tables to stackable lawn chairs.

Nathalie takes a seat in a white plastic lawn chair in

front of the soundboard, and I follow suit. She crosses her legs and leans back in her seat.

"There's coffee over there if you want some," she says, waving behind her.

"No thanks," I mumble, wishing something stronger were on offer. I glance nervously at my watch.

After a few minutes, a stream of girls enters the lounge. They line up against the back wall, whispering and giggling, throwing their arms around each others' necks and poking each other in the ribs.

Eva enters the arena with Joe.

"Quiet!" says Nathalie, raising a hand.

The girls shush each other and fall silent. Sort of.

"Three minutes," whispers a voice from behind me

"Five!"

"Two, tops."

"You can't call two. I already called two."

"No, Kris called two!"

"Then I call three."

"You can't call three—Maggie called three."

"Fine! Four and a half."

"Naw, he'll have her off in one and a half. Remember Elizabeth?"

"I said, *QUIET!*" Nathalie yelps.

Eva leads Joe to the center of the arena and runs down the stirrups. She pulls the right stirrup iron into her armpit to check for length, and then comes back around to the left side and does the same with the other. She checks the girth. She fiddles and adjusts, checking the buckle on the noseband, and then rechecks the girth.

She checks so many things I get suspicious. Has she changed her mind? Is she trying to send me a signal to get her out of this because things have gone too far for her to get herself out without losing face?

I shift forward on my seat, suddenly on full alert.

Oh, baby, I'll get you out of here. Just let me know. Just give me the signal—

Her cheeks are bright crimson, her lips set in a grim line. She stands directly in front of Joe and straightens the reins before running them over his head. Then she picks up first his left foreleg and then his right, pulling them forward by the knee, making sure his hair lies flat beneath the girth.

"She's stalling," whispers one the girls.

"Do you blame her?"

My face burns. Each time Eva lays her fingers on a buckle, each time she slides them under a strap, I become more convinced that she's telling me to step in and put a stop to this. Finally I make a deal with myself: if she checks the throat latch, we're out of here.

Eva steps up to Joe's head and smoothes his forelock. She leans in close to his face and whispers. Then she slips her fingers under his throat latch.

I whip around to Nathalie. "Nathalie, I—"

"Quiet!" she barks.

My eyes spring open, but I am stunned into silence.

Eva turns and looks through the window of the lounge. Her mouth moves.

Nathalie lunges forward. She flicks the switch on the soundboard with one hand while snatching up the microphone with the other.

"What's that, hon?"

"I said, what do you want me to do?" says Eva.

"Oh, you know. Just warm up. Whatever."

Eva looks horrified. "What?"

"Just warm up. Just do, you know . . . stuff. I'll let you know when I want you to do something specific."

Eva blinks a few times at the window of the lounge. Then she turns and mounts.

My heart is in my throat.

A girly hiss from behind me: "Start the clock!"

"QUIET!" snaps Nathalie.

My head feels light, and I realize I'm hyperventilating. I close my eyes for a moment, trying to remember Lamaze breathing. Once my fingertips stop tingling, I look into the arena.

Eva and Joe float around the perimeter, light as tumbleweed. Eva sits erect and straight, her lower back pumping in time with his stride so that her upper body remains motionless. Her elbow is bent at a precise right angle. Joe chomps on the bit, and between chomps I see the reins snap slightly. He is giving her his head.

Nathalie scootches forward to the very edge of the plastic chair, leaning forward, rapt.

"One minute," whispers someone behind us.

Nathalie swings around on her chair. "If I have to say it again, there's gonna be trouble. *Capiche?*"

There is now utter silence behind us.

I concentrate on the scene in front of me, trying to remember to breathe.

Eva rolls her hands down at the wrist by half an inch and presses her legs into him—this is apparent only by a microscopic change in the width of her calf. Joe's body rounds further, his haunches coming forward. He's still chomping the bit, still giving her his head. His ears are perked, his tail trailing them like a banner.

Shoulder in, shoulder in, shoulder in; then haunches in, haunches in, haunches in. A half halt, and they rock forward into a canter. His back and neck are as arched as a Halloween cat, his hooves drumming the sand like fingers.

"Ahhhhhh . . ." says Nathalie, leaning her chin in her hand. "Oh, that's nice."

"Have I mentioned that Eva can be a real handful?" I say.

"What?" she says, distracted, and without taking her eyes from the arena.

Eva crosses to the left rail using a half pass, a sideways canter in which Joe's legs cross at each stride. Then they begin a *passage*.

Oh God, it's perfect—it looks like someone has filmed a high-stepping trotter and is pressing the pause button once a second.

I lean toward Nathalie. "Eva. She can be difficult," I say with increasing urgency. "You know, boy trouble."

"Ahhhhhh . . ." says Nathalie.

Eva halts Joe without any perceptible movement in her legs or hands. He just suddenly plants his feet squarely and stops. A pause of three seconds, and then he rolls forward into a canter. Eva circles him at the far end. Coming out of it, I see her fingers tighten, his ears perk, and I hold my breath—

They execute a perfect *pirouette*.

"It's not just boys. She smokes. She talks back. Heck, just this week she—"

Nathalie lifts a hand and wiggles her fingers at me, all without looking away from Eva and Joe.

I stare at the back of her head. I've never been shushed like this in my life. And then I wonder why the hell I'm trying to sabotage Eva's audition, and sit back with my mouth firmly shut.

Eva canters directly past the window, so close I get a good look at her face—she's concentrating so hard her chin is jutting and there are lines etched on her forehead. She looks just like Mutti.

She pulls Joe out of the corner, still cantering, and crosses the arena on the long diagonal. Within seconds I see why.

They're doing flying changes, one after another, literally skipping across the arena.

"Did you see that? *Did you see that?*" Nathalie spins on her seat to face me, jabbing her finger at the window.

I am speechless. The girls behind me buzz with excitement.

Nathalie swipes the microphone from the table in front of her. "Thank you, that's enough," she says.

Eva pulls Joe up. "What?"

"That's enough. You can dismount."

"What? You don't want me to audition?" says Eva, horrified. Her fingers tighten on the reins, her face goes pale.

"Honey, you just did," laughs Nathalie. "Nobody else has stayed on Joe for more than six minutes since we brought him here. Congratulations."

Eva's face moves seamlessly from horror to pure joy. She slides her feet from the stirrups and leans over to give Joe an enthusiastic pat. Then she dismounts and stands by his head, sliding her hand under his muzzle.

Joe stands perfectly still, licking and licking and licking the flat of her hand. When the girls pile out of the lounge and skip and laugh their way across the arena, Eva turns, beaming. And when Joe lifts his muzzle, wraps his neck around Eva's, and lays his head on her chest, I realize that there's no turning back.

"Don't worry, Mom."

I turn, startled. Nathalie is staring right at me.

"I heard every word you said about Eva. The interesting ones are always a handful, but I run a tight ship. I only take students who are between sixteen and twenty-one, and they tend to be a pretty self-contained unit. They work ten to twelve hours, six days a week and have no transportation of their own. If they want to go somewhere, they have to ask Margot or me. But mostly, at the end of the day the only thing they want to do is go to bed."

"Oh," I say, looking back into the arena. Eva is accepting congratulatory pats on the back, with a broad, open smile. I realize suddenly that her earlier reticence was not a wish to be rescued, it was a fear of not measuring up. Furthermore, had I followed through on my instinct to get us out of here before she rode, she probably would have taken out a contract on my life.

• • •

Eva waxes ecstatic the whole way home. She has no need for answers from me, and indeed, doesn't leave room for any.

"—and he's just *solid,* Mom. I mean, you can feel it right through the saddle. He's built like a brick shi—" She glances over quickly. "Er, I mean, he's *solid,* Mom. The horse is made of *granite.* Oh, hey! And he looks like granite, too! I mean, have you ever seen such a coat? Well, okay," she says, nodding grudgingly, conceding an unargued but obvious point, "I guess Hurrah still wins the prize for unusual coat, but have you ever seen such a beautiful roan? Honest to God, he looks blue. And all those specks on his flanks and stuff,

Nathalie said they're from fighting with the other horses because he's always got to be the dominant one, wherever he is. Oh! Did I tell you that when they shipped him here he managed to get under—or over, they don't know which—the stall dividers? Not a scratch on him, but that was before he was gelded, so he actually has a foal on the ground. An accidental Smoky Joe Junior. Can you imagine that? Got loose and made the rounds in a slant-load trailer and actually managed to get one of the mares—"

I take a deep breath and try to follow what she's saying. It's not that I'm uninterested—actually it's quite the opposite. I'm trying to absorb the knowledge that I've just lost my daughter to a horse. I was prepared to lend her to the training program, but Smoky Joe came out of nowhere, a freight train on a foggy night.

A fleeting smile crosses my lips. Eric Hamilton won't know what hit him.

"—and there was one point right at the very beginning where I wasn't sure what he was going to do, he was like a coiled spring, and then suddenly he went, like, 'Oh, it's you up there. Okay.' Like he caught sight of me out of the corner of his eye, like he's my horse and he just knew it. Or, no, that's wrong. I'm his *person*, and he knew it. Yeah, that's it. Totally the other way around—"

She's still talking when we park around the back of the house, still talking as we mount the back porch.

"—and did you see when I asked him for the flying changes? No hesitation, nothing. Just skipped right across like it was nothing! Oh, Oma!" she shrieks as she opens the back door and catches sight of my mother.

She rushes over and grabs my shocked mother by both hands, spinning her around in a dance. "She took me! I'm in! And you won't believe my horse!"

Mutti cocks an eyebrow. "Your horse?"

"Yeah! His name is Smoky Joe, and he's a Nokota and he's usually such a terror the rest of the girls call him Smokin' Gun, but we just clicked and OHMIGOD you should have seen us, Oma! We were perfect, just floating. We just *connected* instantly. Apparently he never lets anyone ride him, ever, but the second I laid eyes on him, I just knew—"

I stare open-mouthed at my daughter, and then turn stiffly to hang my purse by the back door.

"Where are you going?" says Mutti.

"Nowhere," I say, turning back around.

But she doesn't mean me. She's facing the hallway.

Eva is gone, thumping up the stairs—two at a time apparently, since her footsteps run out before the stairs should. The door to her bedroom slams shut.

I stare at Mutti.

We hear drawers yanked forth, objects clunking and banging. Chairs shoved aside, and things scooped from surfaces. Her door opens again, followed by more thumping, and then another door opens—is she in the bathroom? Mutti's room? the linen closet?—and then shuffling and clunking as she drags something down the hall.

When I hear the Samsonite's loose wheel, I realize she's lugging all the suitcases into her room.

Mutti moves wordlessly to the fridge and removes the bottle of chardonnay we started last night.

"No," I say miserably. "Thanks, but no."

Mutti pauses, shrugs, and puts the bottle back in the fridge.

As I put my jacket back on, drawers continue to slam open and shut in the room above us.

Chapter 7

Hurrah stands utterly still as I sweep my hands across his body, over and over, round and round, pausing only to brush off the hair that collects on my palms like mats of prickly felt.

His winter coat is shedding out—in response to the increasing daylight rather than a change in temperature—and in my experience bare hands work better than any brush at removing loose hair. But I don't have a brush anyway, because I didn't come in here to groom him. I came in here because I just needed to be with him.

The moon throws only dim light through the bars of his window, and his brindling is invisible. He could be any solid-colored Hanoverian. Well, no, he couldn't—even under the shadow of night, there's no mistaking his magnificent conformation.

I continue running my hands in circles over his body. Eventually he utters a deep, shuddering sigh and allows his ears to droop. When I realize that I'm lulling him to sleep, I move quietly to his shoulder and press my nose up against his neck. I inhale, taking his scent as deeply into my body as I can. Then I slip my hand between his front legs, seeking his cowlick. When I find it, I twirl my fingertips around it, stopping several times to change direction. My face is still pressed against his cool, smooth shoulder, my other hand hooked over his withers.

After a few moments, I position myself by his left side, brace my hands on his rib cage, and leap up so that my weight is on my arms. I push my feet against the wall behind me and wriggle onto his back.

With my legs hanging loose, I lean forward so I'm resting on his neck. I run both hands toward his head— left under mane, right in the open—until I reach his ears, which I scratch in unison. When I'm finished, I grasp them in my fists and let them slide through—first one, then the other—before moving my hands back to his shoulders, smoothing the hair I roughed up only moments before.

Then I lie back, my legs slack and my head resting on his rump. His spine is padded and warm and slightly indented. I love the feel of my vertebrae stretched out along his. We fit like a zipper. I cross my arms on my chest and close my eyes.

"Hey sweetness."

At the sound of Dan's voice, Hurrah's body stiffens and my eyes snap open. I scramble upright, bracing a hand on each of Hurrah's flanks.

"Sorry—I didn't mean to startle you," Dan says quickly.

There's a soft thud as I drop to the floor.

"You didn't have to get off. I can wait for you upstairs."

"No," I say. "It's okay."

"I'm glad to see you on him," Dan says. "Even if it is just in his stall."

My face burns.

"Hey," he says gently. "Are you okay?"

I pause, and then turn and drop my forehead against his shoulder. "Actually I've had an appalling day."

"Why? What happened?"

"Eva was accepted into Nathalie Jenkins's training program."

Dan is silent for so long I look up. He's staring at me. "You're kidding, right?" he finally says.

"No."

"Annemarie?"

"Yes?"

"Perhaps I'm missing something, but isn't this what you wanted?"

I burst into tears. "Yes. I mean, it was the best available option, but my God! You should have seen her! She can't wait to get out from under my despotic rule. She hardly stopped long enough to give Mutti the good news before running upstairs to pack."

"When's she leaving?"

"Not for another three days. I guess she's going to live out of suitcases in the meantime." I turn and throw myself against his chest. "I'm going to be completely alone by the time I'm forty!"

"Oh, baby. Eva won't be far, will she? Nathalie's only in Columbia."

I frown against his shirt.

"That's not the point," I continue. "With Eva gone, the sum total of my life is part-time employment at my mother's riding academy. Most forty-year-old women have a little something more going for them at this point in their lives."

There's a long silence. I might as well have called myself a spinster. I look up at Dan, who has lines etched in his forehead. "Annemarie, are you unhappy with our relationship?"

"Oh, Dan, I don't know . . . It's just you've been away so much this winter. I mean, I know you've saved eighty-seven horses from slaughter since January—"

"Eighty-eight."

"See? How can I complain about that? Forget I said anything."

I try to twist away from him, but he won't let me. He takes me by the shoulders and turns me back around.

"Annemarie, I don't want to forget you said anything. If you're unhappy with our relationship, I need to know. Are you?"

"I don't know," I say, looking at my feet.

"It's a simple question, Annemarie. And one I need the answer to." His voice is harsh, and it shocks me.

I lift my hands and then drop them against my legs. "But the answer's not simple, is it? I love you, but I hardly ever see you, and when I do see you, we never do anything. I know your work is important. I'd never ask you to give it up. I've been trying to be patient and supportive and involved, but I was also hoping that we'd manage to . . . you know . . . spend more time together."

Move in together. Get married. That's what I should say, but somehow I can't make my tongue move the words out of my throat.

"Well, that's my fault then," he says gently. "Maybe I haven't made it clear just how much I appreciate everything you do. The simple truth is without your help, I could never have made those runs to Canada. And there's no question Bella would have died. Heck, just this last week you saved Maisie's filly and performed a solo rescue. That's at least three horses, possibly four, who wouldn't be around right now if it weren't for you, personally." He wraps his arms around me, holding me tight. "I won't be making these runs forever, baby. This winter has been hell on all of us. But in just a few months the pee farms will be closed and the horses dealt with, one way or another. If you can just hang on until then, we'll see a lot more of each other."

See a lot more of each other. That's not quite the level of commitment I was seeking, although, I suppose, technically it's what I asked for.

"Yes, well, all right then," I say miserably.

Hurrah snorts impatiently and shakes. He's ready to fall asleep and wants us out of his stall.

"So," says Dan, assuming a stern tone. "Are we going upstairs, or am I going to have to ravage you right here?"

"Upstairs," I say grumpily.

"Mmmm," he says, slipping his hands inside my vest. He cups my clothed breasts in his hands and runs his thumbs across my nipples. "I have an idea. Why don't I run us a bath?"

I gasp and close my eyes. I'd answer, except that I seem to have forgotten how to breathe.

That's one of the problems with Dan, if you can call it that. Our chemistry is so explosive I can never manage to stay upset even when it would be in my best interest to do so.

• • •

After he's ravaged me—beautifully, gloriously, sinfully—and I've forgiven him everything as I always do, we lie entangled on slightly damp sheets. My pillow is soaked through because my head got dunked several times before we left the bathtub, so I rest my wet head on his chest, feeling his voice rumble through his rib cage. I stroke him, running my hands up the soft skin on the underside of his arm, and then tracing my way back to his sternum, curling his hairs in my fist.

He straightens my wet tresses gently, separating the tangles and smoothing them across my back.

We are silent for a few minutes, caressing each other in the dark.

"Dan, do you remember when I said I'd had an appalling day?"

"Uh-huh."

"Well, there's a little more to it than I told you."

"What do you mean?" he says, still stroking my back.

I pause. "I nearly did something terrible today."

"What?"

"I think I tried to sabotage Eva's audition."

There's a beat of surprised silence before he answers. "You what? Why?"

"I don't know why. I have no idea. She was riding—doing spectacularly well, in fact—and all of a sudden I found myself telling Nathalie about all the things she's done wrong. When I realized what I was doing, I stopped. Nathalie didn't seem to care, but still. That's not the point."

I struggle up onto my elbow and look down at him. "Are you shocked?"

"Well, yes. A little."

"Me too. I couldn't believe what I was saying, and yet there it was, coming out of my mouth."

I look down at the expression on his beautiful face and cringe with shame. "You're disappointed in me. I can tell."

He doesn't answer right away. "Well . . . at least you stopped yourself."

"Yes," I say, my eyes filling with tears.

Dan looks at me for a moment longer. Then he pulls me to him. I fold my arms like wings and let him envelop me.

"Don't beat yourself up, Annemarie. You've got a lot of things going on right now. The important thing is you caught yourself and did the right thing."

• • •

First thing in the morning I creep out of bed and across the hall to the office, pausing just long enough to gaze at Dan. He lies on his back in the center of the bed with his arms outstretched. The dog is pressed against him, a bloated sausage whose legs move in time to her snoring.

The office is directly above the lounge, and, like the lounge, has a window out onto the arena. Sometimes when the lessons for the day are finished, I turn Hurrah out into the arena and steal glances at him while I'm doing paperwork. I don't do much paperwork anymore, having discovered that it's not my forte. Mutti still trusts me with some of it, but after last year, I'm pretty sure she checks it afterward.

As I slip into the chair behind the desk, I wonder if it's too early to call Roger. Then I decide that no, they've got a new baby. Of course they're up.

The phone rings five times before anyone answers.

"Hello?" says Roger. The baby wails approximately an inch from the mouthpiece.

I'm relieved that he answered, because I still grate at the sound of Sonja's voice. I've come to terms with my divorce—and even come to realize that I wasn't any happier than he was—but still. You don't get left by your husband for another woman without some residual bad feelings.

"Yeah, hi, it's me," I say.

"Oh, Annemarie. Hang on just a second." There's shuffling and thumping, a baby's gurgle followed by an earsplitting squeal.

"Honey?" says Roger's muffled voice, and a pain shoots through me because I very nearly answered him. "Can you take Jeremy for a minute?"

More shuffling, a mother's cooing, and then Roger is back. The sounds of Jeremy recede into the background. "Hi there. Sorry about that. He won't let us put him down. We think he might be getting a tooth."

"Isn't that a little early?"

"He's thirteen weeks. It's on the early end of the normal range."

"Is he drooling?"

"Not really."

"Pulling his ear?"

"Gosh, I'm not sure. Are you thinking ear infection?"

"Seems more likely than a tooth," I say. And then I shift into business mode because I'm irritated at finding myself discussing his new baby. "So, listen, we have to talk."

"Uh-oh," he says. "Eva, I presume?"

"Yes. Brace yourself."

I tell him about the pot, the expulsion, and the condom. And then I tell him about the training program.

At the end, there's dead silence.

"Hello? Roger? Hello? Are you there?"

"I'm here," he says.

"You went all quiet."

"I'm a little shocked, that's all."

"I know. I'm sorry to spring this on you."

I hear Jeremy wailing in another room, along with Sonja's gentle murmurings. I picture her pacing in a floor-length satin negligée—and Roger's eyes upon them.

"Are you sure this is the best thing for Eva?" Roger asks. "Because she could come live with us."

"No!" I croak.

"Why? We could get her a horse here. It would be a fresh start."

"Please, Roger. I don't think you understand. Nathalie Jenkins is the best of the best, and there are zero opportunities to get into trouble. And this horse . . . well, this isn't just a horse. You should have seen them, Roger. This is a horse who won't let anyone else ride him, and yet for her he was doing one-tempi changes. I think this might be her Harry."

I hear him suck in his breath.

"Roger?" I say tentatively.

"And you're sure you're okay with this?" he says. "You've always been so . . . I don't know how to put this. Reticent."

"Well, we can't keep going as we have been. I don't see that we have much choice."

I hear his fingers drumming as he mulls: *Rat-a-tat. Rat-a-tat. Rat-a-tat.*

"All right," he says as the baby cries piteously in the distance. "Let's give it a try and see how it goes."

After we hang up I sit staring into space and pondering how very different Roger's life is from mine.

• • •

On Monday morning, I wake to the sound of the apartment's front door crashing into the wall behind it.

"Ma! Ma!" shouts Eva from the living room. "Where are you?"

I groan and press my face into my pillow. Thank God I don't have a naked Dan beside me. A few hours earlier, I did.

Her bright, young head appears in the doorway of the bedroom.

"Oh my God!" she screams in horror. "You're not even up yet?"

"Eva," I say, peering groggily at the clock radio by my bed. "It's only . . . Eva! It's not even seven yet!"

"Ma! Please!" she exclaims, sighing dramatically and staring at me as though my stupidity is beyond comprehension.

"Oh, all right. All right," I say, throwing the covers back and creating a triangle of eiderdown from which only Harriet's head and front paws stick out. A dachshund turnover. Harriet opens her shiny black eyes, takes in the scene, heaves a sigh equal in magnitude to any of Eva's, and goes back to sleep.

I wish I could do the same, but my daughter is yelling at me.

"And brush your hair! And put on some lipstick or something!" she calls after me as I stumble toward the bathroom.

I stop and turn to face her. "Eva! Please!" I say, putting my hands on my waist. "What do you think I am?"

"I just don't want you looking like a—"

"Don't say it!" I snap. "And if you want me to keep getting ready, don't even think it!"

She clamps her mouth shut and looks down. Her toe traces a small circle on the floor. "Sorry, Ma," she says finally. The effort she's taking to control her excitement is painfully obvious.

I sigh. "Just make some coffee, and I'll try not to embarrass you."

"You'll hurry, right?"

"Honey, I'm sorry, but you either get fast and sea hag, or you wait while I get presentable. You can't have both."

Another pause.

"Take your time," she says sweetly and trips off to the kitchen.

I close the bathroom door and approach the sink, which is covered with the various bottles of goop required to make me presentable these days. I have moisturizing cleansers, revitalizing toners, repair lotions, eye serums, lip balms that promise sunscreen protection, even acne medication—because horrifically, I'm still prone to outbreaks even though I have the beginnings of wrinkles. That seems like the cruelest injustice of all, the act of a vengeful God. And that doesn't even begin to address my makeup, which offers its own collection of mind-boggling miracles.

I start the hot water running and glance into the mirror.

My God, she's right. I do look like a sea hag. Or maybe a swamp monster, with my hair all mashed to one side. My left eye is puffy and creased with pillow lines—and to add insult to injury, it doesn't want to focus yet.

I lean forward, squinting at my reflection.

I poke at the line between my eyes, wondering whether Botox would help. I take after my mother in many ways, but I seem to have missed two key genes: the one responsible for good housewifery, and the one responsible for graceful aging. Which is fine. I'll fight it. The Clan of the Sea Hags may be circling, singing their siren song, but I'll go down kicking and screaming and clutching a vial of botulism.

I puff my cheeks full of air and check to see if the creases beside my mouth diminish. To my surprise, they disappear entirely, but my delight is short-lived since I can't walk around all day looking like a blowfish.

Fugu Mama. I can hear Eva now.

I test the running water—this time with my wrist—and, finding it sufficiently hot, plug the drain.

While the sink is filling, I pick up my brush, watching in the mirror. Just as I'm poised to drag it through my Medusa mop, I realize it's full of long black hair. Since Eva's hair is long and black and I've been known to jump to conclusions, I take hold of one, pull it out, and hold it up to the light. It's horse hair.

I turn to the door and bellow. *"Eva-a-a-a-a-a!"*

She appears. "What?"

"Would you please stop using my hairbrush to groom your horse?"

"Sure. Whatever," she shrugs. "It's kind of a given since I'm not going to be living here anymore."

She turns and pads back to the kitchen, leaving me to gawp after her.

• • •

Mutti helps us load the car, dragging suitcases two at a time down the ramp we had put in for Pappa and never removed after his death. It's the second such ramp our family's had, and I'm too superstitious to remove it. I know logically that my recovery from my spinal cord injury did not cause Pappa's illness, but I can't help feeling as though removing the ramp would be poking the fates.

When the many bags and boxes are piled in the backseat, Mutti slams the door and turns to face Eva.

She frowns and wags a finger. "You be good, Eva. And call us." She's trying to look stern, but I can't help noticing a certain moistness about her eyes. Then she suddenly pulls Eva into a bear hug.

"Oma! I'm coming back on Sunday," laughs Eva. She kisses Mutti on both cheeks. Then she scoops Harriet off the ground and tries to plant a kiss on the side of her snout.

Harriet responds with a snarling yap.

"Harriet! Bad dog!" I shout.

"Bah, it's okay, Ma," says Eva, opening the door and tossing my wiener dog onto the passenger seat. "Just for that, she can come along for the ride."

I shrug, and move around to the driver's door.

Despite her earlier enthusiasm, Eva becomes distinctly subdued as we drive toward Columbia. I steal glances at her, wondering if maybe she's feeling a little melancholy about leaving me after all.

She sits with her shoes off and feet propped up, staring out the passenger window so that whenever I glance at her all I see is the back of her head.

Her jet black hair has been carefully straightened in

anticipation of the big day, but she still hasn't done anything about the roots. I daren't say anything for fear of giving her ideas.

Eva heaves a dramatic sigh and wriggles her toes on the dash. She sneaks a glance at me, and then sighs again—this time so loudly it's arguable she employed vocal chords.

"Honey?"

She turns to look at me, playing innocent. "Yeah?"

"You okay?"

"Yeah, sure," she says, turning her head back to the window. There's a long silence—several minutes worth—followed by another long shuddering sigh.

"Honey?" I say carefully. "Is something on your mind?"

"You know, I didn't mean what I said this morning. You look okay for an old lady."

"Gee, thanks," I say, tightening my grasp on the steering wheel.

"Mom, I'm joking," she says. "You look great."

"Oh."

Another silence.

"Mom?"

"Yes?"

"I didn't do it, you know."

"What?"

"You know. *It.*" she says, her cheeks bright red. She plucks Harriet from the seat between us and plants her on her lap. Then she concentrates on Harriet's long ears, turning them inside out repeatedly.

"No, I don't know 'it,' " I say, glancing back at the road. "What are you talking about?"

"With Eric."

I look at her, wide-eyed.

"Mom! Watch out!" she shrieks.

I jerk the steering wheel around just in time to keep from going off into the trees. Harriet lurches sideways and Eva clutches her to her chest.

We drive in silence for a couple of minutes while I try to figure out what she's hoping to gain by telling me this.

"So then why did you have condoms in your purse?"

"Condom. Not con*doms*," she says.

"All right," I say, alternating between looking at the road and at Eva. "Why did you have *condom* in your purse?"

"Mom, can you please just watch the road?"

I press my lips together and stare out the windshield.

"It was a dare," Eva finally says. "Remember that field trip to Concord? We played truth or dare on the school bus. Meghan chose dare, and she had to walk into a Walgreens and buy condoms. So she did. And then . . . well, then we had them. So we each took one."

"Why didn't you just throw it out?"

"I was going to. But I wanted to open it up and look at it first."

"So you haven't—as you put it—'*done it?*'"

"No."

We continue driving, silent once again.

"Do you believe me?" she says finally.

"Yes. I do. But I want you to listen to me very carefully. If you ever do decide to 'do it,' I want you to use a condom. Maybe more than one. Actually I think maybe I'd like you to wear a garbage bag."

Eva smirks and starts tapping her toes against the dashboard.

"I'm serious. Because if you don't, you can die."

"I know, Mom."

"How about the pot?" I say. "Did you do that?"

"Yeah," she says, after a slight pause. "That one I did do."

"Was it your first time?"

"No."

"How often?"

"I dunno. Four, maybe five times." Her head swings around to me. "Mom, did you ever try it?"

"Never," I say firmly. She turns her head slowly back to her window. And then, because I can feel her shame and vulnerability expand to fill the car, I add, "But to be completely honest, that's probably only because I never had the chance."

"Never?"

"Nope. My childhood was somewhat sheltered."

As yours is about to be, my dear, I realize with an overwhelming rush of relief.

I steal another quick look at her. The red spots on her cheeks are dissipating, her body less tense. She suddenly springs forward and turns on the radio. She scans through the stations, pausing long enough at each to hear approximately six notes. And yet somehow she recognizes everything.

She finds something she likes and turns it up loud. Before long, she's staring out the window and singing along, her head bobbing happily.

Forty minutes later, the gatepost at Wyldewood squawks something at me. I squawk something back, and the doors swing open.

Eva drops her feet from the dash and turns the radio off. She spins in her seat to face me, her eyes full of horror.

"Mom?"

"Yes?"

"You'll look after Flicka for me?"

"Of course!"

"No, but you'll groom her? And lunge her?"

I glance over at her huge brown eyes, so full of concern.

"Yes, of course," I laugh. "And besides, you'll see her every Sunday."

"She likes her carrots cut up. And she doesn't like Granny Smith apples, only Golden Delicious. And you have to quarter them. But at least she now eats the skins. Hey! Wait a minute!" she says, her expression brightening. "I have an idea! I can board her here!"

"No you can't, honey."

"Why?"

"Because she's not the right kind of horse!"

"Arabs can be sport horses," she says indignantly.

"Yes, I know that. But Flicka won't be. She's not going to top fourteen hands. Besides, Nathalie would never agree to it."

Eva opens her mouth to respond—even sucks in the breath required to do so—but I hold up a hand to stop her.

"This isn't a barn like ours, honey. Not every rider gets to train here, and not every horse gets to live here. This is a huge opportunity you're being given. I hope you realize that."

Eva looks momentarily crestfallen. I'm considering whether to continue on into a last-minute lecture when she catches sight of Joe in a paddock. She turns so violently Harriet falls to the floor.

"Oh," she says breathlessly. "Oh. There he is." She

presses her face and hands against the passenger-side window, and continues twisting her body until she's looking at Joe through the back window. "Oh, Ma," she croons. "There he is."

When I pull the car into place in the gravel parking lot by the main barn, we are immediately swarmed by girls. They pull Eva out of the car, chattering, giggling nonstop. The back doors open, the bags are removed, their retractable handles pulled out.

"Holy crap! Look at all the stuff she brought!"

"Eva, did you bring a hair dryer? Because we're down to five since Maggie busted mine—"

"Oh, I *so* did not! It totally overheated! And look! It burned out a whole clump of my—"

"Hey, Kris, look at all the shoes she brought!"

"Oh! How adorable! A wiener dog!"

"Oooooh! It's so cute! Come here, *poochie-woochie*—Crap! The little shit bit me!"

I rush around to the other side of the car, snatch Harriet up by collar and rump, and chuck her into the front seat. Then I slam all the car doors and try to identify which girl she bit.

But the girls are receding en masse to the barn. Eva is somewhere in the middle, surrounded so I can't even see her. I move my head from side to side, trying to catch sight of her too-black hair.

I raise my chin, place my hands on both sides of my mouth, and shout, "Don't worry, honey! I'll look after Flicka for you! And I'll . . . er . . . Eva?"

The girls are gone, swallowed by the barn.

As I stare mournfully after them, someone taps me on the shoulder.

"Annemarie!"

"Oh. Nathalie."

"I see Eva's been absorbed."

"Yes, you could say that," I say, still staring at the spot where the girls disappeared.

"I'm glad I caught you," says Nathalie. "There are some papers I need you to sign. Plus I want to make sure Eva has the appropriate gear. I have a reputation to uphold."

"Oh, I think she'll do you proud," I say.

"Black gloves? Shadbelly? Body protector? Decent boots?"

"Yes, everything but a top hat. She sat on her last one."

"You'll need to get her a new one right away. For Strafford."

"You're entering her?"

"Yes, of course. Why wouldn't I?"

"It's just that . . . well, it's only two weeks away. I wouldn't have thought she'd have time to prepare."

"It's a little longer than that. And besides who cares? Nobody expects her to place—although after watching the audition, who knows? Consider it practice. A way of getting her feet wet. Besides, it's not set in stone. I'll watch for the next two weeks and if I don't think she's ready, we'll scratch. But in the meantime, we have to get the paperwork in."

I clear my throat. "At what level are you entering her?" I ask, trying to sound casual.

"Intermediate."

The two-star level. Jumps that are a minimum of four feet in height and—with the exception of the very first round—have no maximum.

My head begins to swim. Nathalie's face moves in and out, circling mine like a gigantic rubber clown.

Shimmering fireworks explode in my peripheral vision and then, *whoosh!*

"Annemarie? Are you all right?"

I find myself on the gravel with my head between my knees.

"There, there. You haven't eaten yet, have you?" says Nathalie, crouching beside me. "You're as bad as the girls. Come back to the apartment and have a piece of toast."

"No, thank you," I say weakly. "I think I'll just go home now."

"Don't be ridiculous. I can't let you drive," says Nathalie, taking my elbow and dragging me to my feet. She leans me up against the car and hovers, her arm on the crook of my elbow. "There now. Are you steady?"

"Yes," I say, staring down at the dented hood of my car as Nathalie opens the door and retrieves Harriet.

When she marches off through the barn with my dog, I have no choice but to follow. We go through the barn and arena, past Smoky Joe's empty stall, and straight through the other side.

• • •

The girls' "apartment" turns out to be a house that is larger than Mutti's. It's in the same style as Nathalie's colonial mansion at the top of the hill, but smaller and tucked behind the indoor arena.

I follow Nathalie inside, glancing around with wide eyes. We pass a heap of Eva's belongings that have been dumped in the entryway.

It's all one level. There was clearly a second storey at some point, but the house has been gutted and rebuilt so that the rooms are tall and airy, with whitewashed rafters crisscrossing the cathedral ceiling, which is dotted with skylights. The floor is hardwood, light oak in alternating wide and thin strips. The kitchen, living room, and eating area are all open, but the spaces have been designed and decorated so that they are clearly distinct. The kitchen has a long granite island with a bowl of fresh produce in the center. The maple table is stretched with an impossible number of leaves—without counting, I'd guess that it probably seats sixteen. The living room has a stone fireplace with a gas insert, but the focal point is an enormous flat-screen television mounted on the wall between two lead-paned picture windows. The bookshelves are piled with books, magazines, movies, and games. The stained-glass lamps on the end tables—in Frank Lloyd Wright style—match the floor lamps. There are plants in the corners, lined curtains of William Morris fabric, and a tinkling, shimmering butterfly mobile that hangs from the center of the cathedral ceiling.

In short, I want to move in.

"*This* is where the girls live?" I say as Nathalie leads me to the table and pulls out a chair.

"Four to a room," she says, going to the kitchen and rummaging around in a bread box. She drops a piece of bread in an industrial-sized toaster.

"When you said apartment, I thought you meant something above the barn."

"That's a reasonable assumption, but no. This used to be the plant manager's house."

"The plant manager of what?"

"This is the original Klaas estate."

"Klaas—as in pickles?"

"Exactly," she says. "My brother runs the company, but I maintain a large interest."

Which explains why money isn't an issue. Somehow I wasn't expecting the famed Nathalie Jenkins to be a pickle heiress.

But then again, I also wasn't expecting to be sitting at her table signing permission slips, waivers, and medical cards so that Eva can compete in about two weeks at the two-star level on a horse who hasn't let anyone else ride him for more than six minutes running since moving to this barn.

Chapter 8

"Um, Mrs. Zimmer? Can we stop now?" huffs a sandy-haired twelve-year-old named Kevin as he whizzes past me on Tazz.

Kevin's hands are on the pommel and he leans precariously forward, taking great pains to keep his bottom out of the saddle.

I shake my head to get my bearings.

The six students in my Monday evening group lesson are cantering around me, the horses puffing, the humans' faces red. I glance at my watch and realize just how long I've left them cantering.

"Oh, geez—yes, of course. Slow to a walk, please. Pull back and sit deep in the saddle, Marina. That's it." My attention is caught by a jerky movement to my left.

I pivot and find Blueprint dancing away from the rail. Then he stretches his neck down, preparing to buck. "Amy! Don't let him do that. Pull him up. Amy! Pull him up! Oh crap—" I say as he skids sideways and across the arena at full gallop. I run after them, screaming, "Amy! Pulley rein! Pulley rein! Amy, yank him around! Grab his mane with one hand and—"

There's a thud as Amy hits the ground.

I sprint toward her, keeping track of Blueprint's whereabouts through his hoofbeats, grunts, and flapping stirrup leathers.

I stop once as he passes directly in front of me, and consider making a grab for the reins. At the last possible moment I decide not to because there's a very good chance I'd dislocate my shoulder, but I regret my decision immediately. The reins have now come over his head and if he gets a foot caught, that'll be the end of Blueprint.

Amy lies on her back with her knees up, her face scrunched into a purple grimace.

"Oh God, oh God," I say, kneeling beside her. My hands frame her face, fingers fluttering, never making contact. "Amy, can you hear me?"

"Amy!" shrieks her mother, tearing out of the lounge and into the arena, leaving both doors wide open. I jerk my head from side to side. Parents and younger siblings will start arriving any second to pick up the students, and the last thing we need is a crazed horse stampeding through the aisles.

Fortunately, Blueprint has come to a stop just behind Domino, a sturdy black-and-white paint whose response is to flatten his ears. He surveys the runaway with great suspicion, but doesn't move.

Blueprint stretches his head forward and sniffs Domino's rump. Then he snorts and shakes, sending a prolonged shudder dancing down the stirrup leathers. Whatever it was, he's over it.

I turn back to Amy, who is sitting with her head slumped over her knees. Her mother, Sherrie, investigates each limb, carefully bending each elbow and then each knee.

"Don't move her!" I croak. "Please!"

"I'm okay," Amy says. "I think I'm just winded."

"That could be just adrenaline," I say, digging in my pocket for my cell phone. "I'm calling an ambulance. Better safe than sorry."

Amy fumbles with the strap of her helmet and then removes it with trembling hands. She moves her head in slow circles, wincing, stretching, testing things out.

"No. Really," she says in a cracked voice. "I think I'm okay."

"Can you get up, honey?" says Sherrie.

"Oh God, I really think we should—" I start, but then I shut up because Amy's mother is pulling her to her feet.

I catch hold of Amy's other elbow.

"How does that feel?" says Sherrie. "Are you steady?"

"I think so," says Amy. "Yeah. I'm okay."

I turn back to the other students, who watch grim-faced from on top of their horses.

"Okay," I say, clapping my hands. "Everybody off. The lesson's over. Please walk your horses until they're cool and then put them away. Loosen your girths first. But not enough that the saddle slides around," I add quickly, remembering Jerry Benson from last week.

When I turn back to Amy, she's limping forward, leaning on her mother.

"Sherrie, can you take her to the lounge? I'll be right there. I need to catch Blueprint."

Sherrie meets my eyes and nods. She's pale and her expression strained, but to my immense surprise, she doesn't seem to be preparing to launch herself at me.

Because she should. Because this was my fault.

• • •

It takes the better part of forty minutes to persuade me that Amy is all right. When it dawns on me that Sherrie is muttering platitudes to *me,* I decide it's time to let the matter drop. As they head for the door of the lounge, Sherrie looks over her shoulder at me, and the look on her face says everything. She thinks I'm crazy. Or neurotic. Probably both.

I fight a momentary impulse to explain myself, to tell her my history and exactly why it is that girls being thrown from horses inspires such panic, but I'm pretty sure that if I did, I'd dig myself even further into that hole labeled "crazy" and might just lose myself a student in the process. And so I mutter a weak goodbye and watch them leave.

• • •

After I've given everyone in the barn more than enough time to leave, I top up all the water buckets, throw a flake or two of hay into stalls that are looking a bit low, and go to the end of the tack aisle to collect the dirty saddle pads.

I lean over and clutch them to my chest. When I stand up, I realize my face is inches from about a dozen tiny rodent droppings.

I shriek and leap backward, dropping all the saddle pads to the floor. Then I stare at them, puffing in horror. I rush to the washroom, start the water full blast, and scrub my face, neck, hands, and as far up my arms as I can without getting my clothes wet.

Ten minutes later, the contaminated saddle pads are safely enclosed in a garbage bag, which I've hermetically sealed before slinging over my shoulder.

I pause at Blueprint's stall on my way out. He stands with his rump to the door, calmly munching hay, utterly oblivious to having nearly killed a girl this afternoon.

What's more astonishing is that the girl herself seems utterly oblivious to having nearly been killed.

And then I remind myself that people fall off horses all the time and that not only do most of them not die, they don't even get seriously hurt.

I sigh, knowing this but not believing it, and then go to the house with my rodent-infested laundry.

• • •

I set the garbage bag beside the washing machine and go looking for Mutti.

She's sitting in the living room with a cup of cocoa, a book, and Harriet wedged between her and the arm of the chair. A large fire crackles beside her.

"Und so," she says, looking at me from over the top of her reading glasses.

"And so," I reply, sinking into the chair opposite her.

Harriet's eyebrows twitch. She's considering whether to switch chairs. Oh, the heck with it, she *is* my dog—

"Come here, Harriet! Come here, girl!" I chirp, patting the chair beside me.

Harriet stares me straight in the eye, sighs haltingly, and shifts her gaze to the fireplace.

Mutti scoops her off the chair and dumps her on the floor. Harriet yelps with surprise and throws Mutti a wounded look.

Mutti removes her glasses and stares right back. After a few seconds, Harriet plods resentfully over and lays herself across my feet.

"Do you want some cocoa?" asks Mutti, folding her glasses and setting them on the table beside her.

"No thanks," I say.

"Something stronger?"

"In a bit," I say. "Blueprint threw a student tonight."

"Is everyone okay?"

"Yup. They seem to be," I say.

"Well, thank the Lord for that," says Mutti.

Both of us stare at the fire for a bit.

"Will you be sleeping here tonight?"

"No, I don't think so," I say.

"Eva's room is free for the next five days."

"No, I'm okay at the barn."

Mutti shakes her head dismissively. "Honestly, Annemarie. I can't imagine why you persist in this silliness. You're a grown woman. What you and Dan do at night is of no interest to me."

"It's not silliness," I say, feeling more than a little defensive.

"Huh," says Mutti in a tone that makes it perfectly clear what she thinks. "Well, anyway. We will have to address the issue at some point."

"Why? What do you mean?"

"Presumably you and Dan will get married eventually and then you'll have to live somewhere. And somehow I can't picture you moving into his trailer."

"Yeah, well, I'm not so sure you should presume anything," I grumble.

Mutti looks up quickly. "What do you mean?"

"Well, we've been dating again for almost a year, and so far he hasn't so much as mentioned the *M* word."

"So you bring it up."

"I can't."

"Why not? For goodness sake, Annemarie—you're nearly forty years old, not some blushing teenager. Talk to the man."

"No! I can't."

"Why?"

"Because what if he doesn't want to marry me? What then?"

"Well, indeed. Wouldn't you rather know?"

We sit in silence, each staring at some other point in the room. Then I get up, go to the kitchen, and pour myself a glass of wine.

When I return, I put the wine down beside my chair, scoop Harriet up by the armpits, and settle her on my lap.

"Mutti, why don't we have a barn cat?"

"Your father didn't like cats. Besides, we never needed one."

"We do now. I just found rodent droppings on the saddle pads I was bringing back to wash."

She flaps her hand. *"Psssh,"* she says. "What's a few little mouse pellets?"

"Hanta virus! Rabies!" I sputter. "Bubonic plague!"

"You forgot one," Mutti says, staring calmly at the rim of her blue-flowered mug.

"What?" I say.

"Ebola virus."

"Mutti! I'm serious! Rodents carry terrible diseases. And I had already picked the pads up. They were right . . . right . . . *here*!" I say, flapping a hand in front of my nose, which is scrunched in disgust.

"Annemarie, barns have mice. It's a fact of life."

"I want a cat."

"So get one," she shrugs.

"Really? You don't mind?"

"Of course not. It was your father who didn't like cats," she says, sipping her cocoa.

"Oh. Okay," I say. For some reason I was expecting her to argue with me. "So, um, do you think the washing machine will get rid of everything?"

"You mean the Ebola virus?"

"Mutti!"

"Annemarie," Mutti says in her take-control voice. "People wash diapers in washing machines. They'll be fine."

I suppose she may have a point. But I must still look dubious, because she suddenly blurts out, "Oh, for goodness sake, Annemarie. I'll do the laundry."

"Make sure you use hot—"

"Annemarie!"

"Okay, okay," I say, raising my hands in surrender. I turn to look at the fireplace with equal parts embarrassment and relief. Then I take a large and unabashed slurp of wine as Mutti marches off to the basement to deal with the Ebola virus.

• • •

Later, when I'm lying in bed with Harriet as my only bedmate and wondering whether Dan will show up, my thoughts wander for the millionth time to our relationship's trajectory.

When Dan and I first started seeing each other again, I just assumed our relationship would follow the natural progression. I know I made a mess of my first marriage, but I did sort of think I'd have another go at it, particularly since Dan is the man I should have married in the first place. But on we go, month after month with no sign of progress, no sign of him being dissatisfied with the state of things, and with me finally beginning to wonder whether marriage is even on his radar.

To be sure, I'm not perfect wife material: I'm neurotic. I'm compulsive. I speak before I think and can't cook worth a damn. I'm messy and germaphobic all at once, and it's not entirely unheard of for me to get hold of the wrong end of the stick and then hang there like a pit bull.

But I have this deep fear that Dan might find all that charming and quirky if it weren't for the one thing I can't do anything about.

While I adore him and would give anything to bear his children, I can't. My type of infertility is absolute and unfixable, and has been a source of terrible grief since the moment I came out of the anesthetic all those years ago and realized that the emergency surgery that saved Eva's life also cost me my uterus. And while he's never said a word about it, I'm painfully aware that Jill's ovarian cancer was discovered during treatment for infertility.

So if Dan marries me, what does he get? A highly opinionated and neurotic wife, a highly opinionated and out-of-control stepdaughter, a highly opinionated mother-in-law who would certainly expect us to live with her, and no hope of ever having a child.

And no matter how many times I turn that over in my head, I can't seem to wrap it in an attractive package.

I lie alone with my dog, so upset I'm grinding my teeth, listening as their edges squeak together. I move my jaw around and try to settle it into a relaxed position, but it doesn't work.

Harriet snuggles into my armpit like a piglet rooting

for truffles. She seems to feel guilty about earlier this evening because she followed me out here of her own accord, and I'm grateful for her presence—almost to the point of tears. Her long warm body is pressed up against me, her snout buried under my arm. She digs with her front paws, as though she'd like to burrow entirely beneath me. I stroke her lightly, fingering her silky ears and gently unworking the beginnings of a mat.

After three hours I realize that not only is Dan not coming, but that I also don't have a hope of falling asleep.

Eventually I slip downstairs and into Hurrah's stall. He stirs and shifts his weight as I bury my face in his neck, breathing deeply of his scent.

Chapter 9

I decide to test the issue and wait to see how long it takes for Dan to contact me if I stop calling him. Three days later, when he has neither called nor shown up, I decide that enough is enough. Mutti is right—I'll be forty years old in nine days. If I can't take control of my life now, what hope is there?

After the last of my students has left, I climb into my Camry and head to Day Break. As I bump my way down the drive, I pass Squire in one of the front pastures.

Appaloosa, indeed. There's not a spot anywhere on his body, unless you count mud flecks. He's still stick-rib skinny—even thinner than before because his bloating is going down, but his ears perk when I drive past. He lifts his proud pony head and sniffs the wind, almost as though he recognizes me.

I can't find Dan anywhere, even though his truck is in its usual place. I check the barns, the office, and finally even his trailer. I'm just about to climb back into my car when he appears from the tree line on Mayflower. She's the only horse on his property who is not a rescue, a beautiful palomino quarter horse mare that belonged to

Jill. And although it fills me with crippling, withering shame, I realize I'm jealous of Dan's dead wife.

Dan is wearing blue jeans, a cowboy hat, leather gloves, and a lumberjack shirt. He rides Western—I never could get him interested in English—and he sits tall in the saddle, his long legs stretched low. Dan makes riding Western look so good I even tried it once, but English is so ingrained in me that I wouldn't let him lengthen the stirrups enough and when we cantered my legs got chewed up by the leather.

When he catches sight of me, he steers Mayflower over.

"Hi, babe," he says, resting both hands on the saddle horn. "Wasn't expecting you. Not that I'm not happy to see you. What's up?"

"Well," I say coolly, "let me see. My daughter left home on Monday, and I got so distracted in a lesson a few nights ago that one of the horses spooked and threw a student."

"Jesus—is she all right?"

"Yes. But no thanks to me. I got distracted and left them cantering for ten minutes. And I haven't seen or heard from you in four days."

Dan watches me for a moment and then dismounts, swinging his right leg over the saddle. He steps down, adjusts his hat, and turns to pull the reins over Mayflower's head. I watch his broad back, waiting for a response.

"I'm sorry," he says, his elbows jerking as he loosens Mayflower's girth. "I've been meaning to call, but we've been working fourteen-hour days trying to gentle this latest load of horses. This is the first human contact some of them have had, other than being forced onto the trailers and getting poked with needles. And for the babies, this was their first time away from their mothers. We've got some of them leading now, but we've still got a long way to go before we can send them to their new homes. But I *am* sorry. I should have called. Why don't you wait for me back at the house? I'll be along in a sec."

A wave of something gathers inside me, surging upward, and before I know it words are rolling off my tongue. "No. I don't want to wait back at the house. I want to go out. Dan, we never go out. In fact, we never do anything but go to bed."

He turns slowly to face me. "Is this about the talk we had the other night?"

"Uh . . . kind of," I say.

"I thought we sorted that out."

I press my lips into a thin line and stare at the ground, because as far as I'm concerned we didn't sort out anything.

"Okay. We'll do something," he says. "What do you want to do?"

"I don't know. I'm just tired of staying in all the time," I say, once again completely miserable.

"Well, okay. Let me ask you something. What's your favorite restaurant?"

I blink in surprise. Then I glance down at my stable clothes. "Sorrento's. But I'm hardly dressed for that."

"No," he says, taking my shoulders in his hands and staring deep into my eyes, "but someone has a birthday coming up in nine days, and I'd like it to be very special."

Very special. The phrase shoots through me like a comet, trailing sparks of luminescent joy.

"Oh," I say, leaving my mouth open. I daren't hope—and yet what else could that mean?

"So is Sorrento's that place in Lincoln?"

"Yes."

"And what makes it your favorite restaurant?"

"Oh, they make the best Lobster Newburg in the world—plus a killer chocolate soufflé," I say, considerably more animated now. "In fact, everything on the menu's good. Pappa loved it, although he said he only went there because there wasn't a restaurant with Austrian cuisine within driving distance. That's where he took Mutti for their fortieth anniversary."

"Chocolate soufflé, huh?" Dan rubs his chin, looking past me. "So where do you want to go tonight?"

"Oh, *psssssh,* we don't have to go out," I say cheerfully. "I'll wait for you back at the house. Say—you got any food? The last time I was here, the cupboard was pretty bare."

"Have a look around. But try not to set anything on fire before I get there."

I whack him on the shoulder, and then, because he's just announced his intention to propose to me, immediately stand on tiptoe to kiss his beautiful, split-plum lips.

• • •

I stand in front of Dan's open fridge, bent at the waist and scanning its contents. As its emptiness sinks in, I lean further, peering under, around, and through the wire shelves in the hope of finding some secret food-bearing compartment at the back.

It's even emptier than it was last time, and in more important ways—this time he doesn't even have beer. I pick up the jar of Kim Chee, more out of curiosity than anything else, and find that the *Best Before* date was more than a year ago. I pick up the Klaas pickle jar and gaze at its label, feeling suddenly blue about Eva.

After I've entirely given up on the idea of finding anything I could possibly transform into a dinner—even a bad one—I close the fridge and head to the living room area.

As I pass the phone, a yellow Post-it note catches my eye.

I pluck it from the vinyl wallpaper. My name is written above an unfamiliar phone number. I frown at it for a moment, then pick up the phone and dial.

After four rings, someone picks up.

"Hello?" says a female voice.

"Hello," I say, twisting the phone cord in one hand. "This is Annemarie Zimmer. Someone from this number left a message for me. I'm afraid I don't know who."

"It was me. I'm surprised you called back."

"I beg your pardon?" I say.

"I said I'm surprised you called back. Considering you stole my horse and all."

"Stole your . . . ?" Understanding dawns on me. "Eugenie? Is that you?"

"Yeah, it's me."

"I didn't steal Squire. You called me to take him."

"Yeah? Well, where's my money?"

Oh God. She's right. I left without paying. Obviously Squire would have been confiscated anyway, but I did agree to pay for him. A vision of her little girl flashes through my head, sitting on the dilapidated porch with no socks on, playing with her bald naked Barbie.

"How are you? How's your little girl?"

"We're fine. So you gonna pay, or what?"

"Uh, yes, of course," I say. "I'm sorry. I really didn't mean to leave without paying. I got distracted by . . . er . . ." I let that particular train of thought fade out, since I have no idea whether she's still with her husband. "So when do you want to meet?"

"Tomorrow morning. Nine o'clock. Do you know the Dunkin' Donuts outside Groveton?"

"Of course," I say. "Nine o'clock. I'll be there. Listen, are you really doing okay?"

There's a slight pause. "I already said we're fine," she says. "You ain't gonna back out, are you?"

"No, no, of course not," I say.

"Good," she says, and then there's a click.

I gawk in disbelief at the receiver in my hand. She hung up on me.

Dan enters just as I set the receiver back in its cradle. I still have the Post-it note stuck to my fingertips.

"I see you found your message," says Dan.

"Yup," I say.

"Anything important?"

"Nope," I say.

He stares at me, clearly expecting some kind of explanation.

"So, anyway, unless you want to eat radioactive Kim Chee with a side of Klaas pickle, we're going out," I say, breezing by him into the living room area. As I pass, I run my hand across his lower stomach. It's meant both as a hint of how we're going to end the evening, and as a way of purging the phone message from his mind. I don't want him to know I messed up the rescue.

"Did you see Fricassee?" he says.

"Frica-what? Isn't that a chicken dish?" I say, grabbing my purse from the coffee table.

"Yes it is, Oh Great and Mighty Chef," he says, bowing solemnly.

"Then no," I say. "I already told you, all you have is glow-in-the-dark Kim Chee."

He throws his head back and laughs. "No, silly, that horse you rescued. Since someone finally began feeding him he's been getting friskier and friskier."

I shake my head, trying to make the connection.

"Frisky. Fricassee," he says.

"Oh. You've got to be kidding."

"You can blame Judy for that one," he says.

"I sort of figured."

After years of lobbying by Judy, Day Break has adopted the "new home, new name" policy. On my insistence, the horses who were already here got to keep their own names; and a good thing it is, too, because so far we have a Rover, a Heartful Promise, a Pookie, and now—apparently—a Fricassee.

"Don't worry," says Dan, reading my mind. "I'd put my foot down if she tried to name anyone Ratatouille."

"How about Goulash?" I say, pulling the door open.

"Nope. Won't allow Goulash either."

"Schnitzel? Rumaki? Cookie?" I say, leading the way to his truck.

He pauses before answering. "On the fence about Rumaki," he says. "Would have to allow Cookie."

• • •

An hour later, we're sitting at a wooden picnic table eating deep-fried clams out of a cardboard box. Gil's Crab Shack is one of my favorite restaurants, although it's definitely on the opposite end of the spectrum from Sorrento's. The concrete floors are splattered with paint, the walls lined with fishing nets and artifacts rescued from flea markets. It's the kind of place where you can show up in your stable clothes with your stable hair and your stable fingernails and nobody gives you a second glance.

"Speaking of ratatouille . . ." I say, dipping a clam in tartar sauce and then popping it in my mouth.

"Were we?" says Dan, sipping boxed wine from a clear plastic cup.

"Fricassee, ratatouille," I explain, using my hands.

"Oh, right," he says.

"Anyway, I need a barn cat."

Dan looks at me strangely.

"Ratatouille, rats. Cats eat rats, right?" I say to bring him up to speed.

Dan stares at me for a moment longer and then bursts out laughing.

"What?" I say.

"You."

"What about me?"

"Your mind. I love the way it works."

He reaches across the table and takes my left hand. As I tell him about my near miss with Bubonic plague, he caresses my fingers. I can't help but notice that he spends a great deal of time on my ring finger, almost as though he were trying to judge its size.

• • •

Although I show up ten minutes early, Eugenie is already at the Dunkin' Donuts. I'm relieved to see she's alone.

Her frizzy hair is pulled up into a silver plastic hair clip. She's in tight jeans, a T-shirt, and makeup; lipstick that's too red, blush that's too severe, and blue eye shadow. She looks like a little girl who has gotten into her mother's cosmetics bag. That, or a cheap hooker.

"Hi there," I say, coming to a stop beside her. "Do you want a coffee or something?" I ask, taking note of the empty table.

"No," she says, her eyes darting up to my face.

I slip into the plastic seat, which is bolted to the floor.

Eugenie leans forward, her eyes slightly narrowed. "I could sue you, you know."

"For what?" I exclaim, sitting back.

"You stole my horse."

"You called me to come get him!"

"Yeah, and then you left without paying."

"For Christ's sake, Eugenie—I already explained that. I was a little distracted. Your husband showed up acting like he was going to kill all of us."

"That don't give you the right to steal my horse."

"Okay. Fine," I say, taking a deep breath because my heart's already pounding. "Let's just get on with it. I have errands to run."

I pull a handwritten bill of sale from my purse, unfold it, and hand it to Eugenie. Then I find a pen, uncap it, and lay it on the table in front of her.

Eugenie stares at the paper. "This says four hundred."

"That's right. That's what we agreed on."

"That was before you stole him. Now I want eight hundred."

"What? No way. Are you crazy?"

"Eight hundred or I take him back. Or maybe I'll get my lawyer to sue, seeing as how you stole him."

I'm so furious it takes me a moment to respond. When I finally speak, my voice is quiet, steady, flat. "You do realize I don't have to pay a cent, don't you?"

"He's my rightful property."

"He would have been confiscated anyway—no question about it. In fact, last I heard the police were going to charge you with animal neglect. I've never seen such terrible conditions as that poor horse was living in. I don't know how you can live with yourself."

She throws me a hateful glance.

I continue. "What's really awful is I'm not at all convinced you treat your kid any better."

Eugenie sits up straight. "My kid is just fine! You leave her out of this!"

"Yeah, I'll bet she's fine. She's fine like Squire is a fifteen-hand athletic Appy."

We stare at each other, the air between us buzzing with rage.

A male voice interjects: "Excuse me."

I jerk around in my seat. The counter clerk and four customers are staring at us.

"You can't sit here if you're not going to order something," says the clerk. He's in his mid-twenties, with greasy hair and deeply pitted face. His voice is high and nervous.

"We'll be finished in just a minute," I say. Then I turn back to Eugenie.

"If you're not going to buy something, you'll have to—"

I swivel around in my chair. "I *said* we'll be finished in a minute."

His mouth snaps shut. I see the beginnings of hurt pride blossom in his widened eyes.

I figure we have about three minutes before he decides to boot us out or call the police.

I pick my purse from the floor, set it in my lap, and pull out my red leather wallet. I unsnap it carefully, pause for effect, and remove a wad of twenties that I know equals exactly four hundred, but I lick my finger and count them one by one anyway.

Eugenie's eyes are glued to the bills. I'm still looking at the money, using the edge of the table to stack it neatly, like a deck of cards, but I'm watching her in my peripheral vision. Her mouth is slightly open. Her tongue comes out slowly, like a lizard's, wetting first her top lip, then her bottom.

I lay the stack on the table and raise my eyes to hers.

"Take it or leave it," I say.

Eugenie stares at me. Then her gaze drops to the money on the table. Finally she reaches out a hand.

"Uh! Uh!" I say, wagging my finger.

Her hand freezes. Her eyes snap up to mine.

"Sign first," I say, pushing the paper and pen across at her.

She looks at me for a long time. Then she picks up the pen and signs.

I fold the bill of sale in half and slip it into my purse. Then I stand and put on my jacket. "Well, that's that," I say. I almost add, Thank God.

"You don't know what it's like living with a man like that," she says. "It does things to you."

"No doubt."

"You shouldn't be so judgmental, you know. You don't have any idea what my life's like."

"No, I'm sure I don't."

"Of course you don't. How could you? You're a spoiled rich bitch."

I had started to leave, but this makes me turn back around. "I'm a what? What did you just say to me?" I stare into her eyes for a moment. "My God—to think, I actually felt bad for you. When I saw your little girl, and especially your husband . . ." I shake my head, almost at a loss for words. "I felt bad for you even though I knew what you did to that horse, even when you called and accused me of stealing him."

Her eyes linger on mine, and then drop.

"Maybe you didn't used to be like this. Maybe he turned you into this. Or maybe you just like to blame him, but I'll tell you what—you don't have to stay like this, and I hope you won't, for that little girl's sake. Because I can save your horse, but I can't do a damned thing about your little girl. I wish I could, because mark my words, if I could take her home with me, I'd do it in a heartbeat."

She stares at me with mouth and eyes open.

I step up to the counter and the astonished clerk. "I'll have a large coffee with double cream and two sugars. To go, please."

The clerk watches me for a second—almost as though he's afraid it's a ploy—and then reaches for a cup.

When he finally hands it to me, my hands are shaking too much to take it. With burning cheeks, I leave both the money and the coffee on the counter and walk out.

Chapter 10

It turns out that barn cats are a dime a dozen. In fact, people seem almost desperate to get rid of them. A quick perusal through the back section of the paper connects me with a family that has six and wants to part with three; but since I've never had a cat before, I decide to dip my toe in the water and start with just one. I pick Freddie, a long-haired silver tabby with seven toes on each foot who comes recommended as an especially good mouser. Certainly his rotundity suggests he has talent.

He's a bit reticent about entering Harriet's crate for the ride home, but his previous owner manages to stuff him in, even if it does require the help of her two older children.

Freddie spends the entire trip home howling at me from the backseat. At one point, when his efforts suddenly redouble for no apparent reason, I nearly cross the center line into the path of an 18-wheeler.

With my heart still pounding, I persuade myself that this is a good thing, that he's got a great set of lungs, and that surely some rats will decamp from the noise alone.

When I get back to Maple Brook I drive right past the house and park my car out by the stable. Then I carry Harriet's crate and the now silent Freddie into the center of the aisle.

I open the door, but no cat appears.

"Kitty?" I say, stepping in front of the crate.

Nothing.

I crouch down and peer inside. Two retinas glow back at me.

"Freddie? You can come out now. This is your new home."

Still nothing.

I retrieve the cat kibble and stainless steel dish from the car, and—after determining that the disembodied green globes are still at the back of the crate—fill the dish noisily while trying the high-pitched and distinctive kitty call I heard the previous owner use.

Apparently I'm going to have to work on that. It doesn't produce a kitty, and my tongue gets tangled in the back of my throat.

I crouch down and peek in. The liquid crystal orbs still float in the blackness.

After spending nearly a quarter hour trying to entice the latest member of our family to *please* get the hell out of Harriet's crate, I get desperate, pick it up, and turn it over.

Cat and towel come sliding out—Freddie splays his wide feet, scrabbling desperately to remain inside, but even his million toes can't get purchase on the smooth plastic. The instant he touches the floor, he scampers off, flush with the wall.

I stare ruefully after him, because I had sort of hoped the little fellow would like me.

. . .

When Sunday morning finally rolls around, I pack Harriet into Mutti's truck and head for Columbia.

I follow a Ford Explorer with a trailer hitch through the wrought-iron gates, down Wyldewood's long drive, and park beside it in front of the barn.

"You picking up your kid?" says the large-bosomed redhead who climbs out.

"Sure am," I say.

"Which one's yours?"

"Eva Aldrich," I answer. "I'm Annemarie Zimmer. I'd ask which one's yours, but I don't know the rest of the girls yet."

"Ah, Nathalie's new star student. I'm Maureen Sinclaire, Colleen's mom. So how did you survive your first week?"

"Ech," I say, shrugging. "Actually I hated it. I hated it so much I think I got a cat to compensate."

"I felt the same way at the beginning. You'll get over it."

"I hope so. How long has Colleen been here?"

"Eight months and I'm loving it. The peace. The quiet. The good grades. And the manners!"

"Really? You've seen a difference?"

"I love this place," she says, clasping her hands together and looking skywards. "All the advantages of a boarding school—and best of all, Colleen thinks it was her idea."

I follow Maureen through the spotless barn, the freshly dragged arena, and out the other side.

As we approach the girls' house, the front door opens. A girl and her mother come out.

"Hey, Mrs. Sinclaire," says the girl. "Colleen's still drying her hair. Maggie busted my hair dryer."

"Well, thank you, darlin'," says Maureen. She throws her arms open and greets the other mother with a bear hug. "Ellen! Girlfriend! Meet Annemarie Zimmer."

The other mother's eyes widen. "Ah, yes! I've heard all about you," she says, shaking my hand. "Maureen, you know who this is, don't you?"

"Yeah, Eva's mother."

"No, I mean, you know who *she* is, right?"

Maureen looks confused.

"Remember that striped horse? Last year? In the papers?"

"Oh! Yes!" Maureen's eyes widen. "Of course! I thought the name rang a bell."

"I . . . uh . . . think I'll go find Eva now," I say, slinking away as a familiar burning sensation creeps across my face and neck.

"Nice meeting you, hon—I'll see you next week at the show!" says Maureen, waving enthusiastically.

Just as I'm reaching for the door, it swings open. The girl behind it takes one look at me and shouts over her shoulder, "Heads up, Eva! Your mom's here." Then she and her mother pass, joining the noisy group that's gathering in the area between the house and the barn.

Eight or nine girls mill about the house in various states of dress. Some are already slinging backpacks, some are still wrapped in towels. As one, their heads spin to look at me. I see a collective widening of eyes.

"Oh hey, Ma."

I spin, smiling, toward Eva's voice. Then I shriek, clapping a hand over my mouth. "Eva! You're bald!"

"I am not," she says, scowling and running a hand across her naked scalp.

"Why, Eva? Why? Why would you shave your head?"

"I didn't shave it. We used clippers."

"Clippers?" I repeat weakly.

The other girls skulk away, giggling, sliding into hallways and bedrooms. I hear the click of an interior door, and then an explosion of muffled laughter.

"We were trimming Joe's whiskers and talking about hair and Karen said mine looked like Ashlee Simpson's, and I *hate* Ashlee Simpson, so I went back to blonde."

I blink stupidly, trying to comprehend. "You shaved your head because you're going back to blonde?"

"I didn't shave it, Mom. I used clippers. Turns out once you dye your hair black, it's black until it grows out. Who knew?"

"Well, I did, actually," I say.

"Then why didn't you tell me?"

"What? After you dyed it?" I exclaim in righteous indignation, because of course she didn't consult me before the fact.

"Well, anyway," she continues breezily, "I definitely didn't want to look like Ashlee Simpson, and since Margot didn't think two-tone hair would go over very well with the judges at Strafford, we buzzed off the black part," she says.

"Margot thinks they'll like bald better?"

"I'm not bald!" she says, clearly exasperated.

And she's not—exactly. She's got about half an inch of hair, which stands straight up and shines almost white against her pink scalp. Fortunately, her head is a nice shape. She's also pretty enough to carry it off. She looks delicate and birdlike, like Sinéad O'Connor.

I wonder if she's even heard of Sinéad O'Connor. I like her, but decide not to mention it in case Eva lumps her in with the out-of-favor Ashlee.

"What?" says Eva, frowning and running a hand across her head from back to front.

"What do you mean, 'what'?" I say. "It's a bit of a shock. I think I'm entitled to have a look."

I circle my frowning daughter slowly and come to a stop in front of her. She looks up from beneath knitted brows.

"Can I touch it?" I say.

Her face brightens. "Sure!" She leans over and offers me her head.

I run my hand across it. It's soft and bristly all at once, and each hair springs back as my hand passes over it. The effect is addictive.

"Mom! Stop it! You're going to rub my hair off!" she giggles, because before long I'm rubbing her head like a genie's lamp.

"What hair? Got your stuff?"

"Yeah, let me grab it from the bedroom. Wanna see it?"

"Sure, but quickly. Harriet's in the truck."

• • •

Harriet pounces on Eva as soon as she gets in the truck, standing on her hind legs and licking her face.

"Seat belt," I say, backing out.

Eva puts Harriet on the bench beside her and buckles up.

"So you've been working hard this week?" I say, putting the truck into gear and heading up the drive.

"Unbelievably. Oh my God, Mom—I'm so tired. I thought I was going to die the first couple of days. But you should see my thighs! I've lost five pounds!"

I glance over. "Huh. Maybe I should come here. I can't quite fit into my blue dress and I have a big date next weekend."

"You haven't gained weight, have you?"

"Not really. But it's migrated."

"So what's the big date?"

"My birthday. Dan's taking me somewhere special."

"Oh. Right," she says. "Hey, is he coming with us to Strafford?"

"I dunno," I say, glancing over at her. "Do you want him to?"

"Yeah, sure. Dad and Sonja are going to be there too. And Jeremy, of course."

"Ah," I say, taking a deep breath. "Well, I'll ask him. So how's Joe?"

"You mean Smokin' Gun?" she grins. "He's great. He's a dream. A big, Nokota jumping machine. Oh, and it's the funniest thing! He's like Seabiscuit—he likes to sleep lying down, and there's this little gray barn cat who comes into his stall and curls up with him."

"We've got a cat," I say, pulling onto the highway.

Eva squeals in delight. "Really?"

"Yup. Picked him up day before yesterday."

"Is he a kitten?"

"No, he's about two."

"What's his name?"

"Freddie. And he's got a million toes. Seven on each foot."

"That's . . . weird. And what does Madam think of him?" she says, suspending Harriet in front of her so they're nose to nose.

"I don't think they've crossed paths yet."

"How can that be?" she says, setting my long-suffering dog back down.

"He's made himself rather scarce since I got him home."

Which is my way of saying that I haven't actually laid eyes on the beast since releasing him from the crate. If it weren't for the disappearing cat food, I might think he'd left for greener pastures.

"She doesn't sniff him out?" says Eva.

"He's a barn cat. And you know Harriet—she only goes into the barn when absolutely necessary, generally on her way to bed."

"Barn cat schmarn cat. He's coming into the house."

I look over at my happy bald daughter, who is bobbing her head to whatever schlock she's found on the radio, and decide to fight that battle later—if at all.

• • •

No sooner do I stop the truck than Eva jumps out and disappears into the stable. I watch her recede from between dog's ears, because Harriet is standing with her feet up on the dash, also staring in disbelief.

When I catch up with her at noon, she's lunging Flicka at the far end of the arena.

"Eva!" I shout, standing in the doorway and cupping my hands around my mouth. "Lunch is ready!"

"I'll be there in a minute," she says, adjusting the lunge line and clicking her tongue. She clicks again, urging Flicka into a trot.

"She looks good," I say, trying to jumpstart a conversation.

"Uh-huh," replies Eva. "Trot, Flicka! Trot! Good girl."

After a while I give up and go back to the house.

• • •

I enter the kitchen just as Mutti sets a plate of sliced tomatoes and fresh mozzarella down on the table. The food is beautifully arranged—alternating slices of cheese and tomato separated by basil leaves, with balsamic vinegar drizzled over top.

"Where is Eva?" she says.

"Lunging Flicka. Said she'd be here in a minute," I say, washing my hands. "Oh, have I mentioned that she's now bald?"

Mutti stares at me for a moment. Then she goes to the table and sits.

Fifteen minutes later, Eva bursts through the back door.

"Hey, Oma," she says.

" 'Hey, Oma?' You don't see me for five days, and all I get is 'Hey, Oma'?"

Eva peels off her boots and drops them by the back door. Then she walks to Mutti and plants a kiss on her cheek.

"That's better," says Mutti.

"What do you think of my hair?"

"I hate it. Anyway, you're late for lunch. I thought you told your mother you'd be just a minute."

"I was! I had to put Flicka away. Besides, I'm here now," she says, slipping into a chair.

"Uh! Uh!" says Mutti, wagging a finger. "Your hands!"

Eva sighs, and heads for the sink.

Mutti goes to the counter to slice a loaf of bread.

Eva slides behind her plate, and stares at it. "Oh," she says. "I don't eat cheese anymore."

Mutti stiffens. She turns slowly with widened eyes. "I beg your pardon?" she says.

"I'm a vegan now."

"You're a vegan now," Mutti repeats flatly.

"Yup!" Eva says happily, separating tomatoes and basil leaves from the cheese. "There are four of us. Most of the other girls are also vegetarians, but we're, you know, more *hard-core*."

Mutti stares evenly at Eva. Then she says, "Are you sure you don't want me to wash those for you, seeing as how they've been contaminated by the cheese?"

"No, that's okay." Eva puts her napkin in her lap, and picks up her knife and fork. She holds them European style, the fork upside down in her left hand and her knife in her right.

Mutti blinks at Eva another couple of times, and then goes to the fridge for wine. I happily accept a glass, because while I'm musing about Eva's new table manners, I'm also wracking my brains for knowledge of vegan food. Other than tabbouleh, I can't think of a single vegan dish. And I'm not entirely sure about tabbouleh.

• • •

In the middle of the afternoon, I take a load of clean clothes up to the stable apartment and find Eva sitting cross-legged on my bed. She's feeding Freddie tuna from a can.

"Eva!" I say, propping the clothes basket on my hip.

She looks up in surprise. "Oh, hi, Mom! Look, I found Freddie."

"So I see. What on earth are you doing?"

"Making friends."

"You're feeding him tuna? On my eiderdown?"

Her eyebrows raise ever so slightly, daring me to be angry. She runs a hand down the cat's back, scratching him near his tail. His back end springs upward.

"Couldn't you have used a plate? Is that packed in oil or water?" I say, inching closer.

She holds the can up and reads. "Water," she says. She reaches into it and tweaks off another little piece for Freddie. He nibbles it from her fingers and then walks in front of her, purring, leaning into her with the length of his body.

"Well, thank God for small mercies."

"You don't have to worry. We've been very neat. Look," she says, letting Freddie lick a smudge of tuna from her fingertips. "It never gets near the bedspread."

"I thought you were vegan."

"I am. Why?"

"Tuna doesn't offend your sensibilities?"

"*Pffffffft,*" she says, waving her hand at me. "Cats aren't vegans. Besides, fish is practically a vegetable anyway."

"And how do you figure that?" I ask.

"Their brains are tiny."

"So by that token, does your brand of veganism include turkey?"

"Mom!"

I set the laundry basket on the floor by my dresser and join her on the bed. The springs squeak under our combined weight.

Freddie rolls around in delight, showing his surprisingly taut belly off to its best effect. Tufts of long gray fur stick from between the toes of his enormously wide feet.

"If you keep feeding him tuna, he won't bother with rats," I say.

"I'm going back tomorrow," she says. "You can feed him rats all week, but I don't see why he shouldn't have a treat when I'm home."

When I'm home.

My eyes prick with tears. I try to contain them for a few seconds and then decide the hell with it. I lean over and hug her.

"I missed you," I murmur into what would be her hair if she had any.

She twists and wraps her arms around me, tuna can and all. "I missed you too, Mom."

I sniffle into her shoulder.

Freddie meows and walks behind me. A moment later I feel padded feet climbing up my back as he seeks the remainder of the tuna.

• • •

While I'm exceedingly grateful for the moment of bonding with Eva, feeding Freddie tuna on the eider-down has spawned several problems.

The first is that now he's had tuna, dry cat food no longer passes muster. His downstairs bowl has gone untouched for days. However, apparently he still finds rodent heads palatable—heads, not bodies—which leaves me in a bit of a quandary. Catching rodents is his raison d'être after all, but I had naively hoped he'd dispatch with them altogether, not just crunch off their heads and leave them in the aisle. The first time I found a headless corpse with its nasty pink twig-like feet yanked up against its body, I screamed and leapt backward—to the great amusement of the stable hands, I might add.

The headless rodents are everywhere—which of course proves my point that we really did need Freddie—but now I can't decide whether I hate the headless bodies so much that I'd rather feed Freddie tuna and let the rodents keep their heads or continue with Operation Anti-Rat.

For the time being I'm staying the course and simply watching where I step. I'm also eternally grateful to the stable hands, who take the horrid little bodies away to I-don't-want-to-know-where. So grateful, in fact, that I've started to keep a supply of donuts in the lounge.

I try to forget all of this when Freddie is turning circles on my lap, rubbing his weapons of mass destruction against my cheek and sticking his prickly-pear paws into my thighs.

But the second—and larger—problem resulting from the tuna on the bed is that ever since Freddie discovered the eiderdown, it's the only place he wants to sleep.

It started on Sunday night, only a few hours after the tuna incident. The howling began shortly after Harriet and I crawled into bed and continued for a full forty-three minutes—I know, because I kept looking at the clock thinking that surely it would have to stop eventually.

I was wrong.

I tried ignoring it. I tried covering my head with a pillow. I tried gritting my teeth and pounding the mattress and praying to the Great Goddess of Cats. But then he began clawing and raking, using every one of his gajillion claws to try to dig his way through the door. And to think!—the extra toes seemed charming when I picked him. The screeching was so caustic, so penetrating, that Harriet turned circles of despair, whimpering and trying to bury her head beneath her paws.

Eventually I did the only thing I could. I let him in.

He trotted straight into the bedroom, leapt onto the bed, and settled quietly at the end—after giving Harriet a gratuitous swipe on his way past. Harriet grumbled and closed her eyes and then all was still. I stared in astonishment, and then slipped beneath the eiderdown, moving my feet from warm lump to warm lump, savoring the silence and wondering why I didn't do this forty-two minutes ago.

But my relief was short-lived. It seems Freddie is nocturnal and naps only for short periods at night, when Harriet and I are trying to sleep. The rest of time he's on the wrong side of the door. If he's outside, he howls to get in. If he's inside, he howls to get out. And when I get out of bed in the middle of the night to open the door because I JUST WANT IT TO STOP he sits on his strangely attractive pear-shaped hips, sweeps his thick tail across the floor, and stares placidly across the threshold. For the first few days I picked him up and tossed him into the hall, but that was pointless because within minutes he was on the wrong side of the door again.

Dan stayed over last night and witnessed this first-hand. And that is why he is coming over in just a moment to install a cat flap.

I'm waiting on the couch—one of the leather ones the previous trainer sold us when he returned to Canada—with Freddie turning circles in my lap, purring like a buzz saw, butting my face with his and leaving long silver hair all over my sweatshirt. I'm not encouraging him—I'm simply too tired to push him away. There's no point anyway, since I don't think he'd make the connection between my grumpiness and his having prevented me from having any REM sleep in four days. And so he purrs and rubs and kneads while I try to catch a nap.

Harriet sulks at a distance, staring daggers at the fuzzy usurper. She's so upset she doesn't even bother to announce Dan's arrival.

He knocks twice and then enters, carrying a red metal toolbox in one hand, a jingling plastic bag, and a large cordless tool. He also has a pencil tucked behind his ear.

As he sets everything on the long table by the door, his eyes light on the plastic Petco bag. He pulls out the cat-flap kit, along with Freddie's new red collar. "What's this?" he says, setting the collar on the table and continuing to hold the kit.

"It's the cat flap."

"I was just going to cut a hole in the wall and put up a couple of hinges. How much did this run you?"

"Oh, not much," I say.

Dan flips it over and locates the price. "Annemarie! Tell me you didn't really spend this much on a cat flap!"

"But look," I say, springing from the couch and coming to his side. "It has nice clear flaps and an airlock to reduce heat loss. Plus, it's got an electromagnetic thingamajiggy so that only Freddie can come in and out." I lay my hand on the crook of his elbow. His flannel shirt is warm and soft, his arm solid beneath it. I'm feeling a bit deprived—for Freddie-related reasons, last night was full of nothing but *interruptus*.

"You're in a stable. What else could possibly come in and out?"

"I don't know," I say, feeling a blush creep across my face.

"This is like the rad shampoo, isn't it?"

He's referring to the last time I got my oil changed and was talked into having my radiator washed with a special organic herbal concoction.

I bite my lip and nod.

He stares at me for a long time. "Okay. I'll put it in. Because God knows, we don't want you to end up with a horse wandering around your bedroom."

Then he turns, opens his toolbox, and removes a metal ruler.

His knees creak and pop as he lowers himself to the floor.

"Do you want a towel or something to kneel on?"

"No, I'm fine. This won't take long."

He holds the metal ruler up against the bottom of the wall, flush with the baseboard. Then he takes the pencil from behind his ear and makes a couple of ticks on the wall. After he connects them across the ruler's edge, he sets the ruler on the ground.

"Can you grab me the level?" he says, sticking his hand out toward me.

"The level?" I say.

"The thing with the bubbles in it."

"Sure," I say, springing into action. Fortunately, it's near the top of the toolbox, along with a bunch of screwdrivers. I lay it across his palm, like a surgical nurse.

He checks his lines and appears satisfied.

"Can you pass me the Sawzall?"

"The what?" I say in horror.

"The reciprocating saw?"

I blink at him, and then swivel around to the toolbox.

Reciprocating saw, reciprocating saw—what in God's name is a reciprocating saw? Here's a saw, but I can't see anything reciprocating about it. But it's the only saw-like thing in here, so I hand it to him.

Clearly it's not what he expects, because he turns immediately to look at what I've just laid in his palm. "That's a keyhole saw. The Sawzall is on the table beside the toolbox. The cordless thing."

"Oh, right," I say, stumbling over Freddie, who has an uncanny ability to always be underfoot, particularly when you're moving.

Dan takes the Sawzall from me, switches it on, and sinks its blade into the drywall.

Freddie streaks from the room.

As Dan cuts, I investigate the rest of the toolbox, familiarizing myself with its contents for future requests. And with the exception of mistaking a Phillips for a flathead, I manage fairly well, handing him the appropriate instruments until my beautiful new electromagnetic cat flap is in place.

I sigh with satisfaction, imagining my first uninterrupted night's sleep in four days.

• • •

The damned cat refuses outright to wear the collar, and by extension, the electromagnetic key. He also seems capable of transforming his skull into rubber, because no matter how many times I refit it—and I tighten it as much as I dare, although admittedly it's hard to tell exactly where his neck is under all that hair and it's not the sort of thing you want to call wrong— he falls spinning to the floor, writhing so much I can't tell one end from the other. Then he streaks from the room, leaving his new red collar and key in a heap on the floor.

To compound matters, the adage about teaching old dogs new tricks appears to be accurate. Although I scream her name every time I see her approach, Harriet keeps bashing her head into the clear flap. She invariably throws me a look of deep betrayal—why, I don't know, because I try to warn her—and then skulks off to the corner with bruised nose and feelings.

And so, two days later, Dan is back uninstalling my cat flap so that I can take the electromagnetic key off Harriet's collar and stop getting up every four minutes to let the damned cat in. Or out.

After Dan replaces my disaster of a cat flap with a plain and functional one, he stands up and wipes his hands. "It's not too pretty, but you won't have to look at it for very long."

I open my mouth to ask why, but then I remember and it nearly knocks my legs out from under me.

Three days to my birthday.

As if reading my mind, he takes my chin in one hand and tilts my face toward his. His blue eyes burn into mine, and just as I wonder whether we're going to retire to the bedroom, he turns to collect his tools.

"I have to go back to Canada on Sunday," he says. "I want you to come with me."

"Oh, Dan! I'd love to! But I can't!"

"We'd only be gone a few days."

"I know, but Eva's three-day event starts on Monday. We have to arrive on Sunday. In fact, she was hoping you'd come with us."

"Was she?" he says. His eyebrows raise in surprise. "Oh, shoot. I had no idea. In that case, I'm doubly sorry about the timing."

So am I, because I had really hoped to face Roger, Sonja, and Jeremy armed with my shiny new fiancé.

• • •

I sleep like the dead that night, falling into unconsciousness almost immediately upon hitting the bed.

When I wake up, the sun is shining, birds are singing, and Harriet is licking my face. I gather her in my arms and let her kiss me. After a while, I drop my arm on the eiderdown.

It hits something that feels . . . wrong.

I jerk my head around. A chewed, headless corpse is inches from my pillow.

• • •

I scream for help from the stable hands, and while they dispose of the body, I boil myself, my bedding, and my dog. I put Harriet in the tub and scrub the bejesus out of her, and then scour her teeth with my spare toothbrush. I'd swish her mouth with Listerine if I could figure out how but I can't, so instead I feed her dog biscuits and other hard things in an attempt to remove all traces of rat. Despite this, I declare a moratorium on dog kisses, which causes Harriet no end of sadness. She can't imagine what she's done wrong, and mopes around behind me trying to apologize.

Later in the day, I drive to Petco and buy three cases of wet cat food because Freddie's days as a barn cat are officially over. There will still be rodents in the stable, but at least they won't end up headless in my bed.

• • •

It turns out I've been wrong all along about the biggest problem with Freddie.

The biggest problem with Freddie is that he had kittens this morning, right here in my bedroom. But since it's my birthday and I've dropped three pounds—which appears sufficient for me to squeeze into my favorite blue dress—I decide to forgive him, even if his three babies do look like seven-toed rats.

Chapter 11

As I head up the drive to the house, Mutti comes out the back door with an armful of calla lilies and roses.

Of course—it's Saturday. She has taken flowers to Pappa's grave every Saturday since his death, without exception. She's more reliable than the United States Postal Service.

"Happy birthday, *Schatzlein*," she says, coming to kiss me on the cheek. "May you get everything you wish for."

"Well, I've already had one surprise."

"What's that?" she says, opening the door to her truck and laying the flowers inside.

"Freddie had kittens."

"Mein Gott," she says, glancing skyward. "So much for your barn cat. Are you feeding them caviar yet?"

"Mutti!"

She climbs into the cab. "I left you something on the table. There's fresh coffee in the pot."

"Thanks, Mutti. By the way, I won't be around for lunch."

"Oh? I thought your big date was for tonight."

"It is. I've got an appointment at a spa."

"A *spa*?" she chortles.

"What? What's wrong with that?"

"Nothing," she says, shaking her head and starting the truck. "Nothing at all. Will I see you before you leave?"

"Yes. Dan's picking me up at the house at six."

"Come a little early. And then you can show me your hair or fingernails or whatever it is you're having done," she says. Then she rolls her window up and backs out.

• • •

There's a vase of tulips in the center of the kitchen table, and beside it, a small gift-wrapped box.

I hold it for a moment, feeling its weight in my palm. Then I slide the ribbon off and remove the paper. The second I see the faded red velvet, I know exactly what it is.

"Oh, Mutti," I say, my eyes filling with tears.

She has given me my grandmother's diamond earrings.

• • •

Despite my previous existence as a patent lawyer's wife, I have never been to a spa in my life.

I'm nervous as I pull into the parking lot, and even more nervous when I enter the lobby.

The counters are glass, the floors marble. There is the tinkling of a waterfall somewhere in the background, and I think I can also make out ocean waves. The women behind the counter are impeccably groomed, with serene expressions, perfect skin, and rosebud lips.

I feel entirely out of place—almost like a different species—and hang back near the door, thinking I might just slip out. After all, Dan decided to marry the me he knows—the me with hands hardened from stable work and short, broken fingernails. The me with bits of hay in my hair and bra and horse slobber smeared across my cheek.

But before I have a chance to escape, I am whisked away by a soft-spoken young thing who hands me a fluffy white bathrobe and a pair of paper flip-flops, and steers me into a changing room.

I spend the rest of the day getting waxed, buffed, massaged, plucked, scrubbed, polished, sculpted, and painted. And the me that emerges at the end belongs to that other species—the fragrant one, the pretty one.

I pay what seemed an outrageous fee when I booked my spa treatments, but now seems barely adequate.

There's a full-length mirror by the door, and on my way out I stop to look at myself. I can't believe the transformation. They've even managed to make my fingernails look nice—I resisted the manicure at first, but finally went for it when I remembered the important role my hands will be playing tonight, and it turns out that spa people are miracle workers. Even though I have no nails to speak of, they painted tiny white lines across the ends so that it looks like I do. I feel like crying in gratitude—but since that would ruin my professionally applied makeup, I simply press my manicured hands against my cheeks until I have regained my composure.

When I get in my car, I pull down my shade visor and have yet another look.

I suppose everything will go back to normal eventually, but tonight I'll still be gorgeous. I imagine Dan's reaction as he lays eyes on me in my blue dress and my grandmother's diamond earrings.

I sigh happily and start the car, because everything promises to be perfect.

• • •

Dan's reaction is not quite what I expected.

"Oh—" he says, coming to a dead stop just inside our back door.

"What?" I say in horror. My hands spring to my head, checking for snakes, antennae, or other alien growths.

"Nothing," he says, recovering. He steps forward and kisses me. "You look absolutely stunning." He turns to Mutti, takes both her hands, and kisses her cheek. "Ursula, it's lovely to see you, as always."

"Dan," says Mutti, smiling and nodding sagely.

I'm suddenly embarrassed, because it must be clear to him that I've figured it out and told Mutti.

Dan pretends not to notice. "Shall we?" he says, offering me his arm.

I take it, even though I have to stop by the back door to put on my coat, which he helps me into.

I have to fight to keep from bursting into delighted laughter. I feel like the star of an ancient courtly ritual, and I love it.

• • •

At Sorrento's, the maître d' comes out from behind his podium and greets us at the door.

"Mr. Garibaldi, Miss Zimmer, it's so lovely to see you," he says as though we're old friends. He snaps his fingers at a waiter. "Gerard, take their coats!" He turns back to us, smiling and solicitous. "Please follow me. Your table is ready."

He leads us to what is clearly the best table in the house. There is a single rosebud in the center of each bread plate.

The maître d' holds my chair out, and I manage that most delicate of balancing acts—lowering myself at the exact time the chair reappears beneath me. But the maître d' is good at his job, and even manages to scootch me elegantly forward. Then he reaches for my napkin, unfolds it with a dramatic swoop, and lays it across my lap.

"Thank you," I say, blushing.

I am handed a menu without prices.

"Would you like cocktails to start?"

"I'd love a glass of chardonnay," I say, blinking my fabulous new lashes.

"I think we'll have a bottle," says Dan, squinting at the wine list.

"May I recommend the Catena Alta?" says the maître d'.

"That would be lovely," says Dan, relinquishing the list with obvious relief.

And then we're alone. Dan reaches his hand across the table, palm up, and I lay mine on top of it. For people who have known each other—and slept together—for as long as we have, we're surprisingly tongue-tied. The truth is, I'm feeling pretty and bashful and a little bit shy, and enjoying the lead-up to the Big Moment.

"Are you ready to order, or would you like a few more minutes?" says Gerard, appearing suddenly at our side.

I pull my hand back, blushing.

"May I?" says Dan, looking at me.

"May you what?" I ask.

He turns to Gerard. "We'll start with a dozen oysters on the half shell, and then the lady will have the Lobster Newburg—"

"Oh, no," I break in. "Sorry, no. I'll just have the consommé."

Dan stares at me. "The *consommé*?"

"Yes," I say, smiling. I can see why he might be confused—I do remember telling him that Sorrento's makes the best Lobster Newburg in the world. But what I can't very well explain to him—especially in front of Gerard—is that despite losing three pounds, I barely got the zipper done up on my dress. Also, I fully expect the evening to end up with us in bed—quite possibly with me on top—and the last thing I want is to be aware of my belly.

Dan clears his throat and glances up at Gerard. "Uh, okay. The lady will have the consommé, and I'll have the filet steak, medium rare."

"And the oysters?"

Dan looks at me, eyebrows raised in question.

I shake my head.

"No, it looks like we'll be moving straight to the entrées," Dan says.

Gerard gives a slight bow, and takes our menus.

We make ridiculous small talk during our meals, which I suppose is natural. I can hardly be expected to be a brilliant conversationalist when I know a proposal is imminent; and to be fair, neither can Dan. And so we end up smiling at each other as shyly as teenagers. I sip my clear soup from the side of my spoon and he makes his way through his steak, both of us exercising impeccable manners.

"Can I interest you in anything else? A little dessert, perhaps?" says Gerard, after our dishes have been cleared.

He and Dan exchange glances.

"Uh, yes," says Dan, flushing. "We'll have a bottle of Perrier-Jouët—"

Ooh! Ooh! Here it comes!

"—and two chocolate soufflés. A little bird told me your chocolate soufflé is to die for."

"Oh, no dessert for me," I say to Gerard, with a gentle wave.

"What?" says Dan. "But you said it was your favorite!"

"It is." I lean forward, lowering my voice. "But I'm watching my weight."

"It's your birthday," he responds—and if I'm not mistaken, there's the tiniest hint of an edge in his voice. "Live a little."

"No, really," I say. "I'm full."

Dan stares at me for a moment, then turns to the waiter. "Uh . . . well, in that case *I'll* have the chocolate soufflé."

A soufflé appears on the table, along with the champagne. Its bottle is beautifully painted, white flowers trimmed with gold on sage green stems, and I decide on the spot that I'm taking it home as a souvenir.

Gerard pops the cork, pours champagne into two flutes, and slides the bottle into a silver bucket of jingling ice. He smiles and disappears.

Dan holds a spoon out across the table. "Here, have a few bites," he says.

"No, thank you. Really."

"Annemarie, a single bite won't make you fat."

"No, but a succession of bites will, and I know I wouldn't be able to stop."

He continues to hold the spoon out to me. Eventually, after it starts to become embarrassing, he sets it down on the edge of the plate.

"Uh, okay then." He pauses, clears his throat, and swallows audibly. "Well, as you know, I wanted tonight to be really special," he says. He reaches into his jacket pocket. "This isn't exactly the order in which I planned to do things, but, uh, well, that's the way life goes sometimes, isn't it?"

A navy blue velvet box—ring-sized—makes its way across the table to me. It seems to float of its own accord.

I take it with icy, trembling fingers, tears already gathering in the corners of my eyes. I smile and sniff, trying to keep my face arranged into something resembling lovely.

I open the box. The lid springs up with a snap, and there, pushed deep into a bed of plush velvet, is a pair of diamond earrings.

I am too stunned to move. Then a hand—mine, presumably—covers my mouth.

I close the box and drop it on the table. As I try to retract my hand, Dan catches it.

"Annemarie, I wanted to give you these later. In fact, I didn't realize you already had diamond earrings, but obviously—"

I pull my hand away and stand up abruptly.

"Earrings?" I say.

"Annemarie?"

I turn on my heel and cross the room to the coat rack. I hear shuffling and bumping behind me, and then

Dan is beside me, his hand on my arm. "Annemarie! Come back to the table."

I wrench my arm free. *"Earrings?"*

He looks stunned. I glance around the room. It's as though someone has stopped time. Gerard stands perfectly still, a soup bowl lowered halfway to a table. A diner holds a napkin to the corner of his lips. A woman has a tube of lipstick poised at her mouth, a compact open in front of her. The maître d' is frozen. Every eye in the room is glued on us.

Dan leans toward me and continues in a lowered voice. "Annemarie, you've got it all wrong. Please come back to the table."

"No. For the first time, I think I've got it right," I say, struggling into my coat. I throw my purse over my shoulder and head for the door.

"Annemarie!"

I turn at the door and look back one last time. Dan stands at the coat rack, his arms slack at his side, his eyes wide. He looks angry and hurt, and all I want to do is throw something at him.

Instead, I run from the restaurant.

• • •

Within seconds, I realize that I have no ride home. I stagger three doors down to Denny's—twisting my ankle in the process because I'm not used to high heels—hole up in a washroom stall, and call Mutti from my cell phone.

"Mutti!" I wail when she answers.

"Annemarie? What happened? What's wrong?"

"I need you to come get me," I snuffle. I wipe my

face with the back of my hand, and—finding it covered with makeup-colored slime—reach for the toilet paper. I gather a wad, wipe my eyes and cheeks, and then honk into it.

"Why? What happened? Where's Dan?"

I fall silent and take three quick breaths. *"Dan. Who."*

There's a slight pause. "I see," says Mutti. "Where are you?"

• • •

My cell phone starts ringing as we reach the end of our drive. I dig it out of my purse with shaking hands.

"Who is it?" asks Mutti.

"Him," I say, spitting out Dan's official new moniker and dropping the phone back in my purse.

As we enter the back door, it starts ringing again. I fish it from my purse and fling it onto the kitchen table. It skids to the center, ringing and spinning. I stand staring at it, my chest heaving.

"Why don't you just turn it off?" asks Mutti, opening the fridge.

The phone falls silent and, a moment later, a large glass of white wine appears in front of me. As I reach for it, I catch sight of my stupidly manicured hands. I shove the wine away from me and drop my head and arms onto the table.

After a moment, Mutti's hand appears on the back of my head, stroking my hair.

"I'm so sorry, *Schatzlein*."

My cell phone starts ringing again. I shriek and jerk upright. Mutti picks the phone up and turns it off.

"There," she says, nodding.

I pick up my glass of wine and snurfle through a sip, crying so hard it's difficult to swallow. My swollen eyelids impinge on my field of vision.

When the phone on the kitchen wall begins to ring, a grim-faced Mutti marches over and turns off the ringer. Then she disappears into the hall.

One by one, all the phones in the house fall silent.

• • •

One hour and two glasses of chardonnay later, I ditch my high heels by the back door and pull on my wellies. Then I cover my blue dress with my quilted vest and stumble down the drive to the stable.

When I get there, I head straight for Hurrah's stall.

I am just pressing my nose into his neck when I hear a truck pull up outside. Dan's, to be specific.

I slide Hurrah's door shut and duck down under his water bucket.

The outside door of the stable slides open. Dan's footsteps rush past me. They turn the corner and thump up the stairs. The door to the apartment opens and crashes shut. A few seconds later it opens again.

"Annemarie!" he bellows.

All around me, startled horses shuffle and blow. A few clamber noisily to their feet.

Hurrah snorts and takes a step sideways. I press a hand against his knee to remind him that I'm down here.

"Annemarie! Where are you?" Dan's voice is deep and hoarse.

He crashes noisily down the stairs, pausing—judging from the *thunk*—to punch the wall.

The aisle lights come on, then the can lights in the

stalls. The horses are all awake now, pacing and huffing in alarm.

"Annemarie!"

I hear him check the lounge, the trophy room, the bathroom. I hear him go back upstairs and check the office. Then he comes downstairs and stops just outside Hurrah's stall.

I hold my breath, still crouched in the corner. My head is pressed against the water bucket's cold bottom, my back against the wall's rough boards.

"God damn it, Annemarie," he says.

He sounds forceful and angry and I'm about to stand up when he suddenly turns and leaves. His gait has changed. His footsteps are tired and slow.

Click!

The can lights go out.

Click!

The aisle falls dark.

He walks slowly to the outside door, pauses, and then leaves, sliding it shut behind him. Moments later his engine starts and he pulls away.

I climb to my feet and fall forward, bawling into Hurrah's mane.

Chapter 12

When my alarm goes off at six the next morning and I find myself alone on the leather couch, I nearly burst into tears. A few seconds later I do.

But since I have to be at Wyldewood in exactly an hour and a half for the "pre-event team meeting"—and I've been told in no uncertain terms that parental attendance is mandatory, showing support for the kids, rah rah rah—I slide off the couch and onto my knees. Then I drop my arms and head onto the musty wool blankets that constituted my bedding last night and have a good cry. The unusual sleeping circumstances were necessary because when I finally emerged from Hurrah's stall last night, I discovered that while I was off getting gorgeous—or maybe it was later, when my relationship with the love of my life was being blown to smithereens—Freddie decided to move her kittens into the middle of my bed. They're so tiny and helpless with their barely-there hair and their eyes and ears fused shut that there was no way on earth I was going to try to move them, particularly after the amount of chardonnay I'd had. And so I dug through the top shelf of the linen closet in the apartment bathroom until I came up with these scratchy horrid blankets, installed myself on the couch, and sniffed and snizzled into the darkness. After three hours of this, I realized I simply wasn't going to get to sleep on my own and reached for the rubber cosh—Thera Flu Night Time.

I had only just gotten to sleep when my stupid alarm went off.

But since I have a good hour's drive in front of me and have not yet packed for the four-day excursion, I drag myself upright and into the washroom.

I stop in the doorway, five feet from the mirror, and observe the swamp creature that stares back at me.

That I spent most of the night crying is obvious —my face is puffy, my nose raw and pink, and my eyes seem to have both red and black rings around them. But to add insult to injury, my cheeks, chin, and forehead seem to have broken out into eczema, probably in reaction to the wool blanket.

I burst into tears again at the sight of myself, and then splash cold water on my face, too afraid to use anything else for fear of making the eczema worse.

And then I pack, because I have to be on the road in eighteen minutes.

• • •

I stop at the house to say goodbye to Mutti. She stops, startled, when she sees me.

"You look awful."

"I feel awful."

"Did you sleep?"

"Not really," I say. "Did he come by here last night?" Mutti shrugs.

"He did, didn't he?"

"I kept the lights off and didn't answer the door," she says. "I assume that means he came to the stable?"

"Yes."

"And?"

"And nothing. He tried to give me *earrings,* Mutti."

"I know, I know." After a moment, she pulls me into a hug. Because she's shorter, I curl my spine so I can lay my head on her shoulder. She strokes my hair and makes shushing noises. After a while, I sniff and pull away.

"Are you okay to drive?" she asks.

"Probably not, but I don't have a choice. If I don't show up, Eva will kill me."

"Even under the circumstances?"

I throw Mutti a look.

She sighs. "You're right. Get in the car. I'll get you some coffee."

I do as she says—life is so much easier when someone else is directing—and start the engine.

Mutti comes out the back door with my travel mug. Harriet follows her out, her short legs tripping like a millipede's down the ramp. She stands on two legs, with her front feet on my car door, asking to be let in.

I unroll my window. Mutti hands me the mug and then looks in the backseat.

"What's that?" she says, pointing.

"It's my stuff."

"You packed in plastic grocery bags?" she says in disbelief.

"Eva took all the suitcases."

"Oh," she says. "Well, she's had time to unpack now. Bring them back with you."

"Okay."

Mutti looks at me with eyes narrowed and arms crossed on her chest. "I'm not sure about this. Do you want me to come?"

"I'll be okay," I say.

"You sure?"

"Yes. Besides, the hotel doesn't take pets."

Mutti looks down at Harriet, who is staring up at me hopefully, her tongue lolling off to the side. Mutti reaches over and scoops her up so their faces are side by side.

"Well, call me when you get there," Mutti says sternly. "And call to let me know how that girl of ours does."

"I will, Mutti."

She leans in the window to kiss me. Harriet wiggles and squirms, slurping the right side of my face gleefully with a soft twisting tongue.

So much for my moratorium on dog kisses.

• • •

I arrive a bit late. I was having a little weep near Bethlehem and missed the exit and was almost in Vermont before I noticed.

The parking lot in front of Nathalie's barn is full of vehicles. The three crimson-and-silver gooseneck trailers are lined up in the center, backed up to the entrance.

I find a spot to park and wander through Nathalie's sparkling clean barn. The horses who are going to Strafford are in their stalls, wrapped from head to foot in puffy red nylon shipping gear. They pace their stalls in anticipation.

I follow Nathalie's voice to the lounge.

She's sitting on a white plastic chair with her back to the door. The girls and their parents are arranged in a semicircle in front of her, as though in an auditorium. There is no way to get into the lounge except straight past her.

Eva is at the back, an empty seat beside her. When she sees me, her eyes pop open.

I try to make myself invisible and slink past Nathalie, but the second I come into view she stops midsentence and turns to face me. "I'm glad you decided to join us, Annemarie," she says, her voice glacial.

"Er, sorry, road trouble," I mumble, facing the floor and snaking my way through the seats toward Eva. She's in the back row, which is both bad and good: bad, because I have to pass every other person in the room on my way, and good because now that I'm here, everyone else is ahead of us.

I take a seat and sigh with relief as Nathalie continues talking.

"Naturally, the first thing you'll do is get the horses situated. Only after they're in the temporary stabling and you've checked each and every one of them for—"

Eva leans over and whispers, "Ma! What's wrong with you?"

"I had a hard night."

Her eyes widen and she keeps staring at me, her eyes moving up and down my body. "Are you okay?" she finally says.

Her concern nearly dissolves me. I was expecting her to call me a sea hag.

"I, uh," I say. "I had a—"

"Annemarie! Eva! Are you paying attention?" barks Nathalie.

Eva and I exchange horrified glances. I straighten in my seat.

"Yes ma'am," says Eva.

I'm too stunned to say anything.

"Good," Nathalie says, leaving her eyes on us for a while before allowing them to continue sweeping across the rest of the assembled people. "Margot's car went kaput, so we're short a few seat belts. Some of you are going to have to catch rides with your parents. Eva, since you and your mother obviously can't wait to catch up, you can be one of them. Kris, Colleen, Danielle—you too."

The chosen girls swing their heads to regard each other in horror, and then turn to stare resentfully at their parents.

When Eva's eyes light on me, I shrug and try to stammer an apology. But she doesn't care: she purses her lips, turns her head to the arena, and folds her arms across her chest.

• • •

In the car, dead silence.

"Look Eva, a covered bridge," I say, pointing out her window. "What's the date on it? They usually have a little plaque right at the top."

She turns to me, scowling.

"What?" I say.

"What do I care about some stupid covered bridge?" she says.

"I don't know. It's old. It's pretty. It's part of our heritage."

"No, it's not. It's part of your heritage. I'm from Minnesota."

"Not anymore, you're not."

She turns her head in disgust. "Whatever," she says.

"Okay, fine—but when we get to the Old Man of the Mountain, I'm showing him to you and you're looking."

"Whatever," she says, looking out the opposite window.

"Do you even know what he is?"

"No," she says, folding her arms across her chest.

"He's our state symbol. An old man's face in the side of a mountain. Look," I say, pointing at his profile on a road sign as we pass. "Heck, look at the license plate of the car in front of us. *That's* the Old Man of the Mountain."

"That thing? Then I've seen it a million times."

"In person?"

She glances at me, her lip curled. "No."

"Eva, why are you so mad at me?"

"Gee, Mom, why do you think?" she snarls.

"Because you had to ride with me?"

"Ya think?"

"Quit the sarcasm," I snap. "I'm not in the mood."

Eva looks momentarily surprised.

I grip the wheel and drive in silence.

"So what happened to you anyway?" she says, looking me up and down.

"What do you mean?"

"Well, to start with, you were nearly an hour late this morning. Plus, your face is covered in an oozing rash, you look like you've been crying all night, *and* you haven't brushed your hair since last Sunday. Yet your fingernails look nice for the first time in your life."

"Eva, just shut up. Okay? Just shut up."

I hear her sharp intake of breath. Then she turns slowly toward the window.

We drive in silence for several miles. I've never told

anyone to shut up in all my life—I tell people to shut up in my head all the time, but never out loud, and never my daughter.

I'm fumbling about for some way to reopen the conversation when Eva suddenly leans forward and points across the steering wheel.

"Hey look, Ma, a painted frog," she says.

Someone has painted a boulder on the side of the road to look like a frog.

I do a double take and chortle.

Another couple of minutes pass.

"Hey look, Ma! A library!"

I throw her a glance that's part warning but mostly gratitude. She's grinning coyly, slouched in her seat.

Half a mile later, her arm flashes in front of my face again: "Hey look, Ma! It's a school bus! No, wait! There's a whole yard of them!"

Finally I snort with laughter. "Okay, fine. But you're going to look when we get to the Old Man. There's a lake right beside him, and when the sun's out, you can see his profile perfectly. In fact, it's called Profile Lake."

She shrugs. "Okay. So what's going on with you, anyway? Don't tell me nothing because I know something's up."

I glance at her, and then back at the road. "I had a bad day yesterday."

She claps a hand to her mouth. "Oops. Happy birthday."

I keep my eyes glued to the road ahead of me.

"That's not it, is it?"

"What?"

"Why you're upset? Because I forgot your birthday?"

"God, no," I say, looking over quickly. "Well, it would be nice if you'd remembered, but no. It's got nothing to do with that."

"So Dan couldn't make it, or what?" she says, looking around the car as though just this moment noticing he's not here.

I take a deep breath and hold it against pursed lips. Then I exhale. "No, he couldn't. He had to go pick up another load of horses." After a pause, I add, "Actually, we're not going to be seeing Dan anymore."

Eva stares at me for a moment. Then her eyes spring open and she covers her mouth with her hand. "Oh, Ma—you guys broke up? I'm so sorry."

My face crumples again. I sniff a couple of times to try to contain it, and then when that doesn't work, I wipe my left hand under my lower lids. When it becomes perfectly clear that I'm going to have another full-fledged breakdown, I wipe my nose on my left shoulder and manage to croak, "Can we please just not talk for a while?"

"Sure, Ma. Yeah, no problem."

I'm not looking at her, but I can see in my peripheral vision that she's watching me closely, her brow rippled with worry. And that worries me, because Eva doesn't worry easily. Especially about me.

• • •

I'm so lost in my thoughts I don't notice that we're coming up to the Old Man until we're right beside Profile Lake. And since my voice still feels as though it will splinter if I try to speak, and within seconds we're past the lake anyway, I say nothing.

About twenty minutes later, Eva says, "So where's this Old Man, anyway?"

I clear my throat. "We, uh, we passed him."

She turns to stare at me.

"He doesn't look like much from this direction," I say, making a concerted effort to act more normally before I actually scare her. "We'll catch him on the way back."

• • •

When we get to the hotel, I find that I either have to park at the very back of the lot or pay ten dollars for valet service. When I called to make the reservation, they said I was getting the last room. Apparently they weren't kidding.

I splurge for the valet service since I'm embarrassed by my plastic bags and oozing face rash and want to travel the least possible distance with them.

As I pull our things out from the backseat, Eva climbs from the car and stretches and yawns. It never dawns on her to help.

I pull the retractable handles out of her suitcases and loop the handles of my plastic bags over them, hoping that this will keep them relatively stable and perhaps even render them slightly less conspicuous. I'm actually a little afraid I might be mistaken for a bag lady. Of course, if there are any embarrassing episodes in the lobby, I can just flash my beautiful ringless fingers. Itinerants don't have perfect French manicures.

As our little car disappears behind a long row of SUVs, I struggle to a brass luggage caddy, shove my shoulder in front of the other woman heading for it, pile on our suitcases and bags, and drag it into line at the reception desk.

"Looks nice," says Eva, looking around. "Think they've got a pool?"

"I don't know, honey."

"Ooh! Colleen! Kris!" Eva squeals. "Are you headed out already?"

A group of girls headed up by Maureen is crossing the lobby. They nod assent.

"Got room for me?" Eva says.

"Sure, hon!" says Maureen. "Climb on in the monster van. Annemarie, we have room for you too, if you want."

"Thanks, but I haven't checked in yet," I say, although the stupidity of stating this while in line at the reception desk strikes me immediately. My oozing face reddens further.

Eva turns to me. "Do you mind if I catch a ride with them instead?"

"Well, I—"

"Because Nathalie wanted us to get the horses settled in before we got settled in ourselves and the vet inspections are this afternoon and I know she's watching me to make sure I do everything right and after this morning I really want to make sure—"

"Go! Shoo!" I say, flicking my hands toward her friends.

Eva pauses halfway across the lobby and turns to face me. "Can you ask if Dad and Sonja have checked in yet?" she says.

"What? They're staying *here*?" I cry in horror.

"Yup!" she says cheerfully. "Hey, this'll be the first

time you've seen Jeremy, won't it?" Then she turns and skips off through the revolving doors.

I stare after her for a moment, on the verge of hyperventilating.

"May I help you?"

I whip around.

A placid-faced clerk is staring at me. Her thin blonde hair is pulled straight back under some type of burgundy fez. Her blue eyes flicker as she takes in my oozing face and plastic bags, but then she recovers her equilibrium. She's a professional. She's seen worse. I hope.

I approach the counter, pulling my baggage caddy. "Uh, yes, I'm checking in. Annemarie Zimmer," I say, straightening up and trying to pretend that my face isn't a seeping mess.

"That's two people for four nights?"

"Yes."

I look around anxiously. Roger and his new family could be arriving at any moment, could be behind me right now. Somehow it becomes imperative that they not see me like this —that *she* not see me like this.

The clerk is muttering about do I want to keep the room charge on the original credit card and it's a nonsmoking room and there are dire fines if I yadda yadda yadda, and I get antsier and antsier because I'm now absolutely sure that Roger, the picture-perfect Sonja, and their Gerber Baby have just pulled up, are headed for the revolving doors at this moment and are going to come through and find me standing here at the counter oozing like a bag lady with no Dan and no ring and no anything, not even Eva.

I keep swiveling toward the door, but the clerk seems

not to notice. She keeps going and going and going—
I'm just about to snap and tell her that I really don't
CARE about the fee for using the safe or the charges for
long distance or whatever the hell else she's going on
about when she suddenly smiles and pushes something
across the counter at me.

I blink down at it.

"This is your room key. The room number is written
inside," she says sweetly.

"Oh," I say, wide-eyed. "Oh. Yes. Thank you. My
daughter just went out again—she'll need a room key
when she comes back. Her name is Eva Aldrich."

"Oh," says the clerk, looking perplexed and pressing
a lacquered nail to her computer screen. "Is it possible
she made a reservation under her name as well?
Because—"

"No, no, no, that's her father," I say impatiently,
swiping my key from the counter. "My name is Zimmer. Please make sure you give her the right key when
she comes back. That would be the one to *my* room."

"Yes, of course, Mrs.—"

I grab the cold brass rail of my baggage caddy and
stalk away from the counter. This would be more effective if one of my plastic bags—the one holding all my
toiletries—didn't slide off and spill all over the burgundy and gold carpet.

• • •

The room door closes behind me with a satisfyingly
heavy click. And then it's just me.

The room is comfortable and unremarkable—there
are two queen beds, a dresser, an easy chair, a table that
doubles as a computer desk, and an armoire that hides a

television, minibar, and safe. The art on the walls is of that peculiar hotel variety—inoffensive, not attractive enough to steal, and bolted down just in case.

I drag our motley luggage over to the dresser, haul the larger suitcase up on top of it, and then line my plastic bags up beside it. I locate the one that holds my toiletries and take it into the bathroom. At some point I'm going to rearrange the contents of the luggage so that I end up going home with a suitcase instead of plastic bags. But now is not the time, since I don't feel up to having Eva accuse me of going through her things.

I choose the bed closest to the window, thinking that if there's an intruder he'd have to get through me to get to Eva. Of course, an intruder might also come through the door. When it dawns on me that I haven't done my man check yet—usually the very first thing I do at a hotel—I realize just how out of sorts I am.

After I've peeked inside the bathtub and closets, looked under the beds, and checked the heavy folds of the curtains for stray men, I strip my bedspread. I do it carefully, rolling it inside out to minimize my exposure to its horrifying outer layer. Then I toss it behind the chair and wash my hands. I saw a television exposé on hotel bedspreads once and I've never gotten over it. The second I lay eyes on one, I have visions of naked drug orgies, and the only way to get rid of them is to fold the participants up inside the bedspread and toss them behind the chair.

I help myself to a beer from the minibar, kick off my shoes, and collapse on the bed. But not before exchanging the top pillows with the bottom ones, since the top ones have touched the underside of the bedspread.

The sheets are not the highest thread count, but

they're smooth and clean and a far sight better than what I slept on last night. I wonder vaguely how the kittens are doing, consider calling Mutti, and then turn my head toward Eva's bed. I blink at it for a moment, realize that I'm watching a holographic naked drug orgy, and get up to give her bed the same treatment.

After I've removed Eva's bedspread, I'm now contaminated enough that I need a bath. Fortunately, this is a nice hotel, and they've provided a mini bottle of bubble bath.

So what if it's Raspberry Ripple. It's bubble bath and it's free.

I run the bath almost up to its rim, and then sink into it. I swish my fingers through the bubbles, patting them flat in some places, and gathering them into puffy mountains in others.

Ah. That's better.

Or so it seems for a few minutes, but before I know it terrible thoughts are creeping into my head, things like how Roger and Sonja are probably in this building at this very moment, down the hall or up the stairs, cooing to their beautiful baby and planning on doing God knows what after they finally get him to sleep. Which, unfortunately, I can picture only too well. I close my eyes and try to sense which direction their room is from ours using my Roger-locator homing beacon, but it doesn't work anymore. I've been away from him for too long.

And then my thoughts drift to Dan, who is probably halfway to Canada, and a great numbing void starts in my chest and spreads evenly through my body. I know I can never see him again because if I did, he'd probably propose. Not because he wanted to but because he's a decent man, and now that he knows how I feel he probably feels obligated. And if we married under those circumstances our whole relationship would be predicated on a power play, and every time we had a disagreement—or even if he just grew quiet—I'd wonder whether it was because he never really wanted to marry me in the first place. And that's no way to live.

Next thing I know, I'm sitting up in my bubble bath sobbing onto my knees.

• • •

It's almost midnight before Eva shows up.

The clickity-clack of the automatic door lock wakes me up, so I have a moment's warning before she throws on the room light.

"Oh hey, Ma, did I wake you up?"

"That's okay," I say, squinting and shielding my eyes with my hands. "Did you get Joe settled?"

"Yeah. But it took some doing. The stabling has Dutch doors and apparently he jumps out of those, so we had to rig something with a mesh stall guard."

I lean up on my elbow. Stall guards are made of webbing, and rigging something for a horse that's inclined to jump out sounds like trouble. "Does Nathalie know?"

"Yup. They bring it along for that purpose. Margot actually bolted it onto the stall. It's got snaps along three edges so we can get him out."

"Oh. Well, then," I say, lying back down. "Did you have dinner?"

"Yeah, we went to a great little—" her eyes pop open and she covers her mouth. "Oops. Say, Ma, you didn't want to come, did you?"

"No, it's okay," I say gloomily. "I wasn't hungry anyway."

"So did Dad and Sonja check in?"

"I forgot to ask."

"What?" she says, her jaw dropping in teenage outrage. "I asked you right when you got to the counter!"

"I'm sorry. I just forgot. We'll check in the morning on the way to breakfast."

"Oh," says Eva, slightly mollified. She wanders over to the suitcase on the dresser, unzips it, and pulls out a large T-shirt.

"Eva, at some point over the next few days we're going to have to rearrange things so that I'm not living out of plastic bags."

"Yeah, sure," she says stripping out of her clothes. She is completely unselfconscious. "There's a mall just down the street."

Buying additional suitcases wasn't quite what I had in mind, but we'll come back to that later.

She pulls the clean T-shirt over her head and disappears into the bathroom with a quilted blue-and-red cosmetics bag. Seconds later I hear her brushing her teeth.

She reappears, plops down on her bed, and fiddles with the alarm clock until she finds some suitably horrible radio station. She turns it up loud, sets the alarm, and then clicks it off.

"What time are you setting it for?" I ask, rolling over and burying my face in my pillow.

"Six."

"Good God! Really?"

"Well, I figured you'd need some time to get presentable, and I also need a turn in the shower."

I sigh deeply. "Good night, Eva."

• • •

When the alarm goes off the next morning, I nearly scream. Eva has set it to both alarm and radio, and so our silent blackened room is suddenly filled with grating thumping music and horrible loud buzzing.

"Oh God, turn it off!" I shout.

"I can't! I can't find the switch!"

"Whack the top! Whack it all over!"

Smack! Smack! Smack!

Finally, she locates the Snooze button.

I take a deep shuddering breath. So does Eva.

I lean over and switch on my bedside light.

"Oh, Ma, do you have to?" she says, her face all scrunched up.

"Yes. Because you only hit the Snooze. If you don't want that happening again in nine minutes, you'd better turn it off for real."

Eva regards me in horror and then flips onto her side to investigate the clock radio.

I drag my sorry body out from under the covers and head for the washroom to make myself presentable.

• • •

An hour later, and I don't look too bad. The eczema has mostly cleared up, although if you look closely at my cheeks and forehead there are still patches of roughened pink. But at least it's not oozing anymore. I bolster everything with makeup, lightening the circles under my eyes, and adding foundation to the pink bits. When I reach for my mascara, I hesitate and then grab the waterproof, since it's bound to occur to me several times over the course of the day that I've just lost the love of my life.

Apparently I pass muster, because Eva is quite chipper as she gets herself ready, babbling happily about the day's events and wondering whether the hotel's breakfast buffet is open yet.

As we head out to the lobby, I brace myself. This is ridiculous—I know I'm going to see Roger's new family at some point, but I can't keep my heart from pounding. What if they're in the breakfast room? Is Eva going to expect us all to sit together? Somehow I hadn't gotten past the moment of recognition in my head. I have no idea what is expected of me.

Eva leads the way to the breakfast buffet, her fuzzy head bobbing in front of me. When we enter the dining room, she scans it and turns back to me.

"They're not here."

"They have a baby. They're probably still sleeping," I say.

"You get a table. I'm asking at the desk."

An elderly waitress in a mustard-colored dress approaches me. She has a coffeepot in each hand. "You on your own?"

"No, there are two of us."

"Booth okay?"

"Perfect."

She leads me to one. I slip behind the table and turn my coffee cup upright so she can pour me a cup. She doesn't bother asking whether I want regular or decaf. Apparently it's obvious.

Eva returns, clearly furious. She thumps down on the bench opposite me and crosses her arms.

"They're not here yet."

"Take it easy. When did they say they'd get here?"

"They were supposed to come last night. They're going to miss my dressage test!"

"Not necessarily. Maybe they're coming straight to the show and checking in afterward. Things don't always go smoothly when you're traveling with a baby. Did they leave a message?"

"No," she says, scowling. "Did they try your cell phone?"

I dig through my purse for my cell phone. Nine missed calls from Dan, but nothing else.

"So did they call?" asks Eva.

"No."

"Then why are you making faces at your phone?"

I flip it shut and stick it back in my purse. "No reason," I say.

• • •

When we get to the lot, we have to park way out near the road and then trudge through three parking lots of cars and SUVs. We're just getting to the usual hundreds of horse trailers and RVs when a golf cart comes to a stop beside us.

"You riding today?" says a gnome of a man from beneath a sunshade.

"Sure am," says Eva, beaming.

"Your number card was a dead giveaway," he says, winking. "Hop on."

Before long, I'm clinging to the side of the golf cart and trying to keep from getting pitched out as we zip past all the pedestrians making their way toward the grounds.

"Hey, check it out, Ma," says Eva, nudging me as we

pass an RV with a portable satellite dish set up beside it.

"Don't even think about it," I say in response.

"Har," she says. "Just wait till I win my first big purse."

I glance quickly at my bald, happy daughter, who clutches the golf cart tightly while her eyes take in everything.

• • •

Nathalie zips around like she's on methamphetamine, barking orders and checking legs and sending girls back to redo braids or trim the hair above a hoof.

One of the girls—Kris, I think, although I still can't tell the girls apart—is having trouble with a braid. Each time she sews it up, it's as fat as a dinner roll. I step up to help.

"Annemarie! What are you doing!" snaps Nathalie.

I stop cold. "I was just helping out with a braid."

"She needs to learn how to do it herself," says Nathalie, striding onward, facing the ground. "Colleen! What do you think you're doing?"

"Putting cornstarch on his socks!"

"And all over his hooves too! Wipe them off!"

Someone grabs my arm. It's Maureen Sinclaire. She leans in close. "What do you say we blow this joint?"

"What?"

"Let's go around and have a look at the vendors. We're just in the way here."

I look around for Eva. She's standing on an over-turned bucket, carefully sewing braids into Joe's mane. Her braids are small, tight, and evenly spaced.

I catch her eye—and through expansive arm move-ments and facial expressions ask her if she minds if I leave with Maureen. She scrunches her nose and shakes her head, all without removing the needle and thread from her mouth. Then she holds both hands by her head and spreads all ten fingers. She closes them again and then holds up a single finger.

"Eleven?" I mouth.

She nods.

Her dressage test begins at eleven.

• • •

At ten minutes to eleven, Maureen and I climb over the low-slung rope that separates the spectator area from the vendors, and take our seats right at the front.

The one-star dressage tests ended at ten thirty, and a man on a tractor is dragging the arena in preparation for the two-star tests. After he leaves, a man comes out on foot, pushing a roller down the center line to flatten it.

The seats are filling up. I twist in my seat looking, scanning the crowd.

"Who are you looking for?" says Maureen, adjusting the brim of her hat.

"My ex-husband."

"Ah. I have one of those too."

"He was supposed to show up last night. I can't believe he's going to miss her test."

Maureen shrugs. "Well, what're you gonna do," she says. "You're not responsible for him anymore."

"No, he's not like that. He's not like that at all."

Maureen elbows me. "Here she comes."

And indeed she does—looking glorious in her tailcoat, shining black boots, and top hat. You can't even tell she's bald. She sits tall and erect, her heels pointed downward and her black-gloved hands motionless in front of her. Her seat is glued to the saddle.

A murmur runs through the crowd, reminding me of the inevitable reaction when I would first appear on Harry.

"What on earth is that?"

"Gracious, what a strange-looking—"

"Oh! My! I've never seen anything quite—"

Joe chomps the bit and throws his head, dancing a bit. They haven't entered the ring yet, but it's not a good sign.

Eva approaches the ring. As she turns to enter, I see her eyes scan the faces for her father. When her eyes land on mine, I shrug and shake my head.

She goes down the center line at a working canter and halts in front of the judges to salute. She dips her head and drops her left arm straight down. As she flicks her hand back, Joe skitters two steps sideways.

There's a collective intake of breath from the crowd.

Oh God. This isn't good. This isn't good at all.

Eva proceeds at a working trot and then executes a ten-meter circle that's more like twelve meters. She's having trouble controlling Joe—her back is rigid, and her hands and legs show obvious strain. He's fighting her for the bit, leaning heavily into it, but every time she tries to ease up he goes faster. It's because her legs and back are so tense, but she hasn't noticed, isn't processing all the pieces.

I try to beam positive thoughts toward her: Come on, Eva. Come on. You can do it. Just relax. Don't think about your father or the crowd or Nathalie. Don't think about anything but Joe.

She pulls him back, jigging her arms. Joe raises his

muzzle, sending little bits of foam flying from the corners of his mouth. His nostrils flare red. He finally halts, but it's not before taking another couple of sideways steps. Eva closes her eyes for a moment, collecting herself.

Good girl. Take your time.

She opens her eyes again, her face resolute. After a slight pause they bolt forward into a canter. They're on the wrong lead, but she's trying so hard to control him, she doesn't seem to notice. After a few strides she finally looks down and immediately asks for a flying change. In response, he shoots both hind legs out.

I glance quickly at the judges. One is shaking his head; another writes something on her score sheet with a sour, pinched expression. Yet another leans back in her chair, staring with a finger pressed to her cheek.

When Eva passes me at an accidental countercanter, her face pale as bone, it's all I can do to keep watching.

• • •

Seconds after Eva and Joe leave the ring, the loudspeaker crackles to life. "Eva Aldrich, number forty-two, has now completed the test."

I wince, bracing myself. Maureen's hand creeps across the divide, seeking mine. When it makes contact, I clasp it in a death grip.

"It looks like Judge H gives her a score of 50.5," the man on the loudspeaker says in a slow drone.

"Oh no," I say, clutching my chest.

". . . and Judge M comes in with a . . ." the man pauses and sighs deeply, disingenuously aggrieved. "Oh dear, it looks like a 51.8 from Judge M, and Judge B gives her a 51.2. And so we have Eva Aldrich, our first two-star competitor, with a provisional score of 51.167."

There's a ripple of sympathy from the audience. I leap out of my white plastic chair, knocking it over in the process.

"It's okay, honey, I'll get it," says Maureen, reaching for it. "You go be with your girl."

When I find her, she is collapsed against Nathalie's chest, sobbing. Margot stands off to the side, holding Joe, whose head and tail hang low. Five or six girls stand watching, their faces long. There's a pall over everyone.

I approach slowly, almost timidly.

Nathalie makes eye contact with me, still rubbing Eva's back. "It's all right, Eva. It's all right. You can make it up tomorrow and the next day."

"But I just don't know what happened!" she wails. "We were fine in the warm-up ring. But then something happened, and I couldn't get it back."

"What was it that happened?" says Nathalie, taking Eva by the shoulders and looking deep into her eyes. "Honey, talk to me. What was it that happened?"

"I have no idea!" cries Eva, her body wracked by sobs.

Oh, but I do. I do.

And so help me God, he's going to pay.

I walk over to Eva, turn her around by the shoulders, and pull her to my chest, claiming her as mine. Nathalie hovers for a moment, and then goes about her business.

Chapter 13

Day Two—the endurance test—and I don't know who's dreading it more. When the damnable, damnable alarm goes off, scaring the bejesus out of us for a second morning in a row, Eva smacks its top with deadly precision, flicks on her light, and goes immediately to the bathroom.

I can't remember ever seeing her this upset. Mad, yes. But this is something other. I'm not sure that she connects her failure yesterday with Roger's absence, but I do. She was looking for him, distraught over his absence. That tension translated to the horse beneath her, and once they were out of whack, there was no recovering.

Roger and his new family still haven't shown up. Nor has he called. I'm not proud of the message I left on his voice mail last night, but there you are. He hurt my daughter—our daughter—and I won't forgive him, no matter what his excuse. He can't pretend he didn't know what this meant to her. He knew.

I crawl out of bed, bleary-eyed, and pull the curtains back to get a take on the day. I should have known. The sky is a deep, even gray from horizon to horizon, like the universe is in sympathy.

At breakfast, Eva pokes at a plate of fruit, sighing and staring off into the distance. She looks pale, and although I know she didn't sleep much last night—she thrashed enough that she kept me up too—I worry about her diet. Despite my hope that she would consider fish and poultry to be a form of vegetable, she has eaten nothing but plant material since we got here, even going so far as to ask the servers what type of fat was used to cook it. How can she possibly be getting enough protein—never mind iron and trace elements and selenium and all the other things bodies need to run? A ripple of worry runs through me as I examine her face, her hands, her hair for signs of malnutrition. I'm going on a research mission when I get home.

In the meantime, in defense against whatever the day may bring, I shore myself up with coffee, pancakes, and sausage. I had a revelation last night—it came just as I opened my mouth to order a grilled chicken caesar, as I always do. I suddenly realized that there was no reason to deny myself, and so I ordered the grilled half-pound black angus burger with blue cheese, bacon, extra pickles (Klaas, of course), and fries on the side. I ate the whole thing too, washing it down with a comforting Guinness. I know without a shadow of a doubt that I've gained back the three pounds I lost, but I don't care. I can gain thirteen pounds and I still won't care. Maybe I'll turn into a blimp and wear tent dresses. Maybe I'll be one of those women who are so big they look like they've got tiny feet. Maybe they'll have to break a hole in the wall to get me out when I die. Harriet and Freddie won't care, and they're the only ones likely to see me naked in the foreseeable future.

By the time Eva and I head out to the car, it has started to rain. The air has an icy edge, and the sky a solid gloomy look that promises more of the same all day.

As we drive, Eva sits looking out the window, her shoulders slumped, her hands between her knees. She says not a word. After giving up on ridiculous small talk that she ignores anyway, I throw her sympathetic looks and occasionally reach over to pat her thigh.

The parking lots aren't nearly as crowded today. I guess the idea of standing outside in near-freezing rain isn't all that appealing unless you've got a friend or relative riding.

The dirt road that leads through the miles of parking lots has turned into slick mud dotted with oily puddles. As my tires thump from one hole to the next, I try hard to keep from picturing Eva and Joe galloping—and slipping and skidding and crashing—on the cross-country course. The images come anyway—each time I smack them down in one part of my mind, they come around and try a different angle, prying, levering their way under the edges. But I am determined to ignore them, to concentrate instead on my daughter's flagging spirits.

When we finally park, she is so slow to climb out of the car that I come around and open her door for her.

I want to say something encouraging, but I can't think of anything that wouldn't sound trite and Pollyannaish. Despite what Nathalie said, Eva and I both know she can't make up enough points to place. She got the lowest dressage score of all the two-star competitors. All she can hope to accomplish today and tomorrow is to redeem enough pride to walk away holding her head up.

This time when we park, there is no golf cart to whisk us past and through to the horses. And so I wrap my arm around Eva's shoulders, give her encouraging squeezes, and hold her tight against me under our one umbrella.

But the moment we get through the chain link fence that encloses the temporary stabling, everything changes. Eva speeds up to the point that I'm stumbling behind her, thrusting the umbrella forward to keep it over her head.

She stops and turns around. "It's okay, Mom, I'm going to get wet today."

And she's right. The stalls have roofs, but the area between them doesn't. The only shelter the girls are going to have is in the gooseneck trailers.

"Put your hood up! I don't want your hair . . . I don't want your head to get cold!" I call after her.

She heads straight to Joe's stall, which is instantly recognizable by the red-and-blue stall guard that is bolted across the open top of the Dutch door. Eva yanks the snaps open and pulls it aside. Joe's muzzle pokes out immediately, seeking her hands, pressing against collarbone and chin. She runs both hands up the side of his face as he rumbles his throaty greeting.

It's like watching lovers reunite. He's apologizing, and so is she, each of them telling the other *No, it was me—No, no, it was me, and of course we're okay.* Eva slides the latch on the bottom of the door and disappears inside his stall.

I stand watching with a lump in my throat. Twelve

seconds with Joe has done more good than any of my attempts at cheering her up over the last eighteen hours.

I suddenly miss Hurrah. And then I miss Dan.

And then I have to turn around and leave because I'm starting to cry.

• • •

I run—*whoomp!*—into Maureen's large chest. She and Colleen are headed for the stabling.

"Honey! Where you going in such a hurry?"

"Oh," I say, sniffing and wiping my eyes in what I hope is an inconspicuous manner. "I thought I'd grab a cup of coffee and wait in the food tent."

"Excellent idea. Colleen, you okay without me?"

"Duh!" says Colleen, striding off toward one of the gooseneck trailers.

"Well, then," says Maureen, perfectly cheerful. "Let's go where it's dry. Is that umbrella from the Misses' or Women's section?"

"I beg your pardon?"

"Got room for me under there?"

"Oh—of course!" I say, scrambling to get it over her head.

We start walking toward the fence.

"So," I say. "Have you watched anyone ride today?"

"A couple of the Prelim riders, but it's pretty mucky out there. A lot of the Juniors and Training-level riders dropped out, and the Prelim times are very slow. Not slow enough, in some cases."

"What do you mean?"

"Two people came off."

I stop. "Anyone hurt?"

She pauses, pressing her lips together. "Well, there's

no official word yet, but rumor is one of the horses had to be put down. He dropped a shoe, slid into a jump, and tried to take it anyway."

Panic surges through my breast. I close my eyes, breathing through my open mouth. I'd do anything to have a wall to clutch.

"Honey, are you okay?" Maureen grasps my hand, which must be outstretched.

I open my eyes and find myself hanging on the end of her arm. I blink a few times, and then hand her the umbrella. "I'll be right back. I have to check something."

I turn and run back to Joe's stall.

"Ma!" says Eva as I barge inside. She sounds indignant, and I understand that—she and Joe are coming to an agreement, are still making up for their lovers' quarrel from yesterday. She's fondling his ears as he rubs his face up and down her chest.

"Sorry, honey. I need to check something."

"What?"

I lean over beside Joe's haunch and pick up one of his back feet. Someone has already screwed studs into his shoes. I check each of the studs and then the shoe itself, running my fingers around the outside edge of his hoof, feeling for the ends of the nails. I sigh with relief—his pedicure is as perfect as mine.

"Ma, what on earth are you doing?" says Eva as I move around Joe and pick up his other hind foot.

"Just checking his brakes, sweetie," I say. Since his other hind hoof also checks out, I dart for the door.

"Wait! Ma!" Eva calls after me.

"Yes?" I say.

"What jump are you going to be at?"

"I don't know yet. You got a preference?"

"I guess not. I just wondered."

"Just tell me where you want me to be, Eva."

"It doesn't really matter. I guess what I was really asking was if you're going to watch."

"Of course!"

"I mean," she says, lowering her voice to a loud whisper, "are you going to keep your eyes open?"

I pause, and swallow deeply. "Of course. Yes, of course," I say, plastering a big fake smile all over my face. But then I lean forward and allow my voice to become urgent. "But please, take the weather into account. No heroics, okay? The footing stinks. Take your time approaching the jumps. Just concentrate on getting through in one piece. Remember, these jumps are solid."

"Yes, Mother. I know, Mother," she intones. I'm considering telling her about the dead horse when she adds, "Sheesh, you sound just like Nathalie."

"Good," I say. I step out of the stall and close the Dutch door behind me.

As I walk back to Maureen, Nathalie and I lock eyes. I give her a single approving nod, and she tilts her head quizzically.

• • •

As soon as Maureen and I settle at a plastic-covered table in the food tent, my anxiety blossoms. The rain continues—the grass outside the tent is saturated to the point that the droplets bounce up again when they hit.

"Did the rat ever show up?" says Maureen, ripping the plastic tab from her coffee cup.

"No. He did not," I say grimly, taking a sip of my own. The coffee is dreadful. It tastes like it's been on a

burner for seventeen hours, and they only have pow-
dered non-dairy creamer. Which, it occurs to me, probably makes this coffee vegan.

"Just as well at this point," she says. "It'd probably
upset her all over again if he showed up."

"Probably. But he's not getting out of this one without a damned good explanation."

"How long have you been divorced?"

"Ten months."

Maureen makes a face and leans back in her chair.
"Ouch."

"You don't know the half of it. Here, can I see your
program?"

"You looking up Eva? She's third out of the start box."

"How about Colleen?"

"Sixth. If I let her run."

I glance up quickly. "You're thinking of pulling her?"

"Maybe." She pauses, and then lifts her eyes to mine.
"I saw that horse go down this morning."

We stare at each other, mother to mother.

"Wanna go check out the course?" I say.

"Let's go," she says, swiping her program and hat
from the table.

• • •

We trudge across the field, feet squishing the rain-
soaked turf. I'm wearing Lands End all-weather clogs,
but they're backless, so my socks are soaked through.
We have also managed to miss the marked walkway,
and have to wait as one final one-star competitor gallops past before we duck under the rope divider and
dash across the course.

"Do you care which jump we're at?" says Maureen, as we reach the other side.

"Not really," I say. "To be honest, I don't usually watch."

"What do you mean you don't watch?"

"Nothing," I say, embarrassed and speeding up.

"No, what do you mean?" she says, catching up and peering sideways at my face.

I sigh. "I mean that I park myself beside a jump, wait until I see her, and then close my eyes. And then when I can tell she's landed, I clap like crazy and hold my breath until I hear that she's finished the course."

"Ha!" says Maureen, turning her delighted face toward mine. "I have to say you're full of surprises, Annemarie. I'm glad we met."

We make our way to the water jump, but there is already such a crowd around it that we wander around in search of another.

"Listen, since you admitted that you close your eyes, can I tell you something?" says Maureen.

"Of course," I say, surprised.

"I'm pretty sure I'm going to pull Colleen even though she'll kill me. So can we find a jump that's close to the start box?"

"Of course," I say nodding emphatically and with encouragement.

I glance at Maureen with genuine gratitude, because she's just shown me that I'm not crazy after all. I'm just a mother. I look around at the other soaking people, wondering how many of them are parents of riders, and how many are considering dashes to the start box.

The PA comes to life. "And coming out on course

now is the first of our two-star riders. Number twenty-six, Johanna Daniels, on Paraffin's Puffet." It's the same voice as yesterday, the man who sounds like he'd rather be doing golf commentary.

Maureen and I stare at each other for a second and then hurry onward.

"Here! Here's a good one," I say, coming to a stop just in front of the rope. It's jump twenty of twenty-three. Judging from the scant number of spectators, it's also not a very popular jump, but that's okay. It's a solid thing that resembles an overturned canoe built onto several feet of logs. In fact, it may well *be* an overturned canoe.

"Where's the start box?" asks Maureen.

"Right over there," I say, pointing across the course and behind some trees.

". . . just the one horse on course now, with a provisional score of twenty and no time faults," the man says in a nasal voice.

I pull the edges of my jacket closer around me, and clutch the cold metal of the umbrella handle with frozen fingers.

". . . and here comes David Shykofsky, number seventeen, on Devil's Angel . . . He's cleared number one, the log piles, and is on his way to the ditch and rails . . . Johanna Daniels and Paraffin's Puffet are now over the brick wall and heading for the in-and-out . . . And there they are, in . . . and out again . . . And here comes our third rider on course, Eva Aldrich, number forty-two, on Smoky Joe, the blue roan Nokota . . ."

I gasp. I can't help myself.

I feel Maureen's arm go around me. I hold the icy

umbrella handle so that we're both covered, and slide my other arm around her waist.

"She'll be okay," says Maureen, giving me an encouraging squeeze. "She's an excellent rider and, Lord knows, that horse can jump anything. He's taken out more fencing at Nathalie's place than any horse she's ever had."

"And Johanna Daniels is over the brush table now, over nineteen and headed for twenty . . ." the man drones. I half expect to hear him yawn.

Maureen's arm tightens around me in excitement. "Oh, look! Here's Johanna!"

A dark bay Thoroughbred comes crashing into view. His ears are plastered back, he's soaked through, and his front legs are slathered with blue grease to help him slide over the top if he hits—it's not much, but it's the only possible defense you can offer a horse against solid obstacles. The girl is riding in forward seat, with rain pelting against her face. She's breathing through an open mouth, her front teeth clearly visible.

The long-legged Thoroughbred gallops right up to the overturned boat and shoots over the top of it. He lands cleanly in a spray of water and continues on at a full gallop.

A small group of people to our right scream in encouragement, their voices raw with excitement and anxiety.

"Woohoo, Johanna!"

"Yeah! Way to go!"

"That's my girl!"

And then they rush off to the next vantage point.

"Good God, she took that fast," says Maureen. "I

mean, I know they're riding two-star, but still, considering . . ."

I lean forward, examining the ground in front of the jump, checking to see if the Thoroughbred ripped the turf up. There are hoof marks in the shape of perfect horseshoes, but no skids. The approach and landing look as stable as they did before he came through, which doesn't surprise me—he didn't hesitate for an instant.

"Oh dear," says the man on the PA in the most dismissive tone imaginable, and my heart plummets because the last time he said those words, it was right before he skewered Eva for her dressage test. "Looks like David Shykofsky has had two stops at the picture frame. One more and he's . . . No, wait, it looks like he's over and on to number fourteen. And it's a good thing because Eva Aldrich and Smoky Joe are making unbelievable time, over the brick wall and on to the in-and-out and . . . uh-oh . . . it looks like maybe they're . . . oh dear . . . sliding a bit on the approach . . . I can't imagine . . . Oh my goodness!"

I clutch Maureen's arm, panic-stricken.

"Absolutely unbelievable! Eva Aldrich and Smoky Joe just took the in-and-out as a single jump. Ladies and gentlemen, that's a spread of more than nine feet, I don't believe we've ever—"

Maureen and I gawk at each other, frozen to the spot.

"—fourteen . . . fifteen . . . sixteen, and, my goodness, they're really flying. Oh! They've cleared the brush table with room to spare, and on to the picture frame. And here comes David Shykofsky to number twenty . . ."

A tall Dutch Warmblood careens around the corner

and into view. The young man on top—still a boy, really—is tall and thin, standing in his stirrups and pulling back on the reins with the weight of his body. The horse's head is high in the air, his eyes wild. At the last second, the boy manages to pull him back into a canter. But the gelding has lost his sense of rhythm. He plants his hooves and throws his legs in front of him, skidding to a stop directly in front of the jump. The turf goes with him, rippling under his feet like carpeting, leaving nothing behind but slick mud.

"Oh God, oh God," I say, clutching Maureen.

The boy is temporarily unseated, thrust forward onto the horse's neck. He pushes back with both hands, leans back and yanks the horse around, circling around to have another go.

"And David Shykofsky has had one refusal at the canoe," says the man on the loudspeaker. He has managed to dampen his excitement over Eva and Joe's feat at the in-and-out. "He's coming around again . . ."

As he approaches again, the young man rides hard, pumping his arms and kicking the horse's sides with each stride. The ground is so saturated that the gelding's feet splash each time they hit the ground.

I can tell from the horse's ears that it's not going to happen. The gelding locks his legs the second his front hooves hit the mud. He skids to a stop almost on his rear within inches of the overturned canoe.

"A second refusal for David Shykofsky," says the announcer.

David Shykofsky flicks his hand against the rim of his cap and trots off around the jump, shaking his head in frustration.

"And that's number seventeen, David Shykofsky on

Devil's Angel, withdrawing after two refusals at the picture frame and two more at the canoe. And just in time, because here comes Eva Aldrich on Smoky Joe!"

Eva crashes into view. She and Smoky Joe are a study in concentrated unison—she stands in her stirrups with her legs bent, leaning slightly forward. They're both soaked through. His legs hit heavily and he's blowing hard with his head raised. The reins are taut, but he's not fighting her. He's asking her.

I glance at the ground in front of the canoe. Devil's Angel has left skid marks of raw mud six feet long.

When Eva sees the long, bald approach, her expression changes to alarm and she pulls back. Joe responds instantly, shortening his stride to a fast canter and lowering his nose, but it's no use—when his front feet hit the mud he slides like a car on black ice. He tries to adjust, but it's too late. He glides almost sideways, his hindquarters coming closer to his shoulders with each stride. He's folding like an accordion and twisting so that he's almost parallel to the jump.

"Sweet Jesus—" I croak as Joe crashes into the canoe.

The noise is terrible—the hollow sound of wood cracking and splitting, muted by the padding of flesh.

Eva lurches forward, off-balance. Then, impossibly, Joe shoots from the ground, attempting the jump even though he is pressed up against it.

He springs upward, almost perpendicular to the ground, catching the top of the jump with both forelegs and somersaulting over top. Eva disappears just as Joe achieves perfect verticality. As his wide belly, hind legs, and tail slide from view like the upturned stern of a sinking ship, I topple over the rope, landing on my hands and knees in the mud.

"Eva!" I scream. "Eva!"

I scrabble forward and up, staggering around the far side of the jump.

"—we have a horse down at twenty . . . Eva Aldrich and Smoky Joe are down at the canoe—"

Eva is on her back, her arms and legs spread. One knee is slightly bent. Joe lies beside her. Both are utterly still.

I am too—it can only be for a split second, but it feels like forever because I'm watching in vain for signs of life.

My mouth opens in a wail. I drop to my knees beside my motionless daughter.

"Eva!"

My hands flutter, my breath coming in short chops through an open mouth. My eyes move from her face to her chest, and then back to her face, seeking movement of any kind.

I turn my head and scream, "Help! We need help! Where's the ambulance?"

Maureen appears beside me. She makes the sign of the cross. "Oh dear Lord. Oh dear Lord."

"Eva! Eva! Can you hear me?" I say, sliding my fingers up and down her wrist, trying to find a pulse with frozen fingers. I can't feel anything—her skin is slick with rain and mud. I switch to the side of her neck, pressing two fingers into the flesh just beneath her chin. I turn my head, bellowing, "Where's the ambulance?"

"Oh sweet Mother of God," says Maureen. She gets to her feet and crashes off through the tree line.

My eyes shift from Maureen's broad back to Eva's pale face. Her eyes suddenly spring open, glomming onto mine.

Something inside me shatters. I drop my head, weeping openly. "Eva! Oh, Eva! Don't move!"

Beside us, Joe comes to life. He heaves and shudders and scrambles to his feet, his stirrups flapping. His entire left side is covered in thick mud.

He takes a couple of steps. Eva turns her head to him, watching with shrewd eyes. Then she reaches for me, her fingers digging into my upper arm. "Help me up, Ma."

"What? Eva! No! Lie still!"

"No way," she says, turning onto her side and pulling her knees up. She struggles onto her elbow and winces.

The crowd behind us claps and whistles.

"Eva! Lie still!" I shout.

"Ma!" she barks, red-faced. "I'm fine!"

"No you're not. That's the adrenaline talking. Lie still and wait for the ambulance."

"Ma—"

"Eva! If something's broken you'll make it worse by moving! Please listen to me. You've got to believe me here. I know what I'm talking—Wait! What do you think you're—stop it!"

She claps her other hand on my shoulder and climbs to her feet, using me as unwilling support.

There's an upswell in the applause behind us. I know they're just glad she's not dead and trying to tell us that, but I wish they'd shut up because I'm afraid they're encouraging her.

I consider, briefly, pushing her back to the ground—for her own good, of course—but decide against it on account of the audience.

Eva stands leaning over, panting, her hands braced against her thighs.

I lean over, searching her face. "How do you feel? What hurts?"

"Catch Joe," she says through clenched teeth.

I glance over. "He's fine. He's not going anywhere. Don't worry about him. Someone else will get him. Come on," I say, taking her elbow. "Let's get you off course."

She jerks her arm from my grasp. "The hell with that," she says, turning from me.

I am filled with overwhelming dread and perfect foresight. "Eva," I snap. "What do you think you're doing?"

"I'm getting back on."

"WHAT?" I shriek. "No. No way. Over my dead body."

"Whatever," she says, limping toward Joe. Scattered whistles and clapping erupt from behind her.

I turn to them. *"SHUT! UP!"*

I feel the spittle fly from my mouth.

I'm momentarily horrified by the expressions on their faces. Then I snap out of it and spin on my heel.

"Eva," I hiss, stumping along beside her. "Eva! I told you to stop! You are *not* getting back on!"

She ignores me completely, gathering the reins, leaning over, and surveying Joe's body.

"Shhhhh," she coos. "There's my boy. Are you okay?" She lays a hand on his neck.

"Eva!"

She leads Joe a couple of steps, watching his legs carefully. Then she becomes all business, slipping the reins back over his head and taking her place by his left shoulder.

"No! No! Absolutely not! I will not allow—"

When she turns the stirrup toward her and lifts her

foot, I grab the iron and yank it backward and out of reach. "I said no! *NO!*"

Eva turns to me with smoldering eyes.

"What's going on? Eva, are you all right?" It's Nathalie, from out of nowhere. She's right beside us, taking Joe's reins.

"Yeah, I'm fine," says Eva with clear relief. "Give me a leg up."

"No," says Nathalie.

"What? Why not? We're fine! I want to complete the course."

"No!" Nathalie repeats. "Eva, it's over."

"But—"

"But nothing. It's over," Nathalie says firmly. "Come on—we've got to clear the course." She thrusts the reins at me. "Annemarie, take Joe."

I do.

Nathalie worms her way under Eva's arm and grabs her around the waist so that Eva is resting on her. Then she steers her toward the rope, which several spectators are holding high enough for them to walk under.

A golf cart pulls up to the jump and three men hop out with tool kits. They kneel in front of the overturned canoe, nailing the loose boards back onto the jump.

I turn away to the sound of their hammers.

Bang bang bang.

Chapter 14

Eva and I head toward the car, both of us muddy, both of us limping.

As we weave our way through the parked vehicles, she makes sure she stays several feet ahead of me. The result is that I'm always staring at the back of her bald head. The few times I try to catch up, she immediately buzzes ahead again, and since both my knees hurt, I decide to accept the single-file formation rather than risk yet another increase in speed.

Although it's still raining, I'm so wet there's no point in opening the umbrella. Instead I use it as a cane, stabbing it into the muddy earth and then leaning on it as I catch up. I haven't bothered wrapping the little strap around it, so it flaps like bat wings with each stride. My knees are killing me, both from toppling over the rope and also from dropping to the ground beside my prostrate daughter. Thank God the ground was as saturated as it was, because the water provided significant cushioning. I think I'd be in serious trouble if it hadn't. Come to think of it, maybe that's why Eva and Joe both fared so well. Then again, if the ground hadn't been saturated, maybe they wouldn't have taken a fall in the first place.

My poor, sweet Eva—I know she thinks she's thirty-six, but she's really just a child, and her pain and humiliation make her seem so small and vulnerable. She has no defenses whatever, and it makes me desperate.

Is this what I was trying to protect her from when I didn't want her to come? Partly. It was this and a broken neck. But I don't feel vindicated. Instead, I feel like an enraged mother bear, lumbering toward whatever is threatening my child, which at the moment is a feeling of failure.

She reaches the car before me and lowers herself tenderly onto the front seat. Apparently I forgot to lock the doors. Not that there's anything to steal anyway, and if anyone wants the car they're welcome to it.

I had been going to suggest that we look in the trunk for blankets or feed sacks to put between us and the seats, but since she's already inside, I go around to the driver's side and climb in. I'm only muddy on the front and side, unlike Eva, who's slathered head to toe.

Eva waits until I close my door, and then sets her muddy boots on the dash. I open my mouth to say something—and then shut it again.

When I stick the key in the ignition, she says, "I want to go home."

"That's where we're going."

"I don't mean the hotel. I mean home."

"But . . . are you sure? There's a whole other day."

"Well, obviously I'm not riding tomorrow."

"No, but your friends are. And besides, what would Nathalie say?"

"I said I want to go home. What part of that don't you understand?" she snaps.

I gaze at her for a moment and then turn the key. "There's no need to be rude, Eva. If you don't want to be here, fine. We can hang out at the hotel tomorrow, and then you can go back the next day with the others."

"I'm not going back."

"I beg your pardon?"

"I'm not going back to Nathalie's."

"Eva," I say, broaching the subject delicately for fear of galvanizing her position, "you've just had a terrible disappointment. But that's no reason to give up on the whole enterprise."

She's silent. But I'm not stupid enough to mistake this for acquiescence.

"If you want to come home for a few days, I have no problem with that. I'll bring you home. But please, don't make any snap decisions about this."

"It's too late. I already have."

I raise my voice in exasperation. "You're going to give up just because you had one lousy show?"

"Lousy show? *Lousy show?*" She pivots in her seat so she's facing me. Her face is red as a beet. "I got the lowest dressage score in the history of the show, and I didn't even complete the endurance test."

"That wasn't your fault! The weather was terrible. People were withdrawing all over the place. Hell, Colleen's mother was on her way over to the start box to pull her too."

"It wasn't the weather. It was you."

I blink, stunned. "I beg your pardon?"

"It was your fault."

"What? Are you crazy? I'm responsible for the weather?"

"No, but you prevented me from completing the course."

"That is totally unfair. Nathalie didn't want you to complete the course either."

"Yeah, but if you hadn't delayed me so much, I would have been up and gone by the time she got there," she says accusingly.

"Eva! Your horse somersaulted over the top of a jump. I couldn't see the far side—for all I knew, he'd *landed* on you!"

"But he didn't, did he?"

We drive in silence for a few minutes.

"For once, I wish you *had* closed your eyes," she adds.

"Eva!" I shout. "Enough! Honest to God, I don't see how you can blame me for this!"

"You never wanted me to do this in the first place. And Dad couldn't even be bothered to show up. I hate you both."

I bite my tongue and drive. There's no point in responding. Besides, I can't even remember the exact kernel of what we're arguing about. We seem to have progressed from deciding whether to stick around for the final day of the show to whether Eva is going to continue training with Nathalie at all because clearly everything's gone wrong and somehow it's *my* fault—

This final irony, this reversal, would be funny if so much weren't dependent on it. Whoever would have imagined that I—the one who didn't want Eva to do this in the first place—would find myself encouraging her to continue? But what other choice do I have? If she comes back to Maple Brook, she's still expelled from thc only school in the area, that damned Eric Hamilton will come sniffing around again, and even if she only kept the condom for the novelty of it, I can well imagine where that would lead.

Oh look! Wanna see what it looks like? How about when you put it on? Oh, my!

My mind cuts to black at this point, can't even carry the thought through.

No. As much as I used to be against the idea, somehow I have to persuade Eva to continue at Nathalie's. The alternative is just too dreadful to consider. In fact, the alternative may well be packing her off to Roger's, which is the last thing either of us wants. Right now, our shared fury over his failure to appear is the only thing uniting us.

• • •

When we get back to our hotel room, Eva heads straight for the bathroom and locks the door behind her. Less than a minute later, the shower starts. It goes on and on and on, and I find myself thinking gratefully of industrial-sized water heaters.

My clothes are so muddy and wet that I can't even sit down while I wait my turn in the shower. I strip and then stand holding my cold, stiff clothes, not quite sure where to put them. In the end I spread them out across the table and wooden chair at the far end of the room. They'll dry by tomorrow. They'll be stiff as cardboard, too.

I'm in my wet bra and underwear and am in the middle of removing the Dreaded Bedspread—which the housekeepers keep insisting on putting back on the bed—when Eva comes out of the bathroom.

"Nice, Ma," she says, glancing in disgust at my near nudity.

"Well, you didn't exactly give me a shot at the bathroom, did you?"

I stand beside her at the dresser, choosing a new outfit from my plastic bags.

Eva stumps around with one towel around her body and one on her head, shoving things into the suitcase. She crumples clothes like Kleenex—even the ones that are still folded. I open my mouth to say something, and again bite my tongue. The muddy boots on the dash, the crumpling of the clean clothes—all of it is designed to draw me into an argument.

"Eva, knock it off," I say walking behind her into the washroom.

"Knock what off," she says.

I set my clean clothes on the counter and lean over, rubbing my aching knees. They feel three times their normal size. "The packing. We're not leaving tonight."

"Yes we are!"

"No we're not," I say. "I'm not starting a drive of that length this late at—"

I'm cut off by a furious pounding on the door.

"Eva! Eva! Are you in there?" shouts a muffled voice.

"Oh shit," Eva hisses, spinning in desperation.

"What?" I whisper.

"It's Nathalie."

I snatch a towel from the rack and fling it over my shoulders. "Open the door!" I say. A quick glance in the mirror shows that I am still not sufficiently covered. I wrap the towel around my middle, choosing to let my bra straps show.

"No!" cries Eva, her eyes panicked.

"Then I will," I say, heading for the door.

"Eva, I can hear you in there. *Eva.* Open the door." Nathalie's voice is a growl, and at the end of it, she resumes pounding.

Eva smacks her face with both hands as I open the door.

"Hi, Nathalie," I say, as she marches right past me without any acknowledgment whatever. I sweep my arm toward the interior. "Please, come in."

She stops beside Eva, who has returned to scrunching up clothes.

"What do you think you're doing?" says Nathalie, putting her hands on her hips.

"I'm packing," says Eva. She spins and goes into the bathroom. She returns with bottles of shampoo and conditioner, which she tosses into the suitcase.

Nathalie glances around the room, takes in my wet clothes on the table, and my current state of dishabille. I blush and look down.

She turns back to Eva. "You left without taking care of your horse today," she says quietly.

Eva continues packing.

"I know you were upset, but that does not excuse you from your duties, and your very first duty—before anything else, ever—is to make sure that your horse is settled."

"He's not my horse," says Eva.

"That's right. He's my horse. And you're my student, and I assigned him to you. And you walked away from him out of temper, leaving others to pick up your slack. That won't happen again. Do you understand?"

Eva grabs a plastic bag, wads it up, and stuffs it into

the suitcase. She has run out of her own things and is now packing mine.

"Is this all you're made of? One bad ride and you quit?"

"It wasn't a bad ride, Nathalie, it was a complete disaster."

"No, it wasn't. Everybody lived. You want to hear about really bad rides? Ask your mother."

There's a silence, long and terrible.

"You're not riding tomorrow," Nathalie continues, "but you *will* show up to support those who are."

Eva's chin juts. She lifts her face to Nathalie's, challenging her.

"I'm finished here," Nathalie finally says. "I don't have time for spoiled brats. You have two choices. You adjust your attitude and show up tomorrow, or you pick up your things from Wyldewood on your way past."

And then she's gone, slamming the door behind her.

Eva stares at the back of the door for a few seconds, and then drops onto the edge of her bed, her face buried in her hands. Then she starts to bawl.

I walk over and sit next to her. Then I try to take her hands, but she covers her head with her arms, batting me off like an insect.

"Oh, Eva," I say. I rest my hands in my lap, thinking I'll wait her out, but when her sobs get deeper and her breathing more ragged, I pry her arms from her head and take her face in my hands.

Tears stream from her swollen eyes. Deep, body-wrenching hiccups follow. She's huffing with the effort of trying to breathe regularly. She fails miserably and explodes, spraying me with spittle.

"Look at me, Eva," I say. "Come on now. Get a hold of yourself!"

"She hates me!"

"No, she doesn't."

"She just fired me!"

"No, she didn't. She gave you a choice. She expects better from you, and quite frankly, so do I."

She looks horrified. "You what?" she says, her voice tinged with the deepest betrayal.

"Nathalie's right," I say. "You're acting like a spoiled brat. Pull yourself together."

Eva stares at me for a moment. Then she rises from the bed and continues packing.

"Eva. Stop it," I say.

She ignores me.

"Eva! I said, stop it. We're not going anywhere to-night."

She turns to me, her face purple, her fists clenched at her sides. "I want to go home!"

"Forget it."

"I'll call Oma."

"Go ahead."

"Fine. I'll call a cab."

I laugh outright, a short, sharp noise. "Yeah, right."

Eva freezes with one hand on top of the suitcase.

I've had enough. I grab my purse, a beer from the minibar, and swing into the bathroom.

Eva's mouth drops in outrage. "Ma! Jeez, you don't think I'm going to *steal* from you?"

"Gee, I dunno. You just threatened to call a cab, and you do have a history of running away."

She stares at me with burning hatred, and then reaches for the clicker.

"—a frothy cocktail of rancid cow's blood, frog's legs, and pig eye—"

I rush the final few feet and slam the bathroom door, because I really, really don't want to know the rest of the ingredients in the *Fear Factor* cocktail du jour.

• • •

Fortunately, Eve didn't pack the hotel's shampoo and conditioner. I linger in the shower, both to give myself some time alone and to give Eva some time to calm down. This is promising to be a very long evening, particularly if I can't persuade her to go out for dinner.

Since the outfit I took into the washroom with me was the only one that didn't receive the Eva treatment, I pull the rest of my clothes from the suitcase and lay them flat on the bed, running my hands over them, trying to smooth them.

"You didn't have to crumple all my stuff, you know," I say.

Eva remains unresponsive, a bed-lump.

"Okay, fine. I'm going for dinner. Want me to bring you back anything?"

"Yeah. A cheeseburger."

"A *what*?" I say, spinning to look at her.

"You heard me."

"Yes, I know I did. But do you think maybe you can choose something that won't make you hate yourself in the morning?"

"I'm already going to hate myself in the morning."

"What do you really want?"

"I want a damned cheeseburger!" she screams. Then she punches her pillow and rolls over.

• • •

Obviously I can't buy her an actual cheeseburger and I don't want to face her without one, so instead I end up driving all over hell's half acre on the recommendation of the ex-girlfriend of the teenage son of the night manager until I find The Red Onion, a restaurant that promises to offer up a reasonable facsimile.

"And this is vegan, right?" I say, as a young freckled thing in Heidi braids hands me a brown paper bag. She has a small gold ring in each nostril and another through her eyebrow.

"Yup," she says, smiling.

"Even though there's cheese. And a burger," I say, peering closely at her, looking for cracks.

"Soy. And texturized tofu."

"And the mayo?"

"Eggless."

"You're sure?"

She laughs, revealing a tongue stud. "Of course I'm sure. Everything we serve is vegan."

"Thanks," I say, snatching the bag from her hands.

• • •

When I get back to our room, Eva is sitting cross-legged in the center of her bed. She's watching yet another episode of *Fear Factor.* It seems to be on twenty-four hours a day.

I toss the bag at her, and then follow it with a loose handful of ketchup and mustard packets.

She looks up in surprise. After a pause of a few beats, she reaches for the bag. She unrolls its top slowly, peers in, and then reaches for the cardboard container. She opens it, stares at its contents, and then sets it on the bed in front of her.

"It's not too late to change your mind," I say. "Because I could still go get you a house salad from the restaurant. Or a bowl of soup. Cream of cauliflower, with not a drop of cream in sight."

She removes the bun and looks more closely. The corners of the orange "cheese" sag around the edges of the patty, melting pretty convincingly. Eva leans over, sniffing. Then she pries off the slice of pickle.

"Is this a Klaas?" she says, letting it dangle between thumb and forefinger.

"I have no idea."

Eva swivels at the waist and tosses it neatly into the garbage.

"Gee, thanks. Maybe I wanted it," I say.

"Did you?"

"I don't know. Maybe." It's just dawned on me that I was so wrapped up in my quest for a vegan burger that I neglected to get any dinner for myself.

On the television, a barefoot woman is grimacing and stomping a tub full of worms. Beneath her, a wineglass catches the resulting unfiltered nectar.

Eva grabs a ketchup packet, squirts it across the slice of cheese, replaces the top half of the bun, and goes to town. She stuffs so much into her mouth I'm afraid she's going to choke.

I watch, both horrified and fascinated.

"Man oh man," says Eva, speaking with her mouth crammed full and juice running down her chin. "This is *so good*. You have no idea how much I've missed meat."

The woman on the television has climbed from the wooden tub of squashed worms. She is holding the glass of red-brown worm guts and taking deep breaths. As the show's host urges her on, she plugs her nose and starts gulping. I turn from the screen.

"*Aaaaah!*" I squeal, plugging my ears. "My God! Do you think once—just once!—we could watch something that doesn't involve pigs' eyes or water buffalo penises or rancid cow's blood? Where's the clicker! Give me the clicker!"

When it doesn't appear, I glance over at Eva's bed.

She's staring at me, stone cold.

"*Pffffft,*" she says. Then she grabs the clicker and tosses it across the divide. "It's just worms, Ma."

"And that's just cow, Eva."

She freezes, crouched over the burger with her pinkies extended. Her eyes grow wide. Then her hands begin to shake.

"*Aaaaaaaaaaaaayiiiiaaaaaaaah!*" she shrieks, throwing the burger overhand at the wall. It sticks impressively before sliding slowly down, leaving a brown trail along the wallpaper. Eva looks at the carton in her cross-legged lap and upends it, sending fries and lettuce and ketchup flying. Then she jumps backward and off the bed. She stands a few feet away, trembling with her mouth and eyes open wide.

"No! Honey! No! It's okay!" I say, scrabbling to get to her. I leap from my bed, cross the three feet to hers, and then scootch across it to the other side. "It was fake! Completely fake! I mean, vegan!"

Eva's eyes turn and lock on mine. She is silent for a moment. "Huh?" she says through ragged breaths.

"Your burger. One hundred percent vegan."

She stares at me, chest heaving.

I swipe an *X* across my front. "I swear to God, Eva. It's vegan. That's why it took me so long to get dinner."

She keeps staring, huffing like a horse who's been stung and doesn't know what the hell hit it.

"Eva?"

I grab her shoulders.

"Eva! I swear to you by all I hold sacred—I swear to you on your grandfather's grave—that burger was one hundred percent fake."

She blinks at me. "Yeah?" she pants.

"Yeah," I say.

She stares at me for another couple of seconds and then falls against me, weeping like a five-year-old.

I sigh and pat her back. What else can I do?

• • •

In the morning, we leave the hotel with Eva once again packed in suitcases and me packed in plastic grocery bags. I argue only halfheartedly when the desk clerk explains that we have to pay for tonight as well because we didn't meet the cancellation requirements. And then we're on our way.

The drive home is predictably long. Neither of us is in the mood for conversation, although we're going to have to have one.

Before we left the room, I tried one last time to persuade Eva to attend the final day, but it was no use. The really stupid thing is I don't believe she was making a decision about whether she wanted to remain in the program. I think she was simply too embarrassed to show up. I tried explaining that Nathalie would interpret that as a decision, but since that was obviously causing Eva to dig her heels in even further, I desisted.

My secret hope is that I can change her mind during the drive. My other secret hope is that Nathalie will be receptive to taking her back.

"Eva, look," I say, leaning over and patting her leg. "When we get around that curve, you'll be able to see the Old Man."

"So what," she grumbles.

"No, here. Look! Look!" I say, pointing as we round the curve.

I look up expectantly. And then I continue staring in disbelief and incomprehension.

"Ma! Watch where you're going!"

Eva's warning comes just in time to prevent me from ramming the car in front of me. It, and a great many others, are stopped right in the center of the parkway.

I yank the Camry onto the shoulder and look back at the rock face.

He's gone. The Old Man of the Mountain is gone. There's nothing but a shapeless hollow where he used to be. His face has fallen off, is nothing now but great cubes of Jell-O granite lying on scree at the bottom of the hill.

"Ma! What is it?" squeals Eva, I assume because I'm staring out the window and hyperventilating through peaked fingers. "Ma! What?"

I scrabble out of the car and stare, leaving the car door open. There's no point in asking what happened, although I find it impossible to comprehend. Immediately I begin wondering how we're going to fix this, how we're going to put him back up. And almost as quickly I realize that we can't. The Old Man is just gone.

A news crew is making its way up the parked cars on the shoulder, shoving their microphone in front of hapless New Hampshire faces. Some have dropped jaws. Some stare in bafflement, shaking their heads. Others cry.

Eva joins me beside the car.

"Is this him?" she says, her voice filled with worry.

"It was," I reply.

"What happened?"

"I don't know. I guess he fell off," I say.

Hearing the words, even saying the words, appears to have no actual influence on understanding.

I hear gravel crunching under feet. The news anchor, in her yellow raincoat and golf umbrella, is making her way toward us. She marches purposefully, followed by a handful of crew members. She's only a dozen feet from my car.

"Get in the car," I say quickly.

"But—" says Eva.

"Go through my side. *Do it!*"

Eva scrambles in and across. I jump in and lock the doors just as the news anchor arrives at my side. I drop my head on my steering wheel, trying to look unavailable.

She raps sharply on the window.

I lift my head and turn.

"Excuse me," she says, leaning over and smiling broadly. Her makeup is thick, and when she smiles, cracks form in her foundation. "I was wondering if you would mind—"

"Buckle up," I mumble to Eva, starting the engine.

"Hey! Excuse me!"

I lay on the horn.

The news anchor jumps back with a horrified expression and I gun it out of there, weaving around the vehicles that are stopped right in the center of the pavement.

I'm blubbering hopelessly within a minute. I stop for gas in Whitefield, whimpering at the gas pump. When I go inside to pay and the cashier asks if I'm okay, I tell him what's happened. He looks stricken, almost as though he, too, will burst into tears.

By the time we reach Lancaster, I'm so desperate to get home I'm driving almost twenty miles an hour past the speed limit, zooming past the cherry blossoms.

Eva finally speaks. "I don't see why you're so upset."

"No, of course you don't," I say, without offering to enlighten her.

"Well, why is it then?"

I turn quickly to look at her. "Because I loved him. Because he symbolized New Hampshire."

"*Pffffft*, that's just dumb," she says. Then she chortles.

"What?" I croak.

"Dumb?" she says, pointing at a sign for the town of *Dummer*. "Get it?"

I take a deep breath. "Eva, do me a favor—just keep your mouth shut until we get home."

"Hey! That's not fair. It's not my fault some old piece of—"

"I said, shut it!"

She drops back against her seat and crosses her arms, her brow furrowed so deeply I bet she's nearly cross-eyed.

• • •

When Maple Brook finally comes into sight, I sigh with relief. I turn down our drive, puffy-eyed, having cried on and off since Franconia Notch Park.

As I pull the car around behind the house Mutti comes out the back door. She has a blue sweater clamped around her shoulders. Her arms are folded in front of her, and her face is drawn. Obviously I don't have to explain to her what the Old Man meant.

I climb from the car. "Oh, Mutti—" I say, hugging her.

"So you know," she says grimly. "How?"

"My God, I passed right by it."

Mutti's body tightens. Then she pushes me away. Her eyes search my face. "What are you talking about?"

"The Old Man. He fell off."

"The Old Man . . ."

"The Old Man of the Mountain. What are you talking about?" I ask as it sinks in that she's upset about something else.

Mutti closes her eyes for a moment. Then she says, "Eva, I want you to go in the house."

"Why?"

"Eva, please!"

"Sheesh, all this for some stupid old rock face . . ." she grumbles, slamming the car door and stomping up the ramp to the back door.

Mutti watches her until the door is shut behind her. Then she turns back to me. She has a hand on each of my shoulders.

"Roger and Sonja were in an accident."

"An accident?" I repeat.

Mutti doesn't say anything else.

"Mutti? Are they okay?"

Mutti's eyes flicker. A quick shake of the head.

I gasp, searching my mother's eyes.

"Sonja is dead."

I cry out. Then, in a shaky voice: "And Roger?"

Mutti glances quickly at the house. "In critical condition," she whispers hoarsely.

"Oh God," I say. Then I close my eyes, afraid to even ask the next question. "And the baby?"

"Stable."

I am silent for a moment, trying to take this in. "Where are they?"

"At the hospital in Lebanon."

"They're here? In New Hampshire?"

Mutti nods.

"Oh no." The back of my throat constricts. "Oh no, oh no. We thought they didn't come."

I blink at Mutti, trying to process all of this. Then I say, "Roger has no family."

"I know, *Schatzlein*. I know."

"We've got to go."

She nods.

After a moment, I turn and stare at the house.

Chapter 15

A few hours later we're back on the road. Mutti is driving, I'm in the passenger seat, and Eva is directly behind me, beside the heap of plastic bags that hold Mutti's and my clothes and toiletries.

If I lean slightly forward I can see Eva in the side-view mirror. I do this occasionally and carefully because I don't want her to catch me. I think she's handling this all right, but who's to say? So far we don't even know the extent of what we have to handle.

We pass the covered bridge, the library, the school buses. I catch sight of Percy's Peaks in the side-view mirror, spread out behind us like the breasts of a supine woman, and all I can think of is were we here or there, passing this or that, when the tractor trailer ripped off the front of Roger and Sonja's rented car, leaving the baby and the rear half spinning on the highway, and barreling forth with Roger and Sonja impaled on its grill.

Somehow it's important for me to know where we were when it happened. It seems absurd to me that Roger's life could be shattered so completely in such proximity to me and I didn't pick up a signal. For better or worse, I spent almost twenty years with the man. You'd think I'd feel some kind of sympathetic vibration, like a drone string. If not actual pain, a zap, a ping—something.

But I didn't. I felt nothing. Eva and I could have been discussing painted frogs at the moment Roger was carried forth next to his dead, smashed wife.

As we join the traffic that crawls past the faceless and fallen Old Man, I think back to the voice message I left on Roger's machine and am filled with eviscerating shame. I didn't know. How could I know? He'd disappointed me before; it wasn't outrageous for me to think that he'd do it again.

And now I want to slither down and melt in my seat for making excuses because I know damn well that Roger disappointing me is one thing—and a mitigated thing at that—and Roger disappointing Eva is quite another. I should have known by his absence that something was wrong.

I will explain to him, probably before he even hears the message. I will beg his forgiveness, and he will understand because I was angry for Eva's sake. Perhaps I can even persuade him to delete it without listening.

I sneak a look at Eva. She stares out the window, her forehead leaning against it. Her eyes are hollow and red-rimmed, but dry.

When Mutti and I first told her what happened she burst into horrified tears, but quickly gained the same stunned focus that drove Mutti and me in our hurried preparations as we located Joan and arranged for her to stay at the house. I have this feeling I should be trying to talk to Eva, to prepare her, but I don't know what to say. I won't know what to prepare her for until we get there.

Dead is dead, but critical can mean anything—I'm not even ready to go there yet. For that matter, so can stable. You can be in stable condition after having your face ripped off—or, say, breaking your neck. Stable means they're hedging their bets. They don't think you're exactly at death's door, but they're also not making any guarantees.

And so we drive, silent, grim, united. There was no question that we had to go. And there's no question that we're driving toward family, even though the only person in the car related by blood to either Roger or the baby is Eva.

• • •

The hospital is huge and sprawling, a complex of new buildings attached by various walkways. Fortunately, the lobby leads straight to an information desk, a semicircle of burnished wood that is directly in front of a waterfall. It is flat, and takes up the entire length of the wall. The water trickles sweetly down, engineered to be comforting. It reminds me of the environment at the spa, and I am hit with a wave of nausea. Roger and Sonja were probably packing and chatting while I was having stupid little lines painted across the tips of my fingernails.

The elderly volunteer gives us directions to the ICU. Eva and Mutti turn and rush off while the woman's hand is still outstretched, pointing. I call a thank-you over my shoulder, and jog to catch up.

The nurses' station is a central island with a wall of monitors behind it. I scan them quickly, trying to identify which one is keeping track of Roger's vital signs. I can't tell, but the variation in heart rhythms is sobering.

"Excuse me," I say, coming to an abrupt stop with my chest against the desk. "We're here to see Roger Aldrich."

"And Jeremy Aldrich," Eva says quickly.

"Yes," I say. My throat is tight as a tourniquet. "Roger and Jeremy Aldrich."

The nurse looks up at us. "Are you family?" she says.

"Yes, this is his daughter. Roger's, that is. And I'm his ex-wife. Please, can we see him?"

The nurse stands up and comes around the other side of the station. She lays a hand on my elbow. "Will you ladies please follow me?"

She leads us into the hallway and through a door into a small waiting room. The lights are dimmed. Airport chairs of padded Naugahyde line three walls, bolted to beams. There are two end tables, made of the same false wood as Dan's coffee table. On one is a fanned spread of magazines—*Golf Weekly, Family Circle, Parenting.* On the other is a box of tissue and a brochure about organ donation.

The nurse turns and addresses Eva. Her face is broad and kind, the skin beside her eyes creased. "What's your name, sweetheart?"

"Eva."

"And you're Eva's mother?" she says, turning to me.

"Yes. I'm Annemarie Zimmer, and this is my mother, Ursula Zimmer."

"My name is Chantal," she says. "I'm one of Mr. Aldrich's nurses. Why don't you have a seat, and I'll go find one of the doctors."

"How is he?" I say. "Is he going to be okay?"

"And my brother? Is he here?" Eva says quickly.

Chantal pauses by the door. "One of the doctors will be in shortly to fill you in. And Eva, I'll see what I can find out about your brother." She smiles in sympathy and leaves.

• • •

Fifty-five minutes later, we're still waiting. My frustration builds, and every time I hear footsteps or voices outside the door I want to leap up and tear it open, shouting for attention, for information, for anything.

Eva sits across from me, perched like a bird with her legs up and her arms wrapped around them. Her chin rests on her knees. She's carrying a load far too heavy for someone her age—she's not just scared to death for her father and brother, she's mourning Sonja. And for all I held a grudge, I have to admit that Sonja was good to Eva, always welcomed her into their home. I was secretly grateful for that, and am stunned with something like grief myself. It seems inconceivable—as the result of a split second, a minute miscalculation in distance, Roger is without his wife, and Jeremy, without his mother. She was twenty-four years old.

I'm sitting beside the brochure on organ donation, hoping Eva won't notice it and wondering whether I can flick it discreetly behind the table. I'm also trying hard not to dwell on the fact that this is a private waiting room. My family has a long history with hospitals, and private waiting rooms don't bode well.

Mutti stands by the door with one arm folded across her chest and the other pressed to her chin. Occasionally she crosses the room, but she always returns to the same spot.

The door opens. I jump to my feet. When I realize it's just Chantal, I sigh in irritation.

"Has anybody been in to see you yet?" she says.

"No, they haven't," I say. "It's been nearly an hour. We've heard nothing." I know I sound bad-tempered, but don't they realize how desperate we are?

"I'm sorry for the wait. I've let them know you're here but as you can imagine, things are sometimes unpredictable on this unit. Can I get you something while you wait? Coffee? Juice, or something?"

"No," I say. "Please—just tell us how he's doing. Please."

Chantal presses her lips together, considering. Her eyes flit from me to Eva, and back again. She comes to some sort of internal resolution and turns to Mutti. "Are you ladies from out of town?"

"Yes, we are," says Mutti.

"Have you found a place to stay yet?"

"No, not yet."

"The hotel right across from the west entrance has a special rate for patients' families. I know they have rooms, because I just called over there for another family. Mrs. Zimmer, why don't you take Eva on over there and get yourselves settled before it gets too late?"

Mutti and I exchange startled glances.

I nod.

"Come, Eva," Mutti says, gathering her jacket and purse. "Let's go get a room."

"I want to see Dad," says Eva.

"You will," says Mutti. She walks over and pats Eva's raised knee. "We'll come right back after we check in."

"And where's Jeremy? Why won't anybody tell us

anything?" Eva says crossly, letting her legs drop to the floor. Her voice is querulous, but she reaches for her jacket and hauls herself to her feet.

"He's on the children's ward," says Chantal.

"I want to see him."

"And you shall," says Mutti. "You will see them both. But it will do nobody any good for us to sleep in the back of the car. Come, Eva."

Eva lets her shoulders drop forward and frowns.

As she passes me on her way to the door, I grab her and pull her to me. She melts against me, a warm and heavy weight. Her bristly scalp tickles my nose as we clutch each other.

"It's going to be okay," I say, although I know no such thing.

"All right," she says in a tiny voice. She sniffs and pulls away. She's crying again, but there is no heaving, no hiccups.

Chantal reaches out and rubs her shoulder. "Thank you," she says softly as Mutti steers Eva from the room.

Chantal closes the door behind them and smiles sadly. Then she gestures toward one of the rows of chairs. "Please, have a seat."

I do, and then wait for her to speak, with my hands steepled and trembling in front of my face.

She takes a seat opposite, perching right on the edge of the chair and inclining toward me. "I'm glad you made it. We weren't sure anyone was coming," she says.

"We didn't know. My daughter and I were at a horse show. And besides, we didn't find out until today," I say too quickly. When I realize I'm proclaiming our innocence, I stop.

"How old is Eva?"

"Sixteen."

Chantal nods and purses her lips. She clasps her hands in front of her. "That's about what I thought. I think you're going to want to see Mr. Aldrich yourself before Eva does."

"Why? Can you please tell me what's going on?"

"Hang tight. I'll be right back with the doctor," she says, rising.

"Please—do you not know what this is doing to me?" My voice is raised. I cannot help it.

She leaves anyway. The door shuts, whisper-quiet.

I turn to look at the muted abstract wallpaper, frustrated and scared.

• • •

A doctor in blue-green scrubs enters almost immediately. His hair is in a cap. A paper mask hangs around his neck. Chantal follows him in and closes the door.

"Mrs. Zimmer, I'm Chris Lefcoe, one of your husband's surgeons," he says, extending his hand. I watch mine rise and perform the familiar ritual. Somewhere in my brain it registers that he called Roger my husband, but I don't correct him. At this point it's irrelevant.

"I'm sorry for the wait, but Mr. Aldrich was just getting out of surgery when you arrived," he says, sitting in the opposite chair. He leans forward, resting his elbows on his knees and clasping his hands with his fingers interlocked. His eye contact is steady, and, I fear, practiced.

Chantal sits silently beside me.

"Surgery . . ." I repeat.

"To relieve pressure on his brain."

I am mute, silenced by an overload of imaginings.

After a while the silence becomes conspicuous. I realize I've let my eyes wander to Dr. Lefcoe's feet. When I look up, he's still staring earnestly, lines of concern etched on his forehead.

"How?"

"We removed a piece of skull to allow room for the swelling."

The utterance that comes from my throat is somewhere between a word and cry. I sit ramrod straight, my fingertips pressed to my mouth. "Is he . . . ?"

Chantal's hand appears on my back. She leans toward me, letting her knee touch mine.

"Mr. Aldrich was in a very bad accident," Dr. Lefcoe continues. "If he makes it, life will be very different."

"If he makes it?" I say. "Oh God . . ."

"He is in grave condition. A lot depends on the next few days. He suffered massive injuries."

Grave condition—a degree worse than critical, namesake of the unspeakable. I can't absorb this. It's like I'm watching from outside my body, and the person we're discussing is certainly not Roger.

"What are you saying? Are you telling me he's going to die?"

The doctor drops his gaze to the floor and then raises his eyes back to mine. "The imaging showed extensive brain damage," he says. "We don't know how much function he'll recover." He pauses. "I'm sorry. We attempted to minimize swelling by inducing a coma, but the trauma was too severe. It happens with this sort of injury. His brain continued to swell after the accident."

"I want to see him."

Dr. Lefcoe nods.

• • •

"Are you ready?" says Chantal, and I nod curtly. I've never been less ready in all my life.

I step into the doorway anyway. I feel like a blind person suddenly sighted, disoriented by color and form as my eyes seek the bed.

When they find it, my knees give way. "Oh," I whimper.

Chantal catches my elbow, supporting me. I grasp the doorway with my other hand and look down, letting my eyes flutter shut.

"Are you all right now? Do you want to sit for a moment?"

I stand still for a few seconds, focusing on the floor tiles, trying to keep from sliding down to them.

"No," I say.

As I regain my balance, she tentatively lightens her grip. "You steady now?"

"Yes," I say. I breathe heavily, and then lift my face to my richest horror.

The bed is surrounded by monitors and equipment that blink and beep. The body in the bed is not recognizable. The head is wrapped, the face beneath it puffy and mashed, the eyes taped shut. It is bloated, swollen, apparently boneless.

(Not it. Him. Him. *Roger.*)

A thick tube runs from his mouth to a respirator. Its blue plastic accordion folds rise and fall, hissing like an asp. Leads and wires are taped to his temples and chest, an IV bag hangs above him, dripping, dripping, dripping. A black pulse oximeter clamped to his forefinger blinks red light like an artery.

My consciousness flickers as I scan his outline in the bed. I take it in once, quickly, and then move my focus to the center of his chest.

Chantal moves quietly, bringing a chair to the side of the bed. Then she stands beside it in wordless invitation.

I approach the bed slowly.

When I'm directly beside him, I look down at his face, still seeking Roger. I don't find him there, but I do find him in the muscles of his shoulders and the shape of his chest. I find him in the angularity of his wrist bone and tapered fingers.

"Does he know I'm here?" I whisper.

"He might," she says. I can tell from the way she says it that she doesn't think so.

I reach out tentatively and stroke his little finger.

I had been preparing myself to comfort Roger over the loss of his wife, but how to comfort him over the loss of himself?

Such grief, such grief—I am speechless under its weight. I caress his little finger with both hands, tenderly, afraid to hurt him any more than he's been hurt and weeping because his hand is as familiar to me as my own.

The doctor's words come back to me.

We don't know how much function he'll recover.

Similar words were once spoken about me. I proved them wrong. But as I stand here looking at Roger's ruined head, I can't help but hope that he never becomes aware again.

• • •

About half an hour later, it occurs to me that I must intercept Eva. I'm pretty sure the nurses wouldn't just let her come in, but I can't risk it. I have no idea how—or even if—I can prepare her for this, but I must forestall until I've figured something out.

I ask a nurse how to find the west entrance, and then run in that stilted every-second-stride gait used by people who are running where they aren't allowed to until I find it. The hotel is directly across the street, tucked improbably under a walkway that leads to the hospital's parking lot. It is a dismal, squat building, surrounded by concrete and the amorphous fear that clings to the hospital.

The hotel clerk is clearly expecting me, and gives me directions to the room. I walk until I'm out of sight of the front desk, but as soon as I turn the corner I speed up until I'm sprinting down the dark hall. I stop just outside the door and wipe my eyes with the edges of my hands. I sniff once, straighten my back, and knock. I wait breathlessly, making silent deals with deities. If Mutti and Eva are not here I don't know what I'll do.

After a moment there's a click and the sound of a chain sliding across. The door opens a crack and Mutti's face appears.

"Oh, thank God," I say.

She swings the door open and I step inside the small dark room. It is both intimate and gauche, with cheap furniture and an air conditioner stuck in the window.

"What did you find out?" says Mutti. "Did you see him?"

"How's Dad?" Eva's voice sails to me from across the room. She's lying on the farthest of the two beds, curled on her side on the bedspread's sprawling vines. She hugs one of the shammed pillows. The television is off—indeed, still undiscovered within its armoire.

"He's just had surgery," I say, forcing my voice to remain steady.

"For what?"

"He had some swelling. They needed to relieve it."

Mutti's eyes widen in understanding, but since Eva is searching my face I cannot respond. I concentrate on looking bland. As I attempt to pull the edges of my mouth upward, I realize I'm wearing the same sickly smile as Chantal. Nevertheless, I pin it in place. My lips quiver with the effort.

"Can I go see him now?" says Eva, sitting up. She brushes an imaginary strand of hair behind her ear and continues holding the pillow.

"He's still sleeping," I say. "What did you find out about Jeremy?"

"He's been upgraded to good condition," says Mutti. "He has a hairline skull fracture and a broken wrist."

An involuntary cry escapes my lips. "That's all? Oh, thank God. Thank God."

Eva stares at me, startled.

"I'm sorry, baby. Don't pay any attention to me," I say, crossing the room and sitting beside her. I lean forward and wrap my arms around her, rocking from side to side. "So, what say we find some dinner and get some rest? We'll see them both tomorrow."

The last thing I want is food, but I must keep Eva occupied until I've figured out what the hell I'm going to do.

• • •

A couple of blocks from the hotel we find a cheap roadhouse that has a good selection of salads. It's a noisy place, with heavily lacquered tables and a sports bar in the corner. As the hostess seats us at a booth, Eva asks about the washroom.

The second she disappears around the corner, I drop my menu and lean forward, grasping Mutti's hands. I drop my head onto my arms, breathing through my mouth and trying not to hyperventilate.

"*Schatzlein, Schatzlein,* what is it?"

"It's Roger. I can't let her see him."

"What do you mean? Why?"

I lift my head and moments later find my mouth moving silently.

"Annemarie, tell me! Please!"

"He's in a coma. They had to remove part of his skull to relieve the pressure on his brain."

Mutti stares at me. After a moment she declares, "There's more. What is it?"

"Can I get y'all a drink while you're deciding?" The cheerful voice crashes into us, the contrast nearly farcical.

Both our heads jerk around. A large-boned waitress stands by our booth. She's smiling expectantly, with a hip thrust out and her pen poised above her pad.

"Uh—" I say. "Uh—"

"Please leave us for a minute," Mutti says sharply.

The waitress's expression sets like concrete. She tucks the pad into her waistband and clicks her pen shut. "Sure, no problem," she says, her teeth still clenched in a smile. She spins on her heel and sails away.

She's offended, and the absurdity of this leaves me open-mouthed. Is our distress not visible? Is it not palpable?

"You can't keep her from seeing him. He's her father," says Mutti.

"I know. I know. Oh, Mutti, what are we going to do?"

"I don't know, but—"

"*Shhh,* here she comes," I whisper harshly. I look into my lap and rearrange both my expression and my napkin.

Eva slides into the bench beside me. She freezes, looks from Mutti to me, and then back again.

"Oma? Are you okay?"

"I'm fine, *Liebchen.*" Mutti picks one of the laminated menus from the table and pushes her glasses up her nose. "Now, what looks good?" she says, staring hard at the menu. After a moment she notices she's examining pictures of oversized frothy drinks and flips it over.

With an anvil in place of my heart, I try my best to read the menu. After repeated attempts, I realize that if someone removed the menu right now I wouldn't remember a single option.

When the waitress returns—only slightly sullen and doing her best to hide it—I order the same salad Eva does. I can't endure the thought of anything related to flesh.

• • •

We pick our way through dinner, none of us making much of an effort at eating or conversation. But sitting in a noisy atmosphere surrounded by people whose lives are still normal provides some distraction. The restaurant itself is cheery enough, with brass rails and fake ferns. There's a television in every corner, each playing a different sport, and I find my eyes drawn inexplicably to the one above Mutti's head.

Mutti looks studiously at her soup, turning it over and over with the spoon. She is still absorbing what I told her. For that matter, so am I, although I'm further along in the process. Eva still has no idea, and I try to imagine what she believes. Does she envision Roger as an intensive care patient a la *The Bold and the Beautiful*? Bandages here and there, and a slim oxygen tube running beneath his nose? A few well-placed bruises on a face that retains its shape?

Perhaps she believes he's got a lacerated spleen, or some other thing that requires surgery but that, once fixed, won't affect his lifestyle. Maybe a gash beneath his eyebrow that will heal into a rakish trophy of his close call. I wonder whether she worries about comforting him over the loss of Sonja—as I did, until I saw the truth.

As we turn into the hotel's entrance, Eva says, "Can we stop in and see if he's awake yet?"

My stomach flips. I rub her upper arm—it's a comforting gesture, but I'm fully prepared to grab hold of her if she tries to head across the street.

"I think we should wait until morning," I say.

"Your mother is right," says Mutti. "It's always hard right after surgery. We'll go over in the morning, after he's had a chance to rest."

As we head into the hotel's lobby I think, What are we doing? Protecting her, or setting her up? At some point I'm going to have to tell her the truth. I just know it can't be now, because I want to buy Eva one last night's sleep before her mind is overrun with ghastly images.

• • •

We watch sitcoms and other light fluff until ten, and then shut everything off. I share a bed with Mutti, leaving Eva on her own because I'm afraid I'll thrash and keep her awake. Truth be told, I'm sure she prefers her own bed anyway.

Before long, Eva is asleep—I can tell from her breathing pattern. Mutti is so still as to be dead, although I know she's awake; I lie with a fevered brain and shattered heart. We're probably thinking the same thing.

If I could sneak over and remove his respirator, I would. I have no doubt it would be the right thing to do. I know the situation is different from Pappa's—he made his intentions clear, participating not only in the decision but in the act—but wouldn't Roger, if he could? The irony is that after I broke my neck and was paralyzed, I wanted desperately to be unplugged. Thank God nobody complied. But everything's different for Roger. My limbs weren't paying any attention to my brain, but at least my brain was okay.

And then it hits me, and I can't believe I haven't thought of it before. Sonja is dead. Roger will probably never wake up; and if he does, he will no longer be the person he was. What in the hell is going to happen to Jeremy?

I need to splash water on my face. I get up quietly, groping my way through the blackness with my arms in front of me. When I turn the corner and locate the washroom, I slip inside and flick on the light.

As I lean over the sink to splash my cheeks, my tongue touches one of my back molars. It feels strange. Hollow, somehow. When I reach into my mouth to investigate, it comes out in my fingers. I look at it, horrified, and then try to stick it back into the hole. I press it in, but there's no root left, and eventually I give up.

While investigating the raw space with my tongue, I accidentally touch the tooth next to it. When it breaks free from my gum, I want to vomit. I move my fingers from tooth to tooth, plucking them as easily as grapes until I'm holding a fistful of teeth.

I huff with increasing frequency, staring aghast at the mirror and pulling my cheeks back with my fingers to look at my gaping, pitted gums, until—

Boom! I'm back in bed. I have my teeth. It was all a dream; a terrible, terrible dream. But now I really do need to go to the bathroom, as much as I don't ever want to face that mirror again.

Four different times I get up and go into the bathroom only to realize—when I find a carnival outside the bathroom's nonexistent window, or a camel in the bathtub, or a sink full of blood—that I'm still in bed next to Mutti.

I'm conscious but completely paralyzed. I scream for Mutti in my head, panicked, convinced I'm dying. If only she would sense my distress and poke me, do something to break the spell. I try everything—I count to three and try to lift my head. I concentrate on my hand, trying to move just a finger, but nothing works. Again and again, I feel the victory of swinging my legs around and going into the washroom only to find that I'm still lying prone in the bed.

The phone rings. It rings a second time before I realize I'm not still dreaming.

I jerk upright, slapping the wall beside my bed in an effort to find the light switch. When I finally locate it, I flick it on and grab the phone.

"Hello?" I gasp into it.

"Is this Annemarie Zimmer?" says a male voice.

"Yes."

"This is Dr. Lefcoe. We spoke earlier at the ICU. Chantal told me where you were staying."

I swing my legs around—for real this time—and clutch the phone to my ear. "Yes. What's up? What's going on?"

Eva is awake now, squinting. She raises herself onto an elbow, staring at me.

"I'm very sorry to have to tell you this, but your husband went into cardiac arrest a little over half an hour ago," the doctor continues. "We did everything we could, but there was just too much trauma. His system simply shut down."

I continue clutching the phone with both hands. My mouth moves, but nothing comes out.

"Mrs. Zimmer? Are you still there?"

"Yes," I whisper.

"Do you understand what I'm telling you?"

There's a long pause. "Yes," I repeat.

"Do you have any questions?"

"No."

"Someone will be in touch tomorrow about making arrangements." He pauses. "I'm so sorry for your loss."

"Thank you," I say.

I set the receiver back on the telephone and stare at it, stunned. When I finally raise my eyes I find my mother sitting next to Eva, clutching her hand.

I look from one face to another, and finally land on Eva's.

"He's gone," I say.

There are a few seconds of silence. Then Eva opens her mouth and screams. She screams again and again and again, earth-shattering, earsplitting screams that rise and fall like a siren until I'm sure someone will call the police. Eventually her shrieking subsides into sobbing. As Mutti holds her from the front and I wrap my arms around her from the back, she wails an endless repetition of denials through an increasingly hoarse larynx.

Chapter 16

A social worker named Sandra Compton calls the next morning. She wants to meet with us, will come to our hotel room if that's what we prefer. She wants to know if it's all right if she brings a hospital administrator, if we're ready to begin making arrangements.

I sit on the edge of the bed, twisting the phone cord around my fingers, and wishing Eva weren't in the room.

"The only thing is that technically I'm not Roger's wife anymore. So I don't know if the arrangements are mine to make. It's not that I won't do it—his current wife died in the same accident—it's just . . . Well, I don't know how these things work."

"Did he have any other family?"

It dawns on me that she's speaking of Roger in the past tense, and I'm still using the present.

"Just my daughter, and she's underage," I say, lowering my voice in the hope that Eva won't hear me, which is just possible because she and Mutti are involved in some sort of heated discussion behind me. "And his son," I add quickly, remembering Jeremy. "But he's just a baby."

"Yes, I know about him. Did Roger's wife have any family?"

"I don't know," I say. "I'm sorry."

"Don't be sorry. I'll look into it and see what I can find out."

The noise behind me increases. I twist at the waist and find Eva putting on her jacket as Mutti fusses and clucks.

"I'll call you back in a little while," the social worker says. "Will you be in your room?"

"I don't know. Hang on a sec," I say, pulling the phone away and covering the mouthpiece. "What's going on?"

"She wants to go see Jeremy," says Mutti.

"I *am* going to see Jeremy," retorts Eva.

I bring the phone back to my face. "We'll either be here or at the hospital. My daughter wants to go see her brother."

"Yes, of course," says Sandra. "I'll catch up with you at one place or another. I also want you to know that grief counseling is available for both you and your daughter. You may have been divorced, but that doesn't mean you're not grieving."

I give my head a little shake, baffled.

I realize that she must think I'm in denial and need permission, but, my God—of course I'm grieving. I spent more than half my life with Roger. He wasn't the man for me, but he was a good man, a decent man, and what he went through is beyond comprehension. What kind of a monster wouldn't grieve? I'm grieving even though I'm glad he didn't survive.

I'm glad he didn't survive.

I feel like someone has slammed a brick into my open chest.

"I . . . uh . . . uh . . ." A flash of color passes in my peripheral vision. It's Eva, with Mutti close on her heels. "I'm sorry, I have to go," I say and hang up.

I grab my purse and rush after them.

• • •

As we get off the elevator on the children's floor, a nurse pushes a portable crib toward us. An IV bag hangs from a pole. Its tube leads to a thin baby's splinted arm. A haggard woman trails behind, holding her forearms, hugging herself. I hold the elevator door open for them.

As they approach, an alarm screeches.

The procession stops, and the nurse turns back to face the nurse's station. Three surprised faces pop up— *boom! boom! boom!*—with the frantic insistence of whack-a-mole.

"It's just me," the nurse shouts, waving at the prairie dog heads, which drop back down.

A security guard rushes round the corner. He stops when he sees the nurse. "Sorry, Rob," she says. "Just me. Taking mister here down for an ECG. Want to unlock the elevator for me?"

The guard nods and turns. He punches a code into a keypad beside the elevator and trudges back whence he came.

As the nurse, crib, and weary mother enter the elevator, I stare in astonishment. The mother gives me a searing look and I realize with horror that it looks like I'm gawking at her emaciated baby. I wasn't, although his condition sends a horrified shock through my core. I was staring at the device attached to his ankle.

Do they really have to put anti-theft devices on the

babies? Are there people really sick enough to steal sick babies? As we pass between flat white panels that look for all the world like the devices at the doors of most clothing stores, I realize there must be.

The three of us approach the nurses' desk. I feel like I'm walking down an ever-lengthening tunnel.

The nurses are expecting us. Sandra warned them, I suppose, although I'm grateful since it saves us from having to explain ourselves. We may be dry-eyed, but we're walking wounded. I know our composure—or mine, at least—wouldn't survive the ordeal of having to explain why we're here. I'd shatter like a Christmas ornament.

But the nurse knows all, and leads us down a brightly painted hall with murals at regular intervals. Cookie Monster and Elmo playing in the sand. Another muppet I don't recognize holding a dozen multicolored balloons. Flowers with faces, ladybugs, and sunshine. Bluebirds dipping down in carefree delight.

Mutti and I flank Eva. We clutch hands, a human chain.

"Most of the children here have family staying with them," the nurse says over her shoulder. She has an odd shape—thin shoulders and a small waist that opens onto large hips. Her legs are bent at an odd angle—they seem to get further apart below the knees. "Since Jeremy has been on his own, we've been taking turns," she continues. "We've come to think of him as our baby," she says. "He's an awfully good boy. Here he is, the poor little mite." She turns into a doorway.

The room is deeper than I expected, with a crib in the center and a window at the back. There's a gliding rocker beside the crib, and there, in another nurse's arms, is the famous Jeremy.

The nurse cradles him close, giving him a bottle. I inch closer. I have seen pictures, of course—Eva flew out to Minneapolis immediately after his birth and brought home about three dozen pictures, which I viewed with Teflon eyes. The framed picture in her room has been updated at regular intervals, and while I've noticed its changing contents, I've avoided looking too closely. It was too painful. It reminded me of what Dan and I could never have.

But here he is, directly in front of me, and I can't take my eyes off him. He's gorgeous. His blond hair sticks up in soft tufts. His cheeks are round, his eyes wide. Their color surprises me—they're a deep crocus purple—until I remember that all babies are born with blue eyes and that they change over the course of the first year. Roger's eyes are—were—of the deepest brown. His daughter has them, and so will his son.

Jeremy's cheeks had been moving in and out as he drank, but they stop as his eyes flit from person to person. His right wrist is in a blue fiberglass half-cast, resting on the nurse's generous forearm. There's a raised purple bruise in the center of his forehead. His hands and fingers are pudgy, and my heart about stops when I realize that his knuckles are inverted, mere dimples. I had forgotten that about babies.

The nurse who brought us here leans over him. "Well hello, sweet pea," she coos, stroking his cheek. His eyes glom onto her face. "How's my little sugarplum?"

Jeremy blinks and then moves his cheeks in and out, exactly once, as he takes another sip.

"Carrie, this is Jeremy's sister," says the nurse who brought us here. "Her name is Eva."

Carrie looks up in surprise. "Well, I'll be," she says softly. She shifts to the edge of the rocker. "Would you like to give him his bottle?"

Eva hovers at a distance.

"Come on now, don't be shy. There's nothing to it."

"Will I hurt his arm?" Eva asks without moving.

"No," the nurse says, shaking her head vehemently. "It's protected by the splint. And besides, that's coming off soon. Jeremy is a lucky boy—his fracture was only a greenstick."

Jeremy is a lucky boy—my stomach lurches at the words.

The nurse holding Jeremy rises as Eva inches forward. "Come on, honey. Don't be shy. You just take a seat right there. Put your feet up on this footrest. That's right. Julie, get her a pillow to put across her lap."

As the baby is transferred to Eva, a chubby pink foot with perfect pea-pod toes pops out from beneath the flannel blanket. He, too, is wearing a house arrest anklet.

• • •

An hour later, I'm in the rocker with Jeremy, having rescued Eva when it became apparent she had no clue how to burp a baby.

It all came back instantly—the warm little Easter egg of a body, his complete and utter trust in me as I leaned him forward and rubbed and patted his rounded back. After a belch of seismic proportions, I wiped his chin and brought him back against me. He simply melted, nestling his downy head beneath my chin. He placed his thumb in his mouth and zoned out; not napping but staring into space with his long-lashed blue eyes.

I haven't moved since.

"Hi there." A petite woman in her fifties with short silver hair has entered the room. Her skirt and suit jacket are in muted eggplant. She has pearl earrings and speaks softly. "Are you Annemarie?"

"Yes," I say.

"I'm Sandra, with the Department of Children and Family Services. We spoke earlier."

She turns to face Eva and Mutti, who are parked on the window seat, watching.

"Are you Eva?"

"Yes," I say, answering for her. "And that's my mother, Ursula Zimmer."

"I'm so sorry for your loss," Sandra says, smiling in a sad and kindly fashion.

Eva's face hardens. I brace myself, unsure whether she's going to break down or fly into a fury. Neither reaction would surprise me—this is far too much for a sixteen-year-old to absorb. It may be too much for this forty-year-old to absorb.

"Thank you," says Mutti, neatly relieving Eva of the need to answer.

Sandra seems to understand. She turns to me. "Annemarie, can I steal you for a few minutes?"

"Yes, of course," I say.

Before I can even shift in my seat, Mutti is at my side reaching for the baby. As she takes him by the armpits and lays him against her, he emits a meep.

"Nein, nein, nein," she says, supporting his bottom with one arm and running the other around and up his

back so that his head rests in her gnarled fingers. She rocks from side to side. When his thin voice rises to a wail she begins to sing: "*Schlaf, Kindlein, schlaf . . .* "

I walk over to Eva, who observes me from beneath crooked brows.

"I'll be right back, sweetie."

She nods.

I kiss her forehead, give her hand an encouraging squeeze, and turn before she can see the tears in my eyes.

• • •

Sandra leads me to the end of the hall and turns right. A short jag, and then a left, down a hall that isn't brightly painted. She raps lightly on a door, waits for a moment, and then opens it. It's a small conference room with a laminate table and six chairs of molded polymer. The lights are fluorescent, embedded in the ceiling behind plastic waffle-weave. A whiteboard hangs on one of the walls. On another is a standard-issue clock and a poster that demonstrates how to perform infant CPR.

"Please, have a seat," says Sandra, gesturing toward one of the chairs. She goes around the table and sits opposite me.

After we're both seated, she looks at me for a while.

"How are you doing?" she asks.

"I feel like I've been hit by a Mack truck." My eyes spring open. "Oh my God. I can't believe I just said that."

"It's okay, Annemarie. It's just an expression."

"Yes, but . . . I'm sorry," I say, as my eyes fill. My hand flaps beside my face. "I think I need a minute."

Sandra reaches across the table. A tissue appears as though by magic. I never even saw the box. "Take your time."

I nod and daub my eyes with the tissue. It's a full two minutes before my throat loses the strained feeling that signals an imminent meltdown. When I'm finally able to speak again I say, "Can you explain something to me?"

"I'll try."

"How is it that Jeremy is virtually unscathed?"

"He was in the back of the car."

"But surely it must have been damaged too. I mean, if you saw what it did to . . ." I blink and swallow hard, trying to maintain control.

"The amazing thing is, he wasn't even hurt in the collision. After the truck carried the front away and the back stopped spinning, Jeremy's car seat simply fell out onto the highway. He hit his head and arm on the pavement."

I blink in disbelief.

After a pause, Sandra speaks. "How's Eva?"

I force myself to shift gears, because I'm still thinking about the back of the car spinning like a top, and the car seat toppling forth. "I don't know. She fell completely apart and then she pulled herself together. But honestly? I have no idea how she is."

"I can give you some referrals to grief counselors in your area, if you like."

"Thank you."

"You might consider going yourself."

I stare at my hands, which are clasped on the table in front of me. They're sweating, and I'm embarrassed by the little spots of condensation beneath them. My skin looks sallow under the fluorescent lights.

"Annemarie?"

I nod. "Uh-huh. Yup. I might."

"The thing is, something like this doesn't hit you right away. Some people get through the early stages of grief just fine, and then fall apart when the reality—and permanence—begins to sink in."

I clear my throat. "I know all about the various stages of grief. I lost my father last summer."

"Oh, Annemarie. I'm so sorry."

"Yeah. Me too," I say.

She nods. A long silence stretches between us.

"Well," she says finally. "In that case you know that there are certain practicalities we need to address even though it's probably the last thing you want to do. I followed some leads on Sonja's family this morning, and I'm afraid there doesn't appear to be much there."

"What do you mean?"

"I mean that it seems she was the only child of a woman with a fourteen-year-old warrant for her arrest. Everyone's best guess is that she's in Argentina. At any rate, she's not on the radar."

I stare in shock. "What about her father?"

"Her birth certificate said 'Father Unknown.' The mother cohabited with a number of men, but only married the last one, whom she since divorced. I spoke with him this morning."

My jaw flaps for a moment before I can speak. "And?"

Sandra looks at me, stretches her lips into a grim line, and glances down at her hands. "His main concern, after wondering whether he might stand to gain anything from the estate, was whether he could get stuck with the interment costs."

I stare in disbelief. "Are you serious?"

She nods.

The import of this begins to sink in. "Does that mean I have to make arrangements for them both?"

"You don't have to, no," she says softly. "But it's beginning to look as though nobody will object if you do."

"Oh." My head suddenly feels as though someone has driven a stake behind my right eye socket. I drop my forehead onto my hands. I cannot imagine how I'm going to survive the next few days.

"I'm so sorry, Annemarie. I'll help in any way I can."

"I'll find out what the wills said. What's going to happen to Jeremy?"

"Wills?" Sandra leans forward, almost eagerly. "Do you really think there are wills?"

"Oh, there are wills. I guarantee there are wills. Roger's a lawyer," I say. Then I repeat, a little more forcefully, "But what's going to happen to Jeremy?"

"Well, actually, that's what I'm sorting out this afternoon."

"What do you mean by 'sorting out'?" I say.

"He's well enough to be discharged, so if there really are wills—"

"I already told you, there are wills," I say loudly.

"—and if they specified guardians, that will help things immensely."

I pause. "And if they didn't?"

"Then I need to arrange for transportation back to Minnesota."

"Minnesota! But why?"

"Because he falls under the jurisdiction of the Minnesota DCFS."

I sit forward in my chair. "Please tell me you're not thinking of putting him in *foster care*."

"Unless the wills made other—"

"The hell with that! I'll take him!" My voice sounds angry, but in fact it's panic. I'm frightened to death for that little baby who had his downy head pressed beneath my chin just minutes ago.

"Annemarie, it's not that simple."

"Of course it is. We're family, and we want to take him."

"It doesn't work that way. We can't just hand babies over to anyone—"

"We're not anyone! We're family!"

Sandra sighs. "Eva is. But legally, you're not. And Eva is underage, so she can't take custody. But if you're sure you want to do this, I can help you get licensed as a foster parent."

"Uh. Well then," I say, slightly appeased.

"But you realize you won't be able to just leave here with the baby."

"Why not?"

"Even if we get started tomorrow, the licensing and training process takes anywhere from four to six months."

I straighten up in my chair. "Four to six months!" I sputter. "That's absolutely insane!"

"Eva will have visitation rights, of course."

"Fat lot of good that will do her if he's in Minnesota and she's in New Hampshire!"

"I'm sorry, Annemarie. I didn't make the rules."

I am stunned, left staring at her face in horror. Eventually I realize the futility of arguing. "No. Of course you didn't. So he's going into a foster home for four to six months no matter what?"

"Unless the wills—"

"Yes, yes, unless the wills, etcetera, etcetera," I say

testily. I slump back into my seat. "So what do we have to do?"

"I'll bring the application forms tomorrow. You'll need to provide me with references and fill out medical forms for everyone in the house. We also have to take fingerprints. We can get all that in motion before you go home."

"And then?" I say weakly.

"And then we'll check your references and run criminal background checks—"

My stomach drops through the floor. Every one of us, including Mutti, has had a run-in with the law over the course of the last year. None of us was actually arrested, per se, but that doesn't leave me feeling very confident.

"—and if everything checks out, a caseworker will come out and do a home study."

"And that takes four to six months?"

"The lengthiest part of the process is the training classes. They only run every three months, so you'll have to wait for the next session to start."

I sit forward, outraged. "Training classes! Why would I need training classes? I've already raised a child! I know what to do!"

Sandra shakes her head. "Annemarie, believe me. I understand your frustration. But you also have to understand that there is absolutely nothing I can do about this."

There's a long silence, broken only by the sound of the clock's minute hand wobbling forward.

I rise stiffly, crunching the tissue in my fist. "I'll find out about the wills."

She reaches into her jacket pocket and pulls out a business card. It is tasteful, unornamented. "If I'm out of my office, leave a message. I'll check in at regular intervals. You can also have me paged."

I turn to leave.

"Annemarie?"

I stop in front of the door, my hand already on the knob. I'm afraid to turn around. "Yes?"

"I just want to say . . . I think that what you want to do is remarkable."

"No," I say, still facing the door. "I'm just doing what anybody else would do."

There's a slight pause before she answers. "I only wish that were the case. Trust me. It's remarkable."

I hope she continues to think so after she sees our background checks.

• • •

I stop by Jeremy's room long enough to tell Mutti that I have to go back to the hotel room to take care of some business.

Jeremy is sleeping in his crib. Eva is passed out cold on the window seat, which has been transformed into a single bed. The blinds have been drawn, and she's curled in the fetal position, wrapped in a thin blanket with her back toward me.

Mutti sits in the rocker by the crib. Its side is dropped, and Mutti's fingertips rest against the baby's.

"I have to make some phone calls," I say, speaking quietly into her ear. "If you can possibly keep Eva away, please do. If you can't—well, I don't know what. I guess I'll go on a walk with my cell phone."

Mutti nods. She looks as awful as I feel, with dark gray circles beneath her eyes and blotchy skin.

"Is there anything I can do to help?" she whispers.

"Other than keeping Eva away, no."

"Are you calling funeral homes?"

"No. I've got to take care of something else first."

Mutti trains narrowed eyes on me. "What?"

I glance first at Eva—who heaves a great shuddering sigh—and then at Jeremy, who sleeps on his back with all four limbs spread out, palms facing the ceiling.

I lower my voice, and then lean so that I'm once again speaking into her ear. "They want to discharge Jeremy into foster care—in Minnesota no less. So obviously I'm applying to become a foster parent."

"Well, *of course* you are," Mutti sputters indignantly.

Again, tears spring into my eyes. "They're trying to tell me it will take four to six months, but I don't believe it yet. I'm going to call some of Roger's lawyer friends and see if there are any alternatives."

"*Mein Gott.* Yes. Obviously. Go, shoo," she says, flicking one hand toward the door. "Go fix things. In the meantime, if I have to chain myself to him, I will. Go!"

I practically run back to the hotel room.

Hell, who am I kidding. I run the whole way.

• • •

Despite its being nearly a year since I last called, my fingers dial Roger's office phone number without so much as a fraction of hesitation. I can choose between Alfred Gaines or Lawrence Scoville. I choose Lawrence, because he was close to Roger, even though he hates me.

It wasn't like this at the beginning, of course. When he and Roger were first made partners, the two of them had big plans for us. We were supposed to be "couple friends"—or even "power couple friends"—since in the late eighties and early nineties that was part of the required wardrobe of an upwardly mobile lawyer.

As couples go, we seemed like a good fit. The two men were rising stars, and Peggy and I were homemakers with babies of about the same age. Roger and Lawrence had starry-eyed visions of dinner dates, bridge games, shared vacations, charity balls, and golf outings. The problem was that the dinner dates and bridge games were supposed to involve gourmet cooking by the lovely stay-at-home wives, the shared vacations were supposed to involve Peggy and me keeping our toddlers from drowning in the surf while Roger and Lawrence went deep-sea fishing, and the golf outings left us—Peggy, me, and our babies—stranded at home on playdates.

I never was any good at playdates.

I'll admit I was having some trouble back then, figuring out what I wanted to do with my life, and it's entirely clear I didn't try very hard at my role in the foursome. Housewifery was my second career, and the main reason I chose it was that it was the furthest thing I could think of from competitive riding. By the time all this was going on, I had already tired of it. And eventually I blew up. Unfortunately, it happened in front of Lawrence. That was fourteen years ago, and he hasn't said a civil word since. But still, he's Roger's partner and best friend, and so I think I need to speak to him.

"Aldrich, Scoville, and Gaines," says a sweet young voice.

"Brenda?" I say.

"No, I'm sorry. Brenda's no longer here."

"Oh. Well, anyway, I need to speak to Mr. Scoville," I say.

"Certainly. May I tell him who's calling?"

"Annemarie Zimmer. Aldrich," I add quickly, realizing he may not recognize my maiden name, to which I've reverted.

"One moment, please," she says.

There's a click and I'm left listening to Pachelbel's Canon, sullied by ocean waves.

After a long wait, there's another click. "I'm sorry, Mr. Scoville can't take your call right now. May I take a message?"

My jaw drops in indignation. I shouldn't be surprised—Lawrence has never made much of an effort at hiding his feelings about me. But to refuse my call? That is simply too much.

"Tell Mr. Scoville this won't take long. I really need to talk to him."

"Uh . . ." says the hapless girl.

"Please. This is important."

She goes off. The Pachelbel returns, fighting hard against the synthesized tweeting of birds.

"Mr. Scoville says that he's in a phone conference that starts in four minutes, and he really can't—"

"Tell *Lawrence,*" I say, hissing out his name, "that if he doesn't take my phone call, I will call his personal line once a minute, on the minute, for the rest of the day; and if that fails, I will do the same to his cell phone. I need to speak to him."

I don't have either of those phone numbers, but I don't suppose he knows that.

The distraught receptionist catches her breath. "One moment, please," she says in a quavering voice.

Another click. Now the birdsong and ocean waves are combined, completely overwhelming the Canon.

"Annemarie!" Lawrence booms, pretending that he

didn't just try to refuse my call. "Long time no hear. How are you?"

"I'm terrible, Lawrence."

His voice changes to alarm. "Why? What's going on?"

"I need to know who Roger's family lawyer is."

"Uh," he says. I can hear the cogs turning in his head. "I really don't think it's my place to, uh . . . Why don't you just ask Roger? I thought you were all at a horse show together?"

"Roger's dead, Lawrence. So is Sonja. And the state is trying to place their child in foster care."

A deep gasp comes through the phone line.

"I can't let that happen," I continue. "I need to find out what the will said, and I mean in the next hour or two."

"How? What happened? And they're both . . . ? Oh dear God, dear God—"

I hear an explosion of crying at the other end of the phone; manly, choking noises that hardly sound human. My animosity melts completely. A lump rises in my own throat.

"They pulled out in front of a tractor trailer on I-88," I say softly. "The truck had a full load and no chance of stopping."

"So it was . . . quick?"

"Sonja died on impact. She never knew a thing."

"And Roger?"

I pause. "He hung on for a while. He died last night. It was . . . for the best."

Lawrence is silent for a moment as he absorbs this. "But the baby's alive?"

"Alive. And fine. Practically unscathed. He's got a fairly impressive goose egg on his forehead and a greenstick fracture of the ulna, but it's almost healed. In fact, he's well enough that they want to discharge him from the hospital. As you know, Roger had no family. Apparently neither did Sonja. I need to find out whether the will said anything about guardianship. Because if it didn't, they're going to ship Jeremy out to some foster home in Minnesota even though I said I want to take him."

"Oh Christ . . . I don't believe this . . . oh shit . . . I wonder if he did it yet . . ."

"What in God's name are you talking about, Lawrence?"

There's a long pause. He swallows hard before he speaks again. "When Jeremy was first born they asked Peggy and me to take him if anything happened. But then . . . Peggy left me a month ago, took off with a cardiologist, so I asked him to change it. I don't know if he did, but knowing Roger . . . Oh God, Annemarie. I'm so sorry. No!" he yells suddenly, taking the phone from his ear and shouting at someone else in the room. "Put them off! I'm busy!"

There's female mumbling in the background.

"Heidi, I don't give a good goddamn. Put them off. In fact, clear the rest of my day. Now go. And close the door behind you." He returns to me. "Okay, okay," he says, breathing heavily, trying to calm himself. "So if Roger didn't sort out something else, they're going to put the kid in foster care?"

"Yes."

"And they won't just let you be the foster parent?"

"Yes, but apparently it takes four to six months to get licensed, and in the meantime, they're taking him back to Minnesota to place him with strangers, never mind that I'm the closest thing he's got to a . . . ." Now it's me who has to pause. "Lawrence, I know you and I never saw eye to eye, and I know that I was . . . oh hell, I was selfish and self-centered and confused and difficult and a whole lot of other things when I was younger, and if I were you, I'm not sure I would have liked me either. But I've changed. I swear to God, I've changed. I want to do the right thing here. That baby belongs with Eva and me. We're his family. Please, please—whatever you may have thought of me in the past, *please* help me."

There's a long silence.

I breathe steadily, waiting.

"Where can I reach you?" he says finally. "I'll look into this right away."

I give him the hotel's phone number.

"Do you also have a cell?"

"Yes, but if I'm in the hospital it'll be turned off. You can leave a message, though."

"Give me the caseworker's name and phone number."

I do.

"Hold tight, Annemarie. Roger has friends. So do I. We'll figure this out. I promise you. We'll figure this out."

When I hang up, I sit on the edge of the bed pressing a fist into the center of my chest.

Day before yesterday I was still angry at Roger for leaving me and I hated Sonja outright. Ten minutes ago Lawrence wasn't willing to take my phone call.

Now I'd do anything to bring Roger back. Even Sonja—for whom I have a new respect now that I know her circumstances, and that she made it through law school anyway. And perhaps most surprising of all, Lawrence and I—and I assume half the judicial system in Minnesota—are now in cahoots to secure custody of Jeremy.

An event like this rewrites everything. Absolutely everything. And then as a final gesture, it chucks the pen in the trash.

• • •

My head pounds so badly I wonder if I'm having a stroke. It would be somehow fitting—one parent after another in our family, popping off like a string of firecrackers. Did Pappa have any idea what he was starting? I am seized with irrational and sudden terror, see an attractive opening, and dive through onto the soft crash pad of superstition.

Things come in threes. So. We're done. I'll analyze no further.

I go into the bathroom and root through my toiletries until I find some ibuprofen. Then, I'm ashamed to admit, I root through Mutti's things, hoping to find some Valium.

And then, as much as I'd love to continue to just lie on the bed (my God! I've been lying on the bedspread! The *bedspread*!), I realize that I really ought to go back to the hospital. There's nothing more I can do until I hear from Lawrence.

As I step into the hallway and pull the door shut behind me, I turn my head to the left. And then I freeze, because four doors down from me, with a suitcase sitting beside him, fiddling with the card that's supposed to give him access to his room, is a tall man with broad shoulders.

His head turns at the exact same moment as mine.

"Dan!" My hands fly to my face. My eyelids flicker.

Before I know it, I'm seeing black-and-white zaps through the fluttering wings of a butterfly. Just as my eyes slam shut, I see him cross the space between us. My knees dissolve beneath me, but it doesn't matter because his arms are already around me.

Chapter 17

I think he carries me to his room. At any rate, the next time I'm fully aware of my surroundings, I'm on the edge of a queen-sized bed in a room that's not mine, leaning against Dan, allowing my body to melt against his and relishing the feel of his limbs, his warmth, his strength.

Whatever happened before is unimportant. It's okay if he doesn't want to marry me. It's a piece of paper. A mere formality. He loves me. I know this. He's here, isn't he? He's here, and I don't give a damn, I don't give a damn, I don't give a damn about anything else. And I'm never letting him go again.

I fall completely apart, blubbering incomprehensible news into his shoulder. I break down like I've never broken down before, and suddenly can't imagine what had previously held me together—whatever it was, it had all the staying power of paper clips and masking tape.

But he grasps all. He understands me even though I speak jagged words with a tongue three times its normal size and take frequent breaks to choke with the violence of my sobs, my body wracked by spasms.

Eventually, my body's survival instincts kick in and I begin to calm down. I lean against Dan, waiting for the stress chemicals to dissipate. They do, subsiding in lessening waves. Dan just holds me.

Finally I am still. We're lying on the bed now, spoon style, with his arms wrapped around me and his knees tucked in behind mine.

"So you're taking Jeremy?" he says.

"I'm trying my damnedest. It looks like I might get him eventually, unless Roger and Sonja made other arrangements. And unless the state finds my circumstances to be less than ideal."

"They won't."

"What about our police records?"

"Don't be ridiculous. You don't have police records."

"We don't?"

"Of course not. Nobody was convicted of anything. None of you was even arrested."

"What about the interrogations?"

"Trust me. They don't show up."

"Are you sure?"

"Absolutely. Don't forget I deal with criminal animal neglect all the time. I see the same people time and time again, but if they don't get convicted, their records are clean and there's not a damned thing anyone can do to prevent them from turning around and getting other animals."

"But what about the home inspection? Our house is so small Jeremy wouldn't even have his own room—unless I kick Eva out of hers, but even if I do that, I'll already be sleeping in the study, so where does that leave Eva? We can't turn every downstairs room into a bedroom. And I doubt they'll be impressed if I install him in the stable apartment with me."

"The stable apartment is perfectly fine. And besides, even if that's where he sleeps for a while, it will only be temporary."

"What do you mean?"

Dan struggles into a sitting position. I roll so that I'm facing him.

He stares at me. Hard.

"Dan, what do you mean?"

"Annemarie, I should have explained this a long time ago because obviously it became an issue between us. I should never have let it go that far. The thing is, I had a vision of how this should happen, and I guess I was a little pigheaded about it."

I think I've stopped breathing.

"We haven't gone anywhere or done anything recently because I was saving up." He digs a hand into his jeans and pulls out a wadded tissue. "I know how you feel about the trailer, and I always assumed we'd adopt, so I've been saving up to build a proper house. I wanted it to be a surprise."

I struggle onto my elbows, staring at the crumpled tissue as he carefully peels away its edges. He stares at it awkwardly, and then hands it to me. "It looked better before I had it baked into a soufflé."

In the center of the tissue is a diamond ring. At least I think it's a diamond. The whole thing is encrusted with chocolate.

"Before you . . . Oh my God. Dan, why didn't you come after me?"

"I followed you as far as the door, but I couldn't leave the soufflé. And to be honest, I was more than a little annoyed. You gave me no chance whatever to explain."

"Oh God, Dan, I'm so sorry. I'm so, so sorry. And then I—" I clap a hand to my mouth, horrified. "Oh, Dan. I'm a horrible human being."

"Horrible, no. Stubborn and completely impossible, definitely."

"You tried to explain, and I wouldn't even listen. Not only did I not listen to you but I . . ." I drop my gaze. "I'm not sure I should tell you this."

"What?"

"No. I can't tell you."

"Why?"

"Because I'm afraid you'll get mad and leave."

"Annemarie, you've done eight million stupid things since I've known you, and where am I?" He puts his finger beneath my chin and lifts my face so that he's staring me straight in the eye. "Hmm? Where am I?"

I look at him sheepishly. "I was hiding in Hurrah's stall when you came to the stable. I was crouched beneath his water bucket. In fact, my hair got stuck in the handle when I stood up."

He stares at me for a moment, and then plucks the ring from between my thumb and forefinger.

My jaw drops.

He rises and goes into the bathroom.

I am speechless, mortified. Paralyzed, even. I realize I acted like a complete and utter idiot, but surely, *surely,* he's not mad enough to flush my ring down the toilet?

"Dan—" I wail from the bed, dissolving once again into tears.

He closes the door and turns on the fan. Despite this

cover, strange noises emerge. Water running, rhythmic swishing. Is he brushing his teeth? He wants to dump me with fresh breath?

The door opens and Dan emerges. He stands in the doorway for a moment, his head cocked to the side, eyes drilling holes through my head.

"Dan, I—" I start desperately.

"Shhh," he says, crossing the room. "You can talk in a minute, but not right now. Right now you're not allowed to say a word."

I shut my mouth.

He lowers himself onto the bedspread beside me and takes my left hand in his. With his right, he produces a minty-fresh and sparkling diamond.

"Annemarie," he says, gazing into my eyes, "will you do me the very great honor of—"

I grasp his head in both hands, and smush my mouth into his.

After all, he did forbid me to speak.

• • •

I feel guilty for the joy I feel and the love we make because its intensity rivals the horror and grief that have filled my heart for two days. But then I realize the grief is still there, and what we just did was life-affirming and good.

"We've got to get back to the hospital," I say suddenly, extricating myself and grabbing my clothes.

"Yes, of course."

I struggle into my bra and pull on my underwear. "But first I need to stop by my room and see if Lawrence left a message."

Dan simply nods. When we're both dressed, he steps forward and opens the door for me.

When we reach my room, the red light on the telephone is blinking.

"Oh God," I say, rushing over. "Oh shit." My hands flap beside my face. "How do you pick up messages? My brain is fried. Dan, help!"

He comes around to the table between the beds and takes the receiver from my hands.

"Dan, wait!"

He freezes, waiting for me to explain myself. Since I don't, he says, "What?"

"I don't know if I want to know."

"Why?"

"Because I don't want them to have made other arrangements for Jeremy. I want that baby. I don't just want *a* baby. I want that one."

Dan watches my face for a moment, glances at the keypad, and then presses a single button. Then he hands me the phone.

"Annemarie, this is Lawrence. I've got copies of Roger's and Sonja's wills. They didn't designate anyone as a guardian for Jeremy, but they did leave fairly specific instructions about burial. They wanted to be cremated and have their ashes interred with those of Roger's parents."

A pang runs through me, because at one point that was where I was supposed to end up. Roger and I fought about it because lapsed or not, I was born a Catholic and felt I should end up in consecrated ground. You know, just in case I'm wrong about the whole God thing. Roger won that one, mostly because I didn't have a whole lot of room for argument. I'd been spewing my belief of dead-as-dead for as long as he'd known me, and my own family didn't even have a burial plot—yet.

So much has changed. And yet, in his unimaginative Roger-ish way, I imagine that part of his will is exactly the same, cut and pasted with just the name of the wife swapped out.

"The executor is Terry Hatchett, someone Roger and I both play golf with—"

Dear God. He's still talking about Roger in the present.

"—I just got off the phone with him. Since he's the executor and Roger was so specific about final arrangements, Terry can take care of all of it, although it's fine if you want to be involved. Now, about that boy. I don't have any specific news yet, but I want you to know that Terry is working on it at this very moment. Meanwhile, I'm checking out another angle. I'll try back in a bit, but if you haven't heard from me in a couple of hours, please call. Hang in there, Annemarie. Oh! God, I think I forgot to mention that Terry is a federal judge. For what that's worth."

There's a click, and then an unpleasant automated voice asking if I'd like to delete, replay, or save the message. I seem incapable of choosing, so I simply hang up.

"What's up?" says Dan. "Was that Lawrence?"

I nod.

"And?"

"And . . . they didn't specify a guardian."

I'm in such a hurry I bang my hip on the bedside

table while snatching my purse from the bed. Then I rush from the room, with Dan following close behind.

• • •

The scene that greets us at the door to Jeremy's room would be heartwarming under different circumstances.

Mutti and Eva are sitting on the window seat with Jeremy sprawled between them. Mutti is at his head, and Eva at his feet. He's wearing a baby-sized hospital gown—one of those flannel things with a tie at the neck and a completely open back. They've lifted it up to his armpits and are taking turns leaning forward and applying zerberts to his exposed tummy.

Jeremy goes into spasms of glee before their lips even reach his belly. His giggles are so uncontained, so delighted, that once again I'm in danger of breaking down.

When Eva and Mutti see Dan, they stop. They turn as one, searching my face for a signal. My hands are steepled, held up against my lips, trembling. Mutti's eyes pop open. Eva's eyebrows rise.

They've seen my ring.

Dan crosses the room and drops down beside Eva.

"I'm so sorry, honey. I'm so sorry," he says, gathering her in his arms.

She twists at the waist to meet him, and has more or less the same reaction I had: she dissolves against him and howls.

Jeremy's eyes widen. Then he opens his mouth and shrieks in sympathy. Mutti scoops him off the window seat, and sets off across the room, singing into his ear and jiggling up and down. I rush to the door, close it, and then return to the window seat. Dan still has his arms wrapped around Eva, so I sit behind them and wrap my arms around both of them as far as I can reach.

Eventually Eva's outburst subsides. Shortly thereafter, Jeremy also falls quiet. Mutti brings him back to the window seat and perches on the edge. And there we sit, the five of us.

After a while, Dan says, "May I hold him?"

Mutti rises immediately and deposits Jeremy on his knee. "His head is still a bit wobbly, so be careful," she says. Dan slides his hands beneath the baby's arms. His hands are so large they meet behind Jeremy's back.

"Well, look at you," he croons, leaning down to look into Jeremy's eyes. Dan is wearing an expression I've never seen before. He's soaking in every detail.

Jeremy's dark blue eyes widen. His bottom lip quivers. And then he opens his mouth and bawls, his tongue undulating behind toothless gums. His fists tremble, his eyes scrunch shut.

"Oh, sorry, sorry!" Dan says hastily, holding him up toward Mutti.

"Here, I'll take him," I say, swooping him away.

Jeremy looks doubtful, but when I murmur and rock back and forth, he relaxes and falls quiet.

Dan lifts Eva's hand and holds it in both of his. She doesn't look at him, but I notice her fingers curl around his.

"Ursula, how are you holding up?" says Dan.

"Ech," replies Mutti. "As well as I can. In situations like this, that's all you can do."

Dan nods. He looks up suddenly, glancing around the room. "I had hoped I'd never see the inside of a hospital again after Jill died," he says.

Everyone is quiet for almost a full minute.

"Say, it's almost two o'clock," Dan says suddenly, releasing Eva's hand and patting his thighs. "Have any of you eaten yet?"

"The nurses brought us trays, but since they couldn't guarantee that the food was vegan, young miss here wouldn't touch it," says Mutti.

"Vegan, huh?" says Dan, glancing at Eva.

She nods. There's just the slightest hint of pride about her lips.

"I think we'd better go out and get some food into you," Dan says, rising.

"No," says Eva. "We can't leave Jeremy."

"You go," I say. "I'll stay with Jeremy. You too, Mutti."

"Are you sure, *Liebchen*?" says Mutti. "I could stay with you."

What she's really asking is if there's any news, other than what is obvious from my left hand.

"No, I'll be fine. Take your time. We'll catch up later."

She nods in understanding and turns away.

"Oh!" she says, spinning back. "If Jeremy gets hungry, there's a kitchen just down the hall to the right. There's no door. You'll see it. There are bottles of formula and disposable nipples in boxes on the counter. He uses the orthodontic kind."

"The what kind?"

"The ones that are not round. The nipples are flat on one side—never mind, you'll see. Just screw one onto a bottle, and you're good to go. And they want us to record how much he drank and when on this chart."

"When did he last eat?"

Mutti consults her watch. "Forty minutes ago. You

can probably put him down for a nap." She turns to face
Dan and Eva. "All right then. Let's go find some rabbit
food."

As they leave, Dan pauses just long enough to kiss me.
He also plants a light kiss on the back of Jeremy's head.

• • •

About ten minutes later, I've just gotten Jeremy down.
He's lying on his side, and I've propped him up with
rolled towels on each side so he won't roll onto his
stomach. I've left the side of the crib down because
I'm sitting right at its edge, gazing upon his sleeping
face and the raised purple bruise in the center of his
forehead.

I can't see Roger in him. Nor can I see Sonja. I suppose that might develop later, but right now he just
looks like Jeremy.

"Annemarie," says a voice from the doorway.

It's Sandra. She's leaning against the frame, a thick
folder under her arm.

I hold a finger to my lips and point at the sleeping
baby. Then I carefully pull up the side of the crib, waiting for each side to click so that it's secure.

I walk toward Sandra, who spins on her heel and
leaves the room. She leads me to the same conference
room as before, always staying ahead of me, which
strikes me as strange.

When we get to the room, she takes a seat and sets
her folder in front of her, still without saying a word.
She straightens its edges so that it's square with the
edge of the table. Only then does she raise her eyes to
mine. She leans backward in her chair.

"So I got a phone call from the Inspector General this afternoon."

She stares at me, her lips pursed in a crabby rictus. She crosses her legs and begins bobbing her foot.

"I beg your pardon?" I say.

"It looks like he got a phone call from the Secretary of State. Congratulations," she says without smiling. "It looks like you'd better get yourself a car seat. Because I can assure you I'll be inspecting it personally before you leave the hospital."

"I . . . I beg your pardon?" I repeat weakly.

"There's some paperwork to fill out, but it appears you've been granted temporary custody of Jeremy until we can get out to do the home studies and background checks."

My hand springs to my mouth. "Oh my God! Sandra, thank you!"

"Oh, don't thank me," she says, looking back down at her manila file folder and tracing loop-de-loops on its cover with her finger.

"I'm sorry?"

This time when she meets my gaze, her anger is clear. "You look like a nice enough person, but then again, so did Ted Bundy and Paul Bernardo. And Karla Homolka looked wholesome enough. Would it have been wise to hand babies over to them?"

"Karla Who?"

"The woman who helped her husband rape and kill teenage girls, including her own sister. And video-taped it."

"Sandra, I'm not . . . My God, you don't actually think I'm like that, do you?"

"No. I don't. But evidently you think the normal rules don't apply to you, and I don't appreciate people going over my head."

"I didn't do anything."

"Oh really," she says wryly, leaning back in her seat and folding her arms across her chest.

"I'm a riding instructor! Part-time, at that. I don't hold any sway with anyone."

"Well, apparently somebody you know does."

I look at the table for a moment, considering. "Okay. Here's everything I know. As you know, Roger was a lawyer. This morning, after we met, I went back to the hotel and called one of his partners. I asked him to track down the will and tell me what it said about guardianship. He said he'd get back to me."

Sandra drops her chin to her chest and scowls at me above her glasses.

"Then I got distracted for a couple of hours. My . . . fiancé showed up and I had to fill him in on what was going on. He didn't even know that Roger was dead yet."

Sandra's eyes spring open. She sits forward almost violently. "Your fiancé? Your *fiancé*? Why didn't you mention this fiancé before?"

"I didn't think it was relevant," I say, not wanting to admit that Dan was not my fiancé the last time we spoke.

"It's incredibly relevant. For instance, how does he feel about taking on a four-month-old baby?"

"We've always planned to adopt," I say meekly. "I can't have any more children."

Sandra stares at me, shaking her head slightly. I can't tell if it's in disgust or disbelief. Probably both.

"So anyway, when I got back to my room, there was a

message waiting for me. Lawrence—Roger's partner—had tracked down the wills. They had very specific instructions for burial, which the executor is now taking care of. But they said nothing about guardianship. Anyway, the last thing the message said was that the executor was 'working on it.' That's all I know."

"Working on it," says Sandra. Now she's nodding, her eyes exuding fury. "I'm tempted to ask you what business this executor is in, but I think maybe I don't want to know."

I swallow in embarrassment. "It's not what you're thinking. Not at all. He's a federal judge."

Sandra looks at me for a while. Then she sighs. Her whole body softens. "Oh. Well, in that case, this makes perfect sense."

"It does?"

"Oh yes. Considering the political ambitions of a certain somebody I shall not name."

"I'm sorry you got railroaded," I say. "I swear to you, I didn't know what they were going to do. But I'm not going to pretend I'm unhappy that Jeremy is coming home with us. It's where he belongs. I'm sure the normal set of safeguards makes sense statistically, but I'm not Karla Homolka. Don't you think, in your heart of hearts, that this is better than sending him to yet another home, keeping him there just long enough for him to get used to them, and then tearing him away again?"

Sandra's eyes flicker. Then she looks down at her folder.

"At any rate," I repeat. "I'm sorry you were railroaded."

"So," she says, ignoring my apology. "We'd best get started on the paperwork because the hospital wants to discharge Jeremy tomorrow. I'm guessing it's more likely to happen the next day because I have to get all of this," she stabs the folder with her forefinger, "signed off at my end. And even though it's been suggested to me that I make it a priority"—another quick disapproving glance—"it's still a lot of paperwork."

She pulls out a sheaf of papers almost three inches thick. Each form turns out to be a stack of thin colored sheets—white, yellow, pink, green, and blue—attached at the top by a perforated strip.

"Are there five copies of each of those?" I ask in astonishment.

"Oh, at least," she says, pushing a fine-tipped ballpoint pen across at me. "Hope your wrist is strong."

Two and a half hours later, I press my wobbly signature onto the final form, flip to the blue copy at the back to make sure it's legible, and push it across the table.

"Well," says Sandra, adding it to the stack of finished forms. "I'll have these signed by Mr. Potato Head—er, the soon-to-be Attorney General of New Hampshire—and get back to you as soon as possible." She puts the forms into the folder and stands up.

I stare helplessly, not sure whether a thank-you would just annoy her further.

She glances at me and seems to take pity. "I'm sorry I was so hard on you earlier," she says. "I know you want what's best for Jeremy, and for what it's worth, I do think this will be better for him in the long run. I just hate seeing . . . Well, I won't bore you with my office politics, but let's just say there's a history."

She holds the folder in the crook of her left elbow and

reaches her hand across the table. I shake it, although my hand and wrist are numb with all the writing—or more accurately, the pressing—I've just done.

"I'll see you tomorrow or the next day. I'll bring that list of grief counselors we talked about," she says, heading for the door.

"Sandra?"

"Yes?"

"I'm not sorry about the result, but I'm sorry about the way this happened. I know you were trying to help me, and I appreciate it. Thank you."

There's a long pause. Finally she says, "You're welcome."

• • •

I burst into the baby's room. Dan is sitting on the window seat, jiggling Jeremy on his knee. Eva sits on the floor in front of them, wiggling her fingers and threatening Jeremy with tickles. Mutti sits in the gliding rocker reading a magazine.

They all look up.

"Well?" says Mutti.

I close the door and scream, "We got him!"

• • •

The nurses, who are not nearly as married to DCFS regulations as Sandra, are delighted. I remember the words of the first one, how they'd come to think of Jeremy as their own baby and, by God, I believe them. In their enthusiasm, they sneak us in four dinner trays, each of which holds a lobster tail, a filet mignon, and a swirl of piped garlic mashed potatoes. It's the celebratory dinner they serve to new parents on the maternity ward. They also let it be known that if we were to bring in our own bottle of champagne, it's unlikely that any of them would see it.

I offer to go out and get something suitably green and unbuttered for Eva, but she graciously allows me to eat my dinner while it's still hot. She decides to check out the cafeteria, and when she returns, raves about the salad bar. Her foam box has a few pieces of romaine and sweet peppers on the bottom, which are nearly obscured by a mountain of chickpeas.

Good. Protein, fiber, and probably lots of other good stuff as well.

When the nurse comes back to remove the dinner trays, she says that it would be fine if one of us wants to stay overnight with Jeremy. Although her words aren't specific, she's looking at me. I think it's at this moment that it really hits me.

I am once again a mother.

• • •

It occurs to me that I haven't had a shower in living memory (actually, I believe it was when Nathalie burst into our room at Strafford), so I excuse myself long enough to go back to the hotel to get cleaned up.

When Dan says he'll come with me, at first I think he wants to make love again. But when we get to our hallway, he passes my door and heads for his.

I stop in shocked surprise. "Where are you going?"

"To grab a few things," he says, and then looks at me as though that should be sufficient explanation. I guess I still look confused, because he continues. "I was thinking I'd spend the night at the hospital as well. Since I'm, you know, going to be his, er . . ."

I break into a huge grin. "His daddy?"

He blushes, bashful and happy, and then lets himself into his room.

Chapter 18

Dan and I spend the night perched carefully on the unfolded window seat, which is designed to hold a single person. Each time the baby moves—even though he never wakes up—our heads shoot off our shared pillow.

I get up a few times to adjust the light weave blanket that covers Jeremy from the chest down, but mainly just to look at him. It's all I can do to not pick him up and try to settle in the gliding rocker, but if there's one thing I remember clearly about Eva's days as an infant, it's that you never wake a sleeping baby.

And so I return to the window-seat-cum-bed and slide back against Dan's warm body. He throws an arm around me to keep me from falling off.

When morning comes and Jeremy finally begins to stir in earnest, Dan leaps over my prone form and heads for the door.

"Where are you going?" I ask.

"To get his bottle," he says.

I laugh.

"What?" he says, looking back at me with his hand on the doorknob.

"Nothing," I say, trying to keep from laughing. "Go! Go!"

Eva and Mutti show up while I'm in the middle of a diaper change. I am astonished at how terrible Eva looks. Her face is puffy, and her eyes have dark circles around them. She drags herself across the room and throws herself down on the window seat.

I do the tabs of the diaper up quickly, look at Mutti and incline my head toward the door, asking her to follow me.

Once we're out in the hallway and the door is closed, I turn to her. "What's going on? What happened?"

"She had a bad night. She had a nightmare about Roger, and then couldn't get back to sleep."

"Oh no. Should I have stayed at the hotel with you two?"

"No, *Schatzlein*. Although if we stay another night, you may want to consider letting her spend the night here as well. The only thing she's been talking about since three this morning was when we could come back."

Dan returns from the kitchen with a bottle. "What's going on?"

"Eva had a rough night."

"Where is she now?"

"In the room."

He turns and peers through the small window, tapping his chin with his finger.

"Dan?" I say.

"What?"

"What are you thinking?"

Instead of responding, he opens the door and goes in. Mutti and I follow.

"Come on, Eva, get your stuff," says Dan.

"Huh?" she says, frowning.

"You and I've got some shopping to do. It's a good thing I brought my truck."

For a moment it looks like Eva will refuse. But then she rises and grabs her jacket.

"Where are you going?" I say, turning to Dan, who is struggling to get his second arm into his own jacket.

"Family business," he says, winking. He turns back to Eva. "Come on, Kiddo. We've got a lot of ground to cover."

• • •

It's late afternoon before we see them again.

"Ma!" says Eva, bursting through the door. "Holy crap! You won't believe all the stuff we bought!"

Dan follows her, looking very smug.

"Like what?" I say from my perch on the window seat. The doctor came in this afternoon and removed Jeremy's splint, so Mutti and I have been trying, unsuccessfully, to teach him patty-cake. Peekaboo is much more successful.

"Like a crib, a playpen, a bottle sterilizer, bottles, sleepers, snowsuit, onesies, blankets, slippers, sheets, socks, a changing table, diapers, wipes—oh, and a wipe warmer—a nursery lamp, one of those windup music box mobile thingies, a dresser, bumper pads, a battery-operated swing that plays lullabies, a car seat, a stroller, rattles, stuffed animals, one of those spring-up baby gyms with toys that dangle—Oh! And an Exer-Saucer! Wait until you see it! It's got everything— piano keys, and chewable butterflies, and frogs, and sparkly water bubbles—"

"Whoa! Whoa!" I cry out in alarm. I turn to Dan, dumbfounded. "Dan! Is this true?"

He smiles wickedly. "She missed a few things. But yeah, it's more or less true."

"We didn't need to get all that! At least not *here!*" I lower my voice to a whisper and lean in close. "Besides, surely they'll send us his other stuff at some point."

"Trust me. We needed every last stuffed duck."

I glance over at Eva, who has taken over my spot in the patty-cake lesson, her face shiny and bright.

"Besides," Dan continues, "we're going to need two of almost everything anyway. One for your mother's house, and one for ours."

"Does it all fit in your truck?"

"Not sure. We made several trips. But if it doesn't, we can always rent a U-Haul."

"A U-Haul?"

"Only if we have to," he says, slipping out of his jacket. He pulls a book out from under his arm: *What to Expect the First Year.*

He settles on the rocker and puts his feet up. He flips through the book until he finds the chapter he's looking for, and is lost to the world for an hour and a half.

• • •

In the middle of the next afternoon, Jeremy's doctors, accompanied by Sandra, come to discharge him.

We had been forewarned by the nurses that he was going to be released—and also that, even though we are only walking him across the street to the hotel, DCFS would be inspecting our car seat. Despite this obvious disconnect in logic (after all, they're not also checking the crib or stroller), I don't want to buck any more of Sandra's rules. And so the softly padded car seat sits conspicuously on the floor at the end of the crib.

Sandra takes one look at it—a Britax Marathon in a pattern called "cowmooflage"—and rolls her eyes so hard that if I were her mother I'd warn her about them getting stuck up there. But at least she seems satisfied that we don't intend to bungee-cord the child to the roof of the car.

She hands me a thick manila envelope, shakes my hand, and wishes me luck. Her eyes are stern while she's talking to me, but when she shakes Mutti's and Dan's hands, they're filled with kindness. And when she pulls Eva into a hug, I see the Sandra I first met— the one who wasn't railroaded and humiliated. But while I feel bad about upsetting her faith in the system, I'm still utterly unrepentant about the outcome.

And so, fifteen minutes later, we cross the street to the hotel. Dan leads, carrying the cow-spotted car seat. Mutti and Eva follow, clutching hands. I bring up the rear, grasping Jeremy tight to my chest because he's swimming in his brand-new red snowsuit with farm animals on it, and I can't help feeling he'll slip from my grasp.

• • •

Although there's nothing tying us to Lebanon anymore, we stay an extra night. Partly because it's a long drive home and it's already late afternoon; and partly because Dan now freely admits that we need a U-Haul.

My understanding of the situation isn't complete until Dan swings open the door of his hotel room and I see the sheer volume of things he and Eva purchased. It's nothing short of astounding. Bulging plastic bags cover both beds and the easy chair. Boxes containing the furniture and larger items fill the center of the room. Obviously, we're all sleeping in the other room tonight.

Dan is completely unapologetic.

Although Eva is eager to give the new playpen with its removable full-sized bassinet a test drive, I wait until she and Dan run out to pick up our dinner and then call the front desk to see if they offer cribs.

It arrives just as Dan and Eva return carrying brown paper bags of Chinese food.

Eva takes one look at the hotel's crib and shakes her head. "Uh-uh. No way."

I investigate the inside and find that it is lined with a full-sized sheet. I'm not impressed, but I happen to know that we have several sets of crib sheets in the room four doors down the hall, along with a suspender-type device to keep them in place. But even so, this glaring fault leaves me dubious. "Did you guys get soda?" I ask Eva.

"Yeah," she says.

"Give me a can," I say, extending a hand sideways.

A cold Sprite appears. When it passes easily through the bars of the crib, I turn and tell the hotel employee that we won't be needing the crib after all. I also make a mental note to write a scathing letter to the head of the chain when we return home about exactly what happens when babies' heads get stuck through the bars of cribs.

It takes us forty-five minutes to figure out how to assemble the Pack 'n Play. You're supposed to straighten both the long sides first—or both the short ones—but if you don't do it in exactly the right order, the fourth won't lock. When it collapses on Eva's legs for the sixth time, she bursts into giggles and so does Jeremy.

Chapter 19

Back at Maple Brook, a small war erupts. I want the baby to sleep at the stable with me, and Mutti is insistent that he sleep at the house—with all of us. This issue doesn't arise until most of the things have been unloaded into the house and we're down to the crib, dresser, and nursery lamp. When I instruct Dan to drive the U-Haul down to the stable Mutti puts up a hand and yells, *"Nein!"*

"I beg your pardon?" My voice is weak, because I know the look on her face.

"What on earth are you thinking?"

"But, Mutti," I argue, "there's no room at the house."

"Of course there is. He can sleep in my room. You can sleep in Eva's. I'll move down to the dining room, and Eva can sleep in the study."

"No! No!" I say, shaking my head in horror. "Please! I don't want anyone sleeping in the dining room."

"Fine. Then I'll sleep in the living room."

"I don't want to sleep in the study!" cries Eva.

Dan steps forward with Jeremy on his hip. The baby

is tired, and his head rests on Dan's shoulder. "And where exactly am I going to sleep?"

This new development shuts all of us up.

Mutti recovers before I do. "You're moving in?"

"Well, yes. I sort of figured I would. Especially now that we've got Jeremy. Unless you object," he says.

"No," says Mutti, clearly stunned. "No, of course I don't object."

"Because we could wait until after we get married, but even then we're going to have to live here until the house is built," Dan continues.

"The house?" says Mutti, eyes widening even further.

"We're building a proper house at his place," I chime in.

"The trailer was fine for a bachelor," Dan explains, "but it's no place for a family. I only ever meant it to be temporary anyway. It's just that for a while there was no real urgency. Now there is," he says, taking Jeremy's little fist in his hand and moving it up and down.

"Ah," says Mutti. She presses her lips together and frowns into the distance. Then she turns back to us. "Okay then. You two will take my room. Jeremy will take Eva's. Eva can take the study, and I'll take the living room."

"Oma!" says Eva, turning in outrage. "You can't just kick me out of my room!"

"Why not? You're only spending one night a week there anyway."

"No, I'm not," Eva says miserably.

"What?" says Mutti.

I inhale deeply, realizing that with everything that's been going on, we never got around to telling Mutti what happened at Strafford. And also that I still have to retrieve Eva's things from Wyldewood.

"Well?" says Mutti expectantly, looking from Eva to me and then back again.

Eva kicks the gravel and storms off toward the stable.

I exhale, letting my lips rumble like a horse. "Dan, I guess you'd better bring the crib and stuff into the house." I grab as many of the plastic bags that hold Mutti's and my personal effects as I can, and hold them out to Mutti.

"I want to know what is going on," she says, taking the bags.

I loop the handles of three bags on each of my hands and start walking toward the house. "Come on inside," I say, inclining my head to indicate that she should follow. "I'll explain everything."

"Ahem," says Dan.

"Yes?" I say, stopping.

"If you want me to unload this stuff, one of you is going to have to take this baby."

Mutti and I bang into each other in our rush to ditch our bags back in the car. She beats me to it and ends up with Jeremy.

"Ha," she sniffs, passing me with what can only be described as a look of victory. Jeremy's head bobs up and down as he looks over Mutti's shoulder at Dan, who is trying unsuccessfully not to laugh.

• • •

With Jeremy installed in the ExerSaucer and Dan constructing furniture upstairs, Mutti and I sit in the winged chairs. After a moment, Mutti gets up and lights the fire, like I knew she was going to do all along.

Once the fire is going, Jeremy stares and stares and stares. He occasionally bangs a fist against the edge of the ExerSaucer, setting off a musical toy or sending a rattle spinning, but mostly he is entranced by the flames.

I explain Eva's situation to Mutti.

She gets up wordlessly, and returns with two glasses of wine. She hands me one, leans over to run a hand over the baby's blond tufty hair, and returns to her chair.

"*Und so.* What now?"

"I don't know. I haven't had a whole lot of time to think about it," I say, taking a swallow of wine. I hold the glass up so that I can see the fire through it. I like the way it distorts the flames, giving them a rounded, sensuous look. I also like how the flames reflect off my diamond.

"I suppose we could call the school and see if they'll let her re-enroll next year," says Mutti.

I shake my head. "No. Her school record is horrible. It's also predictable. She already lost last year. If we don't get her a tutor now, she'll lose this one as well."

"Are you going to try to get her back into Nathalie's?"

"I don't know. I don't even know if she wants to go back. Besides, I'm not sure being away from us for six days out of seven would be a good idea right now."

"Well, if she doesn't train somewhere, we have a serious problem."

I look up.

"Think about it, *Schatzlein.* If she's not training, and she's not going to school, what on earth will she be doing? Whatever it is, it won't be good. It won't even be her fault. She can't help herself."

"Ugh," I say, making a frog face. After a moment I slap my hands on my thighs.

Jeremy shakes his little fists in surprise, and for a moment I think he might cry. Then he recovers.

I rise and set my mostly full glass of wine down on the table—slowly, so as not to startle Jeremy again. "Okay. I'll go talk to her."

• • •

"Honey?" I say.

Eva has Flicka out in the cross-ties just outside her stall. Her purple plastic grooming tray is beside them, but Eva isn't grooming her. She's standing at her head, running her hands over Flicka's rounded Arabian cheeks and whispering into her cocked ear.

Eva glances at me, but just momentarily.

I walk behind Flicka, laying a hand on her rump so that she knows I'm there, and come to a stop beside Eva.

"You never told me Freddie had kittens," she says, her tone accusatory.

"Sorry," I say.

She straightens Flicka's forelock and then leans over and chooses a brush. She takes a few steps away from me and begins grooming, sweeping the bristles all over Flicka's body. She throws her whole body into the effort, swinging her arm round and round, and following the path of the brush with the palm of her other hand, smoothing the black hair until it shines like onyx.

"So are their eyes open yet?" I ask.

"Two of them," she says. "The other one's are still closed."

"Are they still on my bed?"

"Yup."

There's a long silence while she continues brushing. Soon she's bent over double, brushing Flicka's stomach. She pauses for a moment, switches the brush to the other hand, and drops her hand between Flicka's rear legs. She's checking to see if the crease between Flicka's teats needs cleaning, because when her udder gets itchy, she tends to rub her tail against walls, trees, and fences, which breaks off the hairs at the top. Eva takes great pride in the state of Flicka's tail, and so she has the cleanest udder in the stable. It's one of the benefits of having a mare, because cleaning a gelding's—or, God forbid, a stallion's—sheath is a whole different kettle of fish.

Eventually I step around to the grooming kit and pick up the long purple comb.

"May I?" I ask.

Eva glances at me. "Sure," she says.

I work on Flicka's tail in silence for several minutes. I work on it until I run out of tangles, and then I keep working on it because I enjoy the way the long hairs fall from my hands, shimmering like a waterfall even though they're coarse. I rub a little Cowboy Magic on my hands and massage it through the length, feeling the hair shafts smooth between my palms. An idea pops into my head, fully formed and from absolutely nowhere: I wonder whether anyone has ever strung a violin bow with black horsehair, and if not, why not.

"So, um," I say. Then I grind to a halt. I have no idea how to approach this.

"What?" says Eva, her face suddenly appearing over the top of Flicka's back, because she's been working on the other side.

"Well, I think we need to talk, don't you?"

"About what?"

"About what you want to do."

Her head disappears again, although I see flashes of dandy brush as Flicka gets the scouring of a lifetime.

"Do you want to go back to Nathalie's?"

There is no answer from the other side of Flicka.

"Okay, well," I continue, "if you don't want to, we can get you a tutor. And you can ride Hurrah. I mean, until we find you another horse, of course."

"I don't want another horse."

"Eva—"

"If I can't ride Joe, I'm not riding anybody."

Eva slams the brush into the grooming kit, ducks under the cross-tie, and marches down the aisle, leaving me alone with Flicka.

I undo the cross-ties and drop them against the walls—*clink, clink*. Then I take hold of Flicka's noseband, lead her into her stall, and remove her purple halter. After I slide her door shut, I hang the halter on the door. If a horse can be described as having a wardrobe, then Flicka's is purple. Grooming kit, halter, lunge line, lead rope, show sheet, brushes, buckets—even bell boots, although she never wears them.

After I get Flicka settled, I climb the stairs to the apartment. As I make my way up the dark wooden stairwell, I feel like I'm climbing the gallows.

Eva is collapsed across the bottom of my bed, bawling. Freddie is curled up against the pillows with her kittens lined up at her belly. They squiggle and squirm, looking, at least from the back, more like piglets now than rats. Their mother watches us with narrowed eyes.

"Eva? Honey?"

"What?" She sits up, takes the tissue I'm offering, and honks into it.

"Do you want to go back to Nathalie's?"

"She won't have me."

"Maybe. Maybe not. But that's not what I'm asking. I want to know if that's what you want."

She turns, her face crimson, clearly ready to yell. I take a step backward, bracing.

"I don't know! I want to have not fucked everything up! I want to not feel guilty because I can't imagine going on without Joe when Dad is dead! And I want Dad to not be dead!" Then she collapses into a crumpled heap on my bed, crying like she'll never stop.

I walk quietly to the foot of the bed and sit beside her. I rub her back for a while, and then drop forward so that my head is next to hers. I whisper shushes into her ear and stroke her mostly bald head rhythmically until she finally calms down. She remains slumped over.

"Come on, sweetie. Come back to the house with me," I say.

"No," says a muffled voice.

"Please?"

"No. I'll come later. I want to be alone for a while."

I sigh deeply, kiss the top of her head, and then leave quietly, taking care not to slam anything on my way out.

Hurrah nickers as I reach his stall. I stop just long enough to kiss his velvet-soft nose, which pokes through his feed hole.

• • •

When I get back to the house, Dan is sitting in my chair drinking a beer. My glass of wine is still on the table, so I grab it and take a seat on the floor in front of the ExerSaucer.

Jeremy looks like he's about to nod off, even though he's upright.

"How did it go?" says Mutti. "Or should I ask?"

"It didn't go very well. But at least now I know what I have to do."

"And what's that?"

"I have to talk Nathalie into either taking Eva back or selling me Smoky Joe."

"And if she does neither?" asks Mutti.

"Then I'm up the crick," I say, turning to stare into the fire.

After a while I realize something else is going on. I whip around and find both Mutti and Dan staring at me.

"What?" I say crossly.

"Perhaps I should leave you two alone," says Mutti, starting to rise.

"No, Ursula," Dan says quickly. "I mean—unless you want to, but I think everything will be, er . . ." He looks uncertainly at me.

"Oh, for God's sake, you two, what is it?"

Dan straightens in his chair. "We have a proposition. Now remember—it's just a proposition. Nobody's going to get upset if you don't want to do it."

"Don't want to do what?"

I'm afraid my conversation with Eva left me a little overwrought, and so I probably sound angry even though I'm just anxious.

Actually, there's no "just" about it. I'm hugely anxious. Obviously they're preparing to tell me something big.

Dan looks me in the eyes. His forehead twitches. "It's just that I was thinking that maybe instead of building a brand-new place over at Day Break, maybe we could just put an addition on this house. So that, you know, Ursula would be living with us."

I blink at them, looking from face to face. "Is that all?" I ask.

"Yes," they say in unison.

I finish my wine in a single slug, and then break into giggles that immediately mushroom into hysteria. I can't tell if I'm crying or laughing. I think maybe I'm doing both, because I thought I was going to be the one talking Dan into letting Mutti live with us.

In a flash, Dan is on the floor beside me, and so is Mutti, but I'm bleating too hard to explain myself. And besides, I'm not sure I could. I'm still trying to figure out how the line between tragedy and comedy can be so blurred.

• • •

I drive to Wyldewood the next day, not at all sure of my mission. What I really want is to make all options possible, so that Eva can choose.

The gatepost crackles something completely incomprehensible at me.

"I'm Annemarie Zimmer," I answer, aiming my mouth at it. "Eva's mother. I'm here to see Nathalie."

"Kecheeweeeii . . . shewuu . . ." it says.

Since this is what it has always said just before the gates swing open, I roll up my window and wait. But nothing happens.

After a moment, I unroll my window and hang over its edge.

"Hello!" I call into the box.

"Kccchchhchcchch e wecchhhh, echy wachhhh ur nachhhh . . ."

Its tone is clearly apologetic, its inflection explanatory.

I lean out my window and shout directly into the box. "Let me make this perfectly clear. I'm not leaving until I see Nathalie. So you can either open the goddamned gate or I can park right here and climb over. Which is it going to be?"

The box falls quiet, although I can tell from the crackling that the channel is still open. Then there's a click, as the person at the other end shuts off the microphone.

Lord, I hope whoever it is decides to open the gates. The brick wall is high, and I'm not at all sure how well I'd handle the dismount.

After a few seconds, the gates swing open.

I find Nathalie in the indoor arena, wearing black breeches and high boots. I stand just outside, beside the door to the lounge, watching.

She's carrying a cordless microphone and is instructing a girl on a dark bay Thoroughbred. Each piece of both girl and horse looks fine when taken separately, but somehow the sum of the parts is not making a whole.

"No, Danielle, that's not it. That's not it at all," Nathalie calls out. She's clearly getting cross. "You've got to get him under you. He's spread out like a pancake. Collect him. Use your legs to bring his hindquarters forward. Yes, there you go—no! You've lost it again!" She shakes her head in frustration. "If you simply push him forward with your legs, it won't work. Period. You've got to keep the *whole* of him balanced. You're not keeping track of both ends of your horse."

There are three girls standing in the arena with Nathalie, listening, watching intently. So far, no one has noticed me. Apparently the gatekeeper did not call down a warning.

"There! There!" Nathalie suddenly shouts, stabbing the air with her finger. "That's beautiful! Do you feel the impulsion? Hold it. Feel it. Memorize it. Beautiful! Beautiful, Danielle!"

As the girl on the horse passes by, Nathalie catches sight of me.

She stares for a moment. Eventually I decide to interpret this as an invitation to enter, since she's clearly not coming over to me.

My heart beats faster the closer I get to the group in the center of the arena. Four sets of eyes are trained on me—even the girl on the horse sneaks occasional glances.

Nathalie folds her arms across her chest. "I was wondering when you were going to show up. Eva's things are already packed. If you need someone to help you load, I'll have one of the girls find Miguel."

I look from side to side, my face burning under continued scrutiny. "Um, can we talk for a moment?"

"Go on," she says.

"In private?"

She glares at me for a moment, and then calls out to her mounted student. "Danielle, keep working. You girls watch, and if Peashooter gets all loose and rambly again, try to figure out why. I don't want you to say anything to Danielle, though, because you might be wrong. We'll discuss theories when she's finished." She turns to me. "Come on," she says. She leads the way to the lounge. Four girls are gathered around the watercooler.

Their eyes widen when they see me.

"Beat it," says Nathalic, jerking her thumb at the door.

The girls file out wordlessly. This time when the door closes, there is silence from behind it. I'm not sure what I was expecting, but it wasn't silence.

"So what's up?" says Nathalie, striding across the room and flopping onto an ancient orange-and-brown-flowered couch.

I take a seat in an old Barcalounger and look her straight in the eyes. "I want to know if you'd consider taking Eva back into your program."

"That depends. Is she still in a snit?"

I stare at her, gritting my teeth and trying to hide it because I know my anger is unreasonable. Nathalie docsn't know what's happened to us; and besides, last time she saw Eva, she *was* in a snit. A world-class snit.

Nathalie spreads her hands, and drops them on her thighs. "Hey, I'm sorry to be blunt, but I call them like I see them. Personally, I'm not sure Eva has what it takes. One bad show, and she bailed."

"She didn't bail. You withdrew her," I say quietly.

"Two entirely different things," she says, leaning forward. "And you're damned right I withdrew her. What would you have donc? Sent her, and your best horse, back out on a coursc that sloppy when there was no hope of placing?"

I look guiltily at my lap, because of course I also had no intention whatever of letting Eva complete the course.

"And she most certainly did bail," Nathalie continues. "She bailed on the rest of us. I made it very clear that if she didn't show up to support the others the next day, she was out. And guess what? She didn't show up."

This is the moment for the atomic bomb. I open the hatch and let her fly—

"Nathalie!" I say sharply. She looks startled, and I let my eyes bore into hers for a moment because I believe this is the first time I've ever had the upper hand. "Eva didn't bail on you. She didn't show up the next day because we learned that her father and his wife had been in a horrific car accident and we had to rush to the hospital in Lebanon. Her stepmother was killed on impact. Her father was in grave condition and died shortly after we arrived."

Nathalie's face morphs completely. I experience a tiny twinge of post-Catholic guilt because I'm fully aware that we didn't find out about the accident until after Eva had already blown off the rest of the show, but I saw an opportunity to flush Nathalie's ultimatum down the toilet and I ran with it. Any mother in my situation would do the same. If it turns out I'm wrong about the God thing, surely he'll consider it a venial sin.

Nathalie leans slowly back into the depths of the couch. It's a long time before she speaks. "I'm so sorry. How's Eva?"

"As well as you might expect. I don't suppose I'll really know for a while."

Nathalie sits with both hands pressed to her cheeks. After a while she gets up and goes to the coffee machine. She pours herself a Styrofoam cup of something that looks more like molasses or tar than coffee, and then lifts the pot by way of an offer.

I shake my head.

She wanders over to the window of the lounge and stands watching Danielle put her horse through his

paces. Horse and rider have now come to an understanding. He's regal and flashy, but he's no Hurrah—
and he's certainly no Joe.

Nathalie sips her coffee with her other hand on her
hip. She stands like that for ages, drinking her coffee
and staring into the arena. Eventually she turns around
and comes back. She flops back down onto the couch
and puts one boot up on a nearby chair.

"Are you sure coming back here is the right thing for
her right now? I mean, wouldn't it be better to be with
her family?"

"I'm not at all sure it's the right thing. But I found her
crying in the barn last night, wracked with guilt because she misses Joe but figures she shouldn't be thinking about anything other than her dead father."

"Aw, Jesus."

"She also says if she can't ride Joe, she'll never ride
another horse as long as she lives."

Nathalie sips her coffee silently. Then she says,
"Well, if it's any consolation, Joe seems to share that
sentiment. He's been sulking since she left, jumping
every damned thing in sight. Paddock fences, that is,
because of course nobody else can get on his back."

"Even you?"

Nathalie throws me a look. "Annemarie, he'd throw
even you."

We're both silent for a minute. "You can tell me to
shut up if you want," I finally say, "but if you can't ride
him, why did you buy him?"

"I bought him because I've never seen a seven-year-
old horse that can do one-tempi changes, and because
Joe can and will jump anything. I saw Yvonne Richards

ride him at Fairhill and bought him on the spot. Sometimes you just have a feeling about a horse, and I had it
about Joe. In spades."

"So why was she selling him?"

"Because even though he let her ride him, he made it
pretty clear he was merely tolerating her. And when he
didn't feel like tolerating her, he threw her. And she's in
her fifties and getting tired of hitting the ground. It's
funny—hubris, I guess. I've known Yvonne for many
years, but I didn't believe her when she said he
wouldn't let anyone ride him. But he didn't."

"Until Eva."

"Until Eva," she replies.

"Would you consider selling him to us?"

Her face swings around. "I thought you said Eva
wanted to come back."

"No. Actually I just asked if you'd consider it." I lean
forward, pleading with my eyes. "I'm in a real pickle
here."

Nathalie turns away in disgust.

"What? What did I say?" And then I realize. "Oh
jeez—no pun intended. Honestly. Look, I don't know
what's best here. I'm just trying to assess the options.
What I haven't told you is that Eva's four-month-old
baby half brother was orphaned in the accident, and
now he's living with us. He means the world to her, so
I'm not at all sure she should be away from home six
days a week. If Eva doesn't come back here—and she
really does refuse to ride any other horse—she's just
going to rattle around at our place until she gets into
trouble. And that's a guarantee. And the only other option I could come up with was buying Joe."

There's a moment of surprised silence. Then she

says, "I'm sorry, but that's impossible. He's not for sale."

"But . . . Will you at least consider it? Eva will come into a considerable amount of money. It will be in trust, of course, and I still have to find out the details, but you can pretty much name your price—"

"Money is not an issue. I haven't seen a horse like this since Beauregard, and Beau is seventeen and ready to retire. Joe is clearly my best prospect, possibly my next Olympian. I'm sure you understand."

"But . . . but . . ." I stare at her for a while, feeling all hope drain from my body. Then I rise to my feet, listening as my forty-year-old knees crack.

"Hold on," says Nathalie. "Where are you going?"

"Home, I guess."

"Don't you want to discuss this?"

I stop, confused. "Do you?"

"Yes, of course. Joe's not for sale, but there's no point having him in my barn if I don't have anyone who can ride him. Let's think about this for a minute."

I plop back down.

"You're only an hour away, right?"

"Right."

"Are you fairly flexible?"

"With regard to what?"

"With regard to bringing her back and forth. Like maybe instead of spending six nights here and one night at home, maybe she could arrive on Mondays and go home Fridays. Or alternate three days here, then two days at home. Or something like that."

"Really? You'd do that?"

"Yes, of course. I think the circumstances call for a bit of flexibility, don't you?"

I stare at her in astonishment. "Yes. Yes, I do." A tear slides down my face. I wish it didn't, but I can't help it. "Thank you, Nathalie. Thank you very much."

Nathalie stands up and comes over to me. After a moment, she lays a hand on my shoulder.

"So," she says gently, "why don't you discuss it with Eva and let me know what she decides?"

I sniffle and nod.

"Give her my love. Tell her Joe misses her."

• • •

Four days later, Mutti, Dan, Eva, Jeremy, and I fly to Minnesota to attend Roger and Sonja's memorial service. It's a shared service, which strikes me as unusual but makes sense considering their instructions were identical, neither had families, and the attendees would have been the same since they both worked at Aldrich, Scoville, and Gaines.

The coffins are closed and the service dignified and short. Both Eva and I cry throughout. I hope this provides some closure for her. I think it probably will—at least she isn't burying her father with unresolved issues, as I did mine. Hell, I'm also burying my ex-husband with unresolved issues.

Roger and I were not meant to be married and both of us deserved better than what we had, but he was a good man and my God I'm sorry he's dead. I'm also grateful that Dan seems to understand exactly what I'm going through, and instead of feeling threatened by it, just keeps his arm firmly around me.

Then the coffins disappear, rolling in unfollowed hearses to the crematorium. The interment of the ashes will happen later, quietly, and a year after that, when the ground has had a chance to settle, a small square of marble will sit on top of each.

We go to Lawrence's palatial home to eat canapés, drink, and reminisce. His house is so conspicuously adorned with the trappings of success that it's pathetic, particularly since I know that Peggy is gone.

Is this what she was fleeing? Is she happier now? Did she and I have more in common than I gave her credit for way back when? I entertain the possibility—and not for the first time—that maybe, just maybe, I really have been an unbearable cow for most of my adult years.

As I look around the mirrored rooms at the expensive paintings and sculptures and couches whose fabric matches the curtains exactly, I can't help wondering what Roger's final house looked like. If he hadn't left me, we'd still be together and I'd still be researching the perfect faux finish, still fussing over dichroic glass sinks, still trying to make my home a showpiece suitable for the lifestyle Roger and I were trying to maintain.

And then—even though I'm fully cognizant that I've been through the wringer and also think that maybe I'm on my third glass of dry sherry—I'm overwhelmed with relief that this is no longer my life.

As it turns out, I won't be living in a moldy trailer with Dan. But I'd choose a moldy trailer with Dan over this with Roger any day. And then I feel guilty and have yet another cry over poor old Roger, who was what he was and couldn't help it.

• • •

Dan and I are married ten days later. Mutti wanted us to be married at her church by her priest, but even though I know how much it means to her, I just can't go along with it. For one thing, I'm so lapsed I doubt the priest would agree to it (although Dan is arguably salvageable). For another, I can't in good conscience receive communion even if I don't believe that there's a God somewhere up there reading my mind. But considering everything that's just happened, I'm hedging my bets just in case.

And so we are wed in Mutti's garden under an apple tree that blossoms most gloriously for us. The other benefit of this arrangement is that I can have Hurrah present—something I doubt very much the priest would have agreed to in the church.

The only people there (besides Dan and me, of course), are Mutti, Eva, Jeremy, and the judge. Eva holds Hurrah, who is bathed, spiffed up, and unbearably bored. Just as the service begins, he trumpets a mournful call to his friends out in the pasture, waits for their response, and then, when he gets it, snorts and falls silent with a great sigh.

The ceremony—only seven minutes long—proceeds with great dignity until the moment Jeremy spits up copiously onto the shoulder of my new blue dress. I should have known better; I was jiggling him on my hip even though I knew somewhere in my brain that his tummy was full and he hadn't yet burped. So I suppose it's a self-inflicted wound.

The dress is similar to my other blue one but a size larger because Mutti's gift to us is a wedding reception at Sorrento's, and I want to be able to enjoy it without worrying about splitting a seam. And since I still don't want to worry about splitting a seam, I decide not to try to squeeze myself into my original blue dress, choosing instead to mop up the milk from the new one and throw a square cloth diaper— which I should have been wearing in the first place—over my shoulder to cover the wet patch and prevent any new ones that might occur over the course of the evening.

The reception is perfect, despite one moment right at the beginning when I wonder whether everything's going to go terribly wrong. It's the moment Luis steps out from behind his uncles—who happen to be our stable hands—and I hear Eva gasp. Dan and I exchange quick glances and I brace myself, because at this point anything could happen.

What was Mutti thinking?

The room falls so silent I hear dishes clinking from the kitchen. The moment stretches on so long that I begin to wonder whether I should hand Jeremy off to Dan in case I have to chase a fleeing Eva. Then she bolts across the room and throws herself into Luis's embrace. His arms close around her and he lifts her from her feet, twirling around as they press their heads together.

I gasp, perilously close to tears, but there's no time for that because it's like someone flicked a switch and the party is back on. Dan, Jeremy, and I are surrounded by noisy well-wishers. The baby is plucked from my arms, and we are hugged, kissed, slapped on the back, and shaken by the hand. In addition to Luis and our stable hands, all of Dan's volunteers are there, along with some of Mutti's friends from church, Joan, and Walter.

Luis and Eva take a table in the back corner and spend the evening canoodling. They lean toward each other, all four hands clutched in the center of the table. She nods a lot, listening. Occasionally she gets teary and drops her head, and when this happens, he raises a hand and wipes her face with his thumb. When I watch what's going on with them, I am grateful that Mutti invited him and embarrassed that I doubted her. I should know better by now—as infuriating as it is, she is almost always right.

The *pièce de résistance* occurs when the maître d' stands in the center of the room and clinks a glass with the edge of a spoon. The room falls silent. I look around, wondering if someone is going to toast us, but then the double doors to the kitchen swing out and Gerard—our waiter from the night of the disastrous nonproposal—marches across the room and presents me with a chocolate soufflé with a plastic bride and groom planted on top.

I stare, shocked, and then look up. Everyone in the room roars with laughter. I look at Dan's smiling face, and then I look at Mutti's, and then I look at Eva—who may well be smiling but I can't tell because she is forehead to forehead with Luis. I feel the solid warm weight of Jeremy against my hip, and experience an upswelling of joy so overwhelming I wonder if it's possible to float right out of my chair.

• • •

Naughty Nathalie. It seems she was not entirely forthcoming with me during our last meeting. She had ulterior motives for wanting Eva back at her barn—or at least even more immediate ones than those to which she was admitting.

A week after Eva returns to training (three days on, two days off), she mentions quite casually that she is competing in the Rochester Invitational Sporthorse Tournament in August—in the jumper division, naturally. It appears that she and Joe were chosen as one of the five "wildcard" invitees on account of what two of the committee members who were at Strafford saw—specifically, Joe and Eva taking the in-and-out as a single jump, and Joe's brave attempt to take the canoe despite sliding into it chest-first.

Eva is over the moon.

I am terrified.

Pappa is probably dancing a jig in his grave.

The invitational has traditionally been a feeding pool for the various equestrian teams that represent the United States at the Olympics.

The family dream may have a pulse yet.

Chapter 20

August 18. Rosemont Stadium, Rochester, New York.

I'm sitting on a hard bench in the stands, one leg jiggering like it's having a seizure all by itself, although my heart is threatening to join in. Dan is perched on the very edge of the bench because he's wearing Jeremy in a Kelty backpack. This gives Jeremy added height, and he reaches out with his little fists and grabs everything, including other spectators' hair, glasses, and hats. Most are good-natured about it. Some are not. When no one else is within reach, he grasps Dan by the ears or tries to stuff both fists in his mouth at once. At one point he has a finger up each of Dan's nostrils, trying to rip them asunder.

We're in a section of the stadium that is unofficially reserved for riders and relatives, although no one says anything to the other spectators who wander in by accident. They quickly realize they're out of place when they hear the conversations going on. Some gather their things and move; others settle back against the hard wood of the benches and listen with greedy ears, hoping for gossip.

We're waiting for the announcer to call Eva. The announcer, in turn, is waiting for some of the jumps to be reassembled. Out of twelve riders in her class, Eva and three others made the jump-off. She's the last to ride, and no one has gone clear yet. The last rider was going too hard for speed, knocked down four rails, and is now—depending on how Eva does—in either third or fourth place.

I'm in the stands rather than at Eva's side for two reasons. The first is that I suddenly understand Nathalie's outrage over Eva's snit at Strafford. Nathalie takes moral support extremely seriously. Although Eva is the only rider from her barn competing, twelve other girls are here, all in matching crimson-and-silver Wyldewood jackets and hats. Seven are up here in the stands—directly behind us, as it happens—and five are down with Nathalie, Mutti, and Eva.

The other reason I'm here is that my therapist suggested that the less similar I made this to my own experience, the better. Ergo, instead of standing at the entrance to the arena and watching from ground level as the horses pass me, I sit perched up here and look down on things; a bird's eye view that is, indeed, new to me.

"Are you okay, babe?" says Dan, squeezing my hand.

I nod.

The PA system screeches to life. "And now for our final contestant in the jump-off for class ninety-two, Open Jumper Division, Eva Aldrich on Smoky Joe, a blue roan Nokota gelding owned by Nathalie Jenkins of Wyldewood Farms."

Eva and Joe canter into the arena, and my heart leaps into my throat. His neck is arched impossibly, his low-set tail streaming behind him. He throws his head and dances a bit, but I can see from both his and Eva's body language that there's no problem here. He's raring to go and just making sure she knows it.

She canters in a small circle, passing the electric eye that starts the clock. As soon as the red numbers flash on the screen, a ticker tape gone berserk, Joe explodes into a gallop.

Jesus, Eva, a gallop? You can't approach a jump like that. Oh God, oh God, I can't take this. I squeeze my eyes shut and slam a hand over them.

Dan continues holding my other hand. He knows the drill—each time she comes down safely, he squeezes my hand to tell me it's okay. Although this coping technique is of my own devising, my therapist has sanctioned it. She says that when I'm ready to watch, I'll know—and that in the meantime, there's no reason in the world not to close my eyes.

I have the course memorized—of course I do, how could I not, especially when it ends with a double oxer? So when I hear a deep horse grunt and Dan squeezes, I know she's cleared the brush box and is headed for the brick wall. I can hear from the hoofbeats that they've slowed to a canter.

A sharp yell from Eva—an aggressive noise—and they speed up again, approaching the brick wall.

"Holy crap! Did you see that?" says someone from behind me.

Another squeeze from Dan, quickly, so I won't leap to conclusions.

I know exactly where she is on the course even though I haven't looked since she began. She gallops between the jumps on the straight, collecting him just in time for the takeoff, and cantering tightly around the turns. With Joe now snorting with each stride, she takes the wishing well, triple bar, and picket fence.

They're coming up to the water jump now. It's a beast of a thing with a fourteen-foot spread. The last horse dropped not one but two rails and then came down in the water.

Apparently Joe's capacity for spreads has become the thing of legend—it was, after all, the in-and-out at Strafford that secured Eva and Joe the wildcard space. I hear people around us murmur things like, "watch this" and "check this out," and find myself peeking through my fingers.

They are flying. Joe's powerful body is pounding the footing so hard it flies up in chunks behind him. His muscles are so defined he looks like separate pieces you could take apart and reassemble, like Lego. He barrels toward that jump like nobody's business and Eva is right there with him, pumping her arms with each thrust of his head. Two strides before, he pulls his head up, brings his haunches under him, shifts from a four-beat gallop to a three-beat canter, and bursts from the ground.

As they arc silently through the air, my eye-covering hand drops to my lap and I stop breathing. Joe rises impossibly, with Eva curled over his back and around his neck, her hands thrust up toward his head.

All around us, people gasp. They clear the top rail by a good six inches. When Joe lands more than a foot past the end of the water, a wild cheer goes up.

I glance at the flashing red numbers. She's flying. She's clear. And the only thing left between her and the finish is the double oxer.

Dan has seen that my eyes are open, and he's looking

at me, not Eva. He knows about me and double oxers. The last time I encountered one, I broke my neck and my horse died. I glance quickly at him, emit a tiny sob, and watch as my daughter approaches my greatest fear.

They're over in a flash, then gallop hell-bent toward the electric eye that will stop the clock.

Eva swings her head around to get a look before she even slows Joe down. As the numbers sink in, the crowd goes wild. I almost leap out of my skin when five or six short blasts of an airhorn go off directly behind me.

Jeremy shrieks, and I jerk around just in time to see Nathalie's girls quickly stuffing the contraband airhorn into the arm of a jacket, leaping about, screaming and hugging each other.

Eva's face is so full of joy, so full of—I don't even know what, it's indescribable, so beautiful I can hardly bear it. She reaches down and slap-pats Joe, whose whole demeanor indicates he knows exactly what he's done.

And then, as Eva takes an impromptu victory gallop around the perimeter of the arena to the enormous delight of the crowd, Dan leans in to me and says, "Do you realize your daughter just won a thirty-thousand-dollar purse?"

I snort. Never had it crossed my mind. Not through any of this. And I'll bet anything it didn't cross Eva's either.

• • •

Dan, Mutti, Jeremy, and I make the long drive home that night, leaving Eva to spend the night at a hotel to celebrate with her friends. Last I saw, she was surrounded by stablemates and sipping a glass of champagne. Illegal, yes—but I don't mind because Nathalie was there, so I have no doubt whatever that her glass wasn't refilled. Eva will travel back to Wyldewood with her friends and horse tomorrow.

It's been a long day, and the drive is grueling. Five hours into it I wonder whether we should have flown after all. When I was planning the trip, I figured that with having to change planes it would take about the same amount of time as driving, but right now it feels like any other option would have been better.

Even though Dan does all the driving, the only person who manages to sleep is Jeremy. Which means, naturally, that when we finally get home—even though it's well after midnight—he doesn't feel like going to bed.

I pace back and forth, back and forth, jiggling and singing until I finally get him to sleep, but each time I try to lay him in his crib, his eyes pop open and I have to start all over again. At one point, when he's fallen asleep for the sixth time and I lean over the crib to try to deposit him, I consider spending the rest of the night exactly as I am—bent over at the waist with my arms between him and the mattress, because I know for absolute certain that he'll wake up when I try to pull my arms out and I'll have to start all over again.

But it turns out to be impossible to sleep standing up with a crib rail running across your midsection and nowhere to rest your head. And so slowly, slowly, I pull my arms out.

Silence.

I wait, frozen, disbelieving.

He jerks awake and begins to shriek.

When Dan appears and takes him from me, I almost weep with gratitude. Then I make a beeline for bed.

I'm out instantly, and just as instantly am flying over jumps on Harry—one after another after another—stadium jumps, set up in a field of wildflowers. Each time we approach, he says, Let me, and I wait until the moment is right and then say, All right, because that's the way we work.

But suddenly we're approaching a double oxer. My body, vision, limbs, and veins flood with stress. I stiffen, realizing with dreadful clarity that I'm dreaming, but that's no comfort at all because I know perfectly well how this dream ends.

I'm begging now: No, no, no, Harry, no, not that. But he doesn't listen to me and then I do what I've never done with Harry—I yank hard on the reins and lean back in the saddle, thrusting my legs forward and trying to pull him back. But it's no use. He just charges forth.

Let me, he says, as though we're approaching a normal jump. My hands and calves and lower back scream No! For God's sake, No! and then his ears prick forward, together this time. Trust me, he says, and next thing I know I'm flying over the crest of that oxer.

And then we're over it. We're just over it.

I awake with a start. When my eyelids flicker and I realize I'm staring at the ceiling of my bedroom, my breathing and heart rate start to normalize. I lie staring up at the rabbit-shaped crack in the plaster, trying to process what just happened.

This is the first time in more than twenty years that Harry and I have come safely down on the other side of an oxer. It's our first safe landing since his death.

• • •

I begin my early morning ritual in utter silence, pulling my tan breeches on over cotton underwear and long socks, and completing the effect with the T-shirt that Dan wore at the show yesterday and left tossed in a heap in the corner.

I creep down the hallway, pausing just long enough to peek into Jeremy's room. Dan is in the gliding rocker with Jeremy sprawled across his chest. They're both out cold.

Hurrah is expecting me—as though he, too, dreamed of his brother.

I enter his stall with his bridle slung over my shoulder. I run the reins over his neck and then stand at his shoulder, holding the bridle's headband up with one hand and guiding the bit into his mouth with my other.

Then I stop.

With the reins still draped around his neck, I put the bridle back on my shoulder and lead him from his stall. When I say lead, I mean I walk and he follows, his shoulder at my hip, because I have nothing on his head at all, just reins slung around his neck.

I walk into the arena and come to a stop just past the mounting block. When Hurrah stops beside it, I remove the reins from his neck and toss the whole bridle into the corner. It hits with a thud.

I've never ridden completely without tack in my entire life. I have a brief moment of misgiving, but then decide that if Pat Parelli can do it, why not me?

The center of the arena is set up with jumps—from one of Joan's lessons yesterday, I guess, and the guys haven't taken them down yet to drag. This will make things easier, since by default we'll have to stick to the rail.

And so I climb the mounting block and slip onto Hurrah's red-and-white-striped back.

Even though he knows I have no equipment with which to control him, he waits until I ask him to walk. And then he does. And when I ask him to stop, he does that too. And I laugh because I can't imagine why I've ever used tack in all my life, and next thing I know we're cantering around the perimeter of the arena. I have my eyes closed and my arms stuck out like wings, which is appropriate because we're flying and there's not a moment of hesitation, not a hiccup of misunderstanding. Hurrah and I are in at least as much harmony as when he's got a snaffle in his mouth. Perhaps more.

When I open my eyes, I see a flash of movement through the window that leads to the lounge. Dan has brought Jeremy down from the house. They're both in pajamas, both sleepy, with tufts of hair sticking up at odd angles.

Dan freezes when he realizes I've seen him, because this is usually when I turn bright red, slip from Hurrah's back, and disappear until I've recovered my equilibrium. But since I'm cantering without a saddle and without a bridle and with my arms out to the side like a little kid playing airplane, I burst into laughter instead and press my left calf into Hurrah's rib cage.

His left ear drops in surprise. Are you sure? he asks. And I bring my right leg back a bit and press harder with my left and say, Yes. He leans into the turn, heading for the triple bar even though I can tell he still doesn't believe me because his ears are swiveling independently.

Are you sure? he asks again.

Yes, I say emphatically, urging him forward with both legs and my upper body.

His ears perk forward, together this time, and his pace picks up and I feel the joy of flight in his body. We're nearly there now and I look up at Dan's astonished face just as Hurrah gathers his strength for the massive push, a hundred thousand pounds of compressed energy exploding forth before—

Silence. As we arc over the fence, I raise my face and close my eyes and hope that Pappa's out there somewhere, watching.

FLYING CHANGES

DISCUSSION QUESTIONS

1) At the beginning of the book, Annemarie doesn't let anyone in her family watch her as she rides Hurrah, preferring to keep this side of herself private. Do you think that everybody has a secret self, and can hiding an important part of yourself from your loved ones ever be a healthy thing?

2) Annemarie is shocked to learn how hard it was for her mother to send her away to train with Marjory when she was a teenager, just as Annemarie is afraid to send Eva away to train with Nathalie. How hard do you think it is for women to understand their mothers and what they went through in raising them, even when they are going through an identical situation? How difficult do you think it is, in any situation, to get out of your own head and put yourself in the place of the other person?

3) Annemarie runs out on her romantic birthday dinner with Dan after he presents her with earrings instead of an engagement ring. Do you think she overreacted, or do you understand why she was so upset?

4) When Eva fails at her first event, she initially wants to quit riding, just as Annemarie did following her accident more than 20 years before. How difficult do you think it is to brush yourself off and move on after a serious failure? Do you think failure is more likely to ultimately make a person stronger or break a spirit forever?

5) How do you think the loss of the Old Man of the Mountain foreshadows the events that are about to take place in Annemarie and Eva's lives? Can you think of any other examples of foreshadowing in the book?

6) Annemarie is sure, almost from the start, that she wants to take custody of Jeremy following the death of Roger and

Sonja. Do you think that most women would be able to move past their resentments (especially if, as in this case, their husband left them for the other woman) in order to raise the child of their ex and his new wife?

7) After her father's death, Eva feels guilty for being upset about missing her horse, Joe, instead of focusing solely on her father. Why do you think guilt is so often tied in with grief?

8) At the end of the book, Annemarie finally lets Dan watch her as she rides Hurrah, and she also makes a jump for the first time since her accident. What life change leading up to this moment, from her marriage to new motherhood to watching Eva make a successful jump at her second big event, do you think was most crucial to Annemarie's healing?

BOOKS BY SARA GRUEN

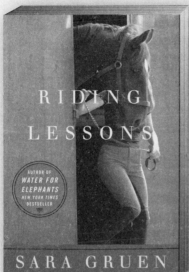

RIDING LESSONS

ISBN 978-0-06-124108-6
(trade paperback)

ISBN 978-0-06-058027-8
(mass market)

Annemarie is coming home to her dying father's New Hampshire horse farm. Jobless and abandoned, she is bringing her troubled teenaged daughter to this place of pain and memory, where ghosts of an unresolved youth still haunt the fields and stables—and where hope lives in the eyes of the handsome, gentle veterinarian Annemarie loved as a girl . . . and in the seductive allure of a trainer with a magic touch.

FLYING CHANGES

ISBN 978-0-06-124109-3
(trade paperback)

ISBN 978-0-06-079095-0
(mass market)

Twenty years after her competitive riding career died, Annemarie Zimmer worries that her relationship with the man she loves is off course, and fears that daughter Eva's own dreams of Olympic glory will carry her far from home. When the teenage Eva is invited to audition for a world-class trainer, Annemarie realizes that she must give Eva a chance to soar. But when Eva falls in love with a blue roan who hasn't let anyone ride him since his arrival at the barn, Annemarie's doubts come crashing back.